FINDING THE ELSEWHERE

FINDING THE ELSEWHERE

GREGORY ALLEN MENDELL

Cover Art by Lisa Hill
Cover Design by Fiona Jayde Media
Interior Design by The Deliberate Page

For Jeanette and Skyler

About the Book

Ket, a vibrant math genius, jokes about quantum bras. Rube, an introspective virtual-body designer, worries about past fiascos. Both are graduate students in India in the Mars Program. Both must avoid personal entanglement to make the cut for the next mission. But sparks fly when Rube gets near Ket at a demo meant to defy Einstein.

Rube is warned not to pursue Ket; though he rationalizes he cannot avoid a potential crewmate. Then Ket's brother-in-law arrives to make her his second wife. Rube intervenes and spies on her family in the virtual body of a doll, only to learn of a mysterious plan that threatens the program.

Meanwhile, Ket struggles to analyze data from a new antenna while wondering if the program's founder wants her as his Eve on Mars. After she accidentally contacts aliens, she learns they want something from her too: DNA sequences to create human embryos throughout the cosmos.

The pressure increases. Everyone wants something from Ket. Everything Rube does ends in disaster. If they make the wrong decisions, not only will they end up worlds apart, with humanity's future ruined, they'll end up dead.

PART I

ENTANGLEMENT

Chapter 1
Soahls and Confusion

"Space is the enemy."

Rube entered the Grand Reception Hall of India's spaceport repeating the mantra, "Space is the enemy. Space is the—"

He stopped. Down the foyer stairs, across the crowded cathedral-sized room, he saw the soft orange glow of a dress. Its color matched the hall's decor, and the radiance of its wearer's curves swept through him. He raised his hand as a shield, but it didn't help. She reminded him of everything he'd traveled so far from home to forget … and to find.

Through parted fingers he watched her converse with a lanky, white-haired man. Her face came to life, and the tropical flower in her long hair quivered while she bounced from foot to foot. Rube imagined she was the smartest, most unattainable woman in the entire universe.

Unless? What if they were together on Mission Fourteen to Mars? Sure, it was fun to think about, but that launch was over two years away. He'd have to get through the extensive selection process first, and to let his mind drift off-course zero seconds into day one was crazy. Besides, he was twenty-six. Too old, he'd promised his brother Vic, to screw up again.

He lowered his hand and let his eyes wander up the high silver and saffron wall behind her. A red banner celebrated the Martian base and the middle of the twenty-first century. Above this, a well-known advertisement played on an enormous holo-screen. A figure-eight shaped metallic band emitted streams of words and equations. The band untwisted into a loop that shrank to a small rectangle. Cascading images of beautiful people and places filled the air while familiar messages floated by:

"I think, therefore I am," –René Descartes

"I hear my thoughts, therefore I have a soul," –Mobius Monk

"I possess the sum of all human learning, therefore I have a ***soahl****," –brought to you by the Math Monks of Mars*

People from around the world appeared. Each held a thumbnail-sized case, which they slipped into their clothing, jewelry, or beneath the skin. Then they each picked up a small cloth square and put it into their pocket or purse.

A voice said, "Every movie ever made, every song ever sung, every word ever written: the Math Monks' new gold soahls, now available with n-cloth 12.0 displays."

The screen faded into a message and a chime sounded.

Proceed to the auditorium for the demonstration. Download MathMonksMars::brochures::newstudent and turn off your soahl.

Rube squeezed the soahl in the hem of his shirt underneath his fleece jacket and adjusted the straps of his backpack. The morning's coolness had not yet given in to India's climate. He looked down. The dress and its wearer were gone.

He started to turn when something ran into him. Solid as a wall, it crushed against his shoulder and pushed his hand into the cold flat region of … of its crotch.

He leapt back to see a tall, headless, armless v-bod standing before him.

"Sorry," a voice called out.

From behind the v-bod a rotund figure—maybe a technician—appeared. He wore green dungarees and work boots. Next to him the v-bod's arms and hard-shell head sat on a robo-cart. "Sorry," the maybe-technician called out again. He winced. "I was trying to get it to the basement. I'm Harlow Featherton, from Alberta. But my friends call me Crater. And you?"

"Uh … Reuben Dual … from Seattle."

"Reuben? Like the sandwich?"

Rube stopped massaging his arm. "I think I was named after an inventor." He inched closer to Harlow, who looked friendly. Or was it hungry? "Anyway, my friends call me Rube."

"All right, inventor." Harlow stuck out a hand. "I'm afraid you missed most of the food."

Rube hesitated then gave it a firm but awkward shake. He had arrived late to avoid mixing in with the competition. But maybe this was a start. "Sorry for asking, are you a recruit?"

"The Monks prefer the term learnling or student. Now that regular folks can try out, I've decided to give it a go. I've worked here since graduating from Ag school last year. I'm kind of a farmer-engineer." Harlow paused. "I saw you staring at the syrup pot—"

"The what?"

"That daughter of Achelous across the room. A trap set by the Monks, I'll bet."

"Daughter of who?" Rube observed Harlow's boyish grin. "You can't believe—"

"Probably not. And I don't like to judge a cake by its frosting." Harlow laughed. "But even if she's not a trap, she's a flame—the kind that attracts a moth and fries it." He glanced around and inhaled. "That reminds me, the naan bread here is intoxicating."

Rube checked his fingertips for past singe marks. He realized how this might look and snapped his hands to his sides.

"Don't worry, I know the rules. No couples allowed on the missions, no entanglement that might interfere—"

"Speaking of which, I've got to get this v-bod to the lift in the alcove over there. It's for the second demo later this week. I've never been clever at steering these things."

"It helps if you have the gloves and the mask. What are you using for the controls?"

Harlow picked a paper-thin display screen off the robo-cart and handed it to Rube.

"Let me see … I guess I can do this the old-fashioned way." Rube pinched the middle of the display. A tiny joy-stick popped up, and he wiggled it with his thumb to walk the v-bod down a couple of stairs to the main level of the hall. Then he maneuvered it like a ballroom dancer, dodging several students and a robo-waiter on the way to the service elevator.

"You're pretty good at that. Thanks."

"All in a day's work," Rube mumbled. "So, what are the demos about?"

"Something that'll make Einstein roll over in his grave is all I know. It's all monk talk."

"Uh, huh." Rube stepped to the robo-cart. "I should get to the auditorium. I'm meeting a couple of friends there. Though I do have another question." He set the display by the v-bod parts. "I understand the arms are here, because of the regulations, but why the head?"

"Oh, we're upgrading that. You'll see once we finalize the design." Harlow started toward the alcove. "I'll miss today's demo, but I'll be around. Be careful Rube. To make the first cut we can't get our hand caught in the cupcake jar, can we? The Monks are watching us." He headed to the elevator. The robo-cart followed him down a ramp by the wall.

Rube decided Harlow must think about food, a lot. He almost called out he knew getting involved was a recipe for disaster. But then again, such recipes were *his* specialty.

* * *

Rube approached the small auditorium recalling the past year spent lost in a virtual world. That was, until he'd heard Mobius Monk's lecture about sending people without a Ph.D. to Mars. "Space is the Enemy," Mobius said, but he had a plan. That had led Rube back to reality, back to his dreams. After reconnecting with his two best friends from college, they all applied to the Mars Program. Somehow they were all accepted ... somehow. Now if he could only find them.

He went through the doors. There was the dress again, in the front row. This time he raised his brochure to block its glow and proceeded down the aisle. He was about to ask if anyone had seen a Lacy Lin Wu and a Quasi Lagage when he turned and spotted them in the last row. Rube slipped off his backpack and squeezed into the empty seat on Lacy's right.

Lacy peered over dark glasses and stroked the face of a man pictured in Rube's brochure. "Very smooth," she said. On her index finger was the tattoo of a tiny pointing hand.

"He looks like a monk," Quasi said from Lacy's left. He touched the rolled-up brim of his bowler hat. Then he coaxed her tattooed hand into his.

Lacy snuggled toward Quasi. "And very Zen."

"You mean Brahman, my dear." Quasi looked past her. "What do you think, Rube?"

Rube studied the tattoo and the hat. Both were new, though not unusual accoutrements for his friends. It dawned on him that perhaps both were intended to mark this occasion. His neck twitched and he tried to reconcile how he felt—the quiet thrill of the outsider let into the fun persons' club versus the sensible urge to run and hide. He scrunched down and shut his eyes. His jacket curled up his spine. He angled his feet onto his backpack. "Well, he is a Math Monk."

"Hey, don't disappear on us again," Lacy said.

Rube opened his eyelids a crack but kept silent.

Lacy took her hand from Quasi's and brought her index finger close to Rube's nose. "Because our destiny is up there." She pointed to the ceiling. "Mars, baby."

Quasi lowered Lacy's hand. "Right now Mars is closer to the horizon."

Lacy's cheeks puffed out and she exhaled. "Engineers." She shrugged and tapped the temple of her glasses. "I can always find out more."

Rube took a deep breath. "You're supposed to turn off your soahl."

"He looks rather serious in that picture," Lacy continued. "The nonverbal genius type."

Quasi patted a leather satchel on his lap. "A sip of my rocket fuel might loosen him up."

Lacy smiled at Quasi. "I doubt it, but maybe he'll be interested in my brains."

"You're a supreme brain builder, but we'll see if he notices more than your—"

"Shh—you're the one that said he looks like a monk." Rube scrunched down more. He gazed up at the decorative steel ceiling … and saw a glint of orange.

"The Monks are academics," Quasi said, as if this wasn't known. Then he added, "That dress up front is a bit over the top, wouldn't you say?"

"Dress? I've been ignoring it." Rube unzipped his jacket. He needed to let some air in.

"I think her father is Abraham Boni." Lacy's tone was very matter-of-fact.

"Huh?" Rube sat straight up. "How do you know that?"

"She came in from the stage before you got here." Lacy reached down and pulled up a large handbag. "When I saw that dress, I had to take a picture." She took out a small cloth square. With a flick of her wrist it grew into a solid display. The words 'connecting to your soahl' appeared on its screen, followed by an article. "I scanned for her—"

"And voila," Quasi said. "No one can search their soahl faster than Lacy."

"I know." Rube shook his head in dismay. "But her father is Abraham Boni, the preacher? Doesn't he want to shut down the Mars Program?"

Quasi furled his eyebrows around a squint. "You watch him?"

"Not really—just while soahl-surfing. He broadcasts from an island in Fiji."

"The thing is, I found her picture," Lacy said. She swiped to the next page, but the lights dimmed and everyone stopped talking. She bent her display and it shrank back into a small cloth square. "Sorry boys, the show's about to start. I'll send you the article."

Over the sound system a voice said, "A message from Mobius ..." Then a deeper voice continued, "We have begun a great journey. While the world falls apart we go to Mars to explore, but also to take the first step toward the stars, to ensure that humans survive far into the future. Even if only the last of these is accomplished, it will have meaning for millions of years."

Lights flooded the stage. Out came an Indian man in comfortable tan clothes styled by his homeland for a life in space. It was the man pictured in the brochure but with white hair. Rube realized it was the man he'd seen Abraham's daughter talking to earlier.

Holo-screens on either side and at the front showed him as he walked to the podium.

"I am Prasham," he said. "Welcome to Sriharikota Island, India's spaceport." His voice was high-pitched, but strong. "Congratulations to all one hundred ninety-two of you on your acceptance into the Mars Program. As you know, at this week's end each of you will be assigned to one of four universities where you will complete a master's degree. After ten months, thirty-two of you will be selected for further training in Antarctica. And finally, eight will be selected for the next thirty-two month mission to Mars, Mission Fourteen, which lifts off twenty-six months from now. Also, this week will culminate in the two launches for the current mission, Mission Thirteen—a grand way to revel in the twenty-sixth anniversary of our first mission."

"I think he's reading from the brochure," Quasi said.

Prasham paused. "As I was saying, twenty-six years since the first mission, twenty-six months until your launch—nice how it works out. But as we say on Mars, you do the math."

Rube repeated his own scary calculation, done on his birthday last week. Born the year of Mission One, a source of undeserved pride, he'd be over thirty when Mission Fourteen returned.

The auditorium lights came up. Prasham stretched his long arms out wide. "Let me begin with a question. Among you," his voice boomed, "who likes to be confused?"

"He's more dramatic than I expected," Lacy whispered.

Before Rube could make sense of the question, an orange flash blinded him.

The dress's wearer had stood up. "My name is Betti Keturah, but I go by Ket." Rube now saw the coils of her hair were their own natural shade of orange. She moved as if to brush away bangs. "If you mean," she continued, "who likes to stare at the beauty of the universe, feeling confused to the core of their being, then yes, I like to be confused."

Rube found his hand was up. He put it down.

"Thank you, Ms. Ket, for that terrific answer." The roll of Prasham's r's sounded like a purring lure meant to tame a tiger. "Please join me up here."

Ket strode up the stairs to the left, onto the stage. Her soahl-powered dress framed bare legs with matching flats. Prasham greeted her and said, "Who else likes to be confused?"

Most of the students raised a hand, reaching for the ceiling. Rube kept his down.

"Young man at the back, in the shirt with 'soahl man' all lit up. Your hand was raised."

Rube touched his chest and sighed. He gave his soahl a stronger squeeze and managed to stand up. "Uh … I was going to say, I don't like to be confused. I like to solve problems. And my name is … uh … Rube." There was no response. "But maybe I do like to be confused?"

"Good, Mr. Rube. Could you also join me?" Then Prasham addressed everyone. "We are going to start today with a very important demonstration. Mobius cannot talk with us in real-time since he's on Mars, alone, except for his wife, Sandra. But here is a hint. This demonstration could change that. We will see who likes to be confused more, Mr. Rube or Ms. Ket."

Rube left his backpack behind and walked to the front. When he reached the stairs to the right, rotating blue lights swept the room and klaxon bells rang out. He stumbled onto the stage.

A student shouted, "Is this the demonstration?"

The bells stopped. Large words flashed across the holo-screens.

… TSUNAMI ALERT … WAIT FOR INSTRUCTIONS …

"Did anyone feel an earthquake?" Prasham called out. "I suspect it is a drill. However, the system will let us know whether to go to the roof or take the robo-bus to the mainland."

"No earthquakes reported anywhere."

That was Lacy. Rube saw her standing at the back. Many other students also stood up.

A man in a corduroy suit appeared on the stage. He said something to Prasham who then turned to the students, stretched his arms out wide again, and said, "To the roof."

Rube stayed put while the students shuffled to the exits. Since there wasn't an earthquake maybe this was a test to see who would panic. Maybe Harlow was right. Maybe the

Monks were watching his every move. He sat down and looked toward Ket.

Prasham had vanished, leaving her seated like an abandoned magician's assistant. She lifted her dress to reach for her soahl. Rube wasn't sure why she was doing this now, but a voice went through his head, "Panties aren't the best thing on Earth, they're next to the best thing on Earth." It was something he'd heard his brother say. "Vic, you're not helping," he muttered. The view didn't embarrass him, but Rube averted his eyes. He pictured himself talking to her, telling her that from the moment she'd spoken about the universe he knew his attraction to her was more than physical.

Something crackled. Rube peeked. He saw Ket heading backstage. Huge sparks flew from her dress and she fell behind the exit curtain. With a frantic turn, Rube looked for help. He saw only the backs of the last students leaving. The next thing he knew he was kneeling at Ket's side. Then everything went dark and the emergency lights flickered on.

There was a crash farther backstage. Someone grumbled, "... white ..."

Rube glimpsed a shadow darting away, like that of a hunted animal. His stomach hardened, anchoring him in place. "Prasham?" No answer came.

Ket stirred. "OK? You're here to save me?" Her eyes opened. "You're not OK."

"Maybe you really are confused," Rube said. His anxiety lessened. "You probably bumped your head." He reached out. "Your soahl must've had a short, but I think you're fine."

Ket looked down and smoothed her dress. "I was trying to switch it off."

Rube thought she was trying to hide a blush, or maybe fear. Without help she stood and ran up the backstage stairs. He moved to follow her ... but returned to the stage. He saw the flower from her hair. With care, he put it in his pocket. Then he faced the seats. He was alone.

"Mr. Rube, you are still here?"

Correction, Prasham was back. The lights came on.

"I thought I should stay calm." He wanted to ask, what the hell was going on?

"Let me give you two pieces of advice, Mr. Rube. First, don't get any ideas about Ms. Ket. We can't send people to Mars who aren't focused or—how should I say it—self contained."

Rube forced himself to not blink. He wanted to go to Mars. He wanted to go for all the reasons Mobius had laid out. But a more pressing reason had led him to India, the contradictory one. The one he had to keep hidden from Prasham, like the far side of the moon. He wanted to love again. If he tried to explain that, he knew he'd lose everything. Instead, he asked, "Second?"

"We are under a tsunami alert. Now is not the time for calm. Now is the time to run."

Rube sped to the back. He scanned for his backpack. It was gone. He turned. Prasham was gone too. How had this happened? He reached for the cloth square in his jacket pocket.

"Don't get your n-cloth in a twist." It was Quasi standing in one of the entrances. "I've got your backpack," he continued. "Come on, let's go."

Rube wondered which would be worse, another failure or a lonely success? Maybe death. He ran for the exit.

Chapter 2
Her List

All the way up the backstage stairs, Ket pictured her dress bursting into flames and the irony of having to jump into the sea from the refuge of the roof to prevent herself from becoming a burnt offering—that is, if the gods had smiled on her and the building was surrounded by a tsunami. However, after scrambling into the fifth floor bathroom and pulling off her dress, she found it was dead and harmless. She flung it over the doorknob and locked the door.

Tsunami. Offering. The words resonated within her while she stared in the mirror at her orange underwear. It was ridiculous. For now, she wanted to know if her soahl still worked. She reached for the flap of n-cloth sticking out from her left bra cup and pulled it free. It expanded into a display and connected to her soahl. Good, that meant the problem was with the dress only. She was about to carry on when two messages popped up.

soahl-touched::private::to Ket::from Prasham:: "Tsunami alert cancelled. Not a drill but a false alarm."

soahl-touched::private::to Ket::from Prasham:: "PS. I've made sure Rube won't bother you."

Why would Prasham be concerned about that? But she knew why, and she would deal with it. A third message popped up.

secret::to Bad Wave::from OK Drunk:: "Corvus is in India."

Corvus was here? Her arms went numb. Then she couldn't help noticing it—the scar, above her left breast. Faded but visible, its tendrils connected to the memories of why she'd run away from home. A scream boiled inside her. She was about to let it out when someone knocked. Her display dropped into the sink and rattled. "Who's there?"

"Ah, there you are. Verrrry good." It was Prasham outside the bathroom door.

"I was checking messages. And something's wrong … with the dress."

"Not to worry," Prasham called back. "I'll have Harlow fix it tonight. Mobius wants you to keep wearing it until after the demonstration. It will look good in the press photos, he says."

Ket stood still for a moment.

"Is there anything else wrong? Should I come in?"

"No … no, everything's fine. I'll see you tonight." She heard Prasham walk away and let out a long sigh. She retrieved her display. She had to settle down. Viewing her to-do list would help. She pulled it up:

1. ~~Find the perfect quantum bra.~~ Find the good people of the universe.

2. Get to Mars. Why? No mosquitoes, no Corvus, and brains matter there.

3. Calculate Clebsch-Gordan coefficients.

She laughed at the first item. It had stayed on her list since arriving in India four years ago. She reviewed the second. It renewed her motivation. In any case, she told herself, twenty-four was too old to ask for help again. If Corvus showed up, she would deal with that too. After finishing the third item, today's task, she would go to the beach, the dreaded beach, to face her fears—alone.

CHAPTER 3
COW POW

"Where are you going?"

Rube called out to Quasi, who waved at him from across the ornate lobby of their hotel in Sri East. No one else was around.

"To the beach," Quasi replied. "Didn't you get my message?"

"Uh … no." Rube froze. "I don't have a swimsuit."

"Neither do we."

Rube flinched at the sound of Lacy's voice. He turned to see her coming up behind him from the elevators. She pushed her dark glasses up onto her curls and jogged past with a wink. After reaching Quasi she stopped.

Rube realized he was having one of those days. First you're warned the sea wants to take you fully clothed, then you're asked to give yourself to it, completely naked. One moment you're dreaming about the next mission to Mars. The next you're dreaming about something even more impossible. He looked down at the article Lacy had sent him. It mentioned Abraham had debated Mobius once, and it quoted Abraham's famous line, 'the only *sum of all human learning* I need is the good book—no *soahls* for me, only souls.' And there she was, pictured next to a man with jet-black hair wearing a vest and a bolo tie. The caption read, 'Abraham Boni's daughter with his son-in-law and public relations manager, Corvus McClough.' What? Was Ket married?

"Well, are you joining us?" Lacy asked.

Rube fiddled with his display. "Uh … I was checking my messages." He checked them now. There was one from his brother, which could wait, and one from Quasi about the beach. He wanted to sit down. He wanted to go over the article. He eyed a sturdy chair, covered in plush rugs. Instead, he stowed his display and grabbed his backpack from beside his feet.

* * *

Once outside, a tropical breeze brushed Rube's cheeks while strange birdcalls interlaced with his thoughts. He couldn't believe this was still his first full day in India.

Lengthening his stride to catch up with his friends, he wondered why he hadn't seen Ket or Prasham since the morning. True, there hadn't been much time to look for them. The tsunami alert was canceled minutes after he'd reached the roof. The demonstration was postponed until tomorrow morning, and the students were directed to a tour of the spaceport, followed by lunch, and then a long meeting about the week's schedule.

At least they had met two more of the program's four instructors. Neither had been to Mars, unlike Prasham who had gone twice. One was Twiddle, the man in the corduroy suit. Round and gray, he was not a dee or a dum, he joked, but an Oxford don. The other was Nickie, blonde and lean, from the University of Washington. Rube had met Dr. Nickie before, at an information meeting there. She didn't joke. A third instructor, Mavra, hadn't come. She was busy with work at Harvard. And the fourth instructor—that would be Prasham himself.

Finally, they were told to return to their hotels to rest and to study the lecture by Mobius. Rube had made a set of notes from it before. Hadn't everyone? There was no need to do so again. It was late afternoon, and he had debated whether to walk back to the Mars Explorer Building to look for Prasham or to wander around and maybe run into Ket. The word wanderlust occurred to him. He had to stop thinking like that.

"Space is the enemy," Rube murmured.

Quasi turned. "You've caught up. What were you saying?"

"Uh ... nothing ... except do you think this is a good idea?"

"Mobius and Prasham expect us to be bold," Quasi replied. "They didn't get to Mars by acting scared to jump in when an opportunity arose."

"I'm pretty sure neither has jumped naked into the sea. This is post-rollover India, but—"

"Relax, Prasham won't see you." Lacy faced Rube and took off her glasses, which she tossed into her bag. She smiled. "But maybe some cute girl will."

"Thanks. That wasn't even on my list of worries." Actually it was. Rube noticed Lacy had pushed up her sleeves and undone the top buttons on her blouse to show off her other tattoos. She'd also changed from black leggings into black cutoffs. Her black nail polish glistened in the light. He wasn't sure her retro-goth look fit in with the rich aura of the colorful shops. Quasi, on the other hand, was dressed like a tourist. He wore a straw hat and had changed from casual dress clothes into a flowered shirt, khaki shorts, and sandals. His satchel hung from broad shoulders that underlined his robust jaw and its five o'clock shadow.

Rube's backpack shifted against his jacket. It was a bit warm for fleece, but along with jeans and tennis shoes, he found comfort in his outfit. Thank goodness it was winter and not too hot. Unfortunately, it was warm enough for a swim.

"So what's in your precious backpack?" Quasi asked.

Rube perked up. "V-bods," he said, like he was carrying a sack full of presents.

"Your new ones?" Lacy positioned herself to have a look. "Can I see?"

"Sorry, I don't want to take them out of their boxes. But, if I see Prasham—"

"You're going to give him a doll?" Quasi tilted his head. "Why didn't you leave those at the hotel?" He pressed in next to Lacy.

Rube shrugged. "I thought maybe I'd go find him."

"But virtual bodies for kids?" Lacy asked. "That's not really new, is it? When I was twelve I did virtual travel in the Grand Canyon—much better than the drone tours. But my soahl froze. After a reboot I found my toy v-bod had walked off a cliff. It fell over a thousand feet."

"These aren't toys," Rube said. "These new v-bods operate under the same regulations as the adult-sized ones. It's the n-cloth that's new. The nano-tech is much more sophisticated. It can do more than act as a display or make simple shapes. I can show you a video."

"No, that's all right," Lacy said. "But girls like dolls. Even grown-up women do."

Quasi cleared his throat. "But do they look like dolls or action figures?"

"The point is the new n-cloth lets them look like anything, and look real. I brought them for the instructors. Maybe I'll give one to Ket."

"Er ... right-o." Quasi paused, as if concerned. He started to walk with Lacy again.

Rube matched their pace and thought about how much work he had put into developing the v-bod protocols while inhabiting an avatar. He remembered explaining to Vic, who avoided anything virtual, the difference between operating a v-bod in the real world and a software avatar in a virtual world. What he couldn't explain was how meaningless his life had felt then.

"Hmm," Quasi continued, "you'll have to risk leaving them while we swim."

Rube thought this over. "You know, they're rather expensive. I should stay with them."

"Suit yourself," Quasi said, "though when Lacy and I *unsuit* ourselves we'll blend in with the sand and surf before anyone has noticed. I hear the water temperature is perfect."

Rube followed his friends to the end of town, then down a slope until the road flattened and turned along a beach. In the distance he saw empty tables outside a café. After a few more steps, sand poured into his tennis shoes. He stopped and tasted the air. Listening to the waves, he imagined explaining Quasi's blending theory to the local authorities.

Quasi took off his hat and plopped it onto the beach. Curly bits of hair stuck out from the sides of his premature balding head. He swung the satchel off his shoulder, pulled out a flask, and opened it. "After you wet your snogger, maybe you could play for us."

Rube looked away. "I think I'll stay dry, all around. And I'm not playing here." He took in the glittering sea. This wasn't the cold Washington coast.

"You're not getting off that easy," Quasi said. "You have to at least get your wee footsies wet. To get to Mars I reckon you'll have to loosen up a bit." He pulled two towels out of his satchel and sat on one. Lacy joined him.

Rube remained standing. "Mars isn't exactly the party center of the solar system. Besides, I left my harmonica back in my room. I haven't really played since we were last together."

"And a right good v-bod player you were," Quasi said. "But your next show should be live—on Mars. We'll all have to offer things beyond our techie skills."

Lacy looked pleased. "I'm going to have the first baby on Mars."

"Well that sort of thing might require a bit more negotiation."

"Who says you'll be the father? Fate might not want him to be an engineer."

"Very funny." Quasi took a sip of his drink and gave Lacy a long smooch.

Frustration filled Rube's face. He knew his friends worked and played hard. But did they understand what was at stake? "Will you two take this seriously?" He kicked the sand so hard Quasi covered his flask. "The Monks are testing the waters to see how ordinary people adapt."

"Ah, testing the waters. Seems right," Quasi said. "You sure you don't want a dip?"

Rube didn't respond. Then something caught the corner of his eye. Saved by a dress!

"Sorry, I'll leave you two to your ocean foray." Rube pointed toward Ket at the café.

Quasi stood and blocked Rube. "Are you serious? After the Princeton fiasco and Tulip, or your escape from the Queen of Thord? And you were lecturing *us*? I'll go talk to her."

Rube felt nailed. "Tulip's in California. I know I won't see her again. And I won't have to see *Queen* Evelyn again either, once I have the money for virtual court." He brightened his tone. "But don't you always say the early worm gets the bird?"

"Early cat," Lacy whispered.

Rube pushed past Quasi. "I know what I'm doing. And *don't* wait for us."

Quasi pulled Lacy up. "Holy *vache* … he's doomed. But let's not miss our swim."

* * *

Rube knew what he was doing. Right? He could focus on Mars, but why couldn't he focus on two things at once? After all, Prasham hadn't said to stay away from her. Because completely avoiding a possible shipmate, wouldn't that be disqualifying too? As Rube neared Ket, he stopped questioning himself. He only knew he needed to ask her things.

When Rube reached the café, Ket stood. She had on the same dress, sans glow. She hadn't seen him, but was looking at a boy coming from the opposite direction. As the boy drew near he grew into a man. He carried a walking stick with a silver handle and looked like a sheriff from an old, deserted ghost town. Ket seemed startled but began talking with him.

Rube realized it was Abraham's public relations manager and saw him grab Ket.

"You idiot," she complained. "Let go of me."

"Your father wants you home. If I have to bring help, I will."

Rube tried to reverse course. He should call the police, not get into trouble. Not—

Ket's scream ripped like a meteor through the air. The man had bent her wrist back.

All thoughts of retreat flew out of Rube. He stepped forward. "Hey!"

The man turned toward Rube. His eyes shined a deadly blue charm. "Soahl man? You look more soulless to me." He jerked Ket's arm as she struggled, her protests reduced to a hiss.

Rube's heart snapped. He made two fists but was shaking. He didn't want to fight, but he would. Right? Though maybe a diversion would be better. He moved in and steadied himself. "Corvus? That last name of yours—is it McCluff as in fluff, or McClow as in cow?"

There was a bright flash. Then enveloping darkness.

* * *

When Rube opened his eyes, he saw stars in the twilight sky. He was on the ground, on his back.

"Tell me that again. You said cow and he went pow?" A damp Quasi stood over him.

"It was something like that. He hit my face. Or maybe my face hit him."

"I think your nose is broken," Lacy said, peering down from Quasi's side. A few drops of water dripped off her breast onto Rube's lips. He tasted salt and remembered why his friends were naked. Well, not completely naked. Their towels were wrapped around their waists.

"No, I'd say burnt." Ket appeared. She knelt next to Rube, and he felt the warmth of her fingertips as she stroked the hair away from his forehead. "Corvus is gone," she continued. "The silver tip of his cane—it doubles as a cattle prod."

"That explains why it feels like a supernova exploded in my head. What did he want?"

"He wants to marry me."

"So, he's not married to you?"

"What made you think that? Never mind—he's married to my sister but has always wanted to make me his second wife. It's insane."

"That's good ... I mean, that he's gone. And I scared him off?"

"Actually, your friends scared him. Then he saw Prasham searching for me and ran off." Ket stood and looked down at Rube. "We need to stop meeting like this."

He kept his eyes on her. "I wanted to ask you something. Sorry, I know it's strange asking this now. But the demonstration—did you understand Prasham's hint?"

"About sending messages faster than light? That was obvious. Prasham says it's to do with entanglement. But I have to go. He's waiting for me."

Rube tried not to look disappointed. "Faster than light? How can that—"

"I don't know. Prasham will explain tomorrow." Ket started to turn away.

"Wait, I just remembered." Rube sat up and found his backpack on the ground. He unzipped it and pulled out a white box. "I have something for you."

Ket seemed unsure what to say. "Something for me?"

"Uh ... I brought these for the staff. Prototype v-bods. I want you to have one." Rube handed her the box. "They're like dolls really. But show it to Prasham if you want."

"Well, thanks ... but I do have to go." Her eyes looked away then met Rube's again.

"It was great to meet you." Rube realized how dumb this sounded.

"We'll take care of him," Quasi said.

"Yes, we'll take care of you, brave Rube," Lacy said, leaning in closer.

Rube glanced around.

Quite a crowd had gathered. "Nice tattoos," someone said. "Are you allowed to take the hotel towels to the beach?" someone else asked. "Children, don't look," a mother said.

Then Rube watched Ket walk off and his nose began to hurt. When she got to Prasham's side, she gave him the white box. Prasham shook his head and the two of them left together.

After a long and painful exhale, Rube lay back down.

CHAPTER 4
MAGIC COINS

Rube stood with Lacy five stories above the Mars Explorer Building's auditorium, away from the hyped-up conversation of the other students.

Everyone had enjoyed the brief view from the roof yesterday and had asked for a better look. So Prasham had let them take their breakfast from the reception hall up in the elevators.

But Prasham was not on the roof. Neither was Ket. Rube had surveyed it several times. Nervous thoughts seemed like cords tightening around his shoulder blades, and he made a conscious effort to take in the view of Sriharikota Island to relax.

He pictured his position about two-thirds the way down the island's fifty-kilometer length. Here, its width narrowed from over twenty kilometers to a few. He looked west and saw tiny fishing boats sailing on Pulicat Lake. Then he looked east. There, the Bay of Bengal met the rising sun at infinity. The roof seemed to tilt, tipping him toward the void, before he spotted the shoreline and the illusion disappeared. There was Sri East and his hotel … and the beach café. He squinted but couldn't see a tsunami wall anywhere.

Next he looked north. The two MLV rockets for this week's launch were barely visible. He imagined his back pressed downward from atop such a rocket in a little over two years, a warm hand at his side, her smile melting the tension. He reached for her … and refocused.

There was the island's main highway. He traced it to the split, where the east fork went north to the launch pads, while the west fork turned to follow the lake. He had taken the robo-bus down that branch two nights ago, after crossing the viaduct onto the island from Sullurupeta. It had been dark, but now he could see the vast carpet of green eucalyptus plantations he had read about, and he tried to spot the flamingos that came here every year.

He saw none. The most exotic covering he'd seen so far was Ket's dress. He gave up trying to distract himself and wondered how many of the students knew about last night.

Based on what he was hearing, all of them.

"She must have tattooed quite the image onto his brain," someone said.

"You betcha," Lacy whispered to Rube. Her dark glasses were buried in her hair.

Rube touched his nose. The good news was it just needed a small bandage.

"At least you're less scraped up than after we took you concrete tobogganing," Lacy continued. "And you've still got your eyebrows."

Rube knew Lacy was referring to the time Quasi poured liquid methane into the Chem-E department's holiday punch bowl and lit it on fire. He turned and was relieved to see Quasi was not offering sips of his 'rocket fuel' to the others but was walking toward him.

"I assume you're ready to impress Prasham with your incredible confusion."

"Uh …" Rube failed to counter Quasi's remark.

"But have you taken in the other students?" Quasi nodded at the crowd. "They look far too smart. I'll bet half of them already work for the Mars Program and have the inside track."

"Some are outdoors types," Lacy said. "That might work against them."

"What about the scone-headed booby-steppers?" Quasi waited for Lacy to catch on.

She shrugged. "The military wannabes? I don't see them in a colony run by professors."

"At least no one from the babbling-soahl crowd made it in," Quasi said.

"I agree," Lacy said. "Who wants to hear someone talking to their soahl all day long."

"Like it's their best friend? I know," Rube said, joining the game.

"Or a person's long lost love?" Lacy gave Rube a sympathetic look. "Not that it would be wrong to do so in private. But in public, I prefer a silent soahl." She squeezed Quasi's hand.

"Good to not see any scarlet-eyed cyber soahls, either," Quasi said. "Right, Rube?"

Before Rube could respond, he glimpsed someone by the roof's edge. "That's Harlow Featherton over there. He works here, so he's a definite insider. Oh, and he goes by Crater."

"I can see why," Quasi said. "Looks like he's contemplating whether a ton of feathers can float. But hey—no railing—shall we give it a go?"

"You stay here," Lacy said. "I don't want you wobbling off the roof."

"I'm as stable as a gyroscope." Quasi grinned. "That one's for the nerd types."

Rube thought some of the 'nerd types' looked like they had spent their whole lives in their parents' basements watching old sci-fi videos. "I guess I'm in that group."

"What about the artisans?" Quasi indicated a group in striped bell-bottoms.

Lacy shrugged and studied her nails. "Not sure about the men's waist-length hair."

"They're probably genius coders," Rube said. "On the other hand, some of the students look like dropouts who think going to Mars might be easier than getting a real job."

"Does he mean us?" Lacy drawled, batting her eyelashes like laced fans at Quasi.

"Well, you two only dress like dropouts sometimes," Rube said. He hoped it was clear he was kidding and added, "You're also obviously very, very intelligent."

"You're the one that got us here." Quasi tipped his hat, the bowler, now with a ruby band.

Lacy smiled. "We're a team, led by an unlikely Rube."

Rube heard a clatter. In came Twiddle with a mango crate followed by Prasham.

Prasham stood on the crate and gave his characteristic arm-wave. "Sorry we were not able to have the demonstration yesterday. I think some of you from cold climates might say the ice is now broken. On Mars we say the dry ice has a lattice defect."

The students gave a polite chuckle.

"However," Prasham continued, "we can now proceed. To the auditorium."

"Right," Rube said. "I'll show him I'm ready." He lurched across the roof and came up next to Prasham sooner than he expected. There was no choice but to follow him to the stairs.

"Ah, Mr. Rube. Are you confused yet?"

The asynchronous staccato of the other students' shoes echoed behind Rube. It seemed no one was taking the elevators if Prasham wasn't. Rube cupped a hand to his ear. "Confused? It's what I like to be, right?" He had to fly over two steps for every one of Prasham's strides.

"I meant about today's demonstration."

"Oh, yes, very interesting—looking forward to the confusion. Er … what's it about?"

"I do not want to spoil the surprise but I heard you asked about my hint."

"Uh …" Rube found it too hard to continue to speak over the clatter. He watched Prasham pull ahead. Then he burst into the auditorium lobby and found Prasham off to one side.

"There you are." Prasham swept his arms out in a greeting. "To answer your question, think of the possibilities. We could talk to Mars. We could talk to people across the universe."

Rube put his hands on his knees. He wondered if Prasham ever got tired of the dramatic gestures. He wondered if he ever got tired, period. Rube forced himself to stand up straight. He didn't want to seem naive, so he asked, "What about Einstein?"

"Oh him—you'll see. Now Mr. Rube, after last night I reviewed your records. Your work on the new v-bods, it is of great interest to us."

Rube tensed up. "It is? You kept the one Ket gave you?"

"No, she said she wanted it. However," Prasham continued, "your records also say you switched from studying astronomy to computer science. Why did you do that?"

Rube attempted to come up with a short answer. "I wanted to do something meaningful. I mean, practical. I mean, without all the ... the physics and math." He knew this was coming out wrong. "Uh ... when you aren't working, what do you do for fun?"

"Physics ... and math."

Great. Now what could he say? He did his best to change the subject. "I was wondering, why did you pick me yesterday? A lot of hands were up."

"You simply looked the opposite of Ket. Not the type she'd find interesting." Prasham showed no sign he was trying to be funny. He turned and headed for the back offices.

* * *

Rube sat on the auditorium stage, across from Ket. She had on the same dress with its soft glow restored. But today she wore it with matching tights. She kept her gaze fixed toward the other students. It was clear she didn't want to talk. However, this gave him the chance to really look at her. Even if she had no interest in him, his gut told him his first impression had been correct. She was smart and desirable, but also approachable. And she'd kept the v-bod doll.

Prasham came to the front of the stage. Behind him, a robo-cart placed itself between Rube and Ket. "Let the demonstration begin," Prasham announced. Everyone became quiet.

On the cart were two shiny metal buckets filled with coins. These also appeared on the holo-screens at the sides of the stage. Prasham took them over to Ket. "Here are two types of coin, but the ones in each pail are identical to each other. Mix them up and take one of each."

Ket swirled her hands around in the buckets. No other sound was in the room. Then she took her coins.

After putting the buckets back on the cart, Prasham returned to Ket. "Can I borrow your coins?" Ket handed them to Prasham and he held them up. A close-up appeared on the holo-screens. "See this copper-colored one-cent coin. It is called a penny. And see this silver-colored ten-cent coin. It is called a dime." He handed the coins back to Ket.

Next Prasham grabbed the buckets and took them over to Rube. "Mr. Rube, mix up the coins in each bucket and take twenty of each." Rube did so. Everyone was mesmerized.

Prasham looked out at the audience. "Remember, the pennies are exact copies of each other, as are the dimes." He pivoted to Ket and said, "Choose a coin and flip it onto the floor."

Ket picked her penny and flipped it high into the air. Close ups on the holo-screens followed the action. It landed, spun around, and fell over heads-up.

"All right, Mr. Rube, flip your dimes, one at time," Prasham said. "Everyone watch."

Rube set his pennies to one side and flipped the first of his dimes. It came up tails. He flipped the second. Tails again. He flipped the third coin. It came up heads …

After Rube had flipped all twenty dimes, there were eleven tails and nine heads.

"Boring," a student near the back said.

"Right, not quite fifty-fifty," Prasham said, "but who knows what would happen, if we flipped more dimes. Let's try again." He took a broom from the cart and swept the coins off the stage. Then he had Ket mix up the coins and choose one penny and one dime again, and he had Rube mix up the coins and choose twenty pennies and twenty dimes again.

Prasham turned to the audience. "Remember," he said, "all the pennies are exact copies of each other, as are the dimes. And these two have picked, completely at random, another set of coins." He waved his hands like a conjurer. "Ket, flip either coin."

Ket picked her dime this time. She flipped it, and it came up heads.

"Now, Mr. Rube," Prasham said. "For fun, flip your dimes again."

The first dime Rube flipped came up tails. So did the second. So did the third and the fourth. Everyone watched the close-ups on the holo-screens.

"It's a cheat," one of the students yelled.

"We'll see," Prasham said.

Rube continued to flip his dimes. He tried harder with each to make the coin go higher and rotate more times before landing. As each one of them came up tails, there were gasps. After the first ten, he took the remaining dimes and threw them up all at once. Silver flashed in the air. Then the harmony of rattling coins, as if on cue, played to a final crescendo.

Dumbfounded, Rube saw all twenty dimes lying tails-up on the stage floor.

Whispers went through the room. Everyone saw this too, on the holo-screens.

"Magic," someone said.

"How so?" Prasham replied.

"The probability is less than one in a million." This came from Ket.

Prasham whirled to her. "So, are you confused?"

Ket appeared to ponder the question carefully. "They must be weighted to come up tails ... except they came from the same pail as the first set of dimes, chosen at random—"

"Rube replaced the dimes somehow," someone shouted.

"No dimes were replaced, and all of them are identical," Prasham said.

"I get it!" It was Lacy at the back. "Taking the coins from the pails put them in a quantum entangled state. When Ket flipped her penny Rube's dimes were forced into a state that had a fifty-fifty chance of coming up tails, but when she flipped her dime, his dimes were forced into a state opposite to hers, so they all came up tails. It's not supernatural magic. It's quantum magic."

Rube shook his head for Lacy to stop.

"Correct," Prasham said. "These do not represent ordinary coins, but quantum coins that have undergone entanglement. Rube's coins knew instantly how to act depending on Ket's choice—instantly, no matter his distance from her. Science is magic, but it's magic that works."

"Of course, she is reading that off her soahl." This time it was Quasi who spoke.

"Well, good," Prasham said. "Before we take a break, I want everyone to know that there is a very deep problem with what I have shown you. But think of the possibilities if we can get around it. All right, like Ms. Lacy has already done, everyone can turn on their soahls now."

Rube was about to ask Ket what she thought about this. But she was gone.

* * *

"That was confusing," Rube said. He and his friends stood outside the auditorium with earpieces in so they could pick up the soahl chatter of the others.

Quasi gave Lacy a pretend glower. "Or it was, until Ms. Soahl Searcher filled us in."

Rube waved a hand and put it up to his ear. "Wait, this is important. Quantum copies are not allowed. Search for theorems against quantum cloning."

"That's from one of the articles I was reading," Lacy said. "You should take a look."

Rube took out his display. He saw links to a list of references:

[1] "Can Quantum-Mechanical Description of Physical Reality Be Considered Complete?" Einstein, Podolsky, Rosen, Phys. Rev. 47 777 (1935)

[2] "FLASH—A Superluminal Communicator Based upon a New Kind of Quantum Measurement," Herbert, Foundations of Physics 12 1171 (1982)

[3] "A Single Quantum Cannot Be Cloned," Wootters and Zurek, Nature 299 802 (1982)

[4] "On the Einstein Podolsky Rosen Paradox," Bell, Physics 1 195 (1964)

Then his soahl shook with an incoming message.

soahl-touched::private::to Rube::from (blocked):: "Meet me for dinner tonight at the beach café. —Ket"

Any calm remaining in Rube's body evaporated.

Chapter 5
The Other Shoe Drops

Rube couldn't believe it. He would finally get to talk to Ket, alone.

She had missed all the afternoon workshops, but soon he could ask her why. At least she wasn't avoiding him. Her message also said Corvus had left India. She was likely more unnerved than she'd let on during the morning's demonstration.

As he walked by the beach, he went over again his conversations with Prasham, how Prasham had said he seemed the opposite of Ket. A strange thought occurred to him. Could Prasham also be worried Ket might get ideas about him? Rube looked up the road.

Ket stood by the café, facing the sea. She wore a different dress—violet and shimmering like satin. He started a ride up Fantasy Mountain and walked faster, noticing it had rained hard. He almost began to dance when a soccer ball rolled across the road toward her. She made a graceful catch. He prepared to clap, to let her know he was there, but a boy came along.

Rube's sense of frisson morphed into déjà vu. Corvus? But before he could warn Ket, she held out the ball and the boy took it.

It was just a little Indian boy … and with the ball the boy started back across the road.

Rube put his arms down and relaxed. Except his chest remained tight. This made no sense—until the ocean sound became a car engine—behind him—approaching fast. He spun. The car swerved, splashing water onto his trousers. The air in his lungs wanted out—now. But his brain projected the car's trajectory to the boy and he stopped breathing. Rube shut his eyes.

Brakes squealed. Tires skidded. Pain slammed into Rube's body—mirroring the impending impact. Then silence.

When Rube looked, he saw a solitary ball bouncing where the boy had been. He heard crying. This led him to Ket holding the boy in her arms.

Farther along, the car's driver got out and yelled at her.

Rube started to run. Was this Corvus?

No. The man got back in the car and sped off. Rube slowed down and saw Ket put the boy down and dab his face with a small cloth square. She was telling him something, probably to be careful. She picked up the ball and led him across the street. Once there, she started playing catch, laughing with a youthful glee that matched the boy's.

Rube's thoughts whipped around. Could the boy be hers? Was she the wife of a local? It made no sense—but maybe it did? He was about to turn around, when a woman approached Ket and the boy. She talked to Ket then led the child away.

By now Rube was very near Ket. When she turned back toward the café she jumped.

"You were fantastic," he said.

"Sorry, you startled me." Ket pressed her cheeks. "Did you see that? I'm still shaking."

"Do you mind if we join you?"

This time Rube jumped.

Why did his friends always need to sneak up behind him?

* * *

"Rube was a bit short on introductions yesterday. I'm Quasi and this is Lacy. Care for a drink?"

Ket picked up her menu. "I could use one, maybe with dinner. Did you see that car?"

Quasi put his flask away. "I can't believe it didn't slow down for the boy."

"Talk about your front-seat driver," Rube said.

Ket laughed. "Yes, what kind of person drives?"

"Quasi does," Lacy said. "Driving's making a comeback."

"Since when?" Rube tried to not overreact to the revelation Quasi was insane.

Lacy ruffled Quasi's charcoal beret and he reset her glasses at an angle in her black curls.

Rube transitioned back to Ket. "But seriously, do you know the driver?"

"That was Sunjay, my bodyguard. He was mad I'd left the hotel without him. Prasham hired him after what happened last night. But Corvus is out of the country. That's why I wanted to meet—to let you know everything's fine." She looked at Rube. "And we all can move on."

"Uh ... my thoughts exactly." Rube's ride up the mountain slowed to a crawl.

Ket smiled and slid her chair closer to Lacy's. "So let me see your tattoos. Is that the Titanic? What's the explosion on your other arm?"

Lacy put her menu down and held out her left arm. "Most people think it's the Hindenburg, because I have a fascination with fate. But it's the Big Bang. And on my right index finger, see this little pointing hand? It's new."

"She calls it her fickle finger of feng shui," Quasi said.

"My family in Montana doesn't appreciate my humor." Lacy laughed. "Isn't it cute?"

"You're the cute one," Quasi said. His forehead creased like a Venetian blind.

"And is that a replica of 'The Scream' there?"

Rube knew Ket meant the tattoo on Lacy's cleavage. He fixed his eyes on Quasi.

"Sort of—it's a person being stretched and pulled into a black hole. It goes all the way down my front." Rube gave up and turned to see Lacy looking down at her lap.

"Wow," Ket said.

"Enough about me," Lacy said.

Finally, Rube thought. He tapped the cloth napkin under his right hand.

But Lacy continued talking. "What did you think of the questionnaires today?"

Rube folded the napkin in half and twisted one corner. It shrank into a spinning top.

"I'll tell you the one that surprised me," Lacy continued, "the one that asked, if you get selected for a mission to Mars, could you stay celibate for almost three years? You would think they would have asked that on the application. I mean, I know the ideal candidate is a socially adept introvert—but it sounds like they're looking for hermits."

"Monks," Quasi said. "They're looking for monks."

"Probably didn't want to scare you off," Rube said, trying to sound helpful. "Maybe they want you for a ground job." He grabbed the spinning top and it changed into the Eifel Tower.

Lacy ignored Rube and leaned closer to Ket. "What about Mobius and his wife?"

"You mean Sandra?" Ket asked.

"I'll betcha it's not all celibacy for them," Lacy continued. "Why the exception?"

"Think about it," Rube said. "The missions return to Earth after fifteen months on Mars and it's eleven months until the next one arrives. Without Sandra, he'd be alone. Besides, Mobius is Mobius." The Eifel Tower was now a tiny Sphinx.

"But if future colonists stay on Mars, I'm sure they'll change the rules for them," Lacy said. "That's why Quasi and I could still get in. Right?"

"For now, Mobius is the only permanent resident," Rube said.

"Along with Sandra," Ket said. "That is, since she joined him on mission nine."

"I remember a wee hubbub about that," Quasi said. "She's not a Math Monk."

"Exactly," Lacy said. "So why haven't they done some baby making up there?"

Rube shook his head and collapsed the Sphinx back into folds of cloth.

Lacy twirled her glasses around and took in everyone's reaction. "Well la de da. How can they start a colony without babies? And don't remind me about how they want to start things out slowly before letting couples go. If Quasi and I get in, we'll change their minds."

Rube used this as an opening. "You were great with that boy, Ket. Do you like kids?"

"Yes … though I never plan to have any." She looked away for moment.

"Me either." Rube thought maybe he'd been too quick. "Well, maybe one day."

"My sister has two," Ket continued. "That's enough. Besides, I'm on my way to Mars."

Quasi gave Rube an innocent look. "So, if you were still with Evelyn—"

"Who?" Ket asked.

"Rube's old girlfriend," Quasi said. "Evelyn Hatter. He gave up astronomy for her."

"Shh. Ket doesn't want to hear about the *old* girlfriend," Lacy said.

Rube saw Lacy cut her fickle-finger-of-whatever across her throat.

"How old?" Ket asked.

"And in high school," Quasi continued, "there was Tulip Patel. Rube left her for Princeton, then gave up a full ride and returned home to Seattle … except she had moved to Free

California. Caused Rube to rush in a wee bit too fast with Evelyn, I reckon, if you catch my—"

"Old, as in Evelyn's gone," Rube said to Ket. "Mad too, insane, with a cyber soahl."

"Fused to the base of her skull," Lacy said. "And her corneas have LED implants—you know the kind. She has other implants too." She put her chin down. "Not like me."

The waiter came by and everyone looked at the menus.

Rube couldn't have taken much more of Quasi's literal litany of his past. He wasn't sure Lacy had helped either. But now was his chance. He moved his chair closer to Ket's. "I loved what you said about the beauty of the universe. When I was young I thought the most amazing thing a person could do was to try to understand what's out there. I mean the whole enchilada and everything about it." With a swirl, his napkin formed into a miniature Taj Mahal.

"How young were you when you thought this?"

"Uh ... ten." Rube coughed. "Still do. I'm twenty-six now. Born the year of the first—"

"And for you, sir."

Rube had lost track of the waiter. He randomly pointed to number forty-two on the menu.

"Good choice." Ket looked at the waiter and smiled. "I'll have what he's having."

Rube kept his attention on her. "What did you think of the demo? Prasham can't get around the laws of physics, can he?" With a poke, his napkin took on the shape of a wormhole.

"Nice Einstein-Rosen Bridge." Ket nodded at the wormhole. "There's a line in a song my mother used to sing to herself ... about Einstein." She started to hum the tune.

Lacy tapped her display. "*As Time Goes By,* words and music by Herman Hupfeld, 1931. Also featured in the movie *Casablanca,* though not the line about Einstein." She didn't look up. "I'll bet Rube could play it on his blues harp while you sing."

"And are you very good?" Ket asked Rube. "At the harmonica, I mean."

"It's the perfect instrument for a trip to Mars." He started to turn his napkin into a rocket, but decided against it. "Very portable. But I sound like a banshee trapped behind a touch screen."

"Remind me not to go to Mars with you." Ket laughed.

Rube managed to laugh too.

"He's actually pretty good, when he plays as a v-bod," Lacy said.

"It was for our senior project," Quasi added. "A harmonica playing v-bod."

Rube stroked the half-rocket. "Lacy wrote the code. Quasi did the engineering."

"And you ran it," Quasi said. "Rube's a virtuoso when it comes to controlling v-bods."

"You see," Lacy continued, "Rube had Quasi give the v-bod lips, so it could pucker."

Rube wondered how his friends could be so oblivious and so perceptive. "The puckering meant it could play single notes." He formed his napkin into a finger puppet with a large mouth.

Quasi's head tilted. "You unlocked your serviette's stupid n-cloth trick app?"

"I don't even have a robo-dishwasher," Ket said. "I'm not sure about a kissing machine."

"It was a real leap in dexterity and realism," Rube continued. "Much more sophisticated than what this napkin can do. It led to the v-bod dolls. Uh … like the one I gave you."

"Sorry, I haven't looked at it yet." Ket gave her forearm a gentle rub.

Rube glanced down then gazed back at Ket. "Why do you want to go to Mars?"

"As you can guess, there are reasons I don't ever want to return home. But it's much more than that. I like to tell myself,

I left to find the good people of the universe. And the people who go to Mars, I think they must be good."

"I think so too." Rube felt as if his eyes were about to merge with Ket's.

There was a silence. Rube turned to see Quasi and Lacy staring at them, their jaws askew. Rube could see that Ket had noticed them too. "At least we're not cynics," he said.

Then the meals arrived.

* * *

Rube stuck to small talk through the rest of dinner. By the end of the meal, Quasi and Lacy had pulled their chairs around to one side of the table and had become engrossed in their soahls, both using dark glasses and earpieces, while Rube had moved even closer to Ket. It looked like he might get to talk to her in private after all. "Your name. It's so interesting."

"Yes, it's Betti with an 'i'. My parents are from New York, but my mom decided to name me after Laura Betti. She was a French jazz singer and also a film star, I think. I'll have to look that up on my soahl." Ket rapped her fingers on her wine glass. "I couldn't have done that back home. No one has a soahl where I come from. We had videos, which we watched on old TVs."

"You mean back in Fiji?" Rube asked. He realized he had said too much. "Sorry—"

With this, Quasi and Lacy took off their glasses and earpieces.

"So your father *is* Abraham Boni?" Quasi asked. He showed no sense of guile. "Not that I know that much about him. Though Lacy's filled me in."

"Yes. He's famous, I know. That's one reason I go by Keturah, not Boni."

"But does you father really believe everything he says?" Rube asked.

"Everything?" Ket kept an even tone. "You would think I would know, but I don't. Let me say, I've never known him to be anything but sincere. But he doesn't question things. And I do. It's another reason I had to leave—that I had to run away when I was twenty."

"What?" Rube blinked.

"It was four years ago. You see, where I grew up, if you did something bad they didn't just wash your mouth out with soap, they washed your eyes out too. I mean Corvus did."

"Aye," Quasi said. "He's a scunnerous two-legged eel, isn't he? You'd like to sauté the ostrich oysters on that one."

"French father, Swazi mother," Rube explained, "raised in London by a Scottish aunt."

"I couldn't have expressed it better myself." Ket began to rotate her glass. "I'd rather the other students didn't find out about me—who my father is. I thought I had it all locked down. I'm not on book-of-soahls and no one can touch mine without my secret handle."

Rube moved a hand toward Ket's. "But Corvus could still get to you."

"Corvus tried something dumb yesterday. I've found out he was here to talk about India's nukes, and they gave him a tour of the spaceport. He saw a chance to get to me and failed. But he wouldn't seriously injure me. My father wouldn't stand for it. And Prasham will protect me."

Rube saved his doubts about this, for now. "Right, Prasham. How did you meet him?"

"It goes back to that song. It started to make sense to me when I was a teen. I had a pen pal on Mars. It's funny how that term still applies today. You can't get a message to Mars in less than three minutes—as you know. You can never talk. It gets tiresome."

"So Prasham was your pen pal when he was on Mars? Is that why he picked you?"

"For the demo?" Ket put her elbows on the table. "It was partly a set up. I knew Prasham's question was coming. I knew he was going to choose me. He also arranged for the dress. I was kind of mortified, having to wear it again today."

"The dress was a gift from Prasham?"

"He asked me to wear it, said Mobius wanted me to." Ket smoothed her sleeve.

Rube tapped his napkin. "And Prasham got you into the Mars Program?"

"My teacher in Fiji helped me run away. He knew Prasham and sent me here. But I'm a student, just like you. I applied, just like you."

The irritation in Ket's voice stung Rube. He started a rapid ride down the mountain.

"And my answer to Prasham's question," Ket continued. "That was all from me too."

"But what is your relationship? You're always meeting him. Does he really watch everything we do? Is he watching us now?" Rube, in shock, realized he was talking out loud.

"What?" Ket glared at him. "I'm finishing my undergraduate degree. Prasham is my advisor. That's why I'm missing so much of this week. And Prasham doesn't watch us. He works from five in the morning to nine at night, every day." Ket let out an exasperated sigh. "I've got to go meet him—again. We're taking the mag-train to Bangalore tonight, back to RRI."

"Where?" Rube asked. The room began to spin. He sensed the other shoe drop. It fell from the top of Fantasy Mountain and hit him on the head.

"Back to the Raman Research Institute, where I study … where Prasham teaches."

"It's one of the four universities in the Mars Explorer Program," Quasi explained.

"Uh … right," Rube said.

"Sounds like noodles," Lacy said. "Not really, of course. Raman won a Nobel Prize."

"We both have work to do," Ket continued. "We'll be back tomorrow afternoon."

"Uh … right," Rube said again. How could he be so stupid—about everything?

Ket stood up to leave.

"I'm sorry," Rube said.

She looked at him and nodded, but kept going.

It wasn't enough. Nothing would be—unless he took a chance. With the n-cloth-napkin formed into a shoe, he rapped his head. He knew what he had to do.

Chapter 6
Doctor OK Drunk

secret::to Bad Wave::from OK Drunk:: "I'm OK. Are you? Get it?"

Ket noted the message on her display. She sat at her desk in her apartment in Bangalore, where she had arrived by mag-train an hour ago. It was late and she was tired, but she wanted to get some work done before tomorrow. She pulled on the soahl in the waistband of her sweatpants and let it snap. Tiny letters that said 'connected to your soahl' at the top of her display dissolved into 'ouch.' Such a sensitive soahl, she thought. At least she hadn't given it a voice or a name. In any case, it was great to be home and out of a dress. She was about to go to the kitchen when the words 'live reply' blinked on her display. Her heart started to race. She touched the words and an older Fijian man with a large Afro and beard appeared.

"Dr. Mateni, hi ..."

"How are things that side? I hope you didn't mind my joke?"

Ket brushed her hair from her face. "You know I love your jokes. And I'm fine, thanks."

"I'm OK, you're OK." Dr. Mateni smiled for moment. "But this is serious, I know."

"I never thought he'd try something like that. But I'm fine."

"The word around here is that Corvus defended himself from an unprovoked attack. Of course, I got the full story from Prasham and sent you the touch."

"Yes, and I got your earlier one, that Corvus has left India. Thanks for that. I guess I've always known one day he would try something." Ket realized she had not kept in very good contact with her old teacher and a feeling of guilt washed over her. "How have you been?"

"Always OK, like always." He laughed.

"It's been too long." She hesitated. "You really didn't get into trouble?" His messages had said no one knew he had helped her run away, but she was glad finally to have asked.

"Never." Dr. Mateni's face showed a proud grin. "I'd do anything for my best student."

"But if you hadn't told me about Mars—"

"You're the one that started working out Hohmann transfer orbits at age twelve. I posted one film of you doing that, on the share-your-soahl site."

"They'll find it."

"No way. You know there's not a soahl on the island." Dr. Mateni's grin expanded and his eyebrows danced up and down. "Sorry, I can't help it. Anyway Ket, they can't find it. It's called *Bad Wave plans her trip to Mars*, but it's protected with the pass phrase 'Semi Drunk,' so it's not obvious."

"Semi is your middle name, and your last name means drunk."

"But I didn't use my first name, *Sa Rauta*, which I translate to OK in English. Get it?"

"Of course," Ket said. She'd never been sure if 'OK' was just a nickname. "But if someone found out you helped me they could do very bad things."

"Not your father. He's a good man." Dr. Mateni twirled his beard. "And Corvus—there's a lot he's never caught on to. He can't put two and two together." Dr. Mateni's barrel chest rippled with laughter. Then he looked sheepish. "I know, he's not that dumb. I know."

"No, he's not that dumb—just smart enough to do something dumb." Ket drummed her fingers on her desk with irritation. "But he asked the spaceport for a tour to get to me. Right? Someone should tell my father—but not you. You can't stick your neck out for me again."

"He wouldn't listen to me. Maybe your mother would? If only you could talk to her."

"I know she's very unhappy I left. My father is very unhappy. My sister is very unhappy. Everyone's unhappy. But they won't listen to me." Ket pounded her desk with her fist.

"It's because of Corvus." Dr. Mateni remained silent for a moment. "But I love your family. And I love singing in your father's choir."

Nostalgia stirred in Ket. "Thanks to those great voices like yours."

"What about the young man? Did Corvus hurt him much? He saved you, right?"

"You mean Rube? He'll be fine. We've barely met." Ket ran her fingers through her hair. "Not much else to say about him. But I should tell you about Prasham's latest idea."

"You need to stop hanging out with old men."

"Yes, maybe one day." If you only knew, Ket thought. "But I'm set on going to Mars."

"Good. At least Corvus can never get you there. I've heard he's in Free California now. He's due back in Fiji the day after tomorrow, Thursday night for you. So he's far away."

"The Free Part? That's crazy. But yes, good, he's gone and everything's fine. I'm fine."

"That's all I wanted to hear. OK, OK … I should let you work. Bye, Ket. But give the boy a chance." Dr. Mateni smiled again. "Bye … *sa moce*."

Dr. Mateni's image shrunk to a dot. She put her display down. She was fine. Right? So why did she feel out of breath? She took out pages filled with the equations from her desk drawer. She picked up a pencil and started to scribble. Bless Dr. Mateni, she thought, but why did everyone think they knew what she needed?

She stared at the pile of novels on her desk. Maybe she'd read instead. She rolled the pencil in her hands. Someone knocked. The pencil clanked on the floor. Yes, she'd be fine, if she'd just stop dropping things. But could that be him?

"It's me."

Good, it was only Prasham. Ket turned to see he had let himself in.

"I wanted to make sure you were all right."

"I'm fine," she said, putting on her most cheerful voice. "Same as when you checked last night." She thought about changing the access code to her door.

"Yes, but that was back at the hotel at the spaceport, and my room was next to yours. I also wanted to let you know I've posted the guard outside your apartment here too."

Darn it, Ket thought. But it shouldn't matter. "Corvus is in California and then is going back to Fiji. I talked to Dr. Mateni. So there's no need to worry."

"Yes, I sent him a message earlier, telling him about what happened. How is he?"

"Funny … and supportive."

Prasham noticed the paper on her desk. "You're working on the calculations?"

"Just finishing." She leaned over and picked her pencil off the floor.

"All right. You know me. I'll be up early, but I assume you'll want more sleep. I'll meet you for the afternoon train back to the spaceport. Good night." He turned and went out the door.

"Good night," Ket said to the closed door. Right, back to work. She tapped her pencil on her desk to the beat of a jazz tune she liked. She struck the side of desk and then the bookshelf above it. She liked the hard sound, but sought out something different and tapped the white box she'd left on her desk after arriving home. The box Rube had given her.

"I'll have to tell him," she said to herself. She put down the pencil and opened the box.

CHAPTER 7
V-BODDA-BING

Rube ripped open the seal on a clear plastic packet marked 'virtual travel' and spilled its contents—an n-cloth facemask, undershirt, and gloves—onto the bed in his hotel room. He removed his T-shirt, then slipped his soahl from its hem and fastened it to his belt. After putting on the undershirt and gloves, he fell back onto the bed and applied the facemask. It spread over the contours of his face, covering his eyes, ears, and mouth before it solidified. He couldn't see or hear, but his breath poured through holes around his nostrils.

He gave his soahl a squeeze and it powered up. Inside the facemask, messages about options and a list of destinations appeared. With a few blinks, everything changed.

His face began to sweat in the hot sun. Large green leafed plants swayed in front of him and jungle noises drifted in from the bush. Transported to a spot in Africa four thousand miles away, with the subtle motion of his fingers he got up and started to walk—or rather his one-foot tall v-bod body did. He approached a traditional home and stood before its closed front door. There was one problem. He had no arms.

"Vic, open the door. And why did you leave me turned on, lying outside in the grass."

The door swung out. Rube saw his brother look straight ahead then down.

"Whoa, that's weird. That doll looks like a mini-you. What happened to your nose?"

"It's a long story." Rube almost tipped over.

Before he could right himself, Vic put him back on his feet. "Careful little guy, come in."

Rube entered the home. "The n-cloth—it matches my face, but the hair is from a scan and the skin tones are from a photo. I'm sure it looks funny with the bandage."

"Uh, huh." His brother nodded. "Hmm, I gave the doll to Tepi to play with. She must've left it outside before leaving with her mother. Also, don't say things like I left you *turned on* in the grass. I don't want the neighbors spreading rumors while my wife's away."

Rube ignored this and looked around the spartan interior. With his real fingers he could feel the mats on the floor through the doll's feet. "You know, there are only four v-bods like this in the world. I gave two of them to the staff at the spaceport and one to you."

"And the fourth one?"

"I gave it to ..." Rube wanted to raise his missing arms in despair. "She's ... uh ..."

"Hah, I read your letter about chasing after Mars. But if you ask me, this is even better."

"No, no, no." Rube protested. "If I get the chance, I think I will go to Mars."

"Hey, big plans. But here's the important question. Will you get coffee on Mars?"

"Huh?" Rube was baffled. "I'm not worried about getting coffee."

"Maybe that's your problem, little brother. My wife shares about three cups with me per week. Still, the way I see it, the cup's three sevenths full, not four sevenths empty."

"That makes no sense. You're not having an average cup per night."

"Not even close to average. The rising steam, our fingers intertwined, the warmth when my lips touch her rim, her anticipation of—hey, don't give me that look."

"What's your point, Vic?"

"My point, Rube, is I'll bet you haven't had even a fraction of a cup lately. Before you vow to abstain from *coffee* in some godforsaken Martian monastery, a little v-bodda-bing wouldn't hurt, would it?"

Rube had to admit, Vic sometimes had a way of putting things. He also admired his brother's devotion to helping refugees, though Vic's complete disinterest in science and technology, except for medicine, was frustrating. Now Rube wasn't sure what to say. "Uh … how are things here?"

"Life's hard in the camps. The satellite is mostly down. Lucky for you, it's up now."

"I meant to do this before I left for India, to test the new v-bods. Better late than never."

Vic took a seat in a canvas chair next to a simple wooden table. "I knew there was a catch when your letter said you wanted to send me a toy. Want a beer? Sorry, you look so real." He reached down and pushed a finger into Rube's cheek. "And you also feel real."

"Ouch—it feels real to me too." Rube paused. "We haven't seen each other, not since—"

"Mom and Dad's funeral … right … over three years ago … the week you graduated."

"Talk about meaningless." Rube hadn't thought about it for a while. Peter and Pamela Dual, driving through Detroit, crashed and died following their rules: always travel without the kids, avoid sentimental occasions, and never let the car drive itself. But how could that accident happen in the safest city on Earth, populated by automatons? "I shouldn't have said that."

"In that case, you were right."

"I mean I shouldn't have said what I did back then. I never meant your work."

"You mean the little poem you sent me?" Vic recited it:

It matters not what you do
It could seem so meaningless
From another point of view

"Well," Vic continued, "I got it—like you said—you meant your life. But you sort of meant my life too. And some days I think it's exactly true. Things change very slowly here. But you have to look at the individuals you touch."

"I think going to Mars can do that too—I mean help people. And bring meaning—"

"Right, it's what you said in your letter. But let's get back to the girl."

"Weren't you already saying to go for it?"

"I'm being serious. I know you Rube, what *always* happens when you've got big plans."

"What do you mean?"

"Princeton or Tulip? Evelyn or astronomy? Mars or ... what's her name, doll-girl?"

"Ket."

"Cat? Look, before getting scratched, decide what you want this time. If it's Mars—"

"No." Rube's body trembled. He wanted to grab his brother, make him stop talking. But what came out was, "It's not." He gave Vic a headbutt to the shin.

"Hey, watch where you swing that thing." Vic pushed Rube back. "But what? It's not?"

"It's complicated. I know getting to Mars is a long shot."

"So why take it seriously? Have fun. See what happens. Stop thinking it's a failure if—"

"You don't understand. I'd be over thirty after the mission." Rube was overwhelmed with confusion. He longed for love, and meaning, but there was something else. He swallowed. "You see ... if I make another bad decision, I think it will define the rest my life."

"I'm thirty, and I've not turned to stone. You're talking about a self-fulfilling prophecy."

"I know. I also know I promised you—myself really—not to screw up again. But it wasn't a promise to get to Mars, only to give it my best shot, and maybe to find someone. It feels like my last chance. But the process itself has opened up my life to new possibilities."

"Then go for those. But also follow your heart. That's not screwing up—at least not in a bad way." Vic smiled. "Sorry, I just had to say that. But we can't really have a serious talk while you're a doll, can we? So how about I get a beer, and we talk about something else."

Rube shook his head. "I've been thinking, if I get to Mar and stay … we won't—" Something touched his shoulder.

"Rube. Rube," he heard Lacy say. "It's connected. Her v-bod, it's ready to connect!"

* * *

After Rube had said a quick goodbye to Vic, he pinched his mask and pulled it off. He was back in his hotel room, sitting up.

"I've 'touched' the v-bod you gave Ket," Lacy said. "It's ready to connect." She bit her lip. "But what were you doing? You weren't on some sex site—"

"I was visiting my brother. Wasn't my door locked?"

Quasi shrugged. "Lacy hacked the combo. I tried to stop her."

"How did you get Ket to authorize the v-bod?" Rube felt bewildered. "Her soahl, its untouchable. And she doesn't know my handle. How did you find hers?"

"Let's just say," Lacy said, "your prototype v-bods have security holes."

Rube lay back. "All right … but please get out."

"Can't we listen in?" Lacy said. "We won't make a sound."

"No, you can't listen in." Rube sat up on his elbows.

"This goes against my advice," Quasi said. "But I reckon it follows it too." He tugged on Lacy's blouse, pulling her to his side. "So I'm only going to say this. Good luck."

"Yes, good luck Rube," Lacy said.

"But please, get out." Rube watched them leave. Then he fell back and put the facemask on again. Good luck? It sounded more like—be careful. It was his brother's message too, despite his v-bodda-bing remark. There was also Prasham's warning … and the rules.

But Rube hated the rules.

CHAPTER 8
BAD BRA, GOOD SIGN

Ket yelped when the doll sat up.

A moment ago she had lifted the lid from its box to see a spooky blank cloth head. Then, after she pressed where the nose belonged, a programmed voice said, "Authorization to accept connections received." But she had done no such thing. Now it sat staring at her, its face becoming human. "Hi," it said. The voice was clear. It was Rube's.

She had seen other v-bods, full-sized, that tried to look human but actually looked like mannequins. This little doll, though, now had Rube's face and sprouted his shaggy hair with the color of dark honey. Its creepiness diminished. She wanted to scold Rube for invading her privacy, but said, "Don't I have to authorize myself as a tour guide before it can activate?"

"Well, Lacy has her ways."

Ket rolled her eyes. "Here, let me help you out of there." She took Rube out of the box and set him on her desk. "You could have waited to ask me for my soahl handle."

"The v-bod was on—I wasn't sure I'd get the chance to—"

"To what, show up unannounced?" Ket looked away for a moment.

"To say I'm sorry for what I said at the café. I didn't mean to imply—"

"I was thinking about Corvus … that idiot …" She reminded herself she didn't really know Rube. "I'm sorry too. But I hope you're not an idiot—though you look rather harmless, standing there all short and armless and all."

"Sorry, I *am* an idiot. Not like Corvus. But when it comes to trying to meet someone ..."

She saw Rube do a funny little dance, an Irish jig of sorts.

"My hands control the feet on this thing. I wiggle my fingers and ..."

Ket realized she must have given Rube a strange look.

"Sorry, Ket. What do you want? Give the word and I'll leave."

"No, stay. I do want to talk ... to someone." Ket pushed her bangs up before letting them fall back into place. "Did you just ask me what I want?"

"Uh ... I don't know. I was rambling."

"Right ... right ..." Ket gazed at Rube. "You know," she finally said. "I've always had some questions about v-bod regulations. Why no arms? Why does a v-bod need a tour guide? I've never used a v-bod. I guess I could search my soahl." She looked for her display.

"Yeah, the rules are weird, aren't they? What I've heard is that first v-bods had arms and legs and could wander wherever they wanted. After a few were used for robberies, it was decided they could have feet, but no arms, like this one, or arms but no legs, like the ones at store check-outs. Constructing a civilian-class v-bod with both arms and legs is illegal."

"And tour guides? I guess more security—"

"Right. Tour guides became a requirement when I was in college, to make someone local responsible for the v-bods behavior. And rental companies got tired of people stealing them."

Ket watched Rube stroll around her desk in a circle.

"Before that law, I was on a v-bod trip in Italy when a kid grabbed me." Rube play-acted like he was fighting the kid. "He disabled the GPS, dragged me home and hung me upside-down from an exercise bar. I was helpless. The police couldn't find the v-bod. Luckily, I'd bought the insurance."

He stopped moving and looked down. "Interesting. Some sort of math?"

"It is," said Ket. "It's called Dirac notation. He used it to denote quantum states. You've heard of Dirac, haven't you?"

"You don't mean *the* Dirac, the famous physicist?"

"There's another?" Ket picked up her pencil. She wrote where Rube could see: <*m* | *n*>. "Dirac called this a bracket and broke it into its left and right parts. The right part would be this." She wrote: | *n*>. "He called this a ket. You see, perfect for me."

"So you're a ket, Ket?"

"Yes, exactly. It's another reason I go by that—I love its meaning. A ket is one way of representing a quantum state. But so is this ..." Ket wrote: <*m* | . "Dirac called this a bra. Get it? A bra and ket make a bracket." She pointed at the <*m* | *n*> symbols.

"Yep, I think so. Wait, what's a bra again?"

"A bra also represents a quantum state, but it's a companion to the ket, and it can be a good companion or a bad one. I like to think of bras and kets as seeking each other to join."

"I started out in astronomy but didn't get that far into quantum theory."

"It's just how I like to think about it. When a bra joins a ket, the output is a complex number, but its absolute square is a number between zero and one. If it's zero, then that's a bad bra. It's not compatible with that ket. But if a ket meets its perfect bra, its perfect companion, then the output is one ... in other words, perfect unity."

"I like your description. It's romantic. I've always been a sucker for a good love story, which I know is about the strangest thing someone planning to go to Mars could say. Sorry, I'm rambling again. I guess I'm confused."

"Me too." Ket felt herself blush. "It must be the coins ... but ... when I meet a guy, I always try to judge—would he be a good bra or a bad bra for me."

"So, when you meet a guy you imagine him as your bra?"

She could see Rube struggling to keep a straight face. "No, go ahead and laugh. That was supposed to be a joke."

"Uh … then lucky for you this v-bod has no hands, or we could find out how bad a bra this v-bod boy can be." Rube gave her a big day-dreamy smile.

"Don't be cheeky." She had set this up, but she was a little surprised that Rube had taken the bait so easily. She was going to have to make sure she didn't mislead him. "I thought you were kind of shy. But I was joking, so I can take it. Anyway, I don't tell just anyone my way of thinking about bras and kets."

"Not Prasham?"

"Never. He took a vow of celibacy when he went to Mars. He told me he still tries to keep that vow, to stay focused on science. I haven't asked what he means by 'tries' though. He keeps things professional, unlike some guys who stare yearningly at me more than they should."

"What do you do then?"

"Oh, I electrocute them with the orange dress." Ket laughed.

Rube stepped back, off her math papers. "I'll remember that."

"I'm kidding." She hoped Rube wasn't taking her seriously.

"Even as a doll, I've found out this mask can transmit pain to my face."

"How do you know?"

"I was visiting my brother before I came here. He poked me in the cheek."

"There is something tempting about how you look—I mean the doll—so soft and real and … you have a brother?"

"Yep, he's Doctor V in the soahliverse. He's not a real doctor but it's what he goes by. Well, when he goes online, which is rare. So, what's your soahl handle?"

"I guess I can tell you. It's Bad Wave."

"Bad Wave?"

Ket fought to hold her expression steady. Then she smiled. "There's a story behind it. I'll tell you about it sometime ... but Bad Wave also sounds good."

"Why not Good Wave?"

"No way. I'm a preacher's kid. I didn't want to be 'good' anything. Like I said, I'm looking for that good bra—my perfect match. But of course, my good bra will also have to be a little bit 'bad' you see ..." She hoped Rube knew this was all in fun. "Good, bad, bad, good. Anyway, you are?"

"Good Sine." Rube's doll face looked mortified.

"No problem. You can be good. I'll be bad." Ket laughed again. "A trig function, eh?"

"Yes. I had a dream once."

"Corvus takes dreams very seriously. I hope you don't—"

"No, no ... but there is a story behind it. I'll tell you about it sometime."

"Yes ... sometime." Ket realized it was getting late. "I talked with my old teacher in Fiji. He still works for my father. He says Corvus is due back Thursday night. So I'm safe and Prasham has a guard outside." She hesitated. How much should she tell Rube? "Corvus is capable of doing very cruel things. I wish I could get my sister and her kids away from him. If it wasn't for my father ... really, I don't want to admit this, but I wish I knew what he was planning. If Corvus came to get me then maybe my father can't control him anymore. If only—"

"Hah—I've got it." Rube seemed to hopscotch across her desk.

"What?" Ket looked around the room, trying to see if Rube had noticed something.

"How to find out what Corvus is up to. I'll go spy on him."

"What? How?"

"Your teacher—I'll need his full name."

"Dr. Mateni's? It's Sa Rauta Mateni, OK Drunk in English. But why—"

"I can search for his address. Then, after a little help from Lacy and Quasi, we ship this v-bod to him in Fiji. He drops it off at your sister's place as a doll for her kids, and I use it to find out what Corvus is up to." Rube's eyes blinked several times.

"You're mad." Ket stepped back. "Are you serious about going to Mars?"

"Very."

"So am I. But your plan … it's bad, really bad."

"You said you liked bad. But take it as a good sign from a Good Sine."

She could see Rube was giving her his best 'trust me' smile.

"Let's talk about it tomorrow when I'm back to normal," he continued. "Somehow this v-bod makes me feel … different. But while I've got my courage up, what does a guy, uh, maybe when he's not a twelve-inch tall doll, have to do to get you to go out with them?"

Ket had not expected this. Not yet. Though she had her pat answer ready. "I usually give them a math puzzle. If they solve it, they get a date."

"I see. So … when can I have my puzzle?"

There was a knock at the door. Ket almost jumped up to the ceiling. She looked at Rube. "Things are moving too fast in too many directions at once, don't you think?" She went over and opened the door. "How did you get past the guard?"

"Who is it? Prasham?"

Ket looked back and saw Rube trying to see past her. "It's my boyfriend."

The v-bod fell over backwards, and its face changed from Rube's back to blank cloth.

CHAPTER 9
VIRTUAL SPIES DON'T CRY

"This is bad, really bad." Lacy paced around the roof of the Mars Explorer Building.

"That's what Ket said. But it's important." Rube followed Lacy's quick back-and-forth motion. Then he looked over at Quasi, who stared intently at his n-cloth display. Rube had asked them to come here for a seven a.m. 'emergency' meeting. He had not expected this reaction.

"You're the one who keeps reminding us that we're trying to go to Mars," Lacy continued, swinging her arms. "You're the one who talks about hanging out with the smartest, most famous and richest guy in the world, to do something that will matter for millions of years to come. But now you're proposing we sneak out of orientation week, take the train to Bangalore, send an ok-drunk guy a hacked v-bod, and spy on the public relations manager of the second richest and most famous guy in the world? And she has a boyfriend?"

"Technically," Quasi said, "with Mobius on Mars, Abraham is the richest guy on Earth."

"And it's Dr. OK Drunk," Rube said, "not some ok-drunk guy."

Lacy stopped pacing. "If you do this, you really will have crossed the Rubicon this time."

"When did you last think I crossed the Rubicon?" Rube squinted. "Never mind."

"Right-o." Quasi adjusted his hat for the day, a tweed detective's cap. "Doesn't the to-do list also say we have to steal the v-bod you gave to Twiddle?" He began to scroll down the list.

"And you asked her out on a date?" Lacy raised her open hands toward the heavens.

"There was something wrong with that mask. It made me feel like I could say anything."

"And what did Prasham say?" Quasi asked.

Not much, Rube thought. After tossing and turning for hours last night he got up and went over to the Mars Explorer Building. That was just after six. He was surprised to find Prasham, who had taken the early train back from Bangalore, in his office. Ket, he found out, wasn't due back until noon. He decided to tell Prasham that Corvus might still be planning something. Prasham, Rube told his friends, had responded this was nonsense, that Abraham and Corvus had too much at stake to risk a scandal. Corvus had tried his ploy and failed. Then Prasham had laughed and said, "Besides, Corvus has left India. So the guard is more to keep—how should I put it—to keep those who are too easily distracted out of trouble."

"So Prasham doesn't know about the boyfriend?" Lacy asked.

"Prasham is more focused on work than watching her." Rube replied. "Like Ket said."

"Or us, we hope," Lacy said. "That's a point in our favor. But are you sure this plan of yours isn't just to impress her? I know I've been cheering you on, but— "

"But that would be crazy," said Quasi. "However ... however ... I reckon a trip to Bangalore could be fun. There's a mag-train right after the last workshop today. We could eat on the way and return at four the next morning, like you said Prasham did. No harm in doing that. On the other hand, if you're doing this to get to her—well then, you're *aff yer heid*."

"I'm not doing this to get to her." Rube clenched his fists and beat his thighs with desperation. "But I am doing this for her. She needs our help. And I'm convinced if Corvus comes back, the next mission could be at stake too. I need your help."

Lacy relaxed her shoulders and smiled. "Gotcha."

Quasi smiled too. "Right-o, but maybe we should go over the plan one more time."

Rube did so. Quasi and Lacy would get the v-bod from Twiddle's office while he kept watch. This v-bod had arms and hands but no legs or feet, which Ket's did have. Rube felt he might need a v-bod with all of these for a spy mission. After the last workshop, they would head for Bangalore. Once at Ket's apartment, Quasi would perform a little engineering surgery and insert the head of Ket's v-bod through the diaphragm of Twiddle's, pushing it up into its chest cavity, and then interconnect them. Quasi pointed out that there would no local soahl in Fiji to route commands to the v-bod, so they would need to pick up a miniature satellite receiver from a shop, which Quasi could connect internally. Rube suggested that they pick up a long-life battery too. That way the spy v-bod could run for at least a year without a recharge.

Next, Rube explained, after Quasi had done his part, Lacy would change the code so the joint v-bods would work together. She suggested the virtual travel kit's left glove control the hands and its right glove control walking. Rube agreed that would be perfect, since it was exactly how he had controlled his software avatar for most of the past year. She would also disable the security settings, rather than having to hack past them as she had done with Ket's v-bod, to allow remote control without authorization from a local tour guide in Fiji. There was one more thing. Lacy would also give the v-bod a clown face so Rube would not be recognized.

Everything seemed set, but Quasi wanted to know what role Ket would play. Rube told them that Prasham had said that he and Ket were staying in the hotel in Sri East tonight. They could ask her for the pass code to her apartment. Then Rube made a decision. "There's no need to involve her. All she knows is that I had a crazy idea—too crazy for anyone to actually act on it. I have the GPS coordinates of her apartment in my soahl, downloaded from my v-bod visit last night. Lacy, I'll bet you can get past the passcode to enter her apartment."

"Piece of cake," Lacy said. "I mean, no problem. But stealing v-bods, illegally joining them, operating them without a tour guide, and spying—now those are problems."

"Only *my* soahl handle will be used," Rube said. "I won't get caught, or if I am, they'll just have a doll that acts like a robot. No one will realize it's a v-bod. Worst case, I'll say you two helped me prepare it to impress a girl. It's sort of true, despite what I said before. As for the spy mission, I'll contact Dr. Drunk, uh, Dr. Mateni tonight and tell him I'm sending Ket's nieces a present. We'll ship him the v-bod overnight. Then I can do the spy mission tomorrow night from my hotel room—when Corvus is due back in Fiji."

Quasi flicked his display back into its soft cloth state and looked up. "You know, I actually think it will work. Aye, only a wee bit of a doodle for us. I propose we have a toast." He found his flask and passed it to Lacy.

"To friendship." Lacy laughed and took a mouthful. "And to impressing that girl."

"To friendship," Rube said, firmly. He accepted the flask from Lacy and took the tiniest of nips. Then he passed it back to Quasi.

Quasi gulped down a big swig. "Now that's the kicker. To friendship and—"

"We start in five minutes, downstairs."

Rube had heard heavy footsteps before the voice. He turned to see Harlow.

"Five minutes," Harlow repeated. "So what's this, a secret party?"

Rube hoped he and his friends didn't look too startled. They all remained silent until Rube said, "Yes, but you missed the cake."

* * *

Rube took out his virtual travel kit and began to prepare for the spy mission. Everything since yesterday morning had been a blur. The workshops had kept them busy, and he had easily avoided talking to Ket after her arrival. She hadn't sought him out either, and he wondered if she was avoiding him. Why was he doing this? But he had no intention of backing out.

The combined v-bod had been assembled last night, and they'd left it for shipment just before midnight. Dr. Mateni had acknowledged its delivery to Ket's sister an hour ago, and confirmed that Corvus was due to arrive soon. It was all going very well.

Well, there had been two, what Lacy called doodle-hics, along the way.

First, while Quasi was searching for the v-bod with arms, Twiddle had shown up outside his office. But, according to Lacy, she had stepped in and begged him to answer a question about black hole embedding diagrams, allowing Quasi to slip out of Twiddle's office with the v-bod, unseen. Second, when they got to Ket's apartment, the man from the car, Sunjay, had been standing guard outside. Rube replayed the latter incident in his mind.

Sunjay, in his early twenties, maybe, looked like a bored disco dancer who had been asked to watch a ballet. Rube had not anticipated his presence, since Ket was back at the hotel in Sri East. Quasi chatted to Sunjay about the uselessness of guarding someone who wasn't there. Then Quasi's flask came out. "Time to freshen up," Sunjay said in response, and he and Quasi walked off together.

Ten minutes later Quasi returned. For a few quid, Sunjay had agreed to take the night off. He'd told Quasi that a young man had made him a similar offer the night before. Rube wondered if Sunjay was really the best guard Prasham could find. But with Sunjay gone, Lacy disabled the passcode. And the rest of the evening went off without a hitch.

Now, Rube sat on his bed in his hotel room, looking at the picture of the red and white clown face Lacy had programmed the v-bod to display. With a pinch, the picture collapsed into a cloth square that floated from his gloved hands onto the bed. He picked up the facemask and put it on. With a squeeze of his soahl it conformed to his face, and he fell back.

* * *

Rube found himself lying on another bed, one made of moonlit straw. Just above, he saw the snout of a wooden donkey. For a moment he thought it was drooling on him. Then he realized the stickiness he felt was the humidity. He raised his toy head slowly. Mosquito nets hung down from the ceiling, with two figurines in nightgowns underneath. Through the gauze he made out these were little girls. He was in the kids' room.

He sat up. Nightlights lined the floor. Faint candle-shaped lights were also strung along the walls. Several wooden shepherds gazed upon him. Across the room, a brighter light flooded beneath a door. He stood up and turned to face three robed kings made of porcelain, looking up at a large star painted on the ceiling. Their crooked beards almost touched his head. He heard a soft buzzing, and for a moment the kings seemed to break into wicked grins. A blink erased this eerie image, and he looked down at a toy bin filled with dolls. Most were babies in various states of undress. He realized he was the newest doll on the scene, put in the place of highest honor. But he couldn't just stand there. He had to get on with the mission. Tracing the moonlight, he identified the windows. They were louvered and open to the night air. They also let in the source of the buzzing—mosquitos that fortunately had no interest in his bloodless form.

He crawled over a railing and dropped onto a long wooden box. With a small leap, he landed with a light thud on the floor. One of the girls stirred. He picked himself up and froze.

"Is everything all right in there?"

The door opened and a woman leaned in. Rube thought it was probably Ket's sister. No sounds came from the girls and she backed out and closed the door. He let out a sigh. One of the girls rolled over and looked his way. He kept still and she closed her eyes again.

After moving carefully over to the window, he jumped. He could feel the chipped paint of the sill in his firm grip. He was thankful for how silently he could move this v-bod. He slipped under the windowpane, rolled outside, and dropped onto a wooden walkway.

Rube realized he was on a veranda that ran the length of a very long house. He looked up. The full moon almost blinded him. He choked back a curse. Where was the gain control? He fumbled with the heads-up controls. It would have to wait. He was far too visible. He had to keep moving. Farther down, an overhang began, and a bit farther from there, a light came from a window. Several potted plants sat on its sill. Even farther along, a large porch led into a vestibule that must be the house's main entrance.

Rube sprinted into the shadow of the overhang. The sound of crunching gravel caught his attention. A car was pulling into a circular drive between two ghostlike palm trees. It stopped, and a man with cowboy boots and a holstered gun got out.

"Take the car and my bags around back," Corvus said to the driver.

Rube watched him go up the porch stairs and walk inside. After the car pulled away, Rube snuck farther along the veranda to the lit window. It was open. He heard voices and then heavy breathing close up. A wet tongue licked his face … belonging to a scruffy hound.

He waggled his hands at the dog. Then he tried holding very still. After sniffing him over, the dog lost interest. Rube turned back toward the window and made another flawless leap.

After doing a v-bod chin-up, Rube poked his head between two flowers and peered inside. This window was screened, but inside he could see Corvus in a lush office sitting in a large leather chair across from a gray-haired man—Abraham. Rube lowered himself so that his eyes were at sill level. He could see them, but he was in the shadow of the overhang, behind a flower. He was pretty sure the screen would make his image a blur.

"You should have told me your plan," Abraham said. His voice was very calm but somewhat weak. He looked older than the man Rube remembered from Soahl-7.

"I received the sign … the one I said I wanted to tell you about."

"Did you tell Ket about this? I told you the right approach with her would be to remind her about her family—about me. For goodness sake, why didn't you use that public relations charm I pay you for?"

"I did. I told her you wanted her back home. I was going to tell her how much you all missed her, but I was attacked by her boyfriend."

You attacked me! Rube managed to remain still while his mind screamed.

"Some wretched creature without a soul. I fought him off, but didn't want to make a scene. However, I think he is another sign."

"You haven't told me about the first sign yet."

"As you say, pray and pay attention to the dreams." Corvus rapped his fingers on a book.

Rube could make out on its spine, 'The New Age of the Spirit' and 'A. Boni.' Beneath this, he could make out another title, 'The Three Eras of Joachim of Fiore,' and he suddenly wished he had done some research first.

"After much prayer," Corvus said, "Betti told me she'd rather marry than burn."

"In your dream? That was the first sign? That's when you decided to go to her?"

Rube was heartened by Abraham's skepticism.

"Yes. I was going to India already, you know, to negotiate the transfer of the nuke."

"Of course, you were going to Mumbai. Though I hoped you might see her. How is she?"

"She looked like someone brainwashed by those mathematicians." Corvus scowled and turned his head. "You know, it's all witchcraft, from the Greeks."

"Don't sound like a donkey." Abraham stopped and shook his head like he was talking to a school child. "I'm not against science, just its arrogance. I've made that clear, haven't I?"

"Of course, very clear."

"I don't care if Betti likes math, but I don't want her to ... to ... I want her back."

You're her father. Try to contact her.

"Yes, I know. She cannot go to Mars. You have forbidden it. If I could bring her back here to marry me that would solve everything."

Abraham, do you buy this? Who's in charge here?

"We can only pray and look inside for the answers. I cannot go to her." Abraham tried to stand up but sank back into his seat. "I was counting on a sign—a real one."

"You doubt me?"

"Sometimes dreams are simply wishes in disguise. Though I can't for the life of me figure out why you want a second wife. You don't even seem to like women."

Corvus circled around the desk, behind Abraham, and paused for a moment. He rolled his cane between his thumb and index finger. Then he came back to face the old man. "I could take some of the boys. We could kidnap her."

"No—"

"Bride kidnapping is not unprecedented; the Benjamites—"

"No!"

"But if she disobeys, we should shun her and you could disown her. Then we could deal with the Mars Program as we wish."

"No kidnapping. No shunning. That was a different dispensation. She must come back of her own free will."

Good, Abraham.

"I could scare her back here. All legal, of course."

"Now is not the time to do anything, legal or illegal. Nothing must be done to harm the ministry, and nothing must be done to harm Betti."

"But if I take a vow and there has to be a sacrifice? The BS—couldn't it involve her?"

The BS?

"If the signs were right we would do what we had to. Except, not with my daughter."

"But think about Jephthah—that was a great victory!"

Who?

"I said no. But you did say there was another sign?"

"Yes. I met with Dr. Whitesmith on the way back from India. He pointed me to the boyfriend's slog."

"His slog?"

"His soahl log." Corvus bowed down, as if saying the word soahl was a swear word. "His slog, it's called 'I dreamed I was a sin wave."

Not sin, sine. It's pronounced sine.

"A sin wave? Do you mean sine wave? I may be a preacher, but I did learn a thing or two in school. Though I think Betti got her math smarts from her mother."

"Yes, Dr. Whitesmith thought so too. I mean about sin being sine. By the way, he has agreed to the salvage operation for the BS. But the boyfriend … the boyfriend dreamed he was spreading through the universe. It made him change his life's course. It led him to Mobius. So be it, a sine wave. But a sine wave in a dream could be a sign … a sign that evil wants him to spread sin throughout the universe. That's what Mobius wants. That is why we must stop them."

"First get Betti back here …"

Rube couldn't make out what Abraham said next. It was drowned out by a buzz. An out-of-focus insect crawled across his eyes then bounced between them and the screen—a bee. He tried to brush it away. Rube bit his real tongue. The bee landed again on his face.

"Ouch!"

Rube saw Abraham and Corvus look toward him. He cursed at how the n-cloth facemask had managed to transmit the feeling of a sting so effectively. He wanted to cry. *Damn it, what's wrong this mask? Where's the mute control?*

"I'll go see what's out there." Corvus strode out of the room.

Rube dropped to the veranda. He tried to scamper into the bushes, but dog slobber stopped him. After he struggled to push the probing snout out of the way, the dog ran off, revealing Corvus pointing a pistol straight at him.

"Hey, little robo-clown. Did the boys from the village send you?"

Rube saw Corvus return the gun to its holster and pick him up. Then Corvus carried him around the side of the house and tossed him onto the lawn.

"I'll teach them to make fun of me. When they see your headless clown body sitting up on the fence tomorrow, that'll scare 'em." Corvus drew his gun again.

Back in his hotel room Rube tried to pull off the mask. It was stuck! Fear would have poured out of his eyes and ears if they weren't covered. He reached with his gloved hand to turn off his soahl. At the same time, the feel of a wet tongue returned to his face.

"Hey, get away from there, you stupid dog."

Rube saw the dog scamper way. He squeezed his soahl, but the words 'saving data before shutting down' scrolled by. He closed his eyes.

"Corvus, what are you doing? Don't shoot, you'll wake up the girls."

It was Abraham.

"Someone put a robo-clown toy outside your window," Corvus explained.

Rube saw Abraham stare his way and squint.

"That thing? Mateni brought that by for the girls. One of them probably left it outside. I'll have Mateni remove its batteries tomorrow. Now put that gun away."

Corvus uncocked the gun. Rube sighed as quietly as he could. Then one of the little girls, holding her nightgown up, tiptoed across the grass in bare feet.

"Why are you shooting baby Je—"

"And why are you out of bed?" Corvus holstered his gun. "And hush. We were just playing cowboys and … and clowns. Here, you can take him back inside now."

Rube saw Corvus move quickly toward him but felt the dog mouth his face and pick him up. While being carried away, he heard one more thing.

"Come back, you stupid dog. We aren't playing with that now."

Finally, Rube's soahl powered off and he managed to rip the n-cloth mask from his face.

CHAPTER 10
SOUL VERSUS SOAHL

"I think, therefore I am. I hear my thoughts, therefore I have a soul."

Ket pushed pause on the holo-screen remote in her hotel room. The image of Mobius froze with his lips sticking out from the trim, full goatee around his mouth, as if he were ready for a kiss. Cute, but she wanted the part farther along. She pushed fast-forward and Mobius's sturdy frame rolled from side-to-side behind the podium. His arms flapped like the wings of an albatross. Then the camera panned and her father appeared. Ket pushed play and watched.

"What is over there?" Abraham asked a robo-viewer sitting on a stand.

"A curtain, ten point two meters away, chenille-weave of FR cotton-esterwool."

"Very good. Now what color is the curtain?"

"Red," the robo-viewer replied.

"Well, let's think about this," Abraham continued. "This device reports red, but I am sure no one in this room thinks it sees red. It has no soul. Right?" He used the tone of a lawyer.

"Experiencing a color is a conscious experience," Mobius replied.

The camera pulled back to show both men.

"But you have no theory of how it works. To you, it might as well be a miracle."

"There were many things we didn't understand before. In time we will."

"Well, I hear some of your followers think the soahls you invented are alive."

"Cults do exist, but I wouldn't call their members followers of mine." Mobius paused. "Some people think that self awareness is merely a matter of complexity. I do not. Computers today are approaching human intelligence. It's taken more time than we thought it would—but we'll get there. However, I'm not sure a silicon mind will ever hear itself think. Not like we do. So I do believe humans have a soul. I just don't think it's immortal or supernatural."

"But it's beyond science. No experiment can tell if this robo-viewer is conscious or not. Ha! Now that's got to snarkle the cell walls of those reductionist-believing neurons of yours."

The audience tittered and Abraham looked proud.

Mobius stood firm. "One day we'll understand it. For example, we know stimulating areas near the claustrum can turn consciousness off, we've mapped the connectome, and we understand the biochemistry. There are details to be work out, but when they are, we'll know if silicon can do it too. So I am not saying we know the answers, only that one day we will."

Abraham grabbed his suit's lapels. "Only inside can you find deeper meaning. The same way you can hear yourself think, you can hear the Spirit. Look inside, then you will know—"

Ket pushed pause. She thought it was funny how both men would claim to have won the debate, but also praise the other ... how afterward they would work together and later brag their shared influence had helped pass greater privacy laws and drone regulations, correcting years of abuse ... how after that, they would go back to accusing the other of arrogance. She pushed play.

"You have an immortal soul. Just examine someone's eyes." Abraham looked down.

Ket pushed pause again. She knew her father was looking at her, twelve years ago. He seemed old next to Mobius, who was twenty years younger than her father. Though it struck her how less frail her father was then. The dozen years between her father's mid-sixties and mid-seventies had taken a toll.

She imagined her father's touch when she was five. Picking her up, he asked, "How's my little girl?" It was a family picnic on the fresh mowed Bermuda lawn behind the house in Fiji, surrounded by the bougainvillea her mother grew, with sliced papaya and mangos spread out on Chinese bamboo mats. She wondered why these were not the beautiful ones woven by the nearby village.

The mats dissolved into pews, and she watched her father preach. "The family comes first," he said. Her tiny legs in linen stockings fidgeted, and her younger self asked, "Why are you never around?" But her voice was just a whisper. She knew as long as she attended church, or watched recordings of his travels, her father acted satisfied with the parenting job he had done.

Then she saw her mother retreating to her back room to listen to music, and her older sister Sarah startled by a shout from Corvus. She thought about how Sarah was trapped now, taking care of their two little girls.

Ket's thoughts shifted to her sixteenth birthday, the day Corvus told her he knew how she could always be with him and her sister. An uncontrollable shiver went through her body. There was no way to escape.

Except, a month later, tsunami warning sirens rang during the offering, and while the congregation headed for higher ground she thought of a way. After reaching the beach she felt the dry sand between her toes, the last warmth she would ever feel. She watched the sea rush out, as if it were pouring over the edge of the Earth. She waited for it to return, to take away her last breath. But a shout came from behind. She turned. A silhouetted figure was running toward her.

If it hadn't been for her teacher that day, she wouldn't be here … trying for Mars. For a moment, though, she imagined

Mobius running to save her. He was attractive, wasn't he? She pushed play until Mobius stared at her with his lonely, chestnut eyes—eyes that said he'd do anything for someone he loved. A turbulent mix of feelings flooded into her. Hurt over the missed affection from her father, revulsion for Corvus … and an almost forgotten crush.

"What a silly girl." Ket flipped off the screen and spun onto the bed. Mars. She wanted that thought to banish all the others. She tried to sound like Mobius. Deepening her voice, she said, "We go to Mars to explore …" But she sounded comical and sad. Something was wrong.

The breakup. After breakfast in Bangalore she reminded her boyfriend she was going away. It was time to end it. He didn't object, since they'd never been in love. He'd wanted their relationship kept secret too. Which was perfect, except … Rube knew.

She almost laughed. Now there's the rub, she thought. In some ways Rube seemed like the perfect guy. A bit disheveled, maybe, but smart and committed to Mars. Wasn't he? Had he really asked her out? She knew he'd had an eye on her, and she had planned to tell him she was unavailable, too focused on science. Except for some stupid reason she had told him about her search for the perfect 'bra' … and he'd seen the boyfriend. What could she tell him now?

Ket let out a huge sigh. Then her n-cloth chimed. She opened her display to see a reminder to submit her university preferences. The assignments would be posted after the second demo. Wasn't it too late? What she needed was a new list, and she started to dictate:

Mars Program, Academic Phase, List of Universities.

1. Raman Research Institute, Prasham. Leads the Math Monks. Everyone's first choice. But he said I should try somewhere new. I agree, and I need a break from him too.

2. Harvard, Mavra. Harvard is Harvard … but I hear Mavra is even more obsessed with work than Prasham. So no.

3. Oxford, Twiddle. Funny. But is life there too stuffy?

4. U. of Washington, Dr. Nickie. Tall, elegant, smart. Might be interesting to work with a woman. Soahl Headquarters. Mobius's home. And Rube, he went there … so he won't go there.

She saved the list, then filled out the request form: UW, 1st, Oxford 2nd, Harvard 3rd, RRI 4th. Without thinking, she pressed send.

CHAPTER 11
LAUNCH CRAWL

Rube stared at the four high-rope courses. He was inside the Mars Explorer training facility, which spanned the size of six gymnasiums, near the end of the line for the far right course. Quasi and Lacy had already completed their run and were busy laying out the belay lines for his turn. Harlow was the only one behind him. All Rube had to do was get through this course.

He ran his eyes up the 'Cargo Space Net' to the first platform, twelve meters off the floor. This led to the 'Bridge of Zeno' with wooden slats doubling their separation with every step, until reaching the two-meter 'Leap of Reason' needed to get to the next platform. From there one 'Walked the Quantum Planck' then jumped down twenty centimeters to tightropes (the 'Death Rays') using shoulder-high rope railings to follow converging paths to a large central crow's nest called 'The Focal Point.' Here, one switched safety lines and chose a partner. With hands clasped while leaning toward each other to make a human A-frame, each member of the pair stood on one of two parallel steel cables and sidestepped along 'The Launch Crawl' until reaching a swinging steel gantry. Each individual then had to switch safety lines again, climb up the three meter 'Rocket Tower' to another platform, and finally rappel down the fifteen meter 'Escape Wall' to the floor.

"Child's play," Harlow said. 'Like swinging over the quarry lake back home."

Rube felt like smacking him. Who came up with these team-building exercises, anyway? Sure, they had gone through information workshops, been interviewed by psychologists, and attended role-playing classes. In one, he had to resolve a dispute about a leaking oxygen tank before everyone suffocated. In another, Quasi and Lacy had to 'pretend to be a couple' that had lied to get in and now never wanted to see each other again. They were asked to act out how they would cope with never being more than a few hundred meters apart until their return to Earth.

There had also been Prasham's class on solitude and spaceflight, which ended with the students floating in saltwater for two hours, each in a chamber the size of a coffin. They were asked to meditate on spending eight and a half months on the journey to Mars and back. These chambers would be the size of their bedrooms for that voyage, their one place of privacy. Since Rube had spent years in small rooms with only his soahl, this wouldn't be a problem for him.

But heights were different. What was the point of heights, if there was no up or down in space? And surely falling on Mars, in two-fifth's Earth's gravity, inside an enclosed base, wasn't an issue, was it?

At least Ket wasn't there to see him fall flat on his face today. He wanted to tell her what he had learned last night, though, and to ask her something too.

But—there she was … late.

In ballet shoes and black leotards, her hair wet, stretching straight down to her waist, she went to the back of the line next to Rube's. She started to flex like a gymnast who couldn't wait to start her routine.

Rube looked at her, then at Harlow in his tan wrestling outfit. He pictured himself in his white shorts and T-shirt, looking like a skinny marshmallow propped up on two toothpicks. But was he marshmallow or man? "Hey Harlow, switch places with me."

"Huh?" Harlow squinted. "Don't you want me to be last, in case I collapse the course?"

For Rube, that was also a good reason to switch, but he simply said, "I want to go last."

Harlow looked over at Ket and back at Rube. "Oh Rube, make a fist."

"What?"

"That's what I do … whenever I need to keep my hand out of the cupcake jar."

"Next" the belay team called out. Rube ignored Harlow and slipped behind him.

* * *

As he approached The Focal Point, Rube felt encouraged. Somehow he had kept his knees from knocking, and was grateful all eyes were not on him. They had followed Harlow, who so far had danced his way through the course like a circus bear in a cartoon. That is, except when Quasi and Lacy had to swing him across the Leap of Reason while he yelled, "Cannon Ball." Rube thought he heard the floorboards creak, trying to get out of the way, and he imagined the sudden displacement of all the water from Harlow's quarry back home upon his splash down. Thank goodness for friction pulleys, climbing gloves, and leverage.

In fact, watching Harlow had made Rube deliriously happy. He'd made the leap himself with no sensation of nerves, at least not about the heights. He hadn't dared to look toward Ket.

Maybe now, he thought, as he stepped onto The Focal Point. But it was too late. He crashed into her. "Sorry." He reached out a hand to pull her up. "But I'm glad you made it."

Ket rolled her eyes. "Prasham said today's activities were mandatory." She gave Rube her hand. Back on her feet, looking no worse for wear, she began to undo her harness. "I guess we're partners for this next part."

"Funny that," Rube said. "I mean, I thought they were all mandatory." He moved with Ket around The Focal Point and put on a new harness. After facing each other, they moved apart while holding the other's hands at push-up level. Then they stepped onto their individual cables. Like an inverted 'V' they started to shuffle, with their noses inches apart.

"Like I said, I had finals and work to finish up."

"Or a boyfriend to meet?" Rube hadn't planned to bring that up. He wanted to tell her about her father and Corvus. But somehow, pushing his weight against her hands and feeling the warmth of hers against his, he felt able to get this off his chest.

Ket let out a puff of air. "The boyfriend's out of the picture."

"Sorry, that's not what I meant to say. It's not like I travelled to Fiji to try to impress—" Rube stopped. "Wait, he's what?"

Ket had to stop with Rube. She looked annoyed. "You what?"

"She'll be right, mate. Keep going." It was Quasi calling from below. Rube knew he meant the course, not Ket. He looked down. Lacy winked. "Or take your time," she called up.

Rube almost lost his grip and imagined Lacy and Quasi lowering him to the floor in failure. He looked into Ket's eyes and she strengthened her hold on his hands, maybe using more force than necessary. He started to shuffle along with her again. "Sorry, I meant to say … I wanted to tell you about Corvus. Do you remember the plan I told you about with the v-bods?"

"You mean the lunatic one about sending the doll to Dr. Mateni?"

"Yes—yes, that plan … well … I did it."

Ket looked like she wanted to raise her hands in despair, but she could only shake her head. Then she looked at him. "Suppose I believe you. What … what did you learn?"

"That your father cares about you—that he told Corvus not to do anything illegal."

"That's good," Ket said. She didn't look entirely reassured but said, "Thanks."

Rube thought about going into some of the weird plans Corvus had mentioned, and how he didn't really trust him to follow her father's orders. But maybe he would do that later. He wanted to debrief Prasham too, make sure he knew Corvus was planning something to do with the Mars missions, legal or otherwise. For now, he felt there was nothing to worry about, and he asked Ket the other thing on his mind. "So which university did you select as your first choice?"

Ket's legs wobbled. Rube was feeling the burn too, but their crawl was almost done. Finally she said, "Elsewhere."

Rube wanted to ask where 'elsewhere' was, but decided to play along. "Me too," he said. He didn't tell her he'd only weighed the options last night. He didn't want her to think he left things like this to the last minute. He especially didn't want to admit he had wanted to choose RRI, where Prasham was, as his first choice, but hadn't done so when he realized Ket would likely choose somewhere else. Prasham had said the students should choose a new place if they'd already attended one of the four choices. So he'd debated what Ket's first choice would be. Finally he decided, Harvard. Harvard was Harvard after all, and a woman, Mavra, ran the program. He didn't like how sexist that sounded, but he had decided someone as smart at Ket would choose Harvard or Oxford as her first choice, and use that to break the tie. So he'd listed Harvard, Oxford, RRI, and then UW. It was a stupid impulsive decision. But with her boyfriend gone?

With that thought, Rube arms started to shake. He would have to lean closer to Ket. If his arms gave out, only their lips would keep them apart. And they'd fall together ... for eternity ... in a kiss. He closed his eyes, waiting for that wondrous disaster to happen, when he tripped. They'd reached the gantry. "Will I see you at this afternoon's launch?"

"Maybe," Ket replied. She slipped into a new harness. "But the v-bods, how—"

"Let's just say," Rube said, struggling with a buckle, "you won't find that little armless guy back at your apartment."

"Oh, Rube ..." Ket climbed up and looked at him. "There's something I should tell you." But she reached the top of the tower, reversed positions to rappel down, and disappeared.

Chapter 12
Morse Code From The Moon

Rube headed to the roof of the Mars Explorer Building to watch the launch of Mission Thirteen.

Earlier, after leaving the team-building exercise to shower back at the hotel, he had noticed workers taking bleacher parts up in the elevators. He decided to take the stairs.

His feet drummed the steps with a rhythm that increased with his growing anticipation. It wasn't just the excitement of the launch but knowing he would find out soon afterward where he and his friends would go next ... and where Ket would go. He tried to tell himself it didn't matter. What was done was done. If he happened to ended up at Harvard with Ket, he could tell his friends it was perfectly reasonable that he chose the top university, even though they'd probably picked RRI. Whatever happened, he was sure Lacy would call it fate and Quasi would call it a good excuse for a toast.

Emerging into the fresh air brought him back to the present moment. The roof's transformation was amazing. Railings ran around its perimeter, surrounding a smooth wooden floor. Telescopes and cameras faced toward the launch pads on the north side, while bleachers lined the south side. In the center were a podium and two large holo-screens. Above, the sky was like a sapphire crystal bowl wrapped in the high chilled air. The day was as crisp as one could hope for at this location.

Rube raised his hand to block the sun on his left then turned to find his friends. They waved from the top of the crowded stands.

"This is so exciting," Lacy said after Rube sat next to her. "I may have to get a new tattoo. A tunnel to another universe, I think."

"I can't wait for the show," Quasi said. "Two million gallons of fuel burning in fifteen minutes." He turned to Rube. "So, I finally read your message about last night."

"And your latest one about Ket," Lacy added.

Rube resisted an awkward smile. "Uh, we'll have to see—"

"They're supposed to post the lists outside the auditorium after the launch," Lacy said.

"Actually, we'll find out after the second demo, which is after the launch," Quasi said. "But I reckon we'll all get into RRI, right?"

Before Rube could answer, a cheer went up. Prasham was at the podium.

"Today is the launch of the thirteenth mission to Mars. Twenty-six years ago the Western and Eastern Alliances competed to go to Mars. It was hard. So hard that in the end they joined forces for the first mission. And then, after the great economic rollover, the Alliances lost interest. Enter Mobius Monk. He had a vision … and money." Prasham smiled. "And he started his own missions. He and I were on the first of those, and I am eternally grateful for that opportunity. He started the Math Monks and worked tirelessly on his plans for colonization. Then, a bit over eight and a half years ago, we returned to Mars and he stayed. Today, through his efforts, you are here. The missions will continue, but in this new phase, regular people will go. Though, as we have learned this week, 'regular' is not what any of you are."

Rube joined the other students in an uproarious round of applause.

"This launch also marks the beginning of another era. Aboard the manned rocket is one of these." Prasham held up a metallic box with pairs of crossed tubes mounted on rotating disks attached to each side. "This is a mock-up of a gravitino emitter. There is a satellite aboard the crewed ship with one of these that it will put into orbit between Earth and Mars." He waved toward the launch site with his free hand then indicated the box again. "These tubes can swivel and rotate to send entangled gravitinos to us and Mars." Prasham put down the box and picked up a second one, with what looked like an old-fashioned Morse code telegraph key on top. "And this is connected to a gravitino antenna. Impossible, I know."

"So gravitational-wave experiments are good for something?" a student asked.

"Well, yes, they're good for detecting gravitational waves," Prasham responded. "But that corresponds to detecting trillions and trillions of gravitons. In this case, we will detect gravitinos, partners of the graviton." He paused. "Oh, I know what you're thinking ... so many versions of that theory were wrong in the past."

"I hadn't ..." Quasi mumbled.

"I'll look it up," Lacy said.

"Shh," Rube said.

Prasham set the box down. "Let me tell you today, we've recently discovered stable gravitinos, and friends ... these are not your grandfathers' gravitinos." He smiled. "I won't bore you with the details, but we can now make measurements of gravitinos that act like the coin flips in the demo. The coins were magnetically rigged, but this really works." He scanned the stands. "It's all thanks to calculations completed this week by Ket." He pointed. "There she is."

Rube looked at her in the front row, wearing a new dress. It didn't glow, but she did.

Prasham held up the second box again. "We sent one of these and a gravitino antenna to our robo-station on the moon last week." Then he bowed his head until there was silence. "This will allow us," he said in a solemn tone, "to send signals faster than light." After putting down the box, he stretched out his arms. "Today, the theories will end and the magic will begin."

The students applauded and Prasham raised his head.

"I've figured something out," whispered Quasi. "Only crazy people would want to go to Mars. And he's testing us to see if we're crazy. It's one more test."

"Twenty minutes after the launch," Prasham continued, "we'll meet in the auditorium for the second demonstration." Waving his arms, he gave out a jubilant cry. "Now for the launch!"

The large holo-screens showed the two MLV rockets on their pads, a half-kilometer apart from each other. During the week, Rube had learned that the missions were based on plans written up in the nineteen nineties and why there were two rockets. Each would fly directly from Earth to Mars, with the one nearest the sea carrying hydrogen to Mars to synthesize the fuel for the return of the next mission. This rocket also carried with it supplies to expand and improve the base and backup equipment for use in case of mid-mission failure. The other rocket carried a crew of eight, with enough water and food for the thirty-two month mission. Since food was grown on Mars and water was melted from deep permafrost wells, most of this would not be used, except to shield against radiation and then stored as reserves.

Rube couldn't sit still. The excitement rose to a level only someone without a real soul could ignore. That's how Ket had put it in her message, asking to meet him after the demo.

A group of Indian dancers came out in flowing robes. Music, modern and ancient, rich in history and colorful in sound, thundered through the speakers. First the performers brought their hands together in prayer position, which they pushed up like rockets lifting off. Next, the men flexed their broad shoulders, slapped their knees, and stamped their bare feet, while the women crouched and moved their eyes and heads in opposite directions with the beat. Then the men formed the pointed shape of a rocket, while the women formed the round shape of a planet. The formations approached and went through each other—the dancers' bodies performing intricate maneuvers, nearly touching. Finally, both groups fell back with out-stretched arms, like flowers opening to the sun. Springing to their feet, they started again.

The voice of the countdown began over the holo-screen's speakers.

"Ten, nine, eight, seven, six, five, four ..."

Rube watched the liftoff on the screens. Moments later he saw the two brightest things in the sky he had ever seen, other than the sun. Then the roar reached his ears. The speed at which the rockets gained altitude entranced him, and he felt as if he too were rising up. He would have floated away if not for some mysterious force that tethered him to the bleachers. He continued to gaze upward with no sense of his surrounding even after the rockets were no longer visible. Then those around him began to move, and he found his way off the roof and to the auditorium.

* * *

Rube and his friends sat in the back row, as they had for the first demonstration.

"Did you know the Russians sent a radio message in Morse code in 1962?" Lacy had her dark glasses on. "The message came back in four minutes and thirty-two point seven seconds."

"You mean aliens were detected in 1962?" Rube played along.

"No, the radio waves reflected off Venus," Lacy replied. "I think it's funny they used such a primitive form of communication, which it seems Prasham is about to do."

"Though, look up front." Quasi pointed toward the dark stage. "Those aren't primitive."

Rube had noticed them too. Two military-grade v-bods sat in the same chairs he and Ket had been in at the start of the week. And, in particular, these v-bods had n-cloth heads.

"So it didn't take them long to figure that out," Lacy said.

"It seems they got what they wanted from my dolls." Rube blinked a few times.

"And I guess from where Mobius is, he's not worried about patents," Quasi said. "Of course, I reckon it's an obvious idea—using n-cloth instead of elastomers. I'm sure they'll still need that wee brain of yours to top off the design. Sorry ... you said Ket wants to meet?"

"After this, we'll all get together," Rube replied. "I'll tell you more about last night."

"Then, sans boyfriend, you can make your move." An eye appeared in one of the lenses of Lacy's dark glasses. It winked at Rube.

"It's just to talk." Rube squirmed. "Although, I am going to ask her to send me a puzzle."

"A puzzle? She 'tis that, ain't she," Quasi said. "But maybe a wise choice, after all."

"You'll figure it out, Rube," Lacy said, "especially when Prasham is no longer looking over your shoulder. For now, I've found something new on stable gravitinos in the soahlopedia. I'll send the link." She flipped her glasses up onto her hair. "Oh, there's my favorite monk."

Prasham appeared on the stage. He put the second box he'd shown before on the podium. Clicks and clacks were heard through speakers. "That is coming from the moon," he began. "Listen, I'll send a message and the moon will replay it. It is almost a two-second round trip for light." He pressed the transmitter key three times, and the speakers sounded, click, click, click. Then Prasham varied the pattern. Each time the same one came right back. "See, no delay."

"Send a real message," one of the students called out.

Prasham tapped furiously. A short reply came right back. "I said 'goodnight moon robot' and it said, 'oh, mom,' I think." Prasham fiddled a bit with the box. "I'm not very good at Morse code." He turned to the students. "Well, I know, not very impressive. But probably good enough for a Noble Prize," he said with a wry smile. "And, when it's perfected, we'll be able to do this." He pointed to the two v-bods. Lit by spotlights, they stood and came to life.

A collective gasp rolled through the room, as if two corpses had reanimated in the penultimate scene of a horror movie. Then one of the v-bod heads turned into the nerdy and round Twiddle, the other into the fair but serious Nickie.

"Of course, you recognize your instructors," Prasham said. "They wanted to help and are controlling them from their offices. However, think of it. When we can control a v-bod from Mars, instantly, then anyone there can do virtual travel to Earth whenever they want. And vice versa. We are working on the software now and should be able to transmit it to Mars by the time the current mission arrives. Very soon, going to Mars will no longer be a journey to isolation."

Wild clapping came from the students.

Lacy sprang up. "So we could use this to talk to planets around other stars too?"

"Yes," Prasham said. "We could, except we would have to get a gravitino emitter between us and that planet first. And we would have to wait for the entangled gravitino beams to reach that planet and us. It would mean years of waiting. But the possibilities are endless."

"Yes," Rube said to himself. "They are." He tried to see Ket's reaction.

Prasham worked the controls a bit more until there was a loud clack. This was followed by a series of rapid clicks, and then a loud buzzing. Finally, a puff of smoke came out of the box.

"That was interesting," Rube said. He thought Prasham looked alarmed.

"You always have to get a few flies out of the fuel lines," Quasi said.

Prasham regained his composure. "A normal setback. Let's all give each other three cheers. You can then find your university assignments posted outside the auditorium."

After the cheers, Rube saw Ket heading up the aisle. Neither gravity's tether nor fear would bind him. He stood and followed her out of the auditorium.

His adventure was just beginning.

Chapter 13
Space Is The Enemy

Ten minutes after leaving the auditorium, Rube's adventure was over.

In fact, his whole life was over.

The first sign of trouble came when he couldn't find his name on any of the lists for the four universities in the Mars Explorer Program. He found Quasi and Lacy's. They were going to Harvard. And Ket, for some reason, was going to the University of Washington. Then he saw Prasham listed as the leader of that group, apparently doing an exchange with Nickie. It seemed unfair … unbelievable. He scanned the lobby for Prasham.

That was the second sign of trouble. Prasham looked frantic, waving his hands. He led Rube to his office and told him word had come from Mobius, moments before the lists went up, that his name had to be removed—it was something to do with what Rube had done last night and there was nothing that could be done about it. Rube was to leave immediately.

Rube wondered how Mobius had found out. He tried to tell Prasham he had important information about Corvus. But Prasham said he couldn't listen to anything obtained by a violation of privacy laws—laws that Mobius had helped write, he reminded Rube.

After that, Rube stopped protesting. A guard arrived and took him out.

In the hall, Ket approached. She reached toward him but only mouthed the words, 'I'm sorry.' She turned away.

The next thing he knew he was on a robo-bus with a guard, leaving the spaceport.

Then, in a blur of less than twenty-four hours, Rube was in a hotel in Seattle. Strange, Ket would be coming this way. He decided he would have to leave town. He had no idea where to go, except far away. Farther away than any signal, faster-than-light or not, could ever reach.

Out of habit, he checked his soahl for messages. Nothing. He opened a slog entry.

Slog::Good Sine:: Why life is meaningless.

He wrote sine and not sin—to avoid future confusion by the truly confused. But he wrote nothing more. What had led him to dream of Mars, anyway? He used his n-cloth display to bring up the speech by Mobius and played it on a big holo-screen on the wall.

"The question is, in the large scheme of things, are we humans more important than the bacteria in the gut of the lice living on the eyelash of a naked mole rat? As far as the universe is concerned, the answer is no. But as far as I am concerned, our future means everything."

Rube watched Mobius speak, his deep voice filling the lecture hall.

"Let's say you want to get to the nearest star within a human lifetime. Let's take that to be one hundred twenty years, to use an optimistic round number. I'm not sure how long any of you plan to live, but one hundred twenty years works for me. The nearest star, past the sun, is Proxima Centauri, a part of the Alpha Centauri trinary system. It's about four light-years away. So to get to Proxima Centauri in one hundred twenty years means you have to go one-thirtieth the speed of light. The speed of light is 1.08 *billion* kilometers per hour, so one thirtieth of this is three hundred sixty *million* kilometers per hour, or ten thousand kilometers per second.

Now, how much rocket fuel do you think it takes to get one gram of matter going that fast?

For a conventional chemical rocket it's more than all the grams of matter in all the stars in the entire visible universe. "More than one, zero, zero, zero, zero, zero, zero, zero, zero, …"

Mobius wrote as he spoke: *100000000000000 … 0000000 0000000000 …*

Minutes passed. Rube lost track of the zeros.

"That's eight hundred sixty-nine zeros," Mobius said. "To see why, let's understand how a rocket works. I'm sure you've heard, for every action there is an equal but opposite reaction."

"Of course," Rube said to the screen, his tone flat. He'd heard Mobius explain it a million times. He wanted to fast-forward. Instead, he kept watching as a kind of numbing torture.

"In more precise terms, it means that every change in the rocket's momentum corresponds to an equal but opposite change in the momentum of the fuel exhausted out its back. Momentum is mass times velocity. If the rocket of mass m burns delta m of fuel and exhausts it with velocity large V, the rockets velocity, small v, increases by delta v. Equating the momentum changes and using d for delta …" Mobius wrote: $-dm\ V = m\ dv$ and then $dm/dv = -m/V$.

"Note the minus sign," Mobius continued. "It's because the rocket's mass decreases. And note that the rate the rocket's mass changes with respect to its velocity is proportional to its mass. It's like radioactivity—the rate the atoms decay is proportional to the number of atoms, and the number of undecayed atoms at the start is exponentially more than what you end up with. It's the same relationship between a rocket's initial mass, large M, and its final velocity, small v. The result is called the rocket equation." Mobius wrote: $M = m\ exp(v/V)$.

"Now, for a chemical rocket the maximum exhaust velocity, large V, is five kilometers per second. There's no way to beat that. It comes down to the maximum chemical energy per atom. And, as I said before, to get to the nearest star in one hundred twenty years you need to go ten thousand kilometers per seconds. So, put in the numbers. Mobius wrote: $exp(10{,}000/5) = exp(2000) = 10^{869}$. "That's the number of grams of fuel it takes to get one gram of payload to the nearest star in one hundred twenty years. It's a very depressing number."

"Yes, it's a very depressing number," Rube said. "But do tell us, why?"

"Here's why," Mobius continued. "There are roughly Avogadro's number of stars in the observable universe, or 10^{23}, and on the order of 10^{33} grams in each star. Thus, all the stars in the entire observable universe contain about 10^{56} grams of matter. Convert all that to rocket fuel and it's nowhere near the 10^{869} grams we would need to get even one gram to the nearest star in a human lifetime. Thus, using chemical rockets can never work. Even with our biggest rockets, such a journey would take many tens of thousands of years."

"So it's hopeless," Rube said. "Like life."

"Right," Mobius continued. "What about other ways to get there, like using stages and a gravity assist trajectory? It still takes nearly ten thousand years. What about ion drive? Not much better. Nuclear fission? It takes several thousand years. Nuclear fusion? Well, if you eject three hundred thousand typical thermonuclear nuclear bombs out the back of the rocket you can make it to the nearest star in about a hundred thirty years. That is, if you don't vaporize yourself in the process. And that doesn't even include the bombs to slow down, to start the journey back, and to stop at Earth, over two hundred years later. And that's ignoring the fact you need to carry all these extra bombs with you. Best case, you can get up to twelve percent the speed of light and reach Proxima Centauri in thirty-seven years in a rocket with a mass to nuclear fuel ratio of forty to one. It's true. The Orion and Daedalus projects worked it all out. But it isn't going to happen."

"Get to the punch line, Mobius." Rube tapped a clenched fist against his lips.

"And the planets there are too hot for humans. What about the next habitable planet? That's three times farther away. But it doesn't take three times as much nuclear fuel to reach it in the same amount of time—it takes forty cubed, or over a thousand times as much nuclear fuel as needed to get to Proxima Centauri. In fact, the nearest planet we could survive on is five times farther way. To get there, it takes forty to the fifth power, or over two million times as much fuel as needed to reach Proxima Centauri. So you see, a thousand times, a million times ... the amount of fuel you need to get to a star in a human lifetime increases exponentially with the distance. Even if we could make it to the nearest star, we couldn't get much farther."

"What if you used B-41s?" someone in the audience asked.

"You mean one of the most powerful bombs the U.S. ever made? You'd need fewer bombs, but the same amount of nuclear fuel."

"Come on." Rube said. "Say it." He almost expected Mobius to turn to him and respond.

"What about other things?" Mobius continued. "Antimatter? The total amount of antimatter humans have created would run a refrigerator for less than a week. Laser powered sails? You need to use the Earth's entire power supply for years. Interstellar ramjets? The drag is greater than the thrust. How about generation ships, sleeper ships, or we ship embryos or our DNA there, or send self-replicating androids? We'd still hear nothing back for thousands of years. So who cares? What about Krasnikov tubes, wormholes, Hawking radiation, black-hole drives, or modified Alcubierre spacetime bubbles? All are either too weak, too unstable, or require negative energy. What about quantum fluctuations, dark matter, or dark energy jets? Those are worse than trying to grab shadows—physically implausible or mere science fiction."

And then Mobius said what Rube had been waiting to hear.

"You see … Space is the enemy … Space is the enemy. We have to get to Mars first. We have to learn how to live in harsh environments and survive far into the future before we can reach for the stars. Space is the enemy … Space is the enemy."

Rube stopped the video and threw his n-cloth display to the floor. It collapsed into a rag. "No Mobius, you are the enemy! You wrote rules when I was a teenager. How am I supposed to care about that now, when you don't care about anything except what *you* need?"

Rube collapsed too. Curled in a ball, he ached. He knew he would never finish his slog entry. He would never finish anything.

PART II
THE ELSEWHERE

CHAPTER 14
SOAHL-BREAKING NEWS

"I've always said he is a bit hard of thinking."

Ket watched the hibiscus blossoms on Dr. Mateni's print shirt undulate like they were caught in the rolling surf of Fiji as he let out a big belly laugh on her display. She wondered if their friendship had evolved to where she could advise him to lose weight. For now, however, she needed her old teacher's help, again. "Corvus may not have a first magnitude IQ," she said, "but we have to be careful not to think that he's as dim as a minor planet."

Dr. Mateni's laugh became a jovial chuckle. "You learned that one from me."

"Yes, I did. But my father—he's well? Not sick?"

"He moves slower but has good health. His rehearsal of the choir kicked up our spirits, as always." Dr. Mateni raised his palms up. "Listen to the Spirit inside you and join this new age. Amen." He lowered his arms and continued. "Corvus was trying to lasso you back home with a lie. *Oi lei.* If he'd drink grog with the boys, we'd teach him a thing about tall tales—Fiji style." He smiled like a saint.

"Rube did say he might try to scare me. That was months ago." Ket realized she hadn't thought much about it since then, she'd been so busy. "I freaked out when I saw the alert from Corvus about my father having a stroke—on my soahl! He shouldn't have been able to contact me like that. I'm sure my father wasn't pleased."

Dr. Mateni's eyebrows nodded in agreement. "His scare attempt is done and you don't have to come this side, to Fiji.

Your father is well. The good news is he was furious and ordered Corvus to stay here. No more trips to places where he can get someone to send your soahl a message. I heard that from a choir member."

"There was something else that Rube said ..." Ket squinted at her display and opened a side pane. She scrolled down a list of saved messages.

"Too bad that one's gone missing. It must be lonely for you without family ... and no boyfriend now, too? *Isa,* Ket." Dr. Mateni let out a walrus-sized sigh.

She wasn't surprised by her old teacher's exaggerated reaction. But why did he sound as if she'd announced she had a terminal disease? Maybe she'd looked sad when mentioning Rube? If so, it was unintentional. However, she *was* going bonkers. Prasham had kept her cooped up in her new apartment at the top of Soahl Headquarters in Seattle. He said it was safer there than on the university campus and ignored her assurances that Corvus was no longer a threat. He said that it was only a precaution—she could come and go as she pleased. He didn't seem to understand the fact she had to go everywhere with a bodyguard—the same one from India—was beyond annoying. And it didn't help that Sunjay was nothing like his name. No, not sunny at all. He rarely spoke, at least not using words, though he was constantly trying to read her body with his eyes.

But she could handle things. At least she thought she could, until today.

The message header from Rube scrolled into view. Ket didn't open it, but relaxed her face and gazed back at Dr. Mateni. "That *boy,* Rube," she began, "was never my boyfriend—and he's not missing. He's just lost in Africa somewhere. No one in the program is supposed to contact him, so I don't know, really." She flipped the bangs out her eyes and smiled. "Don't worry, I'm good. I'm very good. *Sa vinaka*. And I do get paper letters from Mother and Sarah."

She picked the two latest off her desk and waved them in front of her display. "They hope I'll come home, as always. But they do keep in touch."

As if on cue, her display chimed and a box popped open.

soahl-touched::private::to ... ::from Mobius:: "Tour Guide."

"Maybe that's one message from Rube, now?" Dr. Mateni eye's widened.

"It's from Mobius." Ket pressed two fingers against her temple. "I think I'd better look at this. Thanks for talking. You've been such a help."

"Not a problem ... as always ... yours truly, Ket. Bye. *Sa moce.*"

"Bye ... *moce,*" Ket said. Dr. Mateni vanished. "Thanks for the chat," she said to herself.

* * *

Ket stood in her bathroom. She'd had breakfast but still hadn't read last night's message from Mobius. It was as if she'd been standing on a seesaw all morning.

Earlier, at six a.m., her doorbell had rung. It had been Prasham, who was *amazed* to find her shuffling out of bed after he'd let himself in. He thought she would have adopted better habits by now and apologized for not checking on her more often. Then he told her he had two items of good news.

First, a new gravitino antenna had been set up on the roof of this building, which could sample signals at rates fast enough to transmit audio and video and operate dozens of v-bods between Mars and Earth. Instructions on how to build an identical antenna had been sent to the crew of the current mission, using parts they had taken with them. They had already launched the gravitino emitter into orbit around the sun at their halfway point a week ago. Once the new antenna on the ship was completed, they could try out a real conversation.

Second, the paper on 'Faster than Light Communication Using Entangled Gravitinos' was ready for submission. Ket knew the popular press had reported the story about instantly sending Morse code between Earth and the Moon. This had been greeted with skepticism and scorn. Performing a public demonstration before submitting a paper was considered poor form, and one does not overturn Einstein in a day. The hardboiled research community wanted real measurements published in a refereed journal. For this reason, all tests since the exchange with the Moon had been kept secret.

But the paper would go to a journal soon. And when the current mission reached Mars with its antenna, there would be a press conference. Mobius would address Earth in real-time in a grand demonstration that would leave no doubt. A Nobel Prize would follow. The push for a colony would flourish. And her contribution, Prasham had said, would be acknowledged too.

Then Prasham had told her about another Nobel Prize opportunity. Harlow Featherton would operate the antenna, he explained, but she was to start analyzing the data. It seemed mysterious gravitino bursts had been heard during a test earlier that morning. Before she could ask why she hadn't been invited to the test, Prasham said he had arrived at five a.m. for a morning jog with Harlow, but Harlow had been up all night finishing the installation of the controls. They decided to skip their run and gave the antenna a try. Within minutes, it picked up an intermittent buzzing buried in static. Harlow was trying to shake out the bugs, but if this wasn't a spurious signal, Prasham told her, it would be the greatest accidental discovery since Penzias and Wilson had found microwave radiation from the Big Bang.

Prasham went on to say he wanted Ket to figure out if the bursts where of astronomical origin or an unintended artifact from a particle accelerator somewhere on Earth. He also wanted her to enroll in the University of Washington's new Ph.D. program in astrophysics immediately. He would make sure she was accepted without waiting until the next semester, and she could do this concurrently with the Mars Explorer Program. If she worked hard she could have a Ph.D. before leaving for Mars—an amazing opportunity, he assured her.

This reminded her of the dizzy feeling at the top of the big hill on her first roller coaster ride, wondering if there was another way down. She explained to Prasham that her online classes continued right into the summer without a break. She was already studying eighty hours a week to prepare for Mars and had no social life. How could she finish a Ph.D. if she was going to Antarctica, assuming she was accepted as a Mars novice?

But Prasham had simply replied that she need not worry, she was a sure thing. And, as for a social life, there was good news—Harlow and Sunjay were moving in. The storeroom down the hall was being converted into a second apartment today.

Ket picked up a brush by the bathroom sink and combed her tangled hair while studying her face in the mirror. If she compressed six years of study into one, would she age by the same ratio? She never really thought much about her appearance. If fact, she looked forward to a time when it would matter less to others. But were lines starting to appear on her face? Or were the cracks in her life starting to show?

She had tried very hard since leaving Fiji not to need anyone. And she didn't want mentors to guide her for the rest of her life, either. She was preparing to join an amazing group of people. Good people, peers she'd live and eat with, who'd leave her free to study the universe.

Ket decided the lines were from being tired. After all, she was young and apparently somewhat attractive. And, if she ever did decide she needed someone, she was sure she'd meet someone on Mars who matched her enthusiasm for life.

Her thoughts returned to the message from Mobius. He had never sent one addressed exclusively to her. She perceived a slight thrill and the chance of a fall—a private message from Mobius might not be good news. Maybe she was being kicked out of the program, like Rube. She decided to shower first. This way she could step off the seesaw and melt under a relaxing spray of water before dealing with anything else.

* * *

Ket felt better with clean hair.

She was about to stop toweling off, when the doorbell rang. What now? She went to the door. Maybe it was important.

"Hello, flatmate," a voice said.

"Harlow?" Ket spied his round, distorted face through the peephole. "We're in different apartments," she called back.

"Oh, I guess I thought this floor was called a flat and that made us—never mind. Sunjay confused me when he tried to explain flatting to me. At first I thought he said fatting and I was going to punch him. But I've come by to say hi."

"Right. Hold on, give me a minute." Ket went to her bedroom and threw on a dress. After returning, she opened the door and saw Harlow standing there, all sweaty in shorts and a T-shirt. He'd been working out.

"Hi" Harlow said. "I guess we could call each other hallmates then? That makes sense, doesn't it? And you should call me Crater." He walked in to the center of the room. "Nice apartment. So Sunjay asked me to invite you to dinner at our place. We move in tonight."

Ket closed the door. "Yeah, Harlow … er, Crater …"

The doorbell rang again.

"That could be him," Harlow said.

"He's supposed to be on desk duty in the lobby." Ket knew that Sunjay worked days as part of the building's security staff, though he was called on to escort her any time she went out. She avoided going out in the evening, after the building was locked, since she would have to wait for him to arrive in the lobby and he'd insist on chauffeuring her in his car.

The worst time was when she'd needed him to take her to the store at midnight. When he asked what the 'emergency' was, she hinted it was for a personal product, hoping this would embarrass him back to his usual sullen state. But he stared at her like a mother-in-law inspecting her virginity. Then he went into a story about how he had used the word rubber to mean an eraser when first coming to Seattle, before finding out what it meant here. If those were what she needed, he would be happy to loan her some of his. He was glad to know she was loosening up, and he added he didn't like tight women. Also, he knew a disco where they could go to get fresh, if she understood his meaning. She had politely declined, though considered correcting him in so many ways and rearranging his face in several more.

Ket vowed to stop thinking about Sunjay and started to open the door. If he were on the other side, however, she'd smack him. Instead, what she saw next almost flung her to the floor.

"I didn't know where else to go." A sobbing Lacy walked in.

"How did you get past the security desk? The elevator is off limits without a key card."

"The guy there remembered me from India, of course," Lacy choked out. "Said he could never forget." She put a hand over her cleavage.

* * *

Once Ket had regained her sense of balance, she'd told Harlow she would *love* to come to dinner. Then she'd asked him to excuse her while she caught up with her distressed friend.

After Harlow left, Ket let Lacy rehash everything that had happened since India. Ket knew Lacy and Quasi had resigned after Rube left. Lacy said if their friend had to go, they did too. Quasi had found a job in Seattle with the Chinese rocket fuel company he had worked for previously. Lacy thought about doing more brain building, but instead enrolled in a nursing program. All this time, she and Quasi had been living less than a mile from Ket. She was sorry she hadn't contacted her.

Ket said she was sorry too. She'd been so busy.

They sat on the couch and got into the current situation.

"He's left me," Lacy said.

"What?" Ket noticed Lacy's dark glasses were pushed upside down into her hair.

"He said he had been furloughed from work and wanted a little vacation. I'm on break from nursing school, so I thought we were both going. But he said he wanted to go alone."

"What a jerk." Ket put her hand on Lacy's. "What was the word he used, scunnerous?"

"His aunt would probably call him sheep's dag for pulling a stunt like this. I don't know. Jerk works for me." Lacy rubbed her eyes. "I'm not that good with accents or the way he is with catchy phrases. I told him it was the rocket fuel talking. Except, the next day he was gone."

"Does he drink too much?"

"Actually, he never does. What else could have got into him? He did leave a note, saying he didn't know when he would be back but not to worry about him. Him! That was yesterday. I could only think, where would he go? And then I thought—Africa—where Rube is."

"Yes, I saw your message, before I left India, that Rube had gone there."

"Rube's been completely out of the soahliverse since then. Now Quasi is too." Lacy threw her dark glasses to the floor.

She pulled out a cloth, dabbed her eyes, and collapsed back against the cushions. "I thought maybe you and Rube were in touch, so I came here."

"The students have been told not to contact him. Not that I would let that stop me if there was a good reason. I've wanted to thank him again. But we only talked those few times. It was easier to let it go." Ket felt her cheeks warm. "I've been focused on Mars. But Quasi? Maybe we should call him quasi-jerk, you know, in case he still has some good qualities."

Lacy sat up. "Yeah, Quasi the quasi-jerk. I'll tell him that when I find him. We're meant to be together." She caressed the tattoo on her index finger. "It's fate."

"Do you believe that?"

"In the large scheme of things, I think … I think everything's connected. But whether two people are destined to be …" Lacy looked wistful. "You know, you've given me an idea."

"I did?"

"You said you'd contact Rube if there was a good reason. Well, nursing school doesn't restart until the fall. I'll go to Rube. If Quasi's there, then I'll know I was meant to find him. And as for Rube …" Lacy bit her lip. "I mean—Rube's an old friend. Maybe a visit from me is what he needs too."

"Taking action sounds good—better than waiting around."

"Yeah." Lacy gave a weak smile. "So you and Harlow are friends?"

"We could be, I guess. I don't know him that well, but he and my bodyguard—the guy at the security desk in the lobby—they're moving in down the hall."

"Sunjay, right? I almost forgot his name." Lacy's sad look changed to one of sympathy. She stood up and looked around. "Interesting. I see you like to read real books." She gestured at the stack of novels on Ket's desk. "And you have a lot of posters."

Ket thought about how little notice others had taken of them. She decided she needed to hang out with women more often.

"And what's this?" Lacy walked to a large framed photograph of a sculptured form standing in a window. "Does it suggest ancient fertility?"

"That's 'Gala at the Window,' by Salvador Dali. It's his wife."

"Oh, I thought maybe it was Hindu."

"No. In India I avoided putting up anything religious. I didn't want to offend anyone. Besides, this apartment has no windows. It's like a cave in here. So that's my window.

Lacy surveyed the rest of Ket's living room wall. "Ah, mandatory," she said pointing to a poster of Einstein. She turned to the one beside it. "What's this one with all the symbols?"

"Those are Clebsch-Gordan coefficients. I like the name, and their look, and I use them in my work. And the guy on the next poster is—"

"Oh, I know, Ettore Majorana," Lacy said. "I know about him without having to search my soahl." She looked proud of herself. "After writing down a theory about something to do with sterile neutrinos, he went on a ship and disappeared. I'm not a scientist, but I read a biography about him. There are stories he foresaw a nuclear doomsday, and maybe his ideas could save the world, if we could understand them. I love that kind of mystery. And the sterile neutrinos sound so weird. The theories keep changing. But if the cosmos is filled with them, then it seems to me someone must have given the universe a giant vasectomy."

Ket laughed. "Science terms often relate to sex, or the lack of it for its practitioners."

Lacy laughed too. She indicated the next poster. "And this woman?"

"That's Amalie Noether, another genius. You should read up on her."

Lacy picked her dark glasses up off the floor and put them on. "You've given me another idea. There's something I want to give to Rube. And if Quasi is gone forever, it's something I don't want anymore." She tapped her temples. "Hmm, well here's Gala. Did you know about Dali and her, and his attitude about a woman's lady parts?"

"No, I just liked the sculpture. But Corvus did say he admired Dali's philosophy." Ket thought about how Corvus rarely mentioned anything outside of religion, except for his wish to visit Tombstone, Arizona. "There also was a book of Dali's paintings in the house he seemed to admire. Though sections of it had been cut out. I guess I should read up on him."

"You should." Lacy moved to the door. "Well, it's time I go." Then, with a frantic move, she snapped off her glasses. "Ket, turn on your screen."

Ket did so. Watching the message crawl along the bottom, her gut pinched in.

> *... *** SOAHL-BREAKING NEWS: WIFE OF WORLD'S MOST FAMOUS SCIENTIST DEAD ... SANDRA MONK, WIFE OF MOBIUS MONK, DIED ON MARS YESTERDAY AT AGE 52 ... *** SOAHL-BREAKING NEWS: WIFE OF ...*

"That can't be right. It's unbelievable. I got a message from Mobius last night."

Lacy seemed lost within herself. "You know what Quasi would say: the solar system's most famous scientist, not the world's most famous scientist ..."

Chapter 15
A Voice From The Elsewhere

Ket bent a strand of uncooked spaghetti and watched it break.

Pbrk.

She loved the sound it made. She took another brittle strand and slowly brought the ends together. It formed an arch and then broke into three pieces. The breakage was always into three pieces, never two. She would have to look up the mathematics behind this.

Pbrk.

She had also read about Salvador Dali, and how he had treated Gala. What a jerk. She imagined the spaghetti was Dali, bending, bending, and then breaking into three pieces.

Pbrk.

Speaking of jerks, she imagined the next strand was Quasi, bending, bending …

Pbrk.

What about Rube? Why hadn't he tried to contact her?

Pbrk … ting.

The middle piece bounced off the counter and Ket laughed. She wasn't serious about using spaghetti voodoo on any of them—except maybe Corvus. She bent another strand.

Pbrk.

"Sproing," she called out to the flying spaghetti fragments. She realized her mood was actually good, mixed with a sense of far away sadness.

It had been a week since Sandra's passing. According to the press, she'd had a heart attack and the robo-surgeon on

Mars wasn't able to save her. The outcome might have been different if a specialist on Earth could have used a v-bod to operate remotely. But the time delay made that impossible. It was all very tragic.

After Ket had seen the first report about Sandra, she'd opened the message from Mobius. He made no mention of his wife. Instead, he asked Ket to become an adjunct instructor and do outreach work on Earth. He also wanted her to be his tour guide in four months, during the big press conference. He was not only going to address Earth in real-time—he was going to visit Earth as a v-bod! And he wanted her at his side. He also said she and Prasham would be the first tourists to visit Mars using v-bods. He ended by confirming what Prasham had told her. She would be on the next mission.

Ket had tried to take it all in. The richest and smartest guy in the world—no, in the entire solar system—was offering to fulfill her dream of going to Mars, and more. Ket figured the message was sent before Sandra's death. What should she do now? Responding after the funeral might be more sensitive to Mobius's feelings, but also a less than noble way of avoiding the big question. Had she earned this? No. But how could she say no to a man who had just lost his wife? How could she say no to Mobius? How could she say no when she wanted to say yes?

So she'd sent a brief reply, saying she felt deeply saddened by Sandra's death and knew it must be a very difficult for him. She added it would be an honor to be his tour guide during his v-bod visit. She didn't mention the adjunct position or going to Mars. She'd bring those up later.

Ket poured the remaining unbroken, uncooked spaghetti into a pot of boiling water. It sounded like some of the water had splashed onto the burner, but she realized the buzz was coming from her display—the sound of more gravitino burst data being recorded.

Last night she had worked with Harlow to program the antenna to do an all-sky search. Prasham, watching over their shoulders, said that even though the antenna's mount could rotate and swivel to point to different sky positions, it didn't work like an optical telescope. He had Harlow bring up a cut-away 3-D diagram of the antenna's interior, revealing a pair of long magnets inside. Ket identified the set up as the Stern-Gerlach arrangement she had studied in quantum mechanics. Prasham nodded and explained how the gravitinos entering the antenna were amplified and converted to electrically charged particles that went between the magnets. This bent their trajectories into one of two directions that the detector recorded as either the 'up' or 'down' state. It was like getting a 'head' or a 'tail' from a flipped coin.

"I get that," Ket said. "The antenna measures the incident gravitino's quantum spin. But gravitinos have four spin states. Do you combine these and measure many copies of them?"

"Yes," Prasham replied. "Furthermore, by rotating the axis of the magnets ninety degrees the measurement switches between two polarizations, like switching between flipping pennies or dimes. If the gravitinos are entangled, one either gets all 'ups' or 'downs' *or* fifty-fifty of each. The electronics converts the two cases into ones and zeros, which encode messages, and fast switching of the polarization allows these to go back and forth between two antennas instantly.

Ket was pretty sure Harlow hadn't understood all this. Neither had she, even though she had worked out some of the math. But she hoped the antenna's full capabilities would become clear later today during the first communications test. For now, the antenna ran in passive mode, scanning the sky for naturally occurring astrophysical gravitinos. Ket brought up the data on her large holo-screen, and then returned to stirring the spaghetti. Every once in a while streams of ones and zeros scrolled by on her display, concurrent with a buzzing sound.

* * *

An electronic voice quavered. "Good Sine, your life force is growing weak."

Rube sensed dread in the computer's warning. He flicked a finger to set his jewel-encrusted sword on the ground then opened his inventory.

"You need one hundred gold coins to continue. Hurry, Good Sine," the voice continued.

"Damn it, only ninety-one coins." Rube turned to the fair damsel next to him. "I'm sorry, Ket. I won't be able to rescue you today."

The damsel shrugged. "You always were an underachiever."

"Hurry, Good Sine. One hundred coins to continue," the computer repeated.

In the top left corner Rube saw numbers counting down from thirty, and a reptilian humanoid with spikey brow ridges approached. Rube turned to the damsel. "Why do all the aliens on this planet look like humans with a few modified features thrown in?"

"Aren't you the one that designed them?" she asked. The humanoid ran two clawed fingers down her sleeve. "Hey … careful with the dress!"

"I only designed you," Rube replied. He watched the alien grab her and run off. He sighed. "I don't like games where you have to start over every ten minutes."

"Neither do I."

The disembodied female voice had come from the outside world.

"Ket?" Rube pulled off his mask and sat up.

"Victor said I would find you in here."

"Lacy?" Rube blinked. "You're here?"

"Sorry I didn't tell you I was coming. If Quasi was here, I didn't want him to leave."

Rube studied her. Puffy skin circled her bloodshot eyes. Her dark glasses dangled from matted hair, which stuck out like a bird's nest from one side of her head. She'd probably just arrived from an overnight flight. "Quasi's not here," he said.

"I know. Victor told me. Do you know where he is?" Lacy pulled on her messy curls.

"In South Africa. I haven't seen him. He said he was on a wine tour, and cheers."

Lacy's pupils narrowed into two drops of poison. "That's all the quasi-jerk said?"

Rube had never seen his friends fight. Argue yes, merrily. But in this case, he thought Quasi was lucky to not be around. "I had no idea you weren't with him. He only sends quick texts. Never any pictures. With Quasi, you figure he's having a good time."

"But he hasn't mentioned me?" Lacy collapsed onto the floor and stared at the ceiling. "Oh god, I'm sure he *is* having a good time. He always does. When I would say we were meant to be together, he would say, 'I reckon you're right.' Well, I reckon he's not a quasi-jerk, but a full-on, shoot-the-whole-moon jerk." She let out a wailful cry.

"You don't know that he's not coming back. Maybe he just needed an adventure on his own. And he could be visiting his mom in Swaziland."

"She left a few years after he was born. He's never mentioned wanting to see her."

"Quasi's a fun guy, but he doesn't always think to tell others how he feels. Maybe he wanted to connect with his old roots before—"

"What? More likely he's rooting with someone new, screwing some wild oats, or whatever." Lacy waved her tattooed finger like a wand. "I'll send him to a fate worse than—"

"Maybe he plans to come back and surprise you with a proposal."

"How does he say, 'love ya babe, I'm a rocket and you're the sun I orbit,' and leave?"

"Quasi said that? Uh ... I guess he would when I'm not around."

"And you, dear Rube?" Lacy composed herself and sat up. "You've left reality again?"

"No, not really. I was playing a game, a very old one. I'm helping Vic. The work he does here is so important. I've never done anything like it. But we don't connect to the soahliverse very often. After India, it was easier to close my soahl."

"Gotcha," Lacy said. Then she patted Rube's nose. "I've seen Ket."

"One can work up quite a fantasy about destiny and all that. But it was just a week."

"Ket's not just any woman, Rube. I came here to find Quasi—but also to tell you not to give up." She reached into her bag, pulled out a cardboard tube, and handed it to Rube. "There's a poster inside, one of my favorites. I bought it a long time ago. Now I want you to have it."

Rube pulled the poster out and unrolled it. Across the bottom he read aloud, "You are a child of the universe, no less than the trees and the stars; you have a right to be here. And whether or not it is clear to you, no doubt the universe is unfolding as it should."

"It's from a 1927 poem called the Desiderata."

"This strange guy on the poster—he's the poet?" Rube pointed to the picture of a man with pointed ears and angled eyebrows. One was raised, giving the man a most inquisitive look.

Lacy shook her head. "No, the poet's name is Max Ehrmann. That dude's an actor from decades ago. I think he had his ears reshaped. He was also a singer and a baby doctor. But that poem—it's always been perfect for me. For you too." She looked straight into Rube's eyes.

"Do you really believe that? That the universe really is unfolding as it should?" Rube had to look away. "With all the wars, the refugees here, and now with—"

"With Quasi gone? I do. You see—if you float in an inner tube down a river, like the Bitterroot in Montana, you may swirl around this way or that, but you eventually end up where you're meant to be. I've always been sure of that."

Rube looked back at her. "And I've always been sure of just the opposite. Whatever we do, in a hundred years no one will remember us. In terms of the whole enchilada, the universe, whether it unfolds due to deterministic laws or random fluctuations, it could smack us out of existence tomorrow without stopping to care or notice. And yet maybe *we* can choose to care. So I do believe in something—that something, like going to Mars, can still have meaning."

"That's what I like about you, Rube. You're really an idealist at heart." Lacy took Rube's hand. "I have a new tattoo. It's to do with Quasi. When you see it, you'll understand." She started to pull up her blouse.

"Bro—there's another lady here to see you." It was Vic calling from outside.

In walked Evelyn Hatter, her eyes glowing red.

* * *

Ket sat with her hands on her head. What was wrong with this thing? She tried adjusting the frequency and sample rates and touched the record button again. She saw a long string of ones scroll across her display. It made no sense. The gravitino bursts data was suppose to contain time stamps, sky positions, and counts per second. After collecting data, her analysis suggested the bursts were from astrophysical sources, but she still wasn't sure what kind. Prasham had his ideas. The decay of clumps of a new kind of anomalous dark matter was his favorite. The problem was, this didn't match current theory, though various alternatives had been proposed over the years. But a stream of ones, like this, couldn't be coming from a naturally occurring gravitino burst. And no other burst had ever lasted this long. She kept recording the data, but the droning buzz was starting to get to her. It had to be a malfunction.

Ket turned off the sound and thought about going to the roof to bang on the antenna. How could it fail today? Then she noticed the ones had stopped scrolling across her display. She double-checked that the data had been saved and closed the burst-monitoring software. There was another buzz, this time from her doorbell. She turned to see Prasham and Harlow coming in.

"Ms. Ket, we are ready," Prasham said.

"At least we rang this time," Harlow added.

Ket followed them out and they took the elevator to the control room. Once there, Harlow flicked on the lights and brought up the system display on a big holo-screen. This was where he operated the antenna, when it was not under automatic control.

"I see you have shut down the all-sky search subroutine," Prasham said. "Harlow will now acquire the gravitino beam from the emitter satellite."

Ket put her hands out. "Wait, I think the antenna is broken. It was acting strange."

"All status lights are green," Harlow said. "A copy of the incoming data are stored in this room, so we can check. Maybe the ship sent a pre-test message?"

"Let us see this strange thing," Prasham said.

Harlow pushed a few buttons and looked up at the holo-screen. Across it scrolled thousands of ones. This was accompanied by a grating buzz until Harlow killed the sound.

"Are you confused?" Ket said to Prasham. "I know I am."

"Not at all," Prasham replied. "The circuits may have temporarily jammed."

"No error messages in the logs," Harlow said.

"Or maybe it's a message from aliens," Ket said with a laugh.

"Careful," Prasham said. "After decades of searching, what have we found?"

"I know, I know." Ket sighed. "No sign of intelligent life anywhere."

"Just like here on Earth," Harlow said, without even a hint of sarcasm.

"Besides, you remember the story of pulsars," Prasham said.

"Pulsars?" Harlow looked up for a moment.

"There was a young graduate student, like Ms. Ket," Prasham continued. "Jocelyn Bell. When she discovered the first regular pulsating radio signal, they joked it was an LGM—"

"A Little Green Man," Ket explained.

"Of course they did not report finding such a thing. Instead, they realized the signal was too regular, with no information. And when a second pulsar was found—well, what were the odds that two little green men were sending the same kind of signal at the same time? No, it was shown that pulsars were rotating neutron stars emitting radio beams like cosmic lighthouses."

"Oh," Harlow said.

"So maybe I've found a rotating dark matter star?" Ket hoped she didn't sound too naïve.

"Perhaps," Prasham replied. "In any case, we'll need to confirm the observations. We still depend on support from governments for crucial things, like the spaceport in India. If we make ridiculous claims, the missions could be cut. We have to proceed with caution."

"Like you did with the faster-than-light demo to the moon?" Ket muttered to herself.

"And the response to that supports my warning now," Prasham said. "Once the antenna is on Mars, the Math Monks will do their own survey and we'll see."

"But what do you think it is?" Ket asked.

"Noise," Prasham said. Then, with finality, he added, "Even if it is a signal, it will turn out to be manmade—a stray beam from one of the ultra-colliders."

"I've checked for those," Ket said. "If it's not a fault in the circuitry, it's from space—"

"Actually, it's not from space." Harlow swung his chair around. "And it's not a malfunction." He turned to Ket. "It's a configuration problem. You had the antenna in communication mode, not passive mode, and both detectors were saturated."

"Of course." Ket turned away, trying to hide her embarrassment. "I'm stupid. I was practicing for today's test. I must have accidentally switched into the wrong mode—"

"Which amplified the gravitinos," Harlow continued. "And if they come in too fast, the instrument gets confused and records everything as a one."

"Good. Mystery solved." Prasham appeared proud of his star pupils. "And youthful exuberance, Ms. Ket, is never the same as stupidity. Harlow, are we ready?"

"We're still in communication mode and I've now locked onto the gravitino beam from the satellite. I also sent a radio message to the ship over ten minutes ago that we were ready—way more than enough time for it to reach them at their current distance. They should be ready for the test now too." Harlow handed Prasham a microphone. "Sir, just give the word."

"Go," Prasham said. Harlow pushed a button and gave him a thumbs-up. "Mission Thirteen," Prasham said. "Mission Thirteen. This is Prasham talking to you through the elsewhere. Prepare for the code phrase."

Over the room's speaker system was a brief buzz. Prasham repeatedly squeezed the microphone, as if this would push his words through it faster. Ket chewed her fingers.

"Mission Thirteen. Repeat, this is Prasham talking to you through the elsewhere. The code phrase is, 'science is the magic that works.' Do you read?"

The reply was instantaneous. "Voice from the elsewhere. This is Mission Thirteen. We read you loud and clear. Science is the magic that works, indeed."

"Whoooeeeeee!" Prasham raised his arms to the sky while dancing around.

Ket jumped up and down and whooped too. Then Harlow joined in.

"Whoooeeeeee!" came the call back over the speakers. Ket imagined the ship's crew was trying to jump up and down too, as best as they could in their low-g environment.

Finally Prasham said, "Mission Thirteen. Relay to Mobius. We'll see him on Earth when you reach Mars, and he can let Schrodinger's cat out of the bag."

"Roger that, and roll over Einstein. Congratulations to you and the Math Monks. Will contact Mobius on what is now obsolete radio. Mission Thirteen signing out."

"Right, back to work," Prasham said. Then he told them he had sent Sunjay back to India. He didn't want to chance any word of this test leaking out. "So I will move in with Harlow and act as your bodyguard," Prasham said to Ket. He turned to Harlow. "Five a.m. calisthenics?"

Harlow stopped doing his happy leaps into the air. "Yes, sir," he said. "I'll finish shutting things down."

Ket checked the floor for damage. She should be nicer to 'Crater' but walked toward the control room door. Once there, she turned around and gave Harlow a commiserative shrug.

"Not to worry," Prasham said. "Harlow's an old military son. He knows how to follow orders. But you … you I will have to keep both eyes on." He smiled and joined Ket.

Once in the elevator, she worked up the courage to ask a question. "The elsewhere? I know that's the term for the region outside the light cone of an event. I get that, but …"

"Yes?" Prasham tilted his head.

"According to Einstein, not all observers would agree that the message from Mission Thirteen was sent and received simultaneously. For a superluminal transmission, we could have heard the message before it was sent, meaning an effect preceded its cause. So how can it work?"

"It has to do with the entanglement. At the current distance to Mars, it would take a conventional signal going the speed of light about four minutes to reach us." The elevator opened and Prasham walked with Ket to her door. He made his hands into balls and explained they represented Earth and Mars. "Any signal sent from Mars less than four minutes ago is not yet in our past, since it cannot affect us until it arrives. Similarly, any signal sent by us to Mars cannot affect its future for four minutes. Thus, any signal between Mars and us in this plus or minus four-minute window of time is neither in the past or the future. Not yet. For now, these signals are in the elsewhere." Prasham indicated the space between his hands.

"I understand that," Ket said. "But the entanglement?"

"When we use entanglement for instantaneous communication, like we just did with the gravitinos, by instantaneous I mean everywhere in the elsewhere at once. That means, when I was communicating across the elsewhere with the ship, which is almost as far away as Mars, I was talking to it somewhere between almost four minutes into the past or the future." Prasham lowered his hands. "Exactly which and by how much depends on the current distance from the gravitino emitter to the Earth and the ship. Do you understand?"

"Not everything. Not yet. But does that mean if we were to contact another planet hundreds of light-years away, we could talk to it hundreds of years into the past or future?"

"Yes, Ms. Ket. But like I have said before, we know of no such planets, and we'd have to place an emitter between that planet and us. So don't get distracted by fantasy and fiction." He then gave her his sage look. "We have a lot of work to do. Do stay curious, but also focused on good science. See you in the morning, five a.m. sharp."

Prasham walked down the hall and swiped a key card at the door to Harlow's apartment. Ket took out her own key card and swiped her door. Once inside, euphoria engulfed her entire being. It was all going to work out.

For once she looked forward to waking up before sunrise.

Chapter 16
Tour Guide

"The question is, in the large scheme of things, are we humans more important than the bacteria in the gut of the lice living on the eyelash of a naked mole rat? As far as the universe is concerned, the answer is no. But as far as I am concerned, our future means everything."

Ket heard a voice from the elsewhere. It was Mobius. She wished he would stop repeating himself. She tried to interrupt, but couldn't speak. Her muscles refused to respond.

Then she opened her eyes. It was her third dream in the last two weeks about Mobius. Last time he had become her soahl, saying "Good morning, Ket. Time to wake up … Good morning, Ket. Time to wake up …" and she had tried to swat him right back to Mars. She would swat him now if she could find him. It read four a.m. on the clock.

But then she remembered. Today was *the* day.

In four hours she was due at the University of Washington, along with Prasham and Harlow. The Mars students from the other campuses would be there too, along with the world's press. Unfortunately, Sunjay was also returning today, to guard her. A minor annoyance she'd ignore while the world watched her meet Mobius, on Earth, as his v-bod tour guide.

Lacy would be there too, with Quasi. It was a long story, which included Rube and Evelyn, but Lacy had returned a month ago by herself, followed by Quasi a week ago. He'd told Lacy he was sorry but offered few explanations. Lacy confessed she'd let him move back in. She explained no one could remain mad at someone as cute as Quasi.

Ket realized she had started to rely on Lacy as a confidant during the few visits Prasham allowed. After today's grand event, would Prasham loosen his protectiveness?

She found her way into the bathroom. Why was she even asking herself this? Did Prasham control her whole life? He'd been with her whenever she left the building since he'd moved in four months ago, and he'd allowed this only for quick trips with a specific purpose, except for their morning five a.m. jog with Harlow. Could Prasham really do this, legally? The terms of her position as tour guide did say he was her immediate supervisor, and she had signed the contract.

So maybe he could do this?

It didn't matter. After ushering in the era of faster-than-light communication with Mars, there would be a party with the students tonight. Her isolation from them had not been her fault, but she hadn't made much of an effort to get to know them, either. She would try to fit in.

Also, Sunjay would move back in with Harlow tonight. So tomorrow she'd get to sleep in. She'd also arranged to meet with Lacy at a nearby restaurant tomorrow evening. When she'd told Sunjay her plan to leave him in the bar while she ate with her friend, he hadn't objected. She reminded herself not to mention to Prasham that Sunjay, while exceedingly annoying, had one redeeming feature: he was pretty useless as a bodyguard.

* * *

The library at the University of Washington was designed like a Gothic cathedral.

Ket gazed at it from the back seat of a black limousine driven by Sunjay, who was silent. He'd last spoken the previous night at dinner with Harlow. He talked mostly about the new car he planned to buy once he finished bodyguard duties, and about how it was rare to find someone with his driving skills. He'd also attempted to make a joke. He said he'd heard Harlow had once called her a 'flatmate' but no real 'mate' would call her 'flat.' No one laughed. But Ket reminded him she had an electrified dress, and he went back to talking about cars.

That was not the dress she had on today. An outfit had arrived for her, fit for a princess, with an elegant design that reminded her of the gowns worn for a coronation. A card said it was from Mobius. But it didn't glow. If Sunjay tried anything, she'd just have to quit being nice and report him. He pulled the vehicle to a stop and looked back at her. At least he'd driven carefully for this occasion—better than some robo-cars might have done.

Prasham opened the limo's door and took Ket's hand. He wore a three-piece suit and tie. After she got out, she spun around too fast. She was going to have to be careful in high heels. She steadied herself and felt her hair. It had been professionally styled that morning for the first time in her life. None of it had fallen down. She planted each foot with elegant care and took in the surroundings. Nearby, fountains sprayed water into the cool air—their droplets mixing with the scent of pine. Off in the distance, Mount Rainier watched over her, cloaked in white against azure and green, like Mother Nature's guardian angel.

"You are one stunning adjunct, Ms. Ket," Prasham said.

"I haven't accepted yet," Ket said.

"But you will. You did agree to be the tour guide." Prasham stuck out his elbow.

Ket took it and he escorted her up the steps into the library. Inside, light streamed in through Renaissance symbols set in stained-glass windows. These lined the library's great hall, while gonfalons hung down from its high, arched ceiling, depicting libraries from around the world. Along the walls stretched an endless line of bookshelves. This was a house of academic worship. The middle section was filled with wooden pews, probably dating back to the origin of the university, with soft red cushions. A matching red carpet led to a stage two-thirds the way down the hall. Large holo-screens in wooden frames hung from vaulted beams that fit in with the architecture. On stage, to the left of a podium, was an empty chair. To the right, next to another empty chair, sat a v-bod decked out in a tuxedo. Its head was a shapeless ball of cloth.

An organ played Holst as Prasham brought Ket down the aisle. All the other Mars Explorer students were already seated. More and more it began to feel like a wedding. Hers. She felt a powerful urge to flee, but Prasham took her up to the stage and placed her in the chair next to the v-bod. He crossed the stage and sat in the other chair. In the front row she saw Twiddle and Nickie, and other scientists and staff. She looked out. Members of the press and the public filed in. In the far back row she thought she saw Lacy take a seat. Within minutes the hall was filled to capacity.

Prasham stood up, greeted the crowd, and gave a twenty-minute recap of the Mars missions while a video played on the holo-screens. This was followed by another twenty-minute video about living on Mars, about the isolation, and how everything was about to change.

Ket zoned out and went over her role today. When the recorded speech by Mobius began to play, she was to turn on her soahl, take out her n-cloth display, and bring up the tour guide controls. And after Mobius said, 'Space is the enemy' for the fourth time, she was to touch the 'Begin Tour Now' button. Then she would take Mobius to the podium and return to her seat to let his charisma work the room—live. After that, she and Prasham would stand and join him for another twenty minutes of questions from the press. Finally, she would lead Mobius down the aisle and outside for a reception, following him, while Sunjay followed her.

Panic welled up in her legs. She imagined applying tourniquets. She tried to remember the brilliant comments and questions she had planned for their conversation. All were gone. She realized Prasham had finished and Mobius was talking on the holo-screens. She took out her display and started the 'Tour Guide' application. In her earpiece, she heard it ask for her soahl handle. "Bad Wave," she whispered. Her mind drifted back into a daydream. Who was the groom if this was her wedding? Her ex-boyfriend? Prasham? Harlow? Then baby Craters? She didn't even want babies. Corvus? Was he here to kidnap her? No, no, no, she silently screamed.

Ket pushed the abort button on her thoughts. She was going to live on Mars without being tied down by anyone. She refocused and waited for Mobius to come to the punch line.

"Space is the enemy … Space is the enemy," the image of Mobius said. "We have to get to Mars first. We have to learn how to live in harsh environments and survive far into the future before we can reach for the stars. Space is the enemy … Space is the enemy …"

Ket touched the start button. The v-bod next to her began to metamorphize—its first breath combined with the exclamations of awe in the room. Mobius's head formed, and he stood up. Ket led him to the podium. His movements, she thought, were not like that of most v-bods. Even if he stumbled a bit, he seemed real like flesh and blood. She returned to her seat to listen.

"Space is no longer the enemy!" Mobius said. "I am over sixty million miles away, and yet I am here, right now."

Ket realized his voice was deeper and fuller than in the recorded transmissions.

"The era of isolation on Mars has ended," he continued. "I now want to bring up here my right-hand man, Prasham, and the newest member of the Math Monk team, Ms. Betti Keturah." Mobius motioned for her and Prasham to join him.

He wasn't going to give another speech. He was going right into the press conference.

The hall erupted with applause as she and Prasham went to stand by Mobius.

"In about a year and a half, these two will travel to Mars, maybe to live there forever. And maybe one day some of you will join them. But they will also travel there today, as tourists, using v-bods like this one." Mobius gave his chest a few good thumps. "And soon, very soon, so will all of you. Now, if there are any questions, there are standard microphones in the aisles."

A few people stood up, followed by a spontaneous standing ovation. Commotion filled the room. Displays clicked, emulating the sound of old cameras. Members of the press moved up front. Ket heard whispers about Einstein, about genius, about the story of the century—no, the story of the millennium.

* * *

Once outdoors, Ket pulled the clip from her hair and tucked it into her purse. She gave her head a shake and her long auburn locks flowed again around her shoulders.

Mobius looked over at her and beamed. "I need to come to Earth more often."

Ket threw out the script she had prepared. She decided to be herself. That had always worked for her in the past. "Can you sense the air?" she asked. "It's very refreshing."

"Yes, and the warmth of the sun. I've not done much v-bod travel in my life. The Monks have really souped-up this one. I'm told I can feel not only the warmth, but every detail of another's touch." He reached out his hand. "If you don't mind, I'd like to try that."

Ket wasn't sure how to respond, but she thought: this handsome 'doll' of a man wants to hold your hand—there's no harm in that, is there? She wondered if the Monks had programmed the n-cloth head to remove any wrinkles. His fifty-seven-year-old face had the skin of a young man. It was hard to believe it was cloth. And the brushed-back hair on his head was also amazing—nanotechnology at its highest level. Ket remembered how Lacy had pointed out that all the photos and videos of Mobius in the soahliverse seemed over ten years old. He always looked young in those, but maybe today, in real life, she'd find out he'd become weathered and bald. Lacy had given Ket a hopeful look. But he wasn't. Then Ket noticed his hands. They looked young too. She reached for one.

"Indeed, you do feel warm," Mobius said. "I'm afraid, though, this v-bod has no heaters installed. Maybe next time."

The coldness of his hand permeated Ket's. She pictured the kind of v-bods she'd seen advertised for their warmth—an image she might share with Lacy, but not with Mobius. Instead, she said, "It's still grand. I'm holding hands with someone on Mars!"

"And you're the first person to ever do that while standing on Earth."

Members of the press gathered around them. Ket hadn't realized there would be paparazzi at a scientific press conference. She also hadn't realized there would be so many other young women trying to get Mobius's attention. She caught someone waving at her out of the corner of her eye. Corvus? She glanced left. It was only Sunjay, thank goodness. He was pointing to Lacy, who farther back was waving and pointing at two men much farther back. They kept a low profile, but Ket could tell one was Quasi, without a hat, and the other was someone else—someone that looked like an old man. But then the old man dropped his hands to his side and did an awkward little dance, like an Irish jig.

Ket's heart almost leapt out of her chest. "Oh my god," she muttered.

"Come on, let's get out of here. I want to see the gravitino antenna control room and hear about your work. And I am sure there are things you would like to ask me without the press around." Mobius let go of her hand and looked at her with reassurance.

"Don't you think the crowd will be disappointed the star is leaving so soon?" Ket asked.

"Always leave them wanting more," Mobius replied. Then he did something she'd never seen a v-bod do before. He puckered his lips, stuck two fingers in, and whistled like he was hailing a taxi in an old-time video. And he did it well. "Sunjay—bring the car around."

Ket saw Sunjay scamper off. Lacy, Quasi, and the Irish dancer were nowhere to be seen. She was glad Mobius hadn't noticed them. A moment later the limo approached, and she and Mobius got in.

* * *

Ket was relieved to find Prasham was there to greet them in the control room. After he and Mobius spent a few minutes catching up, Prasham explained how the gravitino antenna now operating on Mars could send and receive data. Ket was a bit surprised that Mobius didn't know this already, but he probably kept his mind on the much bigger picture.

Finally, after an hour's tour, which included a trip to the roof to see the antenna, and a quick peek into Ket's apartment, the three of them had returned to the control room. Prasham opened a panel, pulled out two virtual travel kits, and handed one to Ket. Two twin beds lowered out of the wall.

"Put on the travel kits," Mobius said. "We have two v-bods like mine waiting for the two of you on Mars. It's time for your tour."

Ket opened the kit and saw that in addition to a mask, shirt, and gloves, it had boots, pants, and underwear. Underwear?

"Oh, and forget the underwear. You won't need that. Just slip off your dress and put on the pants and shirt, and the gloves and mask."

Prasham was already down to his skivvies, and started to put on the pants.

"Uh ..." Ket couldn't get any words out.

"Prasham—pull out the divider," Mobius said. "Have you gone daft?"

"Sorry, Ms. Ket." Prasham looked sheepish. He pulled a partition out of the wall that went between the beds. "Sorry. Mobius and I will stay on this side while you get dressed on the other. Then we'll join him on Mars momentarily."

"No problem," Ket said. She could tell Prasham was more embarrassed than she was. She walked with the kit to the bed on the left and saw Prasham and Mobius disappear behind the partition toward the other bed. She quickly changed, removed her soahl from her dress and slipped it into the hem of the travel kit shirt. After she lay down on the bed, she put on the mask. It grabbed her face. She had never done v-bod travel and felt wrapped like a mummy. But virtual controls floated in front of her. "I'm ready."

"Good. See you on Mars in three, two, one ..."

Mobius's voice faded away. Ket found herself sitting up somewhere else. She saw a large desk. Behind it sat Mobius—same face, same hair, but wearing a comfortable jumpsuit with the MathMonksMars insignia on it. Next to her sat Prasham. He also wore a jumpsuit. She corrected herself—his v-bod was wearing it. But where was his hair? She noticed her v-bod was in a jumpsuit too.

"Welcome to Mars."

"It's good to be back," Prasham said.

"I feel the same weight," Ket said. "Because, of course—I'm still on Earth." She reached up and rubbed her head. It was bald. "But I'm here ... on Mars."

"Sorry about the hair." Mobius walked over and motioned for them to stand. Next time we'll have to run you through a scanner first. Then you'll look more like yourself."

"I should have thought about that beforehand," Prasham said. "I apologize, Ms. Ket."

"No apology needed. I just can't believe I'm here. Here through the elsewhere …"

"Indeed," Mobius said. "Come with me. I want to show you both what awaits you."

Ket moved alongside Mobius. "You said before, on Earth, that both Prasham and I would join you in a year and a half." She looked at Prasham. "You're going on the next mission?"

Prasham nodded.

"He'll be an advisor, a ninth person on board. I decided we need that for this first mission of regulars. And you Ket, if you accept our offer, you could be his captain."

"I like that," Prasham said. "Captain Ket."

"I've hardly earned such a title." Ket held up her hand in protest.

"Nonsense," Mobius waved her off. "Your calculations are part of what makes all this possible. But I was joking about the captain part. We don't have military rank here. Those that qualify, though, do get an academic rank. So you'll be an adjunct instructor until the official selection of the novices. After that, you'll be a novice Monk, like the rest—that is, if you pass the exam." Mobius took her hand. "There will be no special treatment, even for our star student."

Ket felt the warmth of his hand and shook it. "All right, professor."

Mobius and Prasham both laughed.

* * *

The tour of Mars lasted three hours. Ket wondered how to explain it. The stadium-sized facilities built into the walls of a domed crater were much more luxurious than she'd thought possible, based on the video tours she had watched before. These had emphasized the state-of-the-art computer design rooms, where plans for the latest soahls were worked out, the labs where Mars rocks were examined, the vast arrays of solar collectors that gathered energy, the heaters and pumps that converted permafrost to water, the gardens where food was grown and oxygen extracted, the techno-buildings where fuel for the next return trip was synthesized, as well as plastics and clay for construction, and the distant pads where the ships landed.

She did get a brief look through a window at these. It was her first look at the Martian landscape, strewn with rocks and sand, painted in hues of pink, orange, and red, with not even the slightest hint of green or blue. It was about as different from Fiji as any person could imagine. She'd seen pictures of this before, of course, and she'd been to the desert region of Australia with her father. But seeing Mars through v-bod eyes, with its total absence of life, wrapped her in a sense of aloneness more eerie than if she'd looked out and seen a thousand ghosts wandering by. The sensation passed, and she asked if they could go outside.

Mobius said one day he'd take her for a walk, but the fine dust everywhere clung to everything. They weren't prepared to deal with it today. Besides, he told her, once you've been out a few times, the views get rather monotonous, except on the days the terrain gets covered in a dry frost or when a dust storm kicks up. When she came to Mars for real, though, he would take her on a trip to see rare carbon-dioxide geysers and to an area with white rocks where water once flowed. For now, he had more impressive things to show her inside.

Then Mobius led her and Prasham to a computer called Maxine, which he said was the most advanced thinking machine yet. She hadn't heard about this. It had ten times the processing power of the human brain, but not yet the 'software' of the mind. Predictions of when robots could think like people had been too optimistic in the past, Mobius explained, and he wasn't sure computers would ever have a soul—a mortal soul, he emphasized, like the one that 'burned' inside the human mind. Ket didn't let on that she'd heard him say this in his debate with her father. Next, Ket learned that Maxine had a dumber cousin, Max, a 3D nano-printer. Max, along with a supply of nano-cubes, could print or program the cubes to self-assemble into all sorts of objects, like spare parts for the antenna and the v-bods, as well as more mundane amenities.

As for the current Monks on Mars, newly arrived from Mission Thirteen, most were polite but only waved from a distance. They had obviously been told to stay out of the way. Mobius explained she could meet them next time, when she had some hair.

Many things about life on Mars were now clearer to Ket. She marveled again at the things that surprised her, like the extent of the gardens under the dome or the fact that rooms existed for over one hundred personnel. Twenty-six years of work had not only made a self-sustaining colony possible, but one with soft furniture, artwork on the walls, and individual bathrooms. It was not all n-cloth displays and hard-shelled robots. Regular people really could live here, she thought.

Just as she was kneading the bed in Mobius's room, admiring its softness, she realized Prasham was no longer there. "He's gone?" she asked.

"I thought you could be more open with me without Prasham around. I wanted to explain further why you are here. Come, let's go back to my office."

Ket took a deep breath and followed Mobius out the door and down a hall to where she had first arrived. He took the seat behind his desk and she sat across from him.

"Now," Mobius said, "I know this has been a whirlwind for you. But I knew you could handle it. Still, I am sure you have some questions."

Ket felt rather undignified. She wished she could toss her hair around. She thought about saying he was wrong, that she couldn't handle it. Instead, she pushed on. If this was about business, that was good. She took another deep breath. "What you have offered is amazing. My dream. But why now?"

"One reason." Mobius paused. "Can I call you Ket?"

"Yes." She realized up until now he had addressed her as Betti.

"One reason, Ket, is that I want you to know this offer has no strings attached. You can say no and go back to being a regular student, with no guarantees of being a novice. You can also remain a student at the university, or a technician, if you show the skills to fill one of those positions. But it would be a waste of your potential. I am so sure of that potential that I didn't want you to spend the next year wondering if you'd make it here. And I needed you on board now, with the tour guide work and all."

"Won't it seem like favoritism to the other students? Won't it look wrong?"

"To tell you the truth, I don't have to worry about what they think. But I do care what you think."

"Before I answer, I did want to say something." Ket gave her most thoughtful look. "About Sandra. I wanted to say again, I'm so sorry."

"Thank you. We had eight marvelous years together. There were no signs of her heart condition when she signed on."

"I didn't know—I thought you were together longer." Ket wondered how stupid that sounded. Had she just implied that eight years wasn't enough to feel the loss of a spouse?

"We had known each other for years beforehand, but eloped, as we liked to say, before my last trip here. But she had been sick for the last year. We didn't let on. We hoped the v-bods could have arrived before it was too late."

"I'm so sorry."

"Don't believe all you read. Even the best surgeon on Earth couldn't have saved her. So I am recovering. You have to have resilience. I've always had that, as do you. But maybe this is happening too fast."

"Right." Ket said. Good, she thought. I can't decide about all this right now.

"Right," Mobius said. "How about tomorrow? I could meet you in your apartment, at your lunchtime. I could take the v-bod down from the control room. It's Saturday. I can arrange it so no one will even know I was there. It will be less awkward for you that way."

Of course, Ket thought, so much less awkward. But she said, "See you then."

CHAPTER 17
A VIRTUAL KISS IS NOT A KISS

"And then that devil-eyed ex of yours showed up? What happened?"

"There's not much to tell," Rube replied. "Evelyn is suing me, that's all." He sat next to Quasi in the back of a robo-taxi. Seattle skyscrapers whirled by. They exited onto Madison Street and headed toward the downtown market.

"She traveled to Africa to sue you? I thought you owed her a bit of virtual money."

The taxi lurched and Rube grabbed the armrest. "I did borrow some virtual gold from her. But she wants more than that. She's suing me for breach of promise. Seems she had some lobbying work to do in Egypt—she's a solicitor now—and for some reason my brother, who never replies to messages, responded to hers. He told her where I was. She's handling the case herself and decided to issue the summons in person—to see the look on my face, I think."

"I know she's a quid-sucking fog shoveler, but breach of promise?" The car swerved and Quasi put a hand on his hatless head. "Taxi, would you ease up a wee bit on the g-forces?"

"It means breaking off a marriage proposal." Rube looked to see if Quasi understood then tried to keep his head from bending back as the vehicle accelerated.

"If only I could mellow this car out with some rocket fuel." Quasi snapped the flap on his satchel. "But it's not only about money? You asked her to marry you?"

"Not in this reality."

"Laws like that went out with wooden teeth, didn't they? Where in the bejeebies do they still … oh, I get it—in the same place you told me she started calling herself queen."

"In the medieval soahlscape."

"And your property in that world is worth real dollars in the real world. If you married her, not only do you have to pay her back, she also gets half of everything you virtually own."

"Yes, not very realistic—medieval laws with a modern sense of equality. She wanted to play on the quest. But they wouldn't let an unmarried couple stay at the inn outside the Caverns of Thord. So we told the inn keeper we were married."

"And he let you stay in the inn together?"

"Yeah. How was I to know the next day I'd uncover the treasure. I'm virtually rich. If I cashed in my gold, it's enough to live on for a few years in the real world."

"But did you ever propose?"

"It turns out virtual sex counts as a common law proposal. Next time I logged in, Evelyn had a signed marriage-proposal certificate and a video log of our animated night."

"What?"

"Which she bought, faked by a virtual con-artist."

The taxi screeched to a halt. Rube and Quasi pushed their faces off the backs of the front seats, got out, and walked to a roped off courtyard with vendor stalls under tents.

"Makes you sick, doesn't it?" Quasi pulled a plaid beret from his satchel and put it on.

"What, Evelyn? I know."

"Nah, I meant you. You look ready to put on a Technicolor display."

"Huh?" Rube could tell Quasi had switched to his London accent, but he didn't get the meaning. "Technicolor?"

"I mean your complexion's a shade of green. But what happened when Evelyn showed up at your bother's home?"

"At first, Evelyn acted like she didn't recognize Lacy," Rube said. "She looked at Lacy and me and said, 'So you're sleeping with hookers in the real world now?' Then it started."

"That's when Lacy decked her?" Quasi sounded hopeful.

"No, Lacy stood up and told Evelyn she had something to show her, outside." Rube sat on a park bench. "I think I've lost my appetite. Have lunch without me. I'll wander back to your apartment and meet you back here tonight. I'll tell you the rest then."

* * *

Ket opened the door to her apartment and saw Mobius in the same tux as yesterday.

A few moments ago, after getting a message from him that he was ready, she had touched the 'begin tour' button on her display. However, upon seeing him, she felt a little underdressed. This was a casual visit, right? In any case, she hoped she looked nice enough in the slacks and top she had chosen for the day. And unless the control room contained a change of clothes, she realized he'd had no choice but to stay in yesterday's outfit. She decided to stop worrying about clothes and started to worry about food. Why had he chosen her lunchtime to meet? She hadn't eaten and couldn't see how she could eat in front of Mobius. More to the point, if he meant this as a kind of date, how would his v-bod self be able to join her for lunch? "Come in," she said.

He walked in, and despite almost tripping, managed to sit on the couch. Very carefully, he put one virtual foot on the knee of the other leg, loosened his waistcoat, and removed his bow tie. "I'm still learning how to operate this thing. It's better if I sit here. I know you've been working very hard and I wanted to hear about that. So, how is it going? Come, sit beside me."

Ket sat deliberately at the far end of the couch and turned to him. He looked as handsome today as yesterday, as good-looking as the man himself had on Mars. Even his hair and trim beard looked the same. She wondered if the real Mobius had nano-hair implants like this v-bod did. Or maybe he had good genes. In any case, he didn't seem vain, just very confident. Her thoughts turned to business. "Has Prasham told you much about the gravitino bursts?"

"Absolutely. It will be a great paper."

"And the strange signal I picked up?" Ket leaned forward to look in Mobius's eyes. Was there an ally in there?

"I heard the detector saturated in communication mode. But then you observed the same sky location and again received a long string of ones?"

"It took some tuning of the sample rate and energy band," Ket replied. "But yes."

"So maybe it's a dark matter pulsar or a flaky circuit after all. I don't want you to get too excited about that." Mobius leaned toward her. "We will follow up on it, when there's time. For now, we need to keep the antenna locked on Mars, for obvious reasons."

"Obviously, right now ..." Ket saw intelligence and wisdom, but not the expression of a concerned mentor. Instead, his eyes seemed to look right into hers. "But maybe in a few days—"

"A good scientist knows when to drop everything and when to avoid going down a rabbit hole. You're going to be a great scientist—and you'll have to follow your gut—but if you think it's E.T., don't get your hopes up."

"I know. It's crazy. Why would there happen to be a gravitino emitter between them and us? And, if they are out there, why no other means of contact before? I'll need to collect more data, and it's probably nothing, of course. It's just I've always wanted to know ..."

"If we're alone? Ket, I—uh ..."

"Yes?" Ket scooted closer to him. For the first time, she thought Mobius looked vulnerable. "I mean, yes, I've wondered that."

"I know you want to come to Mars for the right reasons ... and for one wrong one."

"Wrong?" Ket imagined leaning in even closer to Mobius. "Yes ... it would be wrong."

"One reason you want to come to Mars is to get away from Corvus. If that were your only reason, I would say, don't come. But I know that's not the only reason. The mission is important, and we need you, and ... wait ... wrong? What do you think would be wrong?"

"Nothing ... I mean, I thought maybe you came here to ask me something else." Ket, for the first time, noticed a faint cloth texture could be seen under this man's very nice skin. So the v-bod was good, but not perfect. She felt stupid. Was she blushing?

"I did come here to ask you something else—about the adjunct lecturer position. Have you decided to accept? There are no strings attached."

"Oh, that." Ket let out a huge sigh. "I don't want any favors—no automatic selection for the next mission. But if it means doing outreach work for the Math Monks and continuing to act as your tour guide between now and the launch, then maybe. And if it gets me out a year of freezing my butt off in Antarctica, that would be a bonus. But don't do that as a favor, all right?"

"That would be a rule change not a favor. With this new technology, Mars will no longer be isolated like it was before. After all, here I am." Mobius patted himself on the head. "And, you've been there. As you've seen, the living conditions are becoming more comfortable. So for the next mission, your mission, we could reduce your training in Antarctica to a few months. You could join the other novices during their year there for that. And then there will be the usual four months of safety and rocket training in India, before the pre-launch quarantine."

"That still sounds like special treatment. However, if you are giving me the job because I'm the best person for it ... then I can accept." Ket curled her feet up and relaxed.

"Great. But before you give a final yes, there is one other rule change I want to mention. It comes with a question, and again there are no strings attached. You'll have to go with your gut on this one too." Mobius moved closer to her.

"Yeah?"

"Will you escort me on a date next month?"

"Date?" Wow, Ket thought, here it comes. A moment ago it seemed he might lean over and kiss her. In that same moment, she had entertained the idea and then dismissed it. Maybe down the line, when they got to know each other, something could happen. However, if it was meant to be, it would wait until she was on Mars—not while they were so far apart, regardless of the possibilities opened up by instantaneous v-bod travel. He understood that. Didn't he? So if he was about to ask her out, he was going to be very disappointed.

"Look, here's the logical spiel. I know I've been against relationships on Mars. Now, though, we are setting up a permanent colony. We'll need children. You said that's not for you on your questionnaire, but you're young. You also said you were willing to stay on Mars permanently. If you stay long enough, you might change your mind. I think you'd be very good with kids. It's one of the reasons I think you're perfect for our outreach work. And take a look at me. I'm getting older. I'm starting to wonder, am I an evolutionary dead end? We're both alone, but we don't need to be." Mobius shrugged. "Screw that. This isn't about logic. You're the most interesting, incredible women since Adam met Eve. I can't expect you to stay single—"

"Wait—escort you on a date? You've lost me."

"With Nickie. I'd like you to fly to India and act as my tour guide while I have a date with Nickie."

Ket fought against showing outrage while also quickly blocking the impulse to look disappointed. Instead, she managed to act like Mobius had said something about the weather. "Oh, I see … actually, I don't."

"Sorry, let me get to the point. The other rule change is that persons who agree to settle on Mars will be allowed to bring a partner with them. That is, as long as the partner passes certain security, physical, and psychological requirements. After the relationship is shown to be stable, these couples will be allowed to have children. Then we can start a real colony on Mars."

"What about letting the existing permanent staff on Mars form relationships? Certainly some might already exist—behind your back?"

"I'm sure some do, but it's strongly discouraged. Also, unfortunately, we're still a male dominated project. After all these decades of promoting equality, I'm not sure why. But the fact is, the existing staff on Mars could not effectively pair-up for procreation. Even if the sex ratio was favorable, it's also not realistic to expect people will find their preferred partner amongst the staff or students. Now, a couple can come to us from the beginning."

"You had your chance for that."

"You mean Quasi and Lacy? They chose to quit, and they never planned to stay on Mars. But with the new rule, even if you start out single and later find a partner, and even if you're on Mars and the partner is on Earth, that person can join you."

"If they pass certain requirements?"

"Yes."

"Otherwise, we can choose anyone we want? What about mission resources?"

"I assume few will take advantage of this at first, and persons staying permanently reduce the fuel needed for the return flight. So some weight can be shifted to the uncrewed ship allowing more supplies on the crewed one. Thus, we can squeeze a few more people on board. The details are to be worked out. The point is, dating will now be allowed—for those that plan to stay on Mars."

And you're not asking me out on a date? For a moment Ket wasn't sure if she had said this or thought it. Relieved it was only a thought, she said, "And you're asking Nickie out?"

"I'm opening myself up to the idea of finding a new partner. I will be giving live v-bod conferences around the world for the next month. There are also v-bods like this one in the Mars Explorer Building at the launch site, so we won't have to fly this one there."

"Yes, we saw them during the first demo with the Moon."

"Right, and in a month I'll use one of the v-bods there to visit Nickie in person." Mobius leaned again toward Ket. "And you'll fly there with Sunjay beforehand to prepare things."

"Prepare things?" Ket rolled her eyes. "Couldn't Nickie be your tour guide?"

"Technically yes, but I want it to stay official that you, and only you, are my designated tour guide. It's great for the press, Ket." Mobius smiled.

"But what kind of date will it be if I'm watching you and Sunjay is watching me?"

"Purely platonic, of course," Mobius said. "Even once heaters are installed in the v-bods, I'm not crazy enough to think a satisfying amorous relationship can happen. Besides, Nickie is thirty-four. She might be too old for me." A gleam appeared in his eyes. "I plan to date lots of women before finding the right mate."

"What?" Ket opened her mouth. She was appalled.

The smile on his face grew into a wide grin, surrounded by his neat, short whiskers. "Just kidding, Ket." He let out a deep laugh and seemed extremely pleased with himself.

"I'm simply saying, I'm on the lookout for the right person, and you are allowed to be on the lookout too."

With the tension released, Ket found herself laughing too. Then, for some reason, she felt her heart racing. What had she thought about her future before? The possibilities seemed to be changing. "Sorry if I look flabbergasted, but this is a lot to take in."

"I didn't mean to scare you. The new rule doesn't force you to do anything. It just opens up possibilities. So, do you accept the adjunct position?" Mobius looked worried.

Ket pulled herself together. He's right, she thought, this doesn't force me to do anything. With a steady voice she said, "Yes. Yes I do."

"Good. I think I've kept you too long. You need lunch, and I need to leave. Remember, I've chosen you because I think you are by far the best. I also have a hunch that you'll do great things for the Mars Program and never let us down. But whatever happens, know that you'll always be free to do what's best for you. We are good people on Mars, Ket. We are the good people of the universe."

"I've always thought that," Ket said. She tried to believe it.

Mobius reached out and took her hand. In what seemed an old-fashioned sign of respect, he used his v-bod lips to give it a very cold, virtual kiss.

Chapter 18
I've Come For Your Soahl

"Was he an apple or a snake?"

Ket sat in the restaurant atop Seattle's old space needle, studying Lacy. Robed in bountiful curls, Lacy's glasses seemed like a judge staring down from a high bench with penetrating dark eyes. Ket thought she was prepared for the romance inquisition, but her only response to Lacy's question was, "What?"

"Did you want to bite him, or did he want to bite you?"

"There wasn't any biting. But why the circuitous route through the garden?"

"You're a preacher's kid. You had a secret boyfriend in India." Lacy lowered her glasses. "I figure you're an expert at not kissing and telling. But something happened, right?"

Ket wished she could hide. "Well, there was a kiss."

"Pierced tongue or forked tongue?"

"Ick." Ket regretted sounding critical. She knew Lacy was just playing her favorite game. "Sorry. It was a cold one, on the hand."

"More to your garden point," Lacy continued, "do you think Mobius wants you as his Eve on Mars?"

Ket watched the city lights out the window slowly rotate against the darkened sky. She looked over at Sunjay sitting in the bar. She was glad he was too far away to hear. Then she turned back to Lacy. "Do you mean did I feel any sparks with Mobius? I don't know. I really don't. For a moment—one stupid moment—I thought he might kiss me. On the lips, I mean. And I felt a little crush, but I squashed it. I started to find it unsettling. Up close, you can see the v-bods aren't real. And they're cold. And he is too old."

"And rich, and famous, and smart, and wise, and confident. You said lots of young women wanted to meet him."

"None are his type."

"Exactly. But *you* are." Lacy pointed her tattooed finger at Ket.

"I doubt it. It turns out he's going on a date with Nickie, with me as his tour guide."

"Really? I don't see them joined by the Red Thread of Fate. But your message said he's going to install heaters in the v-bods. And there's n-cloth underwear in the travel kits?"

"I mentioned the underwear because I thought it was weird. Why would we need that?" Ket reached for her glass of wine, not expecting an answer.

"With the right man in that kind of underwear, it would make a lot of sense." Lacy nodded toward the crotch of a waiter as he walked past. "You know, all men *are* shape shifters."

Ket did a spit take. "You're right. I've never thought about it like that. They're aliens, really." She and Lacy burst out laughing.

* * *

"And then Lacy decked her," Rube said. He was with Quasi in the plaza across from the entrance to the space needle.

"I've never seen Lacy hit anyone," Quasi said.

"I didn't see it either," Rube continued, "but she and Evelyn came rolling in to my brother's house. Lacy explained later that when she went outside with her, she'd hoped to persuade Evelyn to leave, that she was sure we'd all end up friends at the end of the universe."

"That sounds like Lacy."

"Then she said she noticed Evelyn had a tattoo on her lower back, and maybe they even had something in common. But Evelyn trained her laser-pointer eyes on Lacy's chest and said she remembered her, and the work of art on her back was nothing like Lacy's flash-trash."

"And that was the last straw?"

"No. Evelyn heaved her chest and told Lacy to do the world a favor—to take her tiny brains and go back to milking robo-cows in Montana and become a harmless, barren old maid."

"That would put Lacy up to high doh. She programmed those cows."

"And that's when Lacy decked her. Though after they rolled in, Evelyn scrambled up and accused Lacy of trying to deflate her chest like it was an inner tube. She picked up her purse, which she'd dropped, took out the summons, and threw it at me. She left after threatening more lawsuits. Then Vic and his kids showed up, and we talked more about life."

"And sex, I'll bet."

"Don't you and Lacy talk?"

"About sex, yes. About life, I'm not really into philosophical disquisition."

"You never seem to have any worries."

"Only compared to you. It's just when things get me down, I get up and do something."

"Like going to South Africa without telling anyone?"

"Lacy found me. I knew she would." Quasi sounded pleased with himself.

"You wanted her to track you down?"

"I was worried. Worried that she was using me for sex."

"You were not. Though that's what Vic asked her. My brother and Lacy kind of think alike. And, with her training to be a nurse, they have things in common. So they hit if off."

"What are you saying?" For once, Quasi looked really concerned.

"Vic made it clear he was married. Though Lacy *did* seem to enjoy sharing cups of *coffee* with him." Rube waited for Quasi to react but realized there was no need to clarify he simply meant the hot beverage. "Vic also said she was far better than me with the refugees. If she'd stayed longer, who knows? I'm just saying, don't take her for granted. Make sure she knows how you feel. Right?"

"Right." Quasi appeared to drift off into thought.

"By the way, before I forget …" Rube reached into his backpack and handed Quasi a very realistic looking latex mask of an old man.

Quasi took the mask and put it into this satchel. He pulled out a wig and a moustache, and pushed the items over to Rube. "You know what I was saying about taking action. Go see her, Rube. She and Lacy are probably talking about the same things up there right now." Quasi pointed near the top of the space needle.

* * *

Ket stopped laughing.

"Seriously Lacy, I don't know if I can take it any more. Corvus wants to marry me. Prasham wants me to get a Ph.D. and win the Nobel Prize. Mobius want me to be his tour guide and who knows what else? And Rube, I don't even know what Rube wants. I just know I need to talk to him." She wrapped her hands around Lacy's.

Lacy looked over at the elevator and sat up straight. "Here comes Quasi. Now remember, he'll keep Sunjay in the bar."

"That shouldn't be too hard."

"And then Rube will come over, in disguise."

"As an old man?"

"No, no. You'll see."

A moment later Lacy gave Ket a kiss on the cheek and left. Then a man with blond dreadlocks and a matching handlebar mustache took Lacy's seat across from Ket.

* * *

"I knew you'd understand about the strange gravitino message," Ket said. She tried to keep a straight face. Rube was fingering his moustache. It looked like it was about to fall off.

"I know Mobius and Prasham are busy," Rube said, "but they might have another reason for ignoring this."

"How so?" Ket put her elbows on the table and rested her chin on her hands.

"If you've discovered a message from aliens you're going to become a little bit more than the daughter of a famous preacher with a psycho brother-in-law. The spotlight will shift onto you and off the Mars Program. Think about it. If we can talk to ET, will we still need to colonize Mars like Mobius plans to do? Will you still need him or Prasham for anything? You could write your own ticket—get funding to build a million gravitino detectors."

Ket had thought about it and was reassured this possibility had occurred to Rube too. But she didn't believe it could be true. "Mobius is not devious. He just wants to do good science and protect me from embarrassment."

"Maybe, though it sounds like he wants more from you than good science."

"Oh, he's looking for someone, but he could have any woman on Earth."

"Ket, when I first saw you I imagined … never mind. Maybe he likes a challenge."

"He's being coy, if he wants me."

"He's smart enough to let you make the first move." Rube glanced away. "So, do you?"

"What? Want to make the first move? Of course not." Ket was not about to admit she had almost leaned over and kissed Mobius. "And I don't want children. I've made that clear."

"Neither do I ... but never? I have a feeling you might be very good with kids."

"Humph ... Mobius thinks so too. He sent me to teach a class about Mars to middle school kids this afternoon. I taught them about Hohmann orbits. But procreation?"

"He wants you to also teach kids about the birds and the bees?"

"No." Ket wasn't sure if Rube was serious or teasing her. "I'm back to me—and having kids. It seems so meaningless—each generation pouring all its energy into producing the next. Some of us have to take the time to push the boundaries of the frontier. Otherwise, we might as well still be roaming the savannah, doomed when the next big meteorite strikes."

"I've always thought so too. But then, if no one did it."

"It? It doesn't have to result in babies, you know."

"But if no one procreated, in a generation there'd be no more humans."

"Mobius tried to tell me that too. No children and in one generation the Mars colony is dead—at least if its goal is to be self-sustaining. But I've never thought about that for me."

"The new rule, though—doesn't it open up new possibilities?" Rube looked hopeful.

"Is it really new? He had Sandra."

"Mobius was the exception to the rule. And now he's made one for you."

"He thinks he's the exception to every rule. But I think you're right, the new rule was made for me. For me to decide if I want to choose him." She looked down.

Rube reached out. "Remember your own rule."

"My rule?" She lifted her chin.

"Yeah, ask yourself if he's a good bra for you." Rube played with his mustache again.

Ket felt cheered. "I could try him on—"

"No—I didn't mean that." Panic wiped the smile from Rube's face and he accidentally displaced his mustache. With a frantic motion he tried to pat it back in place, but failed.

Ket laughed and tried to smile in a way to reassure Rube she wasn't serious. She found herself opening up to him. "Can I tell you something, Rube? Something private?"

"Of course."

"When I was a teen, I stopped pining for my father's return from long trips. Instead, on nights when there wasn't a class with Dr. Mateni, I began to sneak over to the school to do extra math problems and read science books. Returning from those evenings, I overheard my mother listening to old phonograph records by herself in a back room. One night I hid in the bushes to listen too. I didn't recognize the music, but my mother told me she'd spent a summer as a teen on a beach in France, and I somehow knew she was thinking about that beach. Then the bushes rustled and something grabbed me. It was Corvus."

Ket swallowed and continued. "I didn't say anything, but he said he hoped I'd show him more respect when we were married. He had married my sister three years earlier but said he realized he needed a second 'help-meet.' I told him I'd rather burn in the innermost circle of hell than become his help-anything. Then I noticed the cigar, lit, and in his free hand. It was strange, since he didn't smoke. 'The disobedient must be punished,' Corvus said."

"Usually that meant he was going to beat me with a cane switch. He'd do that in public, with my father as a witness, if I did the wrong thing. He'd wash out my mouth with soap if I said the wrong thing, and I already told you he'd wash out my eyes with soap if he thought I'd seen the wrong thing. Instead, he said, 'the church abhors bloodshed, but thankfully burns don't bleed, they blister.' After that, he pulled down the neckline of my dress. I went numb. It was like I'd left my body and was watching him push the cigar against my skin, here."

Ket indicated above her left breast. "Then I felt intense pain. Corvus told me not to cry out or tell, or he'd tell my father what and whom my mother thought about when she came to the back room. Even at the time, while I fought to stay in control, it seemed absurd that someone so consumed with righteousness could do this. I was about to point this out when he lifted the cigar. He said, 'let this mark remind you to not dress like a harlot and to obey me ... and I will forgive your wickedness. But, because of it, I now have to go burn my own eyes with smoke.'

"Then he vanished. All I could do was put one hand over the burn and the other over my mouth. So you see Rube, Mobius might be arrogant, but he's not like Corvus."

Rube looked at her with understanding. She was relieved he hadn't argued with her. She had been intrigued by Rube before but thought they had no future. She couldn't let one week, one conversation, change everything she had ever dreamed of for her life. Now there was a new possibility. What if she 'tried on' Rube? Would Mobius allow that? Could she bring Rube to Mars? Slow down, she thought. He's obviously eager. He's been a big help. But was she losing her mind? For now, she would let the conversation flow and enjoy being with this 'boy.' There was something about him, something that she liked. But she wouldn't let it become serious.

* * *

Three hours later Ket could scarcely believe it was two in the morning.

She'd laughed with Rube about everything, and somehow he'd reduced to zero the viscous tedium that hangs in the air once you run out of things to say. Near closing time she'd finally told him about the attempt by Corvus to scare her home, and she'd asked Rube what else he'd learned about Corvus and her father. Rube had told her he felt that Abraham was in control, and Corvus couldn't really do anything to get to her. Otherwise, he'd said he couldn't remember the details and would have to review his recording of the spy mission. Ket admitted she hadn't looked at Rube's message since leaving India, but wanted to review it again.

"Perhaps," Ket said, "we could meet at Lacy and Quasi's apartment, if I can find a way to completely ditch Sunjay."

"Don't do anything to get yourself in trouble," Rube said.

"Speaking of which." Ket nodded toward the bar, where Quasi appeared with Sunjay resting his head on Quasi's shoulder.

Rube glanced over. "I should go."

Ket gave Rube a quick hug. He sounded so torn. As she watched him exit the restaurant, she realized she'd have to tell Mobius she wanted to see all her friends in the open.

* * *

Down at street level, Sunjay was too drunk to drive, so Quasi had Sunjay put the limo into robo-mode and rode with him and Ket back to Soahl Headquarters. After they were out of the car, Sunjay told the limo to go park itself. It wouldn't. It said it needed an authorized driver. With a bit of coaxing, Ket got Sunjay to burp the code into the steering wheel so Quasi could park it. Ket watched Quasi drive off. Then she suppressed her disgust and attached Sunjay like a leech to her arm. She hauled him inside and up in the elevator. After she delivered him to Harlow at his apartment, she went to her own.

After entering her bedroom, she resolved never to get that intoxicated herself, not by drink, or by Mobius, or by Rube. She also wouldn't let Prasham rule her life, and she'd stop worrying about Corvus. She'd do what she wanted. She felt renewed strength. She would follow up on the gravitino signal by herself. She would go to Mars on her own terms. Nothing would stop her now.

Before she could turn on the light she saw something. In the shadows sat a wiry, bloodless v-bod with a thin face and long white hair down to its knees. It was in her chair. Had Mobius been in here and disconnected his v-bod to return to Mars? No, he couldn't come to Earth without her playing the tour-guide application, unless he'd broken the rules. Those thoughts passed by in a millisecond. Then the thing moved.

She screamed.

"Hello, Ket." A lamp flickered on, showing an old man, not a v-bod.

"Who are you?" She reached for her soahl in her top's hem. "How did you get in here?"

"If you're trying to activate an alarm, I wouldn't do that." He produced a long stiletto knife and smiled, showing a set of ragged teeth. "You'd be dead before anyone arrived."

She froze. He looked like a strung-out zombie who'd been wacked with a waffle iron, leaving an imprint on his half-melted face. "What do you want? Money?"

"Shut up. I'm not here to hurt you … unless I have to. Let's just say, someone sent me to tell you to stop what you're doing and forget about going to Mars."

"I'll scream again, loud enough to curdle the fabric of spacetime. My bodyguard is right down the hall."

"He's drunk. And these apartments are sound proof."

Ket decide to call his bluff. "Then I won't go to Mars." She said this in the most nonchalant voice she could muster. "I'll go home."

"It doesn't matter what you want to do. I'm here to tell you, you have no choice. You're not going to Mars. The ICA is going to shut you down."

"The what?"

"The International Communications Agency. You haven't been quantum encrypting your signals with Mars. That's against treaty. The next mission will be cancelled."

"You don't need to do that. I already said I'd do what you want." How could a junkie influence a lawful agency?

"For some reason I don't trust you. Like I said, it doesn't matter. You're not going to Mars. I'll be going soon ... but I need one more thing."

"What?"

"I've come for your soahl."

"My soul?" Ket touched her chest and thought about making a run for it.

"Not your soul, your *soahl*, your sum of all human learning. Give it to me."

"Don't you have one of your own?" Her voice hinted at anger while she controlled her fear. But she slowly reached for the thumbnail-sized metallic case housing her soahl. For a split second she considered stating the obvious, that she meant his soul or lack of one. Instead, she tossed her soahl at the living dead man and made a dash for the door to her apartment. As she fumbled with the knob she thought about things she'd never get to do. She was sure he was coming for her. But she only heard *it* call out to her.

"Go ahead and run. I'll be gone before you get back."

CHAPTER 19
PIECE OF CAKE

Ket was finally alone in her apartment.

She went to her bedroom closet and pulled out the orange dress. She found a nail sticking out from an unpostered section of the living-room wall and hung it there. With meticulous care she smoothed it, top to bottom. Next, she crossed the room to the kitchen, took out a box of spaghetti, and spilled the contents onto a glass plate. After picking up as many of the raw strands as she could, she faced the dress, showing no emotion. Then, mustering more violence than she thought possible, she hurled the spaghetti like poison darts toward the dress, attempting to pin its perimeter to the wall in a pattern like chalk around a victim's body. To her disappointment, the strands either fell short or bounced off, leaving the dress unharmed.

"Aargh ... *sa lasu na toa.*" Why hadn't she learned to swear better than this? What good were the village boys that used to tease her if they hadn't given her a few choice words to use right now? Her calm father and meek mother were no help, and her sister, who could be mischievous, used polite language. And Corvus? If he found a bad word in a book he ripped out the page, chewed it up, and spit it into the rubbish. Then he'd mutter something about plucking out that which offended him.

Of course she had heard a lot of words she could use since leaving home, but they weren't part of her natural vocabulary. She needed something more than a curse to let out what she was feeling. Her fist slammed into the remaining strands, catching the edge of the plate. Brittle pieces of spaghetti flew around while the plate fell and shattered against the hard floor. She stared at the scattered shards, then at her hand. It hurt but was not cut. In her mind she went over again what had happened since her escape.

Last night, running from her apartment with her heart pounding, she expected to feel the knife blade between her ribs at any moment. Reaching Sunjay and Harlow's door, she banged on it for what seemed only a second short of eternity. Finally, Harlow opened it, and she squeezed under his arm like a collie through a pet door. Then she screamed at him to shut the door.

Forty minutes later, after getting Sunjay's feet under him and urging him to look for the intruder, the police arrived. Sunjay went with them and searched her apartment. No clues were found, but they went back to dust for prints and scan for DNA after the robo-forensics showed up. Before that, one of the officers talked with Ket and told her Sunjay admitted a passkey was missing from the safe downstairs. But the only suspicious person Sunjay could think of was someone in a fake mustache he'd seen last evening. Ket said Sunjay had been drinking and was mixed up. Before leaving, the officer suggested she sleep in Sunjay and Harlow's apartment. Harlow insisted she sleep in his room. He'd sleep on the couch, and, as he put it, flatten anyone who broke into the flat.

Then, this morning, Ket unlocked and opened the door from inside Harlow's room and found Prasham standing there. He told her Harlow had filled him in and Sunjay was suspended. That was a relief. She was surprised, though, when Prasham told her he'd move back into Sunjay's room to again be her bodyguard. He also gave her a new passkey and told her he'd personally changed all the door and elevator codes. And he explained, even though Sunjay had been hired on a separate contract, the rest of building's security would be turned over to a new company, starting that morning. Robo-alarm systems would be installed in the elevator and the stairwell, with image recognition to lock out any unauthorized users. "Can friends, like Lacy, still visit?" Ket asked. "Yes," Prasham said, "but only if they come during hours when the building is open, so they can be cleared when full security is on shift." On the plus side, Ket was told she'd no longer be allowed to go on the morning jog.

After that, Harlow cooked enough eggs to feed an entire corps of Canadian Mounties, and the discussion turned to who had been in her apartment last night. Ket was sure it had to be someone sent by Corvus. She used Harlow's soahl and asked Dr. Mateni if that was possible. He said, as far as he knew, this sounded like the work of the devil, not something Corvus would dream up. She decided her old teacher had no idea the kind of dreams Corvus had. After eating, Prasham checked with the front desk and reported the new security guards had shown up. Everything was perfectly safe now, and he suggested everyone go back to work.

That's when Ket had decided to do some work in the control room. But her new passkey wouldn't open the door. After complaining to Prasham, he explained that the gravitino antenna was robo-locked on Mars, so there was no need for her to access the controls. Besides, the mechanisms to rotate the antenna for an all-sky search had been removed, and the control room computers had also been unplugged from the network, to prevent sabotage. And if anyone tried to use the ICA and a legal approach, the Math Monks would keep them tied up in court forever. Prasham said everyone should concentrate on science from now on.

Anger tore through Ket. Her soahl was gone and the only copy of her data was in the control room. Though Prasham said he would retrieve her data and put it on a new soahl for her when he found time, his stone-cold tone told her he wasn't going to discuss it further.

Once Ket returned to her apartment, it occurred to her it might be easier to talk with Mobius. He'd given her his old-fashioned email address, and she emailed him from a decrepit laptop that came with the apartment. But he was of no help. Prasham would get her data as soon as he could, he'd replied. He also said she could come to Mars as soon as she had a new soahl. He'd have a travel kit sent to her so she could connect directly from her apartment. And if he needed to visit her, he'd have Prasham let the v-bod in and out of the control room. He'd closed by saying he was very much looking forward to spending more time with her when she was his tour guide in India.

As a last resort, she tried to download a soahl emulator onto the laptop, but it was blocked by security protocols. She'd need an actual soahl to connect to anyone besides Mobius, but she couldn't even shop for one online. That was blocked too. That was when she'd begun to wonder if maybe her data in the control room would somehow disappear before Prasham brought her a new soahl. And that's when Ket's anger had ignited into a fury.

Now, she stared at the fragments of spaghetti, the broken wedges of plate, and the dress. Ever since last night she had been fighting the insane thought that maybe the intruder worked for Mobius and Prasham, that this was their plan to separate her from her data—data that could embarrass or upset the Mars Program. They could do something like that, couldn't they? After all, they'd taken Rube's new n-cloth v-bod technology without asking for it, hadn't they? And then they'd got rid of him.

Ket knew what she had to do, but she needed to work up the nerve first. Finally, she went down the hall and asked Harlow to send a message to Lacy. "Tell her to come over for 'cake' at three, before the building closes." She thanked Harlow and returned to her apartment to wait. It meant risking everything, but only the 'team' could help her now.

* * *

"This is bad, really bad."

"Where have I heard that before?" Rube asked Lacy, in response to her comment. He handed the old-man mask to Quasi, who stood next to him staring at his display. Ket was scrunched into a corner of the couch, hugging a pillow. She'd been there since letting them in to her apartment and had just finished telling them her side of things.

"Though you're pretty bold, asking all of us into the heart of the soahliverse," Lacy said.

"Indeed," Quasi said. "So Prasham has you locked in this tower like Ginger Locks?"

"Ginger Locks?" Rube couldn't help sounding incredulous.

"Your nana never told you the story of Ginger Locks and the Tower of Hector?" Quasi replied. He looked over at Ket and tipped his new hat, a felt Fedora. "Never mind. We're not exactly knights in flaming armor, but I reckon we'll do."

Rube suppressed the urge to say how mixed up this sounded.

Ket shoved the pillow away and got up. "I didn't expect everyone to come. Sorry, I about passed out when security knocked on the door and asked me to verify if I wanted to see Lacy, who was on their list, with her husband and his great, great grandpa, who weren't."

"Harlow said you wanted to meet for cake, which I interpreted to mean everyone." Lacy looked down then moved next to Quasi and dug him in the ribs. "Hello husband."

"And this mask is the one Rube used at Mobius's big to-do," Quasi said. "I bought it from Famous Foolers for the cost of a pretty pearl after reading one like it was used to get someone past security and onto an airliner. That was before better bio-scanners were installed. But my hunch was this building wouldn't have those. Good latex still beats n-cloth any day—well, except for the new v-bods."

"I was afraid they might do a pinch test," Rube said. "But Quasi synthesized a revolting liniment smell, which he rubbed over the mask. It kept them from getting too close."

"And you did say cake," Lacy added. "I knew what you meant, but I brought cake mix anyway." She pulled a box from her purse. "The guards scanned this more than anything else."

"Luckily, that worked," Ket said. "The new security system's good, but Harlow had told me about interrupting a 'cake' party. I knew you'd come, Lacy. And I'm glad you're all here."

"Aye," Quasi said, "then we'd better get started before any of the nosy hyenas show up."

"Have you finished looking at my plan?" Rube asked.

Lacy put on her dark glasses. "… I have now and number five won't work."

"Let's start from the top." Ket pointed to the first item on Quasi's display. "First, Rube and I will review the video from his spy mission. Then he'll try to access the toy v-bod in Fiji."

"And if I can at least get audio," Rube said, "we might figure out what Corvus is up to."

"At the same time," Ket continued, "Lacy will search her soahl for pictures of my visitor from last night. Not many people look like … like—"

"Like a zombie," Lacy said, "with a half melted, waffle-ironed complexion and bleached knee-length hair? I wrote that down. But you wouldn't believe how many creeps I've met that fit that description. Some of my favorite tattoo parlors are in the shady parts of town, you know."

Rube did a mock shudder. He also felt sick thinking of what Ket had faced last night.

Quasi cleared his throat. "And I will go out and buy Ket a new soahl."

"We could use one of our soahls," Rube said. "Couldn't we?"

"Except all the computers in the control room are off the network," Ket replied. "We need more than a soahl. We need a way to connect to the data."

"Not a problem," Quasi said. "While I'm out, I'll also get a data cable. They weren't worried about our soahls, so it should pass through security unless they guess why we want it."

"You mean to download my music off my old backup drive?" Ket smiled. "Of course, I shouldn't have been so stupid not to have one, but they don't know that."

Quasi smiled back at Ket. "And Bob's your uncle."

"Huh?"

"He means it should be a piece of cake." Lacy's glasses cleared. She batted her eyelashes.

"Right," Rube said. "Then all we'll need to do is get into the control room and find out what's in the strange data Ket described." He shook his head.

"Well, if it's E.T. I'll be a baboon's uncle," Quasi said.

Lacy's glasses transitioned back to black. "Or a baboon's bottom?"

Rube looked at Ket. "E.T. or not, we can also see if Prasham and Mobius really did try to keep your data from you."

"I hope I'm wrong," Ket said. "I hate thinking of them like that. It's so cynical."

"But here's a problem." Lacy pointed with her tattooed finger at the next step in the plan. "It says I'll break the code to get through the control room door. But that's a super secure door."

Rube waved his hands to object. "We'll cross that bri—door—when we come to it. I have faith in you, Lacy. The universe will unfold as it should. So let's get started."

Lacy sat down on the couch and held the pillow. Though her eyes were hidden, she appeared to stare into nowhere. Ket and Rube sat next to her and Rube opened his display. Quasi closed his and stood by the door. Rube started to play the recording of Ket's father. "I'm not against science, just its arrogance. I've made that clear, haven't I?" Rube skipped ahead. "She cannot go to Mars," Corvus said. "You have forbidden it. If I could bring her back here to marry me that would solve everything." Rube scanned through Corvus's other pronouncements. "I could take some of the boys. We could kidnap her ... Bride kidnapping is not unprecedented ... But if she disobeys, we should shun her ... I could scare her back here. All legal, of course ... But if I take a vow and there has to be a sacrifice? The BS—couldn't it involve her?"

Ket looked perplexed. "I've never heard Corvus say anything close to a swear word. What's up with that?"

"I'd say Corvus talks BS all the time." Rube turned to Lacy. "Anything?"

"There's nothing in the soahliverse. What else do you have?"

"Corvus talks about a salvage operation."

Quasi moved closer to the others. "Didn't you say before he'd been in Free California?"

"California's not mentioned on the recording," Rube replied. "Ket told me that."

"And that's what Dr. Mateni told me," Ket said. "Which reminds me, Corvus mentions meeting someone, doesn't he? Rube, it was in your message to me. I looked for it last time I talked to my old teacher. Can we find that part?"

Rube tapped the buttons on his display. "Here it is. He talks about meeting Dr. Whitesmith and that he agreed to the salvage operation for the BS. Do you know him?"

Ket shook her head. "Never heard of him. He also seemed to know about your slog, Rube, and your dream. He doesn't sound like someone Corvus would visit."

"You mean the time you dreamed you were a cosine function?" Lacy asked.

"Sine wave," Quasi corrected. "Though they're the same, up to a phase shift."

"Never mind that." Rube pushed the buttons on his display again. "It's starting to make sense. Back in India, I heard someone say 'white' backstage when Ket's dress shorted out. What if that was Corvus?" Rube looked at Ket. "What if that was his first attempt to get to you? Maybe he used his cane on your dress. Except, I was there. It means Corvus was talking to Whitesmith backstage, that he was working with Whitesmith even before he went to California. Corvus says that he went to India not to discuss disarmament, but the transfer of one of their nukes. With Whitesmith's help, I'll bet. At the time I thought it was just crazy talk."

"And the rest is sane?" Quasi wrinkled his brow. "How's that to do with disarmament?"

"Beats me," Ket said. "My father's plan has always been to disarm all the nations."

"But if Corvus talked about the transfer of a nuke, could that be to Fiji?" Lacy asked.

"Fiji's not threatened by anyone and it's too small to threaten others. It makes no sense." Rube pondered this for a moment. "So what have we got: Corvus, India, Free California, Dr. Whitesmith, a salvage operation, nukes, and BS. Lacy?"

There was silence. Then Lacy jumped up and turned on Ket's holo-screen. "It's simple." An image of an old man with long hair appeared. On his biceps were the letters BSP.

Ket jumped up too. "That's him. Except his hair is gray in that photo. It's white now."

"So who is that?" Quasi asked. "I see what you meant by the ironed complexion."

"Waffle-ironed," Lacy said. She tossed her glasses into her bag and opened her display. She looked pleased to have corrected Quasi. "It's a Dr. Smith. That's what confused me. There are hundreds of Dr. Whitesmiths in the world, but none matched any of the other key words. But then I broke the name apart and searched just for White. Too many matches. Searching for Smith wasn't much help either, as you can imagine. But Dr. Smith, California, gray hair, and salvage worked. I replaced white hair with gray, as a guess. I'm not sure what took me so long."

"But who's Dr. Smith?" Rube asked. "And BSP? Is that what Corvus meant by BS?"

"Maybe." Lacy read from her display. "It says here Dr. Smith was a Cal Poly physics professor before climate change and civil war made that part of California a free state, followed by Texas, and Florida's removal from the union because of the Orange One, as you know. Afterward, Smith became the head of the Big Sur Privateers. What we'd call pirates. No one goes near them."

"Unless someone wants to minister to the lowest of the low," Ket said. "It's one of the ways my father's church gets new donors. The wretched rich give him money and they get redemption in return. Corvus could have gone to California to minister to the BSP."

"Why are they called privateers?" Rube asked. He moved by Lacy, to see her display.

"Because they run ships up and down the west coast for legitimate salvage operations," Lacy replied. "But also for plunder."

"I've never paid attention to the BSP," Quasi said. "If this Dr. Smith is one them, he won't do anything unless money is involved ... and if it is, then he'll do anything."

"So far we know a Dr. Smith was here," Rube said, "and Corvus met with a Dr. Whitesmith. But what's the connection?"

"Well," Lacy said, "it also says here Dr. Smith dropped out of sight four years ago—supposedly killed. A body turned up, burnt beyond recognition, but its ID was never confirmed. After that, there were rumors he'd been seen now and then, but none were verified. Maybe Dr. Smith bleached his beard and became Whitesmith as a disguise?"

"A bit too obvious of one, don't you think?" Quasi shrugged.

"My impression is he's vain," Ket said. "Not about his looks, but about how smart he is. The white beard and new name could be a joke to him. I think maybe Dr. Whitesmith wants people to know he is also the very clever Dr. Smith."

Lacy danced around. "I think you're right. I see a rumor that last year the BSP declared they have a new leader."

"The photo confirms a Dr. Smith was here," Rube said. "And there's a new leader of the BSP. So it's probably Dr. Whitesmith, same as the old Smith."

Lacy hummed a little tune in agreement.

"Sounds like you're on a bit of a white gallinaceous bird chase to me," Quasi said.

"Uh, right. Except," Rube continued, "Corvus met a Dr. Whitesmith looking for a salvage operation on a trip he told Abraham about. No one else knows about that conversation but us. And they don't know we know."

"So the dots are connecting," Ket said.

Rube was excited. "If we connect Smith to Whitesmith to Corvus—then Corvus is involved with the BSP and culpable in Smith's actions last night. We can put Corvus away."

"But we need more evidence. You'll need to try the toy v-bod again," Lacy said.

"What if my father is also involved?" Ket shrank back.

"Corvus only told him about a Dr. Whitesmith and a salvage operation." Rube said. "I doubt your father knows about anything illegal. In fact, he told Corvus that he must not do anything wrong. He also told Corvus that he must do nothing to harm you, Ket."

"But if Corvus is following my father's order, he can't know about last night."

Rube could tell from Ket's look that she felt despondent, that the whole logic of it might be falling apart. "We'll see. I'll try the toy v-bod next." He patted her shoulder.

Quasi moved back to the door. "Right-o, I'm off to get a new soahl and wire. I reckon this'll be sorted out when I return, and we can commence with the data getting."

Quasi tipped his Fedora and opened the door. Everyone in the room froze.

In the hallway stood Harlow. "Hey, inventor. Is this another secret meeting?"

"No, no," Rube said. He walked toward the door. "Harlow, I mean Crater—come in. We were about to bake a cake, but we're out of an ingredient. Quasi was going to go pick it up. This time we'll save you a piece." He smiled.

"Would the missing ingredient have to do with getting Ket's data?" Prasham stepped out from behind Harlow.

Rube fell backward, but Lacy and Ket managed to catch him.

Ket rushed forward, her face flushed. "Prasham, we need your help. Corvus is up to something. And I need my data back. Sorry, I was starting to wonder if Mobius was behind last night's attack and not Corvus. I wondered if you were too. Sorry."

"I don't know what you're talking about," Prasham said.

"It would explain how Dr. Smith got in here so easily and got away," Quasi said.

"But Prasham," Ket continued, "maybe Mobius wants to scare me too—scare me into choosing him and going to Mars. Because— "

"Who is Dr. Smith?" Prasham asked. He and Harlow came into the room.

"Sorry," Ket continued. "I've been under a lot of stress. I'm going out of my mind. But you have to convince Mobius to take this seriously."

"I do take it seriously." In stepped Mobius.

This time Rube fell way back, tripping over the pillow where Lacy had dropped it. He landed on the couch.

"Who pushed the begin tour button?" Lacy asked.

Ket turned her palms toward the ceiling. "Not me. I don't even have a soahl."

"No one did," Mobius said. "To save the mission, I'm changing all the rules. I'm moving everyone to Antarctica. Now."

"Everyone?" Ket snapped. She put her hands onto her hips. "Do you mean Lacy and Quasi too? Do you think you can just walk in here and order us around? "

"Yes," Mobius replied. "And no. Lacy and Quasi will join us, but it's not an order. Let me explain—"

"Wait, they get to rejoin as students?" Ket asked.

"They'll have to apply again for the mission, after yours," Mobius replied.

"If you're changing all the rules," Quasi said, "including about rocket fuel, if you appreciate my meaning, I might take you up on that." He patted his satchel.

Lacy put her arm around Quasi. "And we could have a baby on Mars?"

"Maybe," Mobius said.

"And Rube?" Ket asked.

"He can apply for that mission too," Mobius continued. "Or Ket, you could choose any one of them."

Rube picked himself up off the couch and took this in, in disbelief.

"Anyone I want, like you said?" Ket looked Mobius up and down.

"Exactly like I said," Mobius replied.

"Could she choose me?" Harlow asked. "That is, for whatever she's choosing."

"You're a current student," Prasham said. "Mobius means Ket can take anyone she wants as her partner to Mars. You might get selected for the mission without her 'choosing' you."

"Which is your best bet, Crater, my boy," Mobius said. "But for now, all of you are going to Antarctica."

"How's that?" Rube said. "We're suppose to drop everything and follow you to the ends of the Earth?" In a surreal moment, Rube felt himself catch Ket's ability to talk back to Mobius.

"You have something better to do? Your brother Victor is doing fine without you. I'm giving you a chance to follow your dream again." Mobius looked around the room. "Quasi, this is your chance to create some real rocket fuel. Lacy, you can start your nursing program again in the spring semester, if you want, but in the meantime I could use your brains. And Ket, there is no way Corvus or anyone can get to you in Antarctica. You can bring your data. Prasham and Harlow will set up two gravitino antennas—one for your work and one for communicating with Mars." Everyone looked happy, except for Harlow, who seemed unsure about what was going on. "Harlow, in Antarctica we serve cake in the cafeteria every night. The novices won't arrive for months, so you can have all the pieces you want."

Mobius seemed to realize he was being a bit unfair. "Oh," he added, "there's also an excellent gym. So everyone, stop standing around like you've witnessed the second coming and get moving."

Chapter 20
Invitation To The Other Side Of The Universe

Ket watched the aurora rip across the sky, whipping the darkness. Its streaming neon currents seemed only meters beyond her reach. She shivered while her breath frosted in the chilled air.

Forty-eight below zero, she noted. Not bad, given that it was always night. She closed the visor on her Mars suit, which was rated for a much more frigid climate than this, and wondered how cold it would feel there compared to here in Beacon Valley, a thousand miles from the South Pole.

She and her friends had arrived at the Mars Explorer Training Base four days ago. She still marveled at how they had secretly flown out of Seattle on a jet to New Zealand, and from there, on a winterized robo-copter to this base in one of Antarctica's dry valleys. Each had a single room in the same wing of the dormitory, and no one else was there. The novices for the next mission, after selection from the students, would not arrive until the sun rose on the first unending day in spring.

She looked to where Prasham and Harlow were working on the antennas on a platform outside the main dome. Soon she'd be able to get back to her research. She'd also have time to get to know Mobius … and Rube. With another shiver, this one deep inside, she realized she could do whatever she wanted without worrying about Corvus for the first time in her life.

Prasham and Harlow moved away from the platform and Harlow used a crane to lower a smaller dome over the antennas. It had a retractable slot, though she knew gravitinos could go right through any structure. The dome was to provide protection from the elements, not to admit light. She turned to go inside.

* * *

The walls seemed to close in on her, making the confined space smaller and smaller.

Ket rubbed her eyes and checked the calendar, expecting to see the tally marks of a prisoner. Had she really been in her room for the past two weeks? Granted, she had emerged now and then to eat, but the clues she found in the data so excited her that only now did she realize she'd been working non-stop. No wonder her friends whispered things like, "Poor thing, she's turned into a nocturnal version of Prasham," and "Lucky she doesn't have to shave," and "Eek, it lives," when she passed them in the hall.

She still wasn't a morning person, whatever that meant here, and it had been easier for her to get food from the robochefs in her pajamas when everyone else was asleep. At least her friends seemed to understand she wasn't being antisocial. Though maybe they were starting to see her as insane. No one had asked her what she was working on. Even Prasham didn't want to know. He'd been absorbed with his own work. Only once did he say, "Even a good scientist has to stretch more than their neurons once in a while." Was he glad he no longer had to watch over her, or did he suspect she was working on something that wasn't worthy of his time? And what about Rube? She could tell he was waiting for a good time to talk to her, but why hadn't he tried to ask her about … about anything?

It didn't matter. She was about to meet with everyone in the lounge to discuss her research. Mobius would attend too—live. His v-bod body had come to Antarctica with them, though since their arrival he'd only talked to them the old fashioned way, by sending email.

She felt a dull tightening beneath her breastbone. Why hadn't Mobius visited before today? It would only take a minute to lock onto the gravitino emitting satellite, which was low on the horizon. Though this didn't matter—the gravitinos could go straight through the entire Earth as easily as they could through the dome covering the antennas. So establishing instantaneous contact with Mars wasn't the problem. It seemed Mobius had chosen not to visit here until now.

Ket knew he had made live visits to Earth since her arrival in Antarctica. Except, now that she was here, she was no longer his official tour guide. Nickie was, and Nickie would take on the double duty of date and tour guide when Mobius visited her next month in India. The idea of watching Mobius go on a date with Nickie had not thrilled her, but being his exclusive tour guide had made her feel special. Ket felt more than a twinge of disappointment.

The good thing was that this had allowed her to concentrate on her data, copied from the control room at Soahl Headquarters before they left, and especially on the weird signal she had recorded in communication mode by accident. Her first breakthrough came after she tried adjusting the acceptance angle in the formula used to translate the raw signals into ones and zeros. She found it wasn't all ones, as it had seemed at first. In fact, if she made the angle too big she got all zeros. And if she made the angle too small, the signal disappeared altogether. Then, after several marathon coding sessions, she found a consistent, repeating pattern: eleven thousand two hundred and sixty-three ones followed by four thousand one hundred and fifty-one zeros, followed by somewhat over sixteen billion ones and zeros. After factoring the numbers, she realized all were multiples of seven. And the last number was the product of seven times seven times seven times the first two numbers. The appearance of a number with a special meaning on Earth—that seemed like too much of a coincidence. It struck her as numerology. But it couldn't all be random chance either. Could it? What did it mean?

Then yesterday she'd figured it out. She was about to tell Mobius and Prasham the biggest "I told you so" in human history. Though what if she were mad? She stood up, threw a turtleneck sweater over her T-shirt and ditched her sweat-pants for matching slacks. Finally, she let her excitement begin to replace her anxiety. She'd face her fears, like she'd done before.

Upon reaching the lounge, she saw her friends' faces. For the first time in her life she felt surrounded by family. She displayed data on the holo-screen and started to explain the patterns she had found. Like family, her friends responded with kindness. But also like family, without hesitance, they pointed out where she might have erred.

"It could be a deception by Whitesmith," Prasham said. "He might have altered the data during his break-in, to discredit the Mars Program."

"He couldn't have got to the data in the control room," Lacy said. "He would have needed to send fake gravitino signals to the antenna on the roof of Soahl Headquarters. But the technology was brand new, invented right before we arrived in India. Even Whitesmith couldn't have figured out how to do it that fast."

Prasham harrumphed. "I agree, it would be too complex for your average scientist. However, a pirate could have stolen the plans for the antenna."

"They only existed on Mars until they were transmitted to India last year," Mobius said.

"But Corvus was in India," Quasi said. "He could have stolen the plans."

"I doubt it. He's a bully, not a spy." Rube winked at Ket.

"Perhaps he had help," Quasi continued. "He was visiting with the Indian military. Could they have stolen the plans for him? Or maybe Whitesmith was with him and stole the plans."

"No," Prasham said. "That would be unbelievable. Corvus asked the navy to give him a tour of the launch site, as a ruse to get onto the spaceport island to get to Ket. But they never would have helped him with espionage. No one in the navy knew about the plans, in any case, and no one else could have been on the island without security knowing about it."

Ket wanted to point out Prasham's assessment of security hadn't always been that good. But she agreed with him in this case. "Corvus was there to get to me," she said. "He thought he would force me to go with him. He had no idea about entangled gravitinos. Neither did any of us. It's far fetched to think he or Whitesmith could have known about the antenna plans back then."

"We are making this too complicated," Lacy said. "Maybe Whitesmith hacked into the antenna data acquisition system in the control room to relay a fake message to Ket's soahl, without having to know anything about gravitinos."

"But even you admitted hacking the door, not to mention the antenna system, would be a challenge ..." Rube stopped himself. "Not that anyone here would ever break into anything."

Ket tried not to laugh at Rube's discomfort and Lacy's attempt to look innocent, while Quasi flashed them his grin. "But if Whitesmith had managed to hack the system, why would he take my soahl?" she asked. "Why would he do that if he wanted to scam me, to get me to embarrass the Mars Program with a hoaxed discovery of aliens?"

"If it's not a hoax, then it was a random event. You said you had to tune the polarization to find your result, correct?" Prasham asked.

"I searched different polarizations and tuned the acceptance angle until the numbers made sense," Ket replied.

"If you search for a pattern in enough random data, you'll find it, Ms. Ket," Prasham continued. "The false alarm rate has to be considered."

"How about I show you it's not random." Ket surprised even herself with her firmness.

"Indeed," Mobius said. "Perhaps Ket has discovered what she's been trying to tell us." He raised a v-bod arm toward a large holo-screen behind Prasham. "So go on, bring up the image you wanted to show us on the screen."

Ket touched a button on her display and up came the full picture.

"Holy mother of the universe," Lacy said. "That looks like a cat."

"With a kangaroo body," Quasi added.

"Kangaroo and cats?" Mobius asked.

"Could it be a pet?" Harlow's hushed tone contained a boyish longing. "Maybe they say hello with a picture of a pet."

"I don't think so," Ket said. "On each hand I count seven fingers, touching as if in prayer, and a long one folded into a triangle-shaped thumb. See how the triangles on the two hands touch tip-to-tip, making an hourglass shape? It's a symbol, something an intelligent being would do."

"How did you get this picture?" Prasham asked. He pulled out an n-cloth square and flicked it into a display.

"I did a little soahl searching," Ket replied. She smiled at Lacy. "I found the usual articles on Active SETI, the Arecibo message, the various Cosmic Calls, and so on. All of these had sent pictogram radio messages to the stars. No reply ever came back, though it would take tens to hundreds of years for even a nearby civilization to respond." Ket brought up two numbers on the screen. "These were the first two numbers, multiples of seven. I thought, what if these were the dimensions of a two dimensional pictogram? I replaced the ones with asterisks and the zeros with dots. At first, I saw just a series of squares, circles, and triangles, followed by a face attached to a stick figure. At least that is what I thought it was. I had to write more code to produce the picture out of the pixels."

Harlow's jaw hung open. "They have eight fingers. Why would they use multiples of seven? Though I did have an Uncle Moose who claimed he'd cracked seven vertebrae when he'd been abducted by aliens. More likely he got lost hunting. But maybe he gave them the idea."

"Are all your rellies named after massive objects?" Quasi asked.

"Shh," Lacy said. "Seven's a lucky number. To my family it means togetherness."

"Don't get too excited. There are eight fingers on each hand," Ket said. "That's a Fibonacci number, as is five, the number of fingers on our hands."

"And nature likes Fibonacci numbers," Rube said.

"But the seven touching fingers and the numbers being multiples of seven—that probably means something," Prasham said.

"The eighth finger is a long thumb bent into a triangle. Right? So I think it means they based their numbers on the remaining seven fingers," Ket said. "It's a coincidence that some humans like that number too."

"Even if it's a coincidence, it will mean something to a lot of people on Earth." Mobius shook his head. "And those triangles look like pyramids. The press is going to have a field day."

"People will see what they want," Rube said. "They're basic geometric shapes."

"But isn't a two-dimensional pictogram too obvious?" Lacy asked.

"A first contact message is supposed to be obvious," Rube said.

"I think Rube's right," Quasi added. "We might miss a message from aliens who think nothing like we do, but that means this message is from aliens who do think something like we do. There could be many other messages out there that we've missed."

"Whatever." Lacy shrugged, then laughed. "I'm so happy I feel like my tattoos are about to glow." She pointed her fickle-finger up. "So they're really out there?"

Rube strode in front of his friends. "If Ket says so, then yes. Here's to Ket and the discovery of the kangaroo-cats!"

Ket was warmed by Rube's burst of energy. Everyone, except Mobius and Prasham, gave her a giant smile.

Quasi reached into his satchel for his flask.

"Scotch is perfect," Harlow said. "Let's break out shot glasses and plates for cake. I'll make a whiskey and maple one—my grandma's favorite. And I have syrup in my room."

"Yes, fine." Mobius grumbled. "Of course, this will all have to be confirmed independently by the Math Monks on Mars. And none of the data can leave Antarctica until we are ready to publish and have a press conference."

"Though from this one pictogram," Prasham said, "we can't say very much."

Ket understood Mobius and Prasham's concern. "That's not a problem," she said. "There are seven hundred and forty-two pictograms after this one." Her smile was as wide as a galaxy.

"Show us," Rube, Lacy, and Quasi said in unison.

"It will take a while to decipher it all," Ket said.

There was silence until Prasham nodded with his own slight smile.

"Well then," Mobius said. "I know a way to speed things up. I suggest you and Prasham join me." Now even he had a grin on his v-bod face.

* * *

Prasham and Ket stood next to Mobius on Mars in front of Maxine.

An hour ago they had scanned all the pictograms into the computer's memory and proceeded to ask questions. For example, what did the series of rotating isosceles triangles mean? Placeholders in a base-seven number system, Maxine replied. And what about the pattern that resembled a star map? It showed, Maxine explained, the alien's planet relative to the galactic center and two wide-beam pulsars. This meant their planet was one hundred twenty-three parsecs away, just over four hundred light-years from Earth, in a system with a known habitable planet found in surveys decades before, orbiting a dwarf star, somewhat less massive and longer lived than the Sun. There was also a series of numbers, which suggested a different frequency and sample rate to use to receive a longer message.

"I think I'll call them the Kay Cees," Ket said, "for kangaroo cats."

"Yes, I like that, Ms. Ket," Prasham said.

"So do I." Mobius beamed. "I can't wait for the two of you to join me here for real. We'll have years together to discover their secrets."

Ket wasn't sure what to say. Prasham looked proud. Mobius looked confident. She knew that none of this could have happened without the two of them. She was grateful for that. But Mobius also sounded like he thought he should lead the study of the aliens.

"I've sent a message to your new soahl, Ms. Ket," Maxine said, "a primer about us that you can send to the Kay Cees." Not only was this computer much smarter than any human at recognizing patterns in unfamiliar data, it also knew how to sound like your friend.

Doubts gripped her mind. Had it been wise to give all her data to Maxine? Mobius had complete control over the computer. Of course, she would work with him and Prasham. The data was coming from their antenna, after all. But besides data, what else did Mobius want from her? He said she was completely free to do what she wanted, with no strings attached. But also, he had brought her to a place where she could not get far away.

This was a silly way to think, she decided. He'd brought her here to protect her. She shook off her doubts and thought about the good people of the universe, about her good friends in Antarctica.

* * *

During the next two weeks Rube realized he'd been brought here for a purpose, and it wasn't to learn that near proximity to Ket in no way improved his chances of even briefly conversing with her. No, he learned from Mobius he was here to give everyone v-bod control lessons. In particular, Mobius had asked Rube for lessons to improve his walking.

As for the others, Lacy was asked to research Abraham's books and sermons for clues about what Corvus might do next and to search for anything that might further link him to Whitesmith. Quasi was tasked with synthesizing additional fuel for the camp from a deep natural gas well. And Harlow's job was to update the menus for the robo-chefs, while continuing to maintain the antennas.

Rube had also read all of Prasham's reports. He'd taken over the study of the naturally occurring gravitino bursts, his chance to do astronomy at last, and concluded, with help from the software Ket had written, that these came from anomalous dark matter clumps, just as Prasham had speculated. It turned out the universe was filled with a natural network of these, and chance alignments were fairly common. Based on the number of clumps and the distance to the Kay Cee planet, there were probably at least ten thousand planets with intelligent life on them in our galaxy at the present moment. That was less than one out of every twenty million planets in the Milky Way,

Prasham explained, but still far more than many experts had predicted.

"But what about other galaxies and the rest of the universe?" Rube asked. He watched Ket join them in the dining room, just as they started another discussion about the aliens.

"There are, perhaps, thousands of trillions of civilizations out there," Prasham replied. "And plausibly millions we might be able to talk with through the elsewhere. The farther away a planet is, the farther into the past or future this could mean." He raised a tofu pikelet toward the ceiling. "If this were a planet on the other side of the observable universe, it would exist in our elsewhere from many billions of years into our past, before Earth formed, to many billions of years into our future, after Earth is gone." He leaned back and almost fell out of his chair.

Rube pictured a tiny Prasham reaching out to the universe while seated upside down on the bottom of a globe. He turned to Ket. "You're here to tell us more about the aliens?"

Ket took a sip of water. "I'm still working on the Kay Cee messages, but I figured it was time I joined your dinner conversations. Well, Mobius asked me to be here tonight."

Rube assessed the knowing look between her and Mobius while poking a potato.

"Contacting other civilizations is unlikely," Prasham continued. "For any civilization much farther away than a few thousand light years, the gravitino beams tend to decohere. Of course, an advanced civilization could set up its own network of gravitino emitters, but it would be complicated. For example, if the Kay Cees decided to set up an emitter near their planet, the beam would take four hundred years to get to Earth, and they would have to point the beam to where the Earth will be in four hundred years. But they could communicate, then, with humans who live four hundred years in their future. Similarly, if we started emitting a beam from here toward them, it would take four hundred years for it to arrive at the Kay Cees planet, and we'd have to point it where their planet will be in four hundred years. But we could communicate, then, with Kay Cees who live four hundred years in our future. It has to do with the relative nature of what we mean by the present, the past, and the future in the elsewhere. As for the likely naturally occurring emitter that exists between the Kay Cees and us, there is no way to know, without other data, where it is positioned between us. They could be communicating with us, from Earth's perspective, anywhere from four hundred years ago to four hundred years from now. It doesn't matter, though. In any case, the communication is instantaneous."

While all of this amazed Rube, he couldn't stop thinking about Ket. She had acquired thousands of additional pictograms once Harlow had tuned the antenna to the new channel Maxine had figured out. But she still hadn't sent Maxine's primer to the Kay Cees. There was a lot of concern about this. Protocol and treaty said Earth should not return contact with an alien civilization until all nations had been informed and offered a chance for input. And the potential consequences had to be considered. If such a civilization were more advanced than ours, would an invasion be likely? And would humans end up like many of the indigenous people on Earth?

Mobius picked up that point now. "Remember, space is the enemy. It would take them over four thousand years using fusion powered rockets to get to us—to get here any faster would require exponentially more energy." He elaborated. "Their star is also longer lived than the Sun. So there is no need for them to come here for survival. Of course, if they are more advanced than us, they might also be further along the acid-etched edge of destruction we humans are always balanced on. If their world is in ruins, their signal might be a beacon to find a place to migrate. But in that case, if we contact them, this will only tell them that there is also intelligent life here, which would make our world less inviting. Invading would mean facing beings that would fight back. Plotting genocide across the galaxy isn't practical, and with so many other planets to choose from—it would make no sense to invade Earth."

"So that means you do plan to contact them?" Ket asked. She used tongs to add a serving of fish and chips to her plate.

"Mars isn't under treaty," Mobius replied. His v-bod eyed Ket's dish, seemingly wishing to take a bite. "We can send the message from Mars, and Earth can go screw itself if it objects."

Rube felt the hubris from Mobius. He pinched his cloth napkin, but nothing happened. "Mars still depends on Earth."

"Though the plan is to start a self-sufficient colony." Ket discreetly slurped in a chip clinging to her lower lip and smiled.

Rube didn't like the way Ket looked at Mobius. But he noticed Quasi, Lacy, and Harlow were very attentive, crunching their food while nodding in agreement. This was the 'Ket and Mobius' show, with Prasham as chief mentor, and Rube saw that his friends understood it wasn't their place to offer opinions.

Rube dipped his potato in sour cream. He told himself he wasn't bothered. He accepted that Ket had to find her own path. If so inclined, she could take a partner to Mars. But even if he was miraculously in the one universe where she asked him to join her, how could that really work out? So, if asked, he'd tell her no. He'd have to earn his own way to Mars, on the mission after Ket's. And if she were shacked up with Mobius by then, that would be that. There was no way he would go to Mars, in that case. Instead, he would go to the farthest corner of the Earth, maybe devote himself to helping others. His life would be great. As great as it could be, with all hope for love stretched infinitely far away by the black hole of loneliness.

* * *

After returning to his room, Rube stared into the dark from his bed. Thoughts of gravity and the emptiness of space continued to weigh on him. That's when his display flickered, and he received the message from Ket. It contained a puzzle and said, once he had it solved, he was invited to meet her for a date on the other side of the universe.

His heart pounded.

The darkness was gone.

Chapter 21
How Ket Got Her Bra Back

The puzzle stated: "You are given twelve bowls that look identical. One, however, weighs less or more than the other eleven. Using only a balance scale, explain how to find the odd bowl after only three weighings and determine whether it is lighter or heavier than the others." Rube worked on it all night.

His first thought was to place six bowls on either side of the balance but realized one learned nothing from this. An hour later, he figured out the maximum number of bowls that could be left as possible candidates by the third weighing and tried to work backward. However, every way he thought about how to divide the bowls into different groups during the first two weighings failed to eliminate enough of them. What was he missing?

Finally, he got it. After he sent his solution to Ket, she replied, "What took you so long?" and then, "Meet me in the control room tonight."

* * *

Rube paced the halls of the base quintillions of times before the next night period.

Because Ket worked on a timetable almost the opposite of everyone else, he hoped she meant the base's night period. She had. He saw her motioning him to the control room.

"It's like the one at Soahl Headquarters in Seattle. But I've got a surprise for you."

"Just being here is a surprise." Rube hoped his internal shaking wasn't visible.

"Look at this pictogram."

Rube saw something on the large holo-screen—himself. Well, not himself, but something to do with him. "A sine wave?"

"Like your dream, spreading out through the universe. Back in India, you said you'd tell me more about it. So?"

"I was working on problem sets every night. One night I dreamed my body was vibrating, oscillating and traveling through space."

"Hmm, not even a Bessel function or a Hermite-Gaussian mode?" She shook her bangs.

"Boring, right?" He looked toward the door.

"Rube, I didn't mean—"

"I know." Rube squared himself with her. "But that dream scared me. I always thought I wanted be an astronomer. Except, the ones I met seemed to have no time for anything but work. And …" He realized Ket might think he was putting her in this category. "Sorry, I know what you're working on now is very important. It makes sense you haven't had time to—"

"Talk? Sorry. I've wanted to talk. It's just—the last four weeks—it's been intense. Finding that signal has consumed me."

"I completely understand," he said. "When you make a great discovery, maybe the greatest ever, you'd be crazy not to give it everything you've got. So I didn't mean you—I meant others—the professors who no longer make discoveries but still worked endlessly, probably out of habit, and maybe to justify having spent their lives writing papers no one will ever read. I feared I would end up like them and I went back home."

"Back to Tulip?" Ket raised her eyebrows. "Sorry, I remember Quasi mentioning her."

"I wasn't going to bring her up," Rube said. "But when I lost her, it made me realize maybe I was spending too much time studying. Then I met Evelyn at the University of Washington. She convinced me to try something more practical, something that would make money. And I changed my major from astronomy to computer science." Rube tempered a well of emotion. "But I've always regretted it. Not because of Evelyn—being with her would have been a disaster even if I'd stuck with astronomy—but because I really do wonder about this universe and why we're here."

"I've always wondered too. However, if I'd had your dream ..."

"You'd have quit too?" Rube wondered if she was serious.

"No, I'd have laughed it off, but—"

"But when I'm around you Ket, I don't think about the universe—or aliens. I think about being with you." Rube's internal shaking rose to the surface. "I mean—"

"Slow down. This is our first date. And don't forget, I'm the one in charge here."

Rube knew he had punched the relationship accelerator pedal too hard. He was relieved to see her smile. He hadn't ruined things.

"I know about pressure too," she continued. "Everything has been happening so fast. I just need to have some fun tonight."

"And that's why our first date is in the control room?"

"Yes ... because we're going to Mars." Ket pushed a button.

Two beds lowered from the wall and Rube jumped back. He hadn't thought about how she and Prasham had gone to Mars. Was it weird they would lie next to each other?

Ket opened a drawer and pulled out two travel kits. "Mobius has granted us the next tour. Quasi and Lacy go tomorrow." She pulled a wand out of another drawer. "Only this time we are going to scan ourselves first. Prasham keeps forgetting to do this, but no more hairless roaming of Mars for me." Ket scanned Rube. Then she handed the wand to him. "Now scan me."

He did, going twice over every curve of her body. "I don't think I missed a spot."

"You didn't. You also lingered in a few places maybe longer than needed. But let's get's dressed in our travel clothes."

Rube opened his kit. "Why is there underwear in here?"

"Never mind."

Rube thought Ket blushed, but she pulled out a partition between the beds and went to the one on the right. He went to the one on the left.

Moments later, he heard her say, "Ready?"

He was, for anything.

* * *

Rube had stayed behind Ket, following her around the Martian base. After they reached a spiral staircase in a dimly lit room, she placed his hand on her hip and guided him up to a domed observation deck. There, he looked through glass at their shadows stretching over the sand.

"It's beyond words."

Ket nodded. "That was the sum-total of my reaction the first time too."

"Is that a v-bod, in the dunes?"

"A test one, to see how it copes with the dust."

Mobius didn't seem to be around and the Monks kept to themselves. Had Ket arranged all this? Then she led him into a room with a large computer and he asked, "Is this Maxine?"

"Yes," Ket said, "and she's been busy. Brace yourself."

Rube grabbed a support handle.

Ket laughed. "Not literally. But what I am about to tell you will blow your mind."

"You mean beyond getting into the Mars Program, getting kicked out, then kicked back in, finding out Einstein didn't have the last say on everything, watching you discover aliens, and now being here with you, through the elsewhere? Believe me, my mind was blown the moment I saw you in that orange dress, and it's been one hell of a ride ever since."

"For me too. But here's the thing. Maxine sent the primer to the Kay Cees."

"On her own? I know Maxine has superhuman intelligence, way beyond the chat-bots programmed into our soahls or the best robo-assistants. But she acted on her own?"

"No, Mobius directed her to do so, like he said he would."

"I thought he might discuss that further with us, at least with you."

"He's the boss here. When he makes up his mind about something …"

Rube drifted into a dream-like trance, staring at Ket's nano-hair, which was almost as beautiful as her real hair. It helped him forget what other things Mobius might have made his mind up about. He realized Ket was looking at him, waiting for him to return to … to Earth? No, Mars. He snapped back into virtual reality. "So, we've contacted the Kay Cees?"

"Yes, and it seems Maxine and the Kay Cees have been talking. The sine wave I showed you in the control room is part of a series of pictures from a longer message that, when animated, shows an oscilloscope-like movie of sound. Maxine quickly figured out the data was digital samples of the Kay Cees speaking, a frequency series showing the amplitude and phase of pressure perturbations. After an inverse Fourier transform, we played the result back through an analog converter and got this." Ket touched a button on Maxine's display.

Out came a high-pitched chirping.

"The kangaroo-cats sound like birds?"

"Yep, I guess that's the best description, though sometimes they also sound like car horns and buzz saws. Not only that, we now have video, and we have this …"

Ket touched another button, and Rube felt his stomach fall. The room whirled around and disappeared. His weightless feeling changed to feeling upside down. New walls appeared and counter-whirled before coming to rest. He found himself sitting in a room that reminded him of his brother's home in Africa, but made of a material he couldn't identify, while strangely colored triangles zoomed around him.

"We've v-bod traveled to their world," Ket continued, "though we haven't learned yet how to walk using their technology. Maxine is trying to understand the instructions. But we can hear and see, and move our arms and heads."

Ket took hold of his wrist. Was she checking his pulse? He thought he might lose consciousness and felt the food he'd eaten earlier searching for a way out. Then the triangles stopped moving and his equilibrium returned.

In hopped two Kay Cees. The smaller one chirped and flashed a row of translucent teeth.

Rube had seen many made-up worlds before and decided that's all this was. He looked for his inventory button or the end-game button. He told himself all he had to do was sit up and rip off his mask and he'd be out of there. He was right. He could do that. But there was something about this place, something real, and the sense this was a computer simulation vanished. Now he felt sure he was on a real world, thousands of trillions of miles from Earth. And, glimpsing Ket, everything felt fine.

He finally allowed himself to really look at the Kay Cees. They were covered in very close-cropped, down-like fur, light purple in color, and wore matching vests and fabric strips around the waist, made of a velour-like material. The skin underneath their fur was silver, the same color as their bracelets, etched with triangle-based moving calligraphy and jewel sliders that probably served as controls. There were other features that weren't apparent in the pictograms and photos he'd seen. Their eye sockets were diamond shaped and their teeth were not only translucent but like blown glass. He also realized that what he thought was the nose, was a fur-covered horn, while air holes and whiskers were under the chin. They were like nothing on Earth—kangaroos and cats were simply the best analogies his Earth brain could come up with. It was the same with how they sounded, like birds, but not like any bird he'd ever heard.

There was another chirp and Rube heard Maxine's voice in his ear. "Young adult."

"Maxine is trying to translate," Ket said, "but she only understands a few thousand of their words, so far, mostly nouns and verbs, based on pictures. I think they understand us more."

The other Kay Cee chirped, and Maxine said, "Female? Give breeding DNA?" It turned to the other Kay Cee and launched into an excited and extended conversation.

"What?" Rube looked at Ket. Her head was normal, but her body was covered in fur. He looked down and saw his was too. He almost asked her if they meant mating. It was like the worst science fiction stories he had ever read—and some of the best too. He gave Ket a look that must have betrayed his thoughts.

"Relax," she said. "From what we can tell so far, the Kay Cees exchange DNA with other species. They are in contact with millions of them across the universe and based on what they've shown me, most of the other species are incomprehensible to us. We are just lucky, very lucky, that the Kay Cees' planet is close enough for our crude antenna to pick up their signal."

"Millions? And these other species go along with this DNA swapping?"

"Let me explain. They do want DNA from other species, and from us, but they're willing to wait thousands of years to get a breeding pair of sequences. They're not going to put us in cages and extract it. They couldn't do that if they wanted to, given we're not really here, right? So, it seems they're interested in gaining our trust first, even if it takes thousands of years, as I said. Well, whatever a year means to them. The more precise word is orbit."

"And after thousands of years … thousands of orbits … then what?"

"According to Maxine, if and when we learn to trust them, a pair of individuals can upload their DNA sequences to them. At the same time, a pair of Kay Cees will exchange their DNA sequences with us. We would also need to send each other all the information needed to produce and raise the offspring."

"I think I'm following you, but—"

"But, if we give them our DNA sequences, such as yours and mine Rube …" Ket paused for a moment. "Hypothetically, I mean … then they can make little Rube-Kets out of it and raise them on their planet. And we can make little Kay Cees on Earth. It's the ultimate foreign exchange program, don't you think?"

Rube didn't think. Not only was his mind blown, it was lost and scattered across the universe. "I thought you never wanted to have kids."

"I don't. And I'm not planning to give them my DNA, or yours, or anyone's. I'm just telling you what they're interested in."

Rube looked at the two Kay Cees. They started licking each other's fur. It wasn't unsettling, but somehow endearing, and he thought they seemed very content.

"And other aliens? How many species have you met?"

"Not too many. Not up close. They've given me some information to consider, and shown me some amazing things. With time they say they will show me more. But like I said, most other species are incomprehensible to us, at least for now. And I'm pretty sure some will never have much appeal. For example, there's what the Kay Cees call the O's."

"In English?"

"Er, no, but they drew a circle to illustrate. I guess O's is my interpretation, because the O's have a single orifice, and everything goes in and out of it all day long. There's both a tongue and other things inside ... fingers ... and other appendages."

"Uh, I get the picture."

"It's too unbelievable for words." She looked into Rube's eyes. "I needed to tell someone about what I've learned, what I've seen. And I wanted to talk to you."

Rube wanted to talk to her too, but the timing was wrong. "Shouldn't we talk more with our hosts?"

"They don't seem to mind. I think they're studying us and like to listen to our voices. We can't really converse with them directly, since we can't vocalize their chirps, at least not without sounding really stupid. And, so far, I haven't heard them try to speak like us. We need the computer to translate."

"You said Maxine is learning."

"Yes. But even with her help we can't talk fluently with the Kay Cees. Not yet. It also gets a bit sing-songy for me, listening to them for more than a few minutes, and darned annoying when they start honking or making sawing sounds."

"Hmm, it's kind of sad really. We meet aliens, but maybe we'll never be able to talk with them, like other ... like other people. I wonder what they think of us?"

"Well, they've studied the basic information in the primer we sent them. That included some of Mobius's speeches and pictures to illustrate. It seems they got inspiration from one of the speeches and now refer to us, at least according to Maxine's translation, as, well, as the naked mole rats of the universe."

Ket started to laugh. Rube did too. He felt her squeeze his hand.

"Come on, let's go," she said.

"Where?"

"You'll see."

Rube felt the room whirl around him again. After a few moments of vertigo he found his body wrapped in a black gooey fumarole and saw Ket's head sticking out of a similar mound. They were outside and alone. He looked up at a sky filled with stars and glowing gas bubbles. Two other galaxies seemed to be colliding overhead. This couldn't be the Milky Way.

"Where are we?"

"According the Kay Cees, we are tens of billions of light-years from their home and tens of billions of years in the future. I like to think of it as the spa on the other side of the universe."

Rube laughed and looked down. "So this is mud? And Earth's gone?"

"Maybe, though any news of Earth's demise would not have reached here yet. That news would still be in the elsewhere … like us." Ket seemed to look out, trying to find home.

Rube looked for home too. Then after a moment he said, "But we're on Earth."

"Right. Time to go back."

* * *

After they left the control room, Ket took Rube to her room. They sat on her bed and talked for hours, at first about the universe, then about their likes and their dislikes, and then about trivial things. He asked about her dress. Was it another gift from Mobius? No, it was a peasant dress from Fiji she'd rarely worn. Then they talked about growing up.

"What did you say the mean kids called you?" she asked.

"Rubik's cube-head. It wasn't a terrible insult, but I didn't like it. And you?"

"When I was sixteen the boys from the village used to call out, hey Betti Boni, you give us boners. That's when I switched to Betti Keturah."

"Did that help?"

"No, then they said, here Ketty Ketty Ketty … we want to pet you."

"Couldn't you have just given them the finger?"

"That wouldn't have meant anything to them. It's funny, they didn't swear, and neither did I. Swearing wasn't part of my growing up." She angled her body more toward his.

"So what did help?"

"Dr. Mateni. He went to the chief of the village. Those boys never bothered me again. I felt bad, having a grown-up do that for me. I never got to know the kids in the village very well … because of my father. Otherwise, maybe things could've been different." She tucked her legs under herself.

"You weren't allowed?" He self-consciously mirrored Ket's position like she was leading a dance and he had two left feet.

"Oh, the villagers came to our church, but the kids were shy there. Only expatriates living on the ranch socialized with me, but they were so narrow-minded. I ended up avoiding them. Then Dr. Mateni showed me a few things, about Mars, and learning, and life … and I went to India and met Prasham and … and here we are."

Rube thought maybe he'd ask her again about Corvus and how she'd run away, but out came something else. "What about friends in India? You had a boyfriend."

"I guess I'd call him a training bra." Ket burst out laughing.

Rube did too and fell off the bed.

Ket stood, took his hand, and pulled him up. "You are a Good Sine, Rube, and I'm feeling like a Bad Wave tonight. I want to go somewhere new with you."

"You've already taken me to the other side of the universe."

"You know the bra I'm looking for—the perfect match, the perfect bra-ket equal to one? I've wanted, for a while, to see if we're like that."

"You have?" Rube immediately added, "I mean, I've wanted that too."

She turned away from him and reached back to unbutton her dress. It fell from her shoulders. "In India, I thought you were a bit cheeky, but maybe also someone that could be good for me. Later, I wondered, how I could get you back into my life."

Rube became aware she was waiting for him. He approached her and placed his hands over her real bra. Everything she was saying could have sounded corny, but it sounded right. Besides, he was so excited he could almost feel his own heart beating through her chest. She had taken him to the other side of the universe. Now she was taking him where he so wanted to go. He gave her a very long, soft kiss on the back of her neck.

"I thought maybe you were going to be *the* bra for me in India," Ket continued, "and I wondered … I wondered, how I was going to get my bra back?"

They laughed and fell over together onto the bed.

CHAPTER 22
SOUL COLLAPSE

When Rube awoke he felt like he was on top of the world. But after last night, how could he know up from down? Then Ket rolled over and rose on her elbows. She was naked.

Gently, she put his hand on the scar above her left breast. "It's mostly faded now. But it also gave me some cover. After Corvus did this, when he came near me, I'd point to it. He'd warn me about the consequences if I said anything, but he kept his distance. It seemed that cover was gone, though, when he came for me in India."

Rube and Ket hugged for a long time.

After a while he left to shower and change clothes in his room, but returned to Ket's room. She got up, put on a robe, and crossed the tiny room to the shower. While the water ran, he looked at the robe on the floor and played a song on his harmonica about cornfields and Kansas. He couldn't remember it's exact name, but it sure wasn't the blues.

A few minutes later Ket came out in a towel. They had decided to neither confirm nor deny anything. "Why don't you go out first," she said, "while I get dressed."

"Good idea." Rube kissed her until she playfully pushed him toward the door. He opened it, and felt her towel snap him. He looked back. "Don't make me come back over there."

She smiled. "Go."

He did. When he entered the lounge he saw Lacy and Quasi sitting on the couch, absorbed in their displays. He sat next to Lacy.

She lowered her dark glasses. "How was the cake?"

"Shh." Quasi waved Rube off. "Don't say anything."

"It was just a date," Rube said. "All right, she took me to the other side of the universe."

"I'll bet," Lacy said.

Before Lacy could say any more, Prasham and v-bod Mobius came in and sat, followed by Ket, who leaned against a support with her arms crossed. Prasham turned on the large holo-screen and displayed a list with the latest news about the Kay Cees. Next to the list, he started a video showing their planet.

"There is no doubt now," Mobius began, "this is bigger than any of us. We have to think carefully about how to present this to the world. What seems best is for me to do so from Mars. Then those that don't want to believe it can dismiss it. Others will have time to adjust. And no treaty violations can be brought up."

"I thought I would lead the press conference." Ket didn't try to hide her irritation.

"You could, but the press would hound you. I'm not even sure I could keep them out of Antarctica. And some nations may want to debrief you. They'll subpoena you, if you don't agree. But it's your decision." Mobius looked sympathetic.

"I guess you're right." Ket bit the edge of her thumb.

Rube could tell she was nervous. Who wouldn't be? In the last month she'd not only discovered aliens, she'd travelled as a v-bod to their world. However, Mobius was still in charge and could pull the plug if he wanted.

"Maybe we should wait until I am on Mars," Ket continued.

"Yes," Rube said. "Hold the press conference from there, and the world can't get to her." He nodded at Ket, as if to say he'd be there too, with her.

"I think that would be wise," Prasham said.

"Please agree," Ket said to Mobius. "There's so much work to do between now and then. There's no time to go public. I'm glad my friends here know. But the world can wait."

Mobius nodded. "If that's the plan, then that's the plan. I've got to get back to work."

"I, too, must work," Prasham said. "I need to help Harlow finish the stabilization code for the second antenna. We don't want a failure with such important data coming in. He glanced at Rube and Ket. "Unlike some of you, that boy was up with me at five a.m. and is working now."

Prasham left the room. Mobius followed him to return the v-bod to the control room, and Rube thought it gave him a strange stare when it passed.

"Aye, all play and no work makes me healthy, happy, but poor. Not that we're getting a farthing to be here. But I also must get back to work, on fuel synthesis." Quasi inched to the edge of the couch and patted the bald space between his curly tuffs. "Where's my hat?"

"Hey, before everyone leaves, do you want to see my new tattoo?" Lacy asked. She looked at Rube and Ket. "You know, the one I told you about months ago?"

Ket took Quasi's place next to Lacy and Rube moved around behind them.

"Here it is." Quasi reached between the cushion and armrest to pull out a sports cap with the MathMonksMars logo. "I've been trying to ferment fruit juice too, though I can't seem to get the reaction going." He slid over next to Ket.

Lacy lifted her blouse to reveal her tummy. "This is new." She pointed to her bellybutton, which showed a star-filled funnel entering her body, while the spaghettified scream figure went around it to one side before continuing on down. She ran her finger around the funnel and stopped at the bald, hunched cartoon character falling into it. "That's Quasimodo, for my Quasi."

"Like in the poem," Rube said. "The universe is unfolding as it should."

"It is?" Quasi tilted his head.

"I know it is now," Rube replied. He placed a hand on Ket's shoulder.

"Right-o." Quasi sighed. "But at the beginning of the year we thought we were all headed to Mars to make a name for ourselves. Now most of us don't know where we're headed, and from what I just heard, our lives are likely to be completely scrambled from here on out."

Ket reached her hand back to Rube's.

Quasi tugged on his cap's brim and continued. "But here we are sitting on a story, and when it breaks, some of you will be more famous than any mission to Mars could ever make us."

"I'm excited, we get to go to Mars tonight," Lacy said.

"And maybe one v-bod trip'll be enough for me," Quasi said. "Maybe being this close to you over-achievers makes me want to return to my quiet life—a life I was quite happy with before, thank you very much."

"I've heard Prasham whisper to Mobius that he still thinks we're the know-nothings from the back row," Lacy said.

"You're not," Ket said. "But I understand completely where Quasi is coming from. This is all very overwhelming. None of us are really ourselves anymore."

Rube moved in front of Lacy and Quasi. "We'll see you on Mars, after the next mission."

"And you'll already be there?" Quasi asked.

Rube took a quick look at Ket, but didn't get the nod he expected. The conversation was getting too far ahead of itself. Finally he said, "I hope so."

"I hope one day we'll be there together," Ket said. "Not because of fate, but because we all want to be there."

"Here's to that," Rube said

"Count me in," Lacy said. "To friendship."

"Sorry, I didn't mean to act like I had my kilt on backwards," Quasi said, "Count me in."

The four of them paused for a moment, looking at each other until their glances of affection caused each of them to shift their eyes from the others' faces to something less intimate, like their own feet. At least Rube found himself staring at his.

Ket broke the silence. "Do you want to know my favorite poem?"

"Yes," Lacy said. She sat up and arched her back.

"It's one by Maya Angelou," Ket said. "It's called *A Brave And Startling Truth*."

"I'll have to read it." With delight, Lacy pushed her dark glasses down from her curls.

Rube looked up from his feet at Ket. "You are brave. And startling." He leaned over and gave her a kiss. She did not complain.

"I reckon you two should get a room," Quasi said.

"Too late."

Rube was relieved it was Lacy who said this. He'd almost blurted out the same thing.

"I was playing along with the game of not kissin' and tellin'," Quasi said. He began to dig between the cushions again. "Now, if I can find my flask."

"That's a beautiful poem, Ket," Lacy said. Her gaze seemed fixed on the inside of her glasses. "But I've got to get back to my research. I was studying the three eras, or ages of Joachim." She looked at Ket. "And the new ages your father believes in. This is the New Age of the Spirit. And hey ..."

"There's a spirit of hay?" Rube laughed.

"She did grow up in Montana," Quasi said. "But you mean, hey, hold on, not hay is for zebras, or hey, sacrebleu, look at my mascara's hue, don't you, my dear?"

"I mean hey, what's this. Ket, your soahl—its on! I've been scanning for it, hoping that the passwords had not been changed."

"You still remember them?" Ket asked.

Rube leaned forward and waved his arms with urgency. "Let us hear."

Lacy opened her display and pushed up the volume slider.

"Then we must shun her."

"Corvus," Ket said. She and Rube knelt in front of Lacy.

"I will not shun my own daughter."

"And Abraham," Rube whispered. He squeezed Ket's hand.

Everyone listened with careful attention.

"You're getting weak in the Spirit, old man," Corvus said. "I've got Whitesmith checking things out. He said there's a message on this thing, a secret message being prepared to send to Mars, but he wasn't sure. I think it could be to aliens."

"Aliens?" Abraham's voice was agitated. "Has your string tie cut off the circulation to your brain? And why do you bring that *thing* here?"

"My outfit does compliment your luddite view of the world, doesn't it?"

"I've never heard Corvus question my father like that," Ket whispered.

"Careful," Abraham said. "You know it's not the modernity of it that bothers me. And since when have you become pro-technology? You're even afraid to turn on a TV."

"Except to watch your sermons, of course." Corvus sounded more compliant. "But if this *thing*, this awful *thing*, can help get her back here, does it matter?"

"Why don't you just call it what it is. If you can ignore my ban and bring it here, then just say the name. This soahl, how did you get it?"

"Fine, this awful soahl is from our second attempt to scare her back here."

"Second attempt? I thought you sent Whitesmith to gather info for our court case."

"Whitesmith tried to scare her back here. This is her soahl, not his."

"He did what?" Abraham sounded alarmed. "I've warned you—"

"And I'm telling you, old man, we have to shun her, at least for now. Cut her off from you, her mother, and her sister. Whitesmith has a plan. With it we can scare all of them, and she'll have nowhere else to go but here."

"Whitesmith's asking for repentance is fine," Abraham said. "It's helped our cause. But now you're telling me he's seen Betti. If she's been harmed—"

"Stay calm. You know I always follow your way—the way of the Spirit."

"You've always been on the right-hand side of the ranch with me." Abraham said. "Well, there've been a few slip-ups I've forgiven, but you know I always trust the Spirit. Let's pray."

Rube saw that Ket could barely stand it. "Should we try to cut in and tell your father what Whitesmith did?"

Lacy shook her head. "I've got output, but her soahl is blocking all inputs."

A moment later Abraham said, "This plan, is it based on the Spirit? Is it based on love? You'll have to convince me first."

"It is based on a dream," Corvus said. "Whitesmith looked at the data on this soahl. He thinks it means something, but he doesn't know what. I think I know."

"So?" Abraham sounded tired.

"Remember that boy your daughter was with—is with—according to Whitesmith. He calls himself Good Sine, or Good Sin. Remember? He dreamed he was going to spread out into the universe. I figure that is to join with the aliens. And I had my own dream."

"And?"

"After the aliens receive the message, they are going to be sent here by the evil ones and start the final revelation. Then the New Age of the Spirit will end. The end of times will begin. In my dream I also saw your daughter on a hard bed, a sacrificial table. And your daughter will be sacrificed to the evil ones unless we get her back here. So we have to get her. Right?"

"Well, my dreams and my heart tell me I love my daughter." Abraham was emphatic. "She is strong and is not going to let anyone sacrifice her. I want her back here, but I want her to choose to come back on her own. No more tricks. You had your shot, but enough is enough."

"But there's no other way to stop her from going to Mars."

"Enough I said. I'm going to bed now."

"So be it then. Amen … good night."

Rube heard a door open and close. Then Corvus said, "Good night, old man." There was scorn in his voice. This was followed by a crackling sound over Lacy's display, and Corvus said, "Whitesmith. Are you there?" Another voice replied, "You idiot, I can see you're being monitored." After that, both voices went dead.

"That last voice," Ket said. "It's the same I heard when I was attacked."

"We've got him," Rube said. "We've got both of them. It may take some work with the international authorities, but we've got enough to put both Corvus and Whitesmith away."

"I think I'll still go to Mars," Ket said. "My father and I are already a million miles apart, though it was so good to hear him … hear him say he loves me. But I left home long ago to find the good people of the universe. And I've found them, right here in this room."

Rube squeezed her hand and she squeezed back.

* * *

When Ket awoke the next morning she felt happier than she'd ever thought was possible. Rube had returned to his room that night. The single beds weren't meant to sleep two. Besides, they were only dating. She had no regrets about the previous night, but felt they needed to slow down a bit and see how things went over time, and not just on the day you travel across the universe with someone. That could leave anyone with her head in the stars. She was happy that Rube agreed with this. At least she thought he had agreed.

She was also happy that Quasi and Lacy had gone on their own tour last night. Harlow and Prasham were scheduled to leave for theirs at five a.m. this morning. Thank goodness Harlow had become Prasham's buddy. By afternoon, everyone here would have seen Mars, the Kay Cees, and the other side of the universe. Everyone here would be part of a very special group of humans, sharing in the adventure of a lifetime.

She sat up and checked her soahl for messages. Then she saw it, a message from Dr. Mateni. No jokes this time, just a note to call him.

She did.

"I am so sorry, Ket," a very sad looking Dr. Mateni said. "Your father was a great man, a great soul, the true kind. I'm so sorry. He collapsed last night and died."

PART III

WHAT IS FOUND?

CHAPTER 23
FIJIAN FEAST

"It's too dangerous." Rube tugged on the bottom of his fleece jacket and stared at Ket, who sat on the couch in the lounge. "You can't go." He swept his arm past the others and pleaded, "Tell her. It's crazy."

"I'm sure Whitesmith won't be there." Lacy's glasses were inky black, her head motionless. "His appearance in Seattle was an anomaly. I'm sure he went back to California. Especially now that he knows we're on to him."

"What about the BSP salvage work? Couldn't they send a ship to Fiji?" Quasi asked.

"There's no proof they've done shady operations overseas," Lacy replied. "When their ships are stopped in international waters they've always had licenses, legit IDs, and the UN recognized flag of Free California. No BSP member has ever been caught doing anything illegal out of California, and in California they're the law."

"Exactly," Rube said. "We all know that. The BSP controls everything there. That's why no sane person goes anywhere near California. But if they show up at the funeral—"

"It's in Fiji." Ket stood and dug her fists into her hips. "Thousands will be there. Even if Whitesmith and the BSP are there, they can't try anything."

"Ms. Ket is correct," Prasham said. His tone was measured. "Not only will Abraham's followers attend, but dignitaries from around the world will too. High security will be on hand."

"According to the *Fiji Times*," Lacy said, "over a hundred foreign representatives are expected. A party will spread out over the island from Abraham's ranch, onto the water in a flotilla, and extend all the way back to the main island of Viti Levu. And at the ranch, Abraham's choir will sing a new requiem followed by the biggest feast in Fijian history."

"Feast?" Harlow brightened.

Rube thought Harlow had become much less round and much more square than when they'd first met. The workouts with Prasham were working. He still looked very hungry, though.

"You've not eaten until you've had food from a Fijian *lovo*," Ket said.

"And Lacy showed me an article about Fiji Bitter," Quasi said.

"I've been reading about their tattoos too." Lacy bumped her shoulder against Quasi's.

"And Corvus?" Rube fumed. "He'll be at the head table, in charge, in his own territory."

"I agree with Rube's concern." Mobius had been silent until now, standing as a v-bod statue. "Even if Whitesmith will not be there, we can't trust Corvus. The risk is too great." He spoke like an army general talking to subordinates. "I'll send Prasham as my representative. He can catch up with his old friend, Dr. Mateni, and pass along our respects for—"

"Stop it!" Ket exploded like a boiler. "I am going to my own father's funeral!"

Mobius dropped his n-cloth jaw.

Rube knew Ket was more than a math whiz and dreamer, more than an attractive siren that held the attention of mentors and suitors, more than the daughter of one of the century's most charismatic figures, more than the tour guide of the century's other most charismatic figure, more than the discoverer of the Kay Cees and a potential Nobel Prize winner, more than a guaranteed member of the next mission to Mars—she was a new force in the universe. What was he doing with her?

"Right," Mobius finally said. "Ket, this is your call. I trust you completely."

"Good," Ket said with utter calmness. "So Mobius, keep giving appearances with Nickie as your tour guide, like nothing has happened. The rest of you will come with me. Quasi, check the fuel requirements and emergency evacuation plan. Lacy, set up the travel documents. We'll take a private jet out of Christchurch tomorrow. Prasham, I assume you can book our arrival into Fiji with the authorities. Can the program cover the cost?"

"It can," Prasham said.

"And I'll have Dr. Mateni arrange a boat from his village to take us to my father's ranch for the burial," Ket continued. "Corvus will not even know we're coming."

"Should I wear a disguise?" Rube asked.

"No." Ket laughed. "We'll arrive, en masse, with the other dignitaries. I'll ask the village elders to have my mother, my sister, and her kids join us at a special table for my friends and family, without Corvus. He won't like it, but everyone will do what I want for this occasion. He won't be able to do anything in public except act like a gracious host." She looked at Rube and smiled. "Besides, you'll be at my side to protect me." Then she nodded at Mobius. "The feast will go all night. We'll leave Fiji early in the morning, before Corvus has a chance to do anything stupid." She paused for a moment. "Right then, Harlow, go bring us some cake. Then help Quasi warm up the robo-copter."

* * *

Rube's ears popped and a gurgling sound rushed though his head.

He'd been living out of his backpack for the last month in Antarctica. Now he prepared to land at Nadi International Airport in Fiji, wearing a suit. Below, a turquoise sea streaked with white caps and emerald reefs surrounded the green paradise of a tropical island. Taking it in, Rube felt submerged. But what he heard was not water or the plane; it was his elevated pulse.

He looked down the aisle. Ket sat by herself at the front. Behind her were Lacy and Quasi, and across the aisle from them sat Prasham. Harlow was in his own row. While the plane banked to align with the runway, his thoughts circled back to wondering where he fit in. Ket had seemed distant since losing her father, a man she'd expressed exasperation with, and who, she'd said, had not been there for her. Like many who reached the top, he'd been obsessed with an endless list of outside commitments. Rube imagined none of this mattered to Ket now. She was likely thinking of the good times she'd described with him, like the time he picked her up as a little girl in her Sunday best, showing her off to his congregation. She'd also be thinking about her mother and whether she still coped by listening to music in the back room. Ket also must be wondering who would now act as a buffer between Corvus and her sister. Rube knew her thoughts would be about them and not him, of course. And his only priority was to keep her safe.

Once on the ground, Rube saw dozens of other jets parked in a very long row, with men in suits and mirrored sunglasses flanking the stairways leading down from these. There were cargo planes on the tarmac too, with robo-limos being unloaded. Fijian soldiers patrolled the area, wearing what looked like white kilts that had been cut across the bottom with giant pinking shears. Lacy explained these were called sulus, and the indigenous islanders wore casual versions of these that were a cloth wrap, as well as formal versions made from designer materials and with belts. Rube also noticed the local women had on full-length colorful dresses and wore flowers in their hair, like the one he'd saved from Ket's hair in India.

After their jet parked, Ket let Prasham and Harlow take the lead. She followed, with Lacy and Quasi behind her. Rube took up the rear. He passed by the pilots' cabin and wondered who flew the plane. The pilots had been friendly over the intercom, so it was not a robo-jet. But they kept the cockpit locked and were staying with the plane.

On the gangway, the humid air surrounded Rube like a sauna. After the dry heated air in Antarctica, it felt good. Then a windowless bus pulled up. Plastic shades blocked the view inside, and the sign on its side said "Suva Lodging: Levuka Tours" and showed paintings of coconut shells and palm trees. But Rube knew they were not going to a lodge or on a tour. At least, not according to the plan. If any deviation occurred, Prasham was to hit a panic button to sound an alarm, Harlow would block any frontal attack like a gridiron linesman, Lacy and Quasi would guard the flanks, and Ket would return to the plane. She had on a long, dark green dress with small white flowers, which restricted her movements. So Rube's job would be to run and grab her hand, dragging her away, if necessary.

The bus door opened and Dr. Mateni appeared. "*Ni sa bula*." He vigorously shook Harlow's hand and gave Prasham a big hug. Then he pushed past them and scooped Ket into his barrel chest. His cheeks were moist.

Rube approached and his hand was shaken up and down, and almost off.

"Hello, Rube," Dr. Mateni said. "It's so good you have come. Everyone, please get on the bus. I'll drive you to my village, that side. The boat is waiting for us there. And call me Dr. OK."

* * *

Rube knew Dr. Mateni had practiced medicine before becoming a teacher, but how many patients had the good doctor produced with his driving? It seemed that any vehicle going slower than twice the speed limit was overtaken regardless of the oncoming traffic. But everyone seemed to know how to swerve at the last second. Rube also noticed the mixture of modern life and poverty, and the lush but overwhelming vegetative growth. One good thing, the doctor had seated him next to Ket.

"Listen, mate," Dr. Mateni said to Rube. "You must guard this pearl with your life, if you want to mate for life." He winked and turned to Ket. "And if this one gives you any problems, you call on me, OK? Get it, call me OK—OK?" He laughed.

Once at the village, a whirl of flip-flops, flowered shirts, and men in sulus passed by, while boys and women scampered about with cooking pots and utensils. The men gathered around the border of an array of mats arranged in a large square and invited Ket and her guests to join them. They sat cross-legged, leaving the center area clear, though young boys soon filled it with food and left. Rube was about to sit next to Ket when Dr. Mateni held out his hand and put him next to Quasi and Lacy. He spoke in Fijian and presented the roots of a plant. Lacy whispered to Rube this was the yaqona, or kava plant. On the plane, she'd sent him a film clip of the roots being pounded with a metal spike and mixed with water.

After Dr. Mateni ended his speech, the village men clapped with cupped hands. Then he directed Ket to sit by the elders. Rube thought they would start to eat, but instead, young men appeared with a tan-colored liquid in coconut shells. Each elder drank down a bowl in one go, upon which everyone clapped with cupped hands and yelled, "*Maca*." "It means, it is dry," Ket told her friends. When Rube's turn came, he found the liquid had a mild plant flavor, but also acted like Novocain, making his lips feel a slight, momentary numbness. "In Fiji, kava is called grog," Ket explained. Then, after Ket had her bowl, the eating of what seemed an endless supply of food began. Rube wondered how he would cope with the funeral feast.

Later, Rube saw Lacy and Ket go away with a woman while Quasi went with some of the men to help prepare things for the ranch. Dr. Mateni said there would be many roast beasts from earth ovens, as well as many cases of Fiji Bitter, to load. "And much more grog too," he added. "It is very safe in my village. No strange visitors will come. The men will not allow it, except for jokers like that one." Dr. Mateni went over to Prasham, who was talking with Harlow.

Rube had the uneasy thought that he found it more alien here than with the Kay Cees. He realized that while he'd spent time at his brother's, he'd never really lived in another culture. Then Lacy came up behind him and he jumped. She was with Ket, who said the village women had shown them how they made *masi*, a decorative tapa cloth, from bark.

When Rube explained his thoughts to Ket, she said she knew what he meant, though *they* were the aliens here and when visiting the Kay Cees. And while Fiji seemed like home to her, and she knew the local customs, her life with her family had isolated her. She added, though, that it was unusual that beer and grog were being loaded on the boat, as no alcohol or yaqona were allowed at her father's ranch. "It appears the village is in charge," she said.

Lacy took this as an opportunity to ask things about the ranch she said she couldn't find on her soahl. For instance, how had her father acquired the island, since local law prohibited the sale of land to outsiders? Even the Indians, who were brought to Fiji during the colonial days by the British, and a sizable minority, couldn't buy land. Ket replied, she didn't know how her father got the island, only that it had been the location of a tourist resort in the Mamanuca group and probably had been in expatriate hands going way back. After her family arrived, a hundred plus believers in her father's Third Millennium Movement came to live there and were its only permanent residents. A steady stream of high paying pilgrims arrived to spend time at workshops, while the locals commuted each day by boat to run the cattle ranch on the island. Corvus headed that work. And every Sunday, many locals arrived for the service, forming a congregation of over a thousand, and a choir of over two hundred. The indigenous Fijians had beautiful angelic voices, Ket added, which Lacy confirmed by playing a bit of the choir on her display. Corvus, Ket continued to explain, took videotape of the weekly service on the island, added his own 'charming' appeal for money, and distributed it to rest of the world via the soahliverse. "And my father started every service with the proclamation: The dateline goes through Fiji. This is where each Sunday begins."

"Didn't Joachim write centuries ago about the Age of the Father, the Son, and the Holy Ghost?" Lacy asked. "But your father added the Age of Discovery and the current Age of Doubt, which he said was a spiritual Armageddon now giving way to the final, New Age of the Spirit. Wouldn't that make six ages?"

"Who's counting? Like I've said before, my father was not the type to question things."

"I reckon, after you've sold hundreds of million copies of your book, it doesn't pay to ask yourself too many questions," Quasi said.

"My father wasn't a dishonest man," Ket said with a mild scold.

Rube wanted to hit his friends. This wasn't the time to question Ket about her father. But there was a topic he thought he couldn't avoid. "What about Corvus? What's he really believe?"

"He's the worst kind of believer," Ket replied. "The kind that has so little doubt, he believes he can do no wrong. Whatever he has planned, it can't be good."

* * *

On the boat heading to the ranch, Rube was surprised to find he was relaxed. Perhaps it was because they were surrounded by the flotilla, with some very large navy ships guarding them. He also spotted the Royal yachts from several countries.

Dr. Mateni confirmed over three thousand would attend the funeral, followed by an all-night feast. He'd also been in touch with the village that attended Abraham's church, and Ket's family would be seated with her friends at the table farthest from Corvus. Dr. Mateni added, his own village would sit on mats surrounding her. "My village will not let a finger touch her."

Ket nodded. "My mother and sister would never try to help Corvus, either. They need to see me. And I need to see them and my nieces one last time too."

Rube felt the boat stop. This was too soon. They were only halfway to the island.

"Snorkeling," Dr. Mateni announced, cheerfully. "This thing you have to see, boy." He grabbed Rube's shoulder and gave it a hearty pull. "Fiji's reefs are the best." Men with snorkels, masks, and fins appeared.

Lacy and Quasi started to undress.

"Wait." Dr. Mateni smiled. "I've heard about you two." He reached into a wooden chest. "Look, swimsuits." He passed several pairs of modest designs around. "Also, please *veisau*, I mean change, in the boat's toilets." He laughed hard. "We don't want you to scare the sharks with our naked-mole-rat bodies."

Rube looked at Ket. "He's my teacher," Ket said. "I tell him everything."

* * *

If India had permanently etched his mind with saffron, silver, and gold, Rube's view of the kaleidoscope of brightly colored fish darting around the yellow-tipped, green and white coral threatened to rearrange his brain cells' definition of beauty forever. He almost forgot to breathe through the pipe stuck in his mouth. There was a whole universe to explore, but this world, invisible from land, was as incredible as anything he had ever experienced. And that was saying a lot, considering where he had been recently. Of course, v-bod travel was different from this. He reminded himself he'd barely dipped his toe into what was out there and had the uncanny sensation something was happening to his toe right now. He looked down and saw a reef shark. It was far way. But purple flowers were closer—beautiful purple flowers, stinging his foot.

* * *

Back on the boat, Dr. Mateni treated Rube's jellyfish stings.

"You have to look at Fiji's beauty," he said, "But not always let it touch you." He glanced at Ket then told Rube about fire coral, lionfish, and sea snakes.

Why hadn't Dr. Mateni mentioned those before he got into the water? Luckily, the jellyfish he'd encountered were not very poisonous, and he would be fine. Lacy patted Rube on the back, and Quasi gave him a thumbs-up. Both admitted they would have swum through the purple flowers too, if they hadn't seen Rube's reaction. Harlow said Rube was a real trooper. And Prasham remarked that he was glad to have stayed on the boat.

Then Rube noticed Ket staring out from the bow at the approaching island.

* * *

Everything was going according to plan.

Rube was sure no one from the ranch had noticed them during the funeral, until he and Ket approached the front. He followed Ket in line. Harlow was right in front of her, and Quasi, Lacy, and Prasham, along with most of Dr. Mateni's village, were right behind him. When Ket approached the casket, she reached out and touched it. She shed no tears, but whispered a short prayer. Corvus, sitting nearby, watched. He showed absolutely no sign of surprise. Maybe Corvus was expecting her? It didn't matter.

After the precession and the burial, Corvus preached about how a great spirit had crossed over into the land of dreams. In this New Age, he said, we can find a personal relationship with the Spirit, one of universal truth, and not lose our way in math and mechanisms that lead to the dark reaches of space, where evil lies. Those that followed that path would end up in hell, he said, since hell was not a place of heat, but cold and barren, like the surface of Mars.

Rube was a bit shocked that Corvus took this moment to make such a direct attack. But Rube wasn't very surprised when Corvus said that with the help of the Spirit he could guide the world to peace and prosperity. All one had to do was cast away the chains of society and sow a seed. And a gift to this ministry could be that seed—while the joy of giving, without knowing more, would be a sign of faith. And faith was always rewarded. Rube had heard Corvus make this appeal before on Soahl-7.

* * *

After the locals took charge with another yaqona ceremony, the feast began. Dr. Mateni led Ket and her friends to a table at the back, far from Corvus. A group of elderly Fijian men led two women and two children to the same table. It was Ket's mother, Maria, her sister Sarah, and the two nieces,

Ruthy and Margie. Ket had gone over their names and pictures before their arrival.

"Betti," Maria said. She broke down in tears and put her arms around Ket. Sarah joined in. Then they sat to Ket's right, with the two children in their laps.

Rube sat to Ket's left and tried to make small talk with Harlow, who was busy eating and getting approving nods from a Fijian woman. "*Kana vaka levu*. That means eat big," the woman said. She refilled his plate. "I will," replied Harlow. Across the table, Rube saw Dr. Mateni and Prasham staring at Ket. Rube glanced her way and listened in, feeling very out of place.

"I could try to take over," Maria said. "I could tell the deacons that Abraham wanted me to replace him."

"You could come home to us," Sarah said. "Mom would keep Corvus in check and you could come back to faith and not have to go to Mars."

Rube thought they probably understood Ket wouldn't come back to Fiji, because they didn't press her too hard about this and switched to small talk. Then Ket gave her nieces a hug. They were young enough to care mostly about the food—like Harlow.

"Your meat, miss," a Fijian girl said to Ket, holding out a platter with steaks.

"*Sa vinaka*," replied Ket, and patted her stomach to show she was full.

But then came glasses of beer.

"Time to freshen up."

Rube jerked his head around to see who had said that. It sounded like someone familiar.

"Cheers!" Quasi yelled out.

"Hey Rube," Dr. Mateni called out. "Do you hear that pounding?" Rube did. He saw some of the boys pounding yaqona root, preparing more grog. "That pounding," Dr. Mateni continued, "is the sound of the *tuki*. Ask not for whom the *tuki* tolls. It tolls for thee. Get it? The grog is coming for you." The other men around the table laughed with the doctor.

Rube laughed too, but he turned his attention back to Ket and her family.

"Aunt Betti, come play hide and seek," Ruthy said.

"I love hide and seek," Ket said. She smiled and jumped up and grabbed hold of her niece's hand. They skipped together away from the table. "Go hide in the bush. But not under any coconut trees." She covered her eyes and began to count. "One, two, three ..."

"Shouldn't you stay near us?" Rube called out.

"I'll be fine. They won't go far," Ket replied.

They didn't. The two girls crawled under a large plant with crimson flowers.

Ket finished counting and pretended not to see them. "Ready or not, here I come." She started off in the wrong direction and her two nieces squealed with glee. After wandering around a bit, Ket disappeared into the bush.

Rube felt like spiders were crawling inside his chest. He started to get up. Then he saw Ket sneaking up on the girls from the opposite direction.

"Gotcha!" Ket touched the girls' shoulders and lightly tugged on them.

Out they came. Both girls wrapped their arms around their aunt's legs, giving her a big squeeze. "Again," they begged.

But Maria said, "We have to go." She turned to Ket. "Will you come back to the house? We'll protect you from Corvus. But none of us can stay out here, now that the drinking has begun. There wasn't supposed to be any alcohol, but the chief of the village insisted."

"Sorry," Ket replied. "I am going to stay here and drink with my friends." Ket kissed her mother, sister, and nieces. They walked off, and she looked completely torn. She returned to her seat, but before sitting, she tapped her glass with her knife. Everyone become silent.

Rube noticed that Corvus and the other expatriates from the church had left.

Then Ket said, "Father, you are a great soul that burns no more, but whose memory will travel forever through the universe. I know now that you loved me and I can leave in peace." Rube realized this was what Ket had whispered while touching his casket.

Ket raised her glass. "And now, to new friends and to the future." She took a sip of beer.

The locals erupted with cheers.

* * *

"Time to freshen up."

Rube heard the voice again. Only what time was it? And why was he lying on his back? He hadn't drunk that much. He and the others had purposely switched to juice after the first toast. Even Quasi had made a big deal out of not drinking more alcohol.

During the drinking there had been a fire walking ceremony, followed by guitar playing and dancing. Prasham, Rube remembered, had laid his head down on the table and fallen asleep. Of course, he wasn't used to late nights. But Dr. Mateni also hadn't lived up to his name. Rube recalled someone saying Dr. OK Drunk drank like a girl and needed to keep up. But behind the doctor's jovial exterior was a very committed man who wouldn't let anyone goad him into letting his guard down. Then Rube remembered Dr. Mateni saying he wanted to go for a walk on the beach. For some reason, this hadn't seemed strange, except why would he do that when they were supposed to guard Ket? It had been very confusing.

What had happened? What was happening?

Rube stood up and searched around the party. A ways off, under a bamboo canopy, Lacy sat at a table rubbing her finger over the forehead of a Fijian man with tattooed bands over his left eye. "I want that," Rube heard her say. The man pulled a jug and bowl from under the table and poured what looked like liquid soot from the jug into the bowl. Then he took a needle out of the small pouch.

Rube ran to get Quasi, but found him drinking from his flask with a Fijian man. He acted drunk and laughed loudly. Rube urged Quasi to come with him. "You've got to stop Lacy."

Next, Rube found Harlow, but Harlow was obsessed with a plate of roasted blue yams. Two Fijian women stroked his belly and admired his ability to keep eating.

One of the women left Harlow and approached Rube. "*Au la'o*" she said. She swayed her hips and motioned for Rube to come closer. It felt wrong, but Rube was momentarily intrigued.

Then Ket tapped him on the shoulder. "I'm going to the beach … tsunami's coming …"

"Good," Rube replied. It felt like a dream. But he was awake, wasn't he? The world started spinning. Or maybe he was spinning? He had to lie down again.

* * *

"Time to freshen up."

Rube sat up. The sun was rising. Everyone else was sprawled out, unconscious or asleep.

"Time to freshen up."

Rube whirled around. It was Sunjay.

"Time to freshen up." Sunjay took a swig from a bottle of Fiji Bitter.

"Sunjay, what are you doing here? Where's Ket?"

"Corvus invited me," Sunjay replied. "I had to find a new job somewhere. Oh, and he asked me to give you this message. He and Ket are getting married today. You'll never hear from her again. And if you ever try to see her, you'll get this, full force."

Sunjay produced the cane with the silver handle and tip.

Rube staggered back, but before he could turn he felt the tip against his chest. His muscles contracted in agony. Spasms ran down his arms and legs.

He fell back, enveloped by darkness again.

Chapter 24
Mobius Strip, Mobius Dip

"Ouch!"

Rube winced as Lacy pulled another piece of burnt cloth from his chest. He sat up in the empty clearing where the feast had been and looked toward the docks. The only boat he saw was the one that had brought him to the island.

"I had one sip, for Ket's toast." Prasham said this like he was confessing to the crime of the century. "Then I passed out."

"Corvus couldn't have spiked the beer," Dr. Mateni said. "It was from my village."

"It wouldn't have mattered," Quasi said. "Sunjay and his minions, armed with those cattle prods, would have taken anyone else down."

"Whatever it was, it was very slow acting," Harlow said. "I was still eating after most people had left. Then at four in the morning everyone remaining was ordered off the island. 'By decree of Corvus,' the chief from the other village said." Harlow bellowed when imitating the chief. "Why was I the only one that could stay up all night? I'd also had some of the grog. The big men from Dr. Mateni's village had egged me on, saying I was the chief drunk. But I wasn't. I wasn't." Harlow looked like he might cry.

"Don't worry," Lacy said. "You're right. It was slow acting ... a sedative." She applied a gauze strip to Rube's wound. "The boat's med-kit is pretty good. I ran a sample of my blood through its robo-analyzer. It wasn't the beer or the grog. It was the air. It contained a narcotic mist causing euphoria and disorientation, and finally sleep."

"Sounds too high-tech for Corvus. But something got up my nose." Quasi took the cloth he'd draped over his head and wiped his face. "If I catch the olid piece of carrion behind this—"

"First things, first!" Rube interrupted. "We need to get Ket."

Dr. Mateni nodded and came over by Rube and Lacy. He took over applying the dressing.

Lacy stood up. Like a blind person with dark glasses on, she walked a few steps and turned around. "I'm afraid I have bad news. According to my soahl the Fijian Navy is to remove anyone left on this island by force, starting … well, starting now." She motioned to the clearing, to men approaching in uniform. "All visitor permits have been canceled. All foreigners have to be out of the country and its territorial waters by evening."

* * *

From the boat's bow, Prasham's head bobbed up and down in front of the setting sun. He looked up. "Our plane is scheduled to leave at midnight. Do you have a fix on her?"

"Her soahl stopped responding soon after four in the morning," Lacy said.

Rube paced on the deck. "Right after everyone was down."

"But I still have the blip coming from the island," Lacy continued.

Dr. Mateni smiled. "Then it's a good thing she agreed to swallow that tracking lozenge."

"Like the horse pills I used to administer on my parents' farm," Harlow said.

"The trouble is," Quasi said, "that lozenge doesn't let us see or hear anything, and we're out here with the Fijian Navy on patrol."

"At least we know where she is," Dr. Mateni said. He pointed to a dot on a map on Lacy's display. "That's in her father's home. Corvus must think we wouldn't dare go there."

"According to radar, there're no ships within ten miles of the island." Quasi held his own display. "I reckon the navy has moved on and we should go get her."

Rube stopped pacing. "We should. But the navy is sure to notice if we head that way."

"Not if we approach from underwater." Prasham pointed to the starboard side of the boat.

The water bubbled. Rube almost fell overboard when a periscope popped up.

"Before we left, Mobius told me to have the mini-sub standing by," Prasham continued. "As a last resort, of course," he added in a matter-of-fact tone.

"But we can't all go." Rube tried to reduce the alarm in his voice. "One false move and we'll all end up in prison. This will take a bit of—"

"I'll go," Dr. Mateni said. "I know the compound. It's my fault. I never should have said it was safe to come here."

"No, " Rube said. "If someone needs to get into the house through a window, it had better be someone …" He paused then continued, "… someone like me. Just tell me the best way onto the compound. I already know the house. Which room is she in?"

"I can't tell," Lacy said.

"It'll be the little ones' room," Dr. Mateni said. Everyone looked at him with surprise. "It can be locked from the outside," he continued. "It also has a time-out bed in it—a sound proof horizontal booth that can also be locked. It's where Corvus puts the kids when he wants them to be quiet. Maria showed it to me once when I told her about one of my chatterbox students. I told her I was OK with the talking after all. Get it? I was OK."

"You're kidding," Lacy said.

"No, I'm not." Dr. Mateni touched his curly dark beard. "He'll have put a drugged Ket in there. When she awakes, she can scream all she wants. If Maria, Sarah, and the kids were already asleep, they might not even know he has Ket."

"We could try going to the authorities," Prasham said.

"Corvus thinks he's the big man now," Dr. Mateni said. "And in the eyes of the locals, he is. Otherwise he would never have risked this. Trust me, if we try going to the police, you'll be made to look like outsiders interfering in a local affair."

"But if he's got Whitesmith and the BSP helping him," Prasham said, "he could become untouchable by the law anywhere. We need to act while we know where he is."

"So far, I don't think the BSP is here," Lacy said. "Though I see a ship under the Free California flag is heading for Fiji."

"That can't be a coincidence," Quasi said.

"So, I'm going." Rube made a move toward the mini-sub.

"There's one problem." Lacy removed her glasses. If worry were a liquid, her eyes were drowning in it. "Even if you make it to where Ket is, Corvus will shoot you, don't you think?"

"Or zap you until your heart stops," Quasi said. His brow became a row of ridges.

"But I have to try." Rube moved to board the sub. He was only somewhat grateful that no one tried to stop him. "If I had shielding and something to stop his—"

"You will find n-cloth armor in the sub," Prasham said. "It will block all forces, rather than transmit them. You will also find a crowbar with an insulated handle and a built-in capacitor. When Corvus tries to shock you, block him with that. It will absorb the shock. Then touch him with it and he'll go down. All supplied by Mobius."

"So Mobius has thought of everything." Rube nodded toward Quasi. "I could use a sip of rocket fuel, if you have any?"

"My Fijian mates drained it dry," Quasi replied. "But she'll be right, mate."

"And we'll put you on soahl surveillance," Lacy said. "If you need help, we'll come get you, navy or no navy."

"Prison or no prison," Quasi added.

"Cake or no cake." Harlow covered his mouth for a moment. "Good luck, I mean."

"He'll have more than luck on his side." Prasham had a knowing look on his face.

Rube realized he was in for more surprises, but only said, "Well then, I'm off."

* * *

Once sealed inside the sub, Rube familiarized himself with the controls. They were easy to understand. He depressed a lever to submerge. Then something pulled on his shoulder—a hand. He made a desperate move to open the hatch, but stopped. That would let the water in. Instead, he turned around.

There sat v-bod Mobius.

"I had Harlow load a v-bod onto the robo-copter before you left," Mobius said. "It was transferred to this mini-sub in Christchurch. Being rich does have its advantages."

Rube considered wiping the self-assured smile off the v-bod's face, but he regained his composure. Still, Mobius had a lot of nerve showing up unannounced. "You're too clumsy in that thing. When we get there, you wait in the sub. I'll get Ket."

"Your heroic urges are noble, Rube. But I have a better idea. Use your soahl to connect to this v-bod and help me. I'll control the feet. You control the hands for the delicate work."

"Why not let me control everything?"

"I have to be logged in for this *thing* to work. And I walk fine, thanks to your lessons."

"You have to remember," Rube said, "I lived in a virtual world for a year. I could make a v-bod dance on the head of a pin."

"Fine, control what you want. But my going as a v-bod is the only safe way to do this. Plus, when Corvus sees me, he might hesitate long enough for me to get to Ket."

"But your v-bod body is too big to fit through a window."

"I'll crash through the door." The v-bod's smile had become even smugger.

"Wait a minute, Mobius. Why don't we both go? You crash the door, distracting Corvus, and I'll come through the window and get Ket."

"Hmm. Two against one might be better. Fine, put on the n-cloth armor."

* * *

Rube adjusted the gloves he'd use to help control the v-bod. Then he put on the armored T-shirt and facemask with slits. He also grabbed the crowbar. He realized his head was not very protected around the eyes or nose, and the back of his head, his arms, and his legs were not protected at all. He thought about letting Mobius go on his own. But there was no way he was going to chicken out now. He updated everyone with the new plan. He would sneak to the unscreened window to the kid's room and peek in, transmitting his view via his soahl back to the ship, and then remove the louvers. At the same time, Mobius would go to the front entrance and smash down the door. With luck, Corvus would go after Mobius. If not, Mobius would enter the house and break into the kids' room. Either way, Mobius would contend with Corvus while Rube went through the window, used the crowbar to free Ket, and helped her escape. Mobius would follow them, defending the rear, until they were on the sub.

For some reason, while Rube went over the plan, Mobius undressed the v-bod. "More ghost-like to scare Corvus," Mobius explained, sitting there in his bare cloth body.

A short while later Rube guided the sub into the lagoon, following Dr. Mateni's instructions, and beached it on a sand bar in shallow water. Dr. Mateni said that this spot was hidden from view and closer to the house than the boat docks. Then Rube and Mobius went ashore and headed through the bush. Soon the trail broke into a clearing and the house appeared.

"You go to the door," Rube said, "and I'll go there." He pointed toward the veranda and snuck quietly along it. After reaching the window, he peered inside. The nightlights were on, but it was too dark to see any details.

"Get Mobius back," Lacy said in his ear. "Put the v-bod infrared sensors on."

Rube motioned for Mobius to come to him. He did, and looked through the window. An infrared image appeared on Rube's heads-up display. "Corvus is in there," Rube whispered, "asleep on top of a long box, the time-out bed. Someone's in the box too." He signaled for Mobius to go back to the main entrance. Then, as silently as possible, he removed two louvers. But the window frame squeaked when he pulled on the third louver. He glanced at Mobius.

The v-bod wobbled and walked off the veranda onto the stone driveway, almost tipping over. Rube wanted to scream, but connected to the virtual controls, to assist the v-bod's movements. Moving steadily now, Mobius made his way to the door and busted the glass.

Rube popped his head through the window, expecting to see Corvus was awake. But he was still asleep, as were the two little girls. Rube guessed that Fiji was such a peaceful place everyone slept like driftwood here. It was quiet too, except for the hum of mosquitoes. Last time, as a bloodless, non-breathing v-bod doll, they had ignored him. Now they bit him.

Rube ducked his head out the window. He removed the third window louver and watched. A moment later, the door to the kid's room shattered into kindling.

Corvus sprang up. An aglet on his bolo tie snapped his face. He turned to the v-bod.

Without thinking, Rube leapt through the window.

"Get out of here!" Corvus was blindfolded and fumbled for his cane. He found it with his right hand, pulled off the blindfold with the other, and shrieked like a demented owl. "The evil one from Mars! How did you get in here?" He switched the cane to his left hand and pulled the gun from his holster with his right.

Rube was glad Corvus was preoccupied with the white-bodied specter in front of him. He quickly moved to the box, passing by the manger. He noticed the v-bod doll, broken and half pulled apart without any legs. He was about to pry open the lock on the box with the crowbar when Corvus swatted the air with his gun.

"Mosquitoes!" Corvus whirled around and fired a shot at Rube's chest.

The momentum of the bullet push Rube back, but the armor worked.

"No," Corvus said, "not blood-sucking mosquitoes, but the soul-sucking boy who wants to spread sin." For some reason Corvus did not shoot again, maybe because the kids were screaming. Instead he holstered the gun and approached Rube.

Mobius tried to follow Corvus but stumbled. Rube had no time to help. He may have said he could make a v-bod dance on the head of a pin, but not while dodging cane thrusts. Corvus lunged and made contact. A strong shock tore through his right thigh—activating a funny-bone sensation from his hip to his knee. So much for counterattacking using the crowbar.

The v-bod thudded behind Corvus, who turned and tried to shock it. Nothing happened. He pulled his gun again and fired a shot, but it ricocheted and hit the bedpost.

Fear coursed through Rube, but it strengthened his rush back to the box. He ripped off the lock with the crowbar. Up popped Ket, wearing a wedding dress.

"Look out!"

Ket's warning was too late. Rube felt the shock in his glutes and went down.

Corvus turned to Mobius, who was having trouble again, careening to his right, almost falling over Ruthy's bed. Rube took the crowbar and moved to the window. He used the controls to right Mobius, who was floundering like a beached whale, and motioned for Ket to join him.

But Corvus put himself between Ket and Rube and pointed his gun at her. "Back off."

Both kids, sitting up, continued to cry.

Rube knew what he had to do. He let go of the crowbar and took complete control of Mobius. "Say something to distract him," he transmitted to the v-bod's earpieces.

"Sheriff," Mobius called out. "I'm backing out of here with my hands up."

Corvus turned to Mobius and lowered the gun. It was the moment Rube needed. Quickly, he used the v-bod to grab each of Corvus's wrists. Then Rube motioned again to Ket. She gathered her dress. Like lighting, she leapt to the window and outside.

Rube grabbed the crowbar and followed. And they both ran onto the driveway.

"Ow." Ket had no shoes and faltered on the stones.

"Here," Rube said. He managed to pick her up and carry her over to the path, but lost control of the v-bod. "It's up to you Mobius," he transmitted. Then he and Ket ran through the bush to the lagoon. It amazed him that no one else had arrived to stop them. He guessed Corvus shooting off a couple of rounds after dark didn't surprise anyone.

Reaching the water, Ket and Rube waded in and looked back. Out of the shadows, Mobius limped toward them. Rube felt Ket brush his sleeve as she fell down beside him.

"My dress, it's waterlogged." Ket struggled to stand. Rube helped her up and they continued heading for the sub.

"Keep going," Mobius called out. "I'll ditch at sea."

Rube was glad to see Mobius coming through the bush on his own. Except, Corvus was behind him. If only Mobius had kept him occupied back at the house. Rube realized Corvus could easily run past Mobius and reach them before they could escape. Still, they had to try. He indicated for Ket to open the hatch. But her orange hair lit up.

Corvus had turned on a bright flashlight. He was moving in a wide arc past Mobius.

Rube placed himself between Ket and the beach while she entered the sub. Mobius tried to get to Corvus, but was too slow. A shot whizzed past Rube's ear. It would take time to reacquire control of the v-bod. But if Corvus got to the sub, he could block the hatch and then shoot them like fish in a barrel.

Rube scrunched down and froze. Should he try to join Ket and close the hatch, or should he try to maneuver Mobius? He realized the only viable option was a third one. He'd have to confront Corvus while Ket got away on her own.

Rube began to rise, steeling himself, crowbar in hand. He heard a blood-curdling scream. Was Corvus that afraid of him, of *Good Sine*?

But Corvus was shining the flashlight on Mobius, not looking toward the sub.

Rube dropped through the hatch.

"Whore!"

"Corvus sounds mad," Ket said.

"Heading out to sea," Mobius transmitted to the sub. "This v-bod will never be found."

"Thanks, Mobius," Ket replied. "Your stripped down v-bod really saved me."

"Anything for you, Ket. Rube helped too, a little. This is Mobius, signing off."

What a dip, Mobius, Rube thought. You had a lot of help from me.

Then a boot clanked up top.

Rube sealed the hatch as fast as he could. "We're tight. Submerge." He dropped farther into the sub and pointed to the controls. With relief, he let the crowbar slip from his hand.

They sank into the sea.

Chapter 25
Burning Her Bra

"I blinded him," Lacy said. She looked very pleased with herself.

"With science?" Quasi asked.

"No, with my body," Lacy replied. "You saw."

Quasi adjusted the sailor cap on his head. "The whole ship saw."

Everyone inside the main cabin burst into laughter.

"So did I," Ket said, "on the sub's display." She was wrapped in a towel.

"I didn't," Rube said. "At least not this time." He looked at Ket.

"Toward the end," Lacy said, "when Corvus reached Mobius, a distraction was needed. I remembered Corvus's reaction to me in India, and realized what had really scared him the most. So I transmitted my naked image onto Mobius's body. Like I said, I blinded him with my body."

"And you just happened to have a naked picture of yourself? And you just happened to transmit it not only onto Mobius's body, but onto everyone's screens too?" Quasi sounded suspicious but looked happy, like always.

"I wanted to let everyone see what was going on," Lacy replied. She laughed.

"Well, all's OK that ends OK," Dr. Mateni said.

"At least we can get out of here," Prasham said. "A friend of mine in the Indian navy forwarded a message from the Fijian navy. It seems Corvus complained someone kidnapped his wife. But when they arrived at his house, they asked how that could be, since his wife was at home with two screaming kids. They told him to go back inside and sleep it off."

"Maybe he can't tell the navy what to do as much as we thought," Dr. Mateni said.

"If he'd thought to tell them we were spies, we'd be in big trouble," Prasham continued. "But he wasn't thinking."

"No he wasn't." Dr. Mateni laughed. "He was up against the Mobius Strip."

"And the virtuoso of the virtual controls," Lacy added. "If Rube hadn't been there to steer Mobius around—"

"You did?" Ket glanced at Rube.

"—none of this could have happened," Lacy continued.

"Mobius set the whole thing up, with the sub and v-bod," Rube said. "Let's face it, without him, where would we all be right now?"

* * *

Back in Antarctica, Ket had a lot to think about. She was very happy about the rescue, but hated how it made her feel indebted. Rube had come to her aid before, but was that why she'd become involved with him? And now that Corvus was in control of the ranch, did that mean she needed Mobius more than ever? She had to get to Mars. She deserved it, didn't she? She'd worked hard and not asked for any special favors. But if grown men fell over each other trying to help her out, was that her fault? No. So, she would have to tell them. Rube first. He would understand.

* * *

"You're burning your bra?"

"I thought you'd understand the humor." Ket turned away to avoid the devastated expression on Rube's face. He sat across from her, in her room.

"I'm not perfect. But I thought I was your perfect bra."

Ket turned to him. "Don't you see? I have to be free. I have to liberate myself."

"I do get it," Rube said. "But—"

"But what?" Ket asked. "But, you love me? How do you know? Things happened too fast. I need some space to follow the path I'm on with no strings attached. We can still be partners on the tours of the universe. We can still see how things develop." Ket liked how rational and calm her voice sounded. "We just need to go back to square one."

"I …" Rube looked very confused. "I don't know. I guess you're right."

Then Ket pulled her bra out from inside her top. "Do you have a match?" She was relieved when he laughed. Rube was so reasonable. She felt a tiny bit disappointed, but pushed that feeling far away, dismissing it as normal second thoughts.

* * *

In his room, Rube lay on his bed. He twirled a pressed flower by the stem, the one from her hair in India. He planned to give it to her in a card, in person. Now he'd mail it before her launch.

What if he had said what was in his heart? But then, if she took him to Mars, he wouldn't know if it was because of a sense of obligation. So he'd have to earn getting to Mars himself. Wasn't that the only way? When it came to Prasham and Mobius, and the Math Monks, and especially Ket, he knew he couldn't compare. When she went on the next mission, when she won the Nobel Prize, when she announced her discovery of the Kay Cees, she wouldn't be out of his league, she would be out of his universe.

He'd crashed and burned for her, in more ways than one. Now, his hopes for the future would perish in the wreckage. Yes, it was better this way. Just like a spear ripping your heart from your chest was better than thousands of razors peeling away your skin, one layer at a time.

Chapter 26
Sunrise Into Darkness

Slog::Good Sine:: Ninety-six hours to midnight. Count the ways.

* * *

Slog::Bad Wave:: Notes about the Kay Cees, continued.

Today I made an amazing discovery. The planet four hundred light-years from Earth isn't the Kay Cees' home planet. It's just one of their colonies. A colony like the one they could set up on Earth. I've also learned a few more strange things …

Ket sat at her desk, entering her latest progress into her display. In the past month, since returning to Antarctica from Fiji, the Kay Cees had been the focus of her research, and she had made many virtual visits to talk with the same two she'd first met.

At first, she thought Mobius or Prasham might help. But Mobius was too busy, as always, and Prasham said he tried showing them a Feynman diagram for matter-antimatter annihilation and they hadn't understood it. "It seems they are not scientists," Prasham observed. "It's a pity they won't be able to answer any of my important questions."

In fact, Prasham had told her he thought the Kay Cees she was talking with might be juveniles. He went on to say if one could communicate through the elsewhere, one could travel through it, using quantum teleportation, maybe. And if one could travel through it, one could do the impossible—one could travel into a black hole and back, and learn whether black holes really did produce baby universes, or whether they recycled themselves by merging horizons and singularities into a quantum fire storm. And, at the end of time, maybe this would result in the rebirth of our universe in a new big bang.

When Prasham talked like this, it amazed Ket. He sounded as crazy as Corvus. Prasham went on to say he knew it would take him the rest of his life to figure it all out. He couldn't waste time talking to teenage aliens. She was the best person to do that. "This research is yours," Prasham said. "However, if you meet any scientists in the elsewhere, let me know."

This seemed to suit the Kay Cees too, who requested they meet with only her from now on. Ket wasn't sure why they felt this way, but her circumstances made it easy for her to go along with their wishes. Even though she'd told Rube he could continue to explore the universe with her, it would have been awkward. Doing it alone would let her get things done more quickly. She went back to working while the others slept.

She continued writing.

Kay Cee History and DNA Exchange: the Kay Cees are the most popular species in the universe, at least according to them. Hundreds of millennia ago they discovered how to communicate using entangled gravitinos through the elsewhere. For the first hundred years they just talked with a few nearby neighboring worlds. During the same time period, they faced many technological and political crises, until they faced the ultimate one. They had mastered biology and increased their lifespan to hundreds of years, but over-population became an imminent threat. War broke out and reduced their numbers. In the process, one nation launched the DNA exchange program with two other worlds, then with dozens. Now, when they encounter a new species, they observe it carefully. After enough time has passed, if the new species is acceptable, they initiate the DNA exchange. They typically wait a thousand years to do this, though I need to clarify what is meant by a year. In any case, according to the Kay Cees, the exchange program has worked, and they've been spreading through the universe ever since.

Kay Cee Reproduction and Sex: …

Ket thought about the many questions she had asked them about this.

"Do you have multiple births?"

"Three is average. But most of us have only one litter. We control things, otherwise," one of the two Kay Cees said while partially unfolding a thumb. The other Kay Cee grabbed it and pushed it down.

Ket ignored this. "Do you have live births?"

The Kay Cees ruffled their neck fur. "What use would dead births be?" one asked. But after showing them pictures of bird eggs on Earth, they got it. "Yes, we have live births."

"What about the process of reproduction? Do you have males and females?" Ket realized she could not tell the sex, if any, of the two Kay Cees she was talking with.

"It is hard to explain, but think of what you call knitting. We like to knit." The two Kay Cees unfolded their thumbs from triangle shapes into chopstick-like extensions and proceeded to strike them together, rapidly. This drove them into a state of extreme excitement. A moment later, this behavior abruptly stopped and they dropped their arms to their sides, looking exhausted. Ket wanted to probe further. Had she just witnessed mating? And, given the look on their faces, maybe Prasham was right. Maybe they were teenagers.

After a minute, one of the Kay Cees said, "We know from the primer about your penises and vaginas." They proceeded to lecture Ket for longer than she cared to hear about human sexual pleasure, but with no mention of the clitoris. Ket made a note to herself to tell Maxine to improve her primer. "But will you choose a partner and give us your DNA now?" the other Kay Cees asked. They were back to their obsession with exchanging DNA. "It is permitted to say no. We will wait. But then, least naked one, Earth's descendants will not be your descendants."

She had bristled at being called 'least naked one' but hadn't complained. Then she started a section on religion in her slog and recalled her last conversation with them.

"Do your dogs talk?" one of the Kay Cees asked.

"No." Ket replied.

"That's surprising," the Kay Cee continued. "Your dogs look smarter than your kind."

For a popular species, Ket thought the Kay Cees lacked tact, but she changed the subject to religion. Unfortunately, it was hard to explain what religion was. She'd showed them people praying. Being quiet with ones thoughts they got, but to hope the dead ones would revive you without your DNA made no sense. Ket tried to explain that prayers weren't to dead people, but to an eternal creator. However, the word creator seemed to get translated into DNA.

Ket had wanted to explain further but had trouble talking to them for more than fifteen minutes at a time. While they could mimic human speech, their chirping drove her crazy. She summarized her observations and decided to rest.

* * *

Slog::Good Sine:: The sunsets mock. Forty-eight hours to go.

* * *

Slog::Bad Wave:: The Kay Cees now speak perfect English.

Ket was told they'd reprogrammed her virtual ears to cancel out their natural sounds. They'd also updated their translation program. She wondered why they hadn't done this sooner, but realized it was wrong to assume just because they were aliens they were technological wizards. They were users of their advanced technology but not engineers. They seemed to have as much trouble getting things to work as humans did, each time a new version of a program was released. Still, she now managed to have several long discussions with them. She continued her explanation of human spiritual beliefs. And, after a while, she thought she better understood theirs. It seemed the Kay Cees worshiped their descendants, and thus, they treated their children almost like gods. They passed on to each generation encapsulated memories of themselves. One day they believed their descendants would use these to bring them back to life.

Then the Kay Cees asked her about human DNA again.

Ket politely said she wanted to learn much more first. She tried asking about travel through the elsewhere. Even if they weren't scientists, they'd certainly know if this was possible, and she could tell Prasham. In response, one of the Kay Cees made a gurgling sound, or was it a giggle? Maybe it was a translator glitch. Then she heard, "one of our descendants tells us if we attempt to travel through the elsewhere we will decohere into dust."

"A descendant?" Ket asked.

The Key Cees looked slightly mortified. "Your English language is too specific about past and future. It confuses us sometimes. Is Maxine working on a better primer?"

"Yes," Ket responded. "English for ET, I think she calls it." She decided to avoid any more science questions until then.

Instead, she asked, "Did finding other worlds bring peace to your home world and unite its nations?"

"No," was the reply. "The home world died long ago."

"From war?" she asked.

"No."

"Disease?"

"No."

"An asteroid? A volcano?"

"No, no."

"What then?" Ket realized her question sounded like a demand. But she wanted to know, what could kill off a species like the Kay Cees?

"Boredom."

This turned out to be a joke. The Kay Cees gurgled again and explained only a small percentage of its species had ever been interested in science or contacting other worlds. And many of those who did had failed to reproduce—they were evolutionary dead ends. "But we are the descendants of those that found beauty in learning and spreading amongst the stars."

Ket paused. Did the Kay Cees seem human or completely different? She knew she couldn't avoid human bias—reading too much into what they said. If only she could learn more.

* * *

Slog::Good Sine:: Bad news. Twenty-four hours to midnight, and the shortest night of my life is today.

* * *

Ket noted the good news in her slog. Rube had finished working out the interface between her travel kit's gloves and the Kay Cees' protocols for operating their v-bods. It was a problem that had been too technical for the Kay Cees to solve.

However, thanks to Rube, she would soon be able to walk out and see the Kay Cees' adopted world.

Tomorrow would be a special day. And tomorrow was only two hours away. Ket got up from her desk and wandered to the lounge. No one else was up yet.

The days were almost twenty-four hours long now. The sun was already up past midnight in the time zone most used in this part of Antarctica. But Mobius had adjusted the local time. It didn't matter what time it was anywhere else. It was ten p.m. at the base and the sun would set in forty-six minutes. It would rise again at exactly midnight—making it the base's first midnight sun of the season—and a sunrise into four months of perpetual light.

Also tomorrow, thirty-two of the Mars novices would arrive to begin the next phase of training and selection for the next mission. But soon, Rube, Quasi, and Lacy would wake up during the shortest night of the year and prepare to return to Seattle.

In so many ways, it would be a bittersweet sunrise.

* * *

Slog::Good Sine:: One hour to midnight, last quantum star I'll see tonight.

Rube stared at his packed bag. The last month in Antarctica had been difficult. He'd almost left after the break-up with Ket. But she'd also made it clear to Mobius that she wanted to remain unattached for now. She'd simply made the logical choice to not let entanglement interfere with her goals, which were studying the Kay Cees, working on her Ph.D., giving virtual outreach tours, and preparing for her launch in just over a year. It was all completely reasonable.

Rube knew she was finally able to concentrate on these things since she was completely unreachable by Corvus here.

Where Corvus was, though, had become a mystery. Rube and his friends had hoped to listen in and track him using bugs left by Mobius in the ranch house. But it had burned to the ground the day after Ket's rescue.

Maybe Corvus knew what Mobius had done, Rube thought. Or maybe Corvus realized the Fijian authorities would find out what he was up to. In a rare conversation with Ket, she had pointed out to Rube another reason. She was sure Corvus had planned to burn down the ranch and leave Fiji all along. Otherwise, she'd have run away again. And the other members of her father's movement would not have readily accepted the marriage. They would have known her father would have objected, or her mom would have spoken up. Ket concluded there was no way Corvus could have married her and kept her in Fiji.

"So where would he have taken you?" Rube asked.

"To California with the rest of the family. It's probably where they are now."

"That makes sense. Once there, you'd never get away."

"I've got to get back to the Kay Cees." Ket turned and left for her room.

Rube thought Ket must be right about Corvus and his plan. But that would suggest Corvus knew in advance she would come to Fiji. Or maybe that had been a good guess. In any case, Mobius had sent evidence to the Fijian police showing that a narcotic mist had been used during the feast. But Dr. Mateni said there were conflicting stories in the *Fiji Times* about Ket's sister: had Corvus taken her away or had Mobius hired someone to kidnap her against her will? Rube knew not everything he and his friends had done to rescue Ket had been legal. Thus, it had been risky, asking the authorities to get involved. However, because no one remained in Fiji, an investigation never took hold. And maybe that was for the best.

The good news was that Dr. Mateni and his family had been able to move to Seattle. Mobius arranged the visas and put them up in Ket's old apartment in Soahl Headquarters. If any letters came from Ket's mother or sister, Dr. Mateni would contact Ket.

When Rube returned to Seattle, at least he would have several tasks to keep himself busy. With Quasi and Lacy, he would continue to build the case against Corvus and Whitesmith. They would also help Mobius with his court battle to prevent the ICA shutdown of communications with Mars. They could help in ways that Mobius's high-priced lawyers could not. Rube had to leave Antarctica for other reasons too. He had to answer Evelyn's ridiculous subpoena. At least he would get to spend some time with Vic.

And Ket? All he had to do was stick out the next four years and he could join her on Mars on the mission after hers. And he could visit her virtually many times before then.

So what could be his problem?

Rube sighed and grabbed his bag. He walked from his room to the lounge and found Ket, standing alone, staring out the window at the blackness.

She turned and looked at him. "So, do you like being confused?"

Rube saw her eyes were wet. "I'm glad this is not easy for you either."

"I don't want to give you any false hope," Ket began.

"Don't worry, you haven't." Rube struggled to keep looking at her. "These last few months … what you want has been clear."

"I mean, I will miss you … but I feel very confident I'm on the right path now and not just doing what others want me to do."

"With no bra restricting you?"

Ket laughed, a little.

"It's too bad, though," Rube continued.

"Why?"

He wondered if she could really not see what was bad about this? He went ahead and explained. "It's too bad you're out of my league."

"Don't say that, Rube. What a stupid thing to say. It's not true."

Without thinking, Rube responded with a bit of pity in his own voice. "But it is true. Though I didn't mean it's too bad for me. I meant, it's too bad for you—too bad you can't see when someone …"

"When someone what, Rube?"

Rube had written down his feeling in his slog over the last four days. It was coming out wrong. He tried to make it right. "I've hardly seen you, Ket. I've tried to count the ways it could work between us. But in sixteen months, you'll travel twenty million leagues under the light of the stars, and out of my depth. And I'll look up and cherish the last quantum glow you'll leave behind, forever. Maybe that's a good thing. You're too smart for me, and—ow!" Rube rubbed the sting from his cheek. He hadn't even seen her hand move. "That smarts."

"Smarts?" Ket put her face close to his. "You've got just as much as me—I don't want to hear any more about who's out of who's league or how many leagues apart we'll be."

Rube stepped back and attempted to smile. "I guess I deserved that."

"You did." It was Quasi. "And the journey to Mars is over a hundred million leagues."

"Did you know Nemo was the son of an Indian Raja?" Lacy had appeared too.

"Though he spoke perfect French," Quasi continued. "Maybe I can teach Prasham. And Ket, he can rocket you on *le sous-marin* to Mars."

"Where you'll meet Dr. Arrogant, I mean Dr. Aronnax," Lacy added. "But beware. If he tries to keep you there, we'll have to come and join you."

"Excellent quick search, my dear," Quasi said. "My soahl appreciates it." He closed his display and joined hands with Lacy, and they gave each other a tender nod.

Ket leaned in and hugged Rube. "Ignore them. I'll see you before the launch."

Rube hugged her back. Out the window he saw the rays of the sunrise break over the horizon. The shortest night of his life was ending, but he was heading, once again, into darkness.

CHAPTER 27
A PRETTY GOOD PIRATE CODE

"There's a tape from Corvus posted on Soahl-7!" Lacy jumped up and down in the living room, causing the scream-like figure tattooed on her chest to bounce around in her low-cut blouse.

Rube tried not to look. He'd shared the apartment at Soahl Headquarters with her, Quasi, and Harlow for the past four months. Harlow was out. But Quasi entered from the direction of the bedrooms.

Lacy flipped on the wall-mounted holo-screen. "Watch. I'll replay it from the start."

"It's been months since a fire destroyed the Third Millennium Ranch in Fiji." Corvus's piercing blue eyes twitched. He'd let his black hair grow out, and long braids flopped across his vest on either side of his bolo tie. "It was the flame of redemption that sent us out, and we've settled into a new home. The Spirit sent us, and in a dream we were led to the Promised Land. This land I talk of is your land. This land I talk of is our land. Pirates took it. But now they've repented and are amongst us. And glory lives on. Brother Whitesmith, prepare ..."

Whitesmith appeared, cleaned up in a collared shirt and dark dress pants but without shoes. He knelt in front of Corvus, who placed the palm of his hand on Whitesmith's forehead and bowed his head. With a push, Whitesmith fell back and sprawled out, shaking with ecstasy on his face. The camera panned back. Seated in large cushioned chairs on a stately looking stage were Ket's mother, sister, and nieces in long flowing, white dresses.

The camera switched to a congregation rising and singing out, "Praise the Spirit!"

Then Corvus launched into a conventional sermon and Lacy turned down the volume.

"So Corvus did shift the family to California." Quasi snapped a photo of the holo-screen. "But hanging out with Whitesmith in public—how will that work for his image?"

"If you seek cult members, seek the most disaffected members of society," Rube said.

"And the hopeless often seek a supernatural forgiveness," Lacy added.

"Not only pirates do that." Quasi smiled and played with his cheese-cutter's hat, then snapped a photo of Rube and Lacy. "Think of how many politicians find 'God' after they're caught lying, cheating, harassing—"

"Or posting an inappropriate picture." Rube cleared his throat.

"But the soahliverse," Lacy continued, "is lit up with the fact the Third Millennium Movement has converted the Big Sur Pirates, and the pirates have pledged to help the movement with its goal of universal nuclear disarmament."

"Ah, so it's the soahliverse that is unfolding as it should." Rube gave Lacy a wry look. "Sorry. At least we can tell Ket her family is fine. That is, if that can be said of anyone in California and living under the control of Corvus." He thought about elaborating—that whenever he was reminded of Ket, nothing about the way his own life was unfolding seemed fine.

"Wait, there's one more thing I want to show you." Lacy hit a button. "After the usual spiel and offers for robes and special water you can buy for spiritual healing, Corvus says something else ... at the end ... he's praying."

"Bring home the prodigal daughter, Betti Boni, to us." Corvus's tone was most reverent. "But if she refuses, we know we must shun her and leave her to the demon's red world. We will listen for your directions and continue our fight to stop them from spreading their wave of sin throughout the universe." Behind Corvus appeared the sine-wave pictogram from the Kay Cees.

Lacy pointed with her index finger, its fickle-finger tattoo pointing in parallel.

"Oh, god," Rube said.

"I reckon a deity has nothing to do with this," Quasi said.

"I thought we'd decided old bird-brain was too dumb to figure out what the data on Ket's soahl meant," Rube said. "At least he thinks that's a message we made to send to aliens."

"That's how it seems." Lacy swiped her display. "I'll keep a watch out to make sure."

"Let's go over what we know," Rube continued. "Whitesmith gave Ket's soahl to Corvus and he told Abraham that Whitesmith had found data on it—a message Corvus decided was for aliens. Now it seems Whitesmith has converted the data into the pictograms from the Kay Cees."

"Aye," Quasi said. "That waffle-faced blighter is the type to figure that out. But I doubt Whitesmith has realized what the pictograms are. Not unless the data files contain sky position information and such … in which case—"

"We'll have to go to California and get Ket's soahl back." Rube wished he could take the words back the moment he spoke them.

* * *

"This is bad, really bad," Lacy's glasses whispered, as she paced in the living room.

"I thought you preferred a silent soahl," Rube said. He wanted to pace too, but his feet felt like they were set in buckets of water, frozen by fear. He suggested they travel in disguise.

"We could pretend to be junkies going to California to be saved," Quasi suggested.

"Or I could blind Corvus with my—"

"He's seen that already," Quasi said.

"—tattoos?" Lacy smiled.

"Right," Rube said. "It's not clear they can get anything off Ket's soahl that could really hurt the discovery of the Kay Cees or the next Mars mission. They've just turned some weird data into weird pictograms. And Corvus thinks it's a message we plan to send to aliens."

Quasi dropped his hat and ran his fingers through his non-existent hair. "But if Whitesmith studies the data further—"

"According to my research, Whitesmith's not interested in data or aliens," Lacy said. "He's more into money and drugs. He's probably just humoring Corvus, for his own plans."

Rube felt he could move again. "So Whitesmith's probably not studied the pictograms or tried to figure out what they are, and there's nothing to worry about."

Lacy stopped pacing. "Except Ket's reply to my message says the gravitino bursts data contains time stamps, sky positions, and counts per second. And we know Whitesmith not only found the data, he's understood some of it corresponds to pictograms."

"And," Quasi said, "even if Corvus has latched onto his interpretation of the data and Whitesmith doesn't care, we still can't go nap in the pub. Corvus will say we've created it to send an unauthorized message to aliens, to help the case to shut down communications with Mars through the ICA. And it will become part of the record."

Rube's feet froze in place again.

"That case will take years." Lacy seemed vexed and her voice rose. "The big worry is they'll figure out Ket's discovery, or someone will, and use it to contact the Kay Cees."

Quasi shook his head. "The second part of your worry is rubbish, according to Prasham. Building a gravitino antenna to talk to aliens is not something that can be done overnight. Prasham has said none of the plans for the antenna have been published, and no one could build one without years of research. So even if someone had a hint of what Ket has discovered, they couldn't repeat what she's done. Her work with the Kay Cees is safe."

"Perhaps," Rube said, "if we take the hypothesis that neither Corvus or Whitesmith think this has anything to do with aliens, this may be another attempt to scare her home. It's like they're saying to Ket, 'Don't forget, we've got your soahl and we know what's on it. Now come and get it.' Only they don't really know. It's an attempt to get her to come to them."

"All righty," Lacy said. "In a year she'll leave for Mars. And a little over two years after that, so will we. In the meantime, the Big Sur Pirates are wanted outside of California. There's no need to go there and they are not coming here. And Mobius has this place sealed off like it's a fortress. It's not like it was when Whitesmith got in here." She stroked the tattoo on her index finger like she was rubbing a lamp with a genie in it. "So everything's copacetic."

"Which calls for some anesthetic," Quasi said. He took out his flask.

Rube let out a huge sigh. "Maybe you're right. It's like we're the first family of the Soahl Empire, with guards following us everywhere. Let's lay low for now."

* * *

The next day Dr. Mateni came down the hall with a letter from Maria Boni. "She had the address from when Ket was here," he explained.

Rube was about to say he would forward it to Antarctica when he noticed it said on the envelope, 'To Reuben Dual c/o Betti Boni.' He opened it.

Rube gathered the gang and read, "Thank you for being a good friend to my daughter. Enclosed is a picture of her when she was two. She was so cute. I used to call her Mrs. McGillicuddy." Rube tipped the envelope. Out fell a back and white print on old-fashioned photographic paper showing a little girl in a dress with frills, twirling her hair around her thumb.

Lacy ran her finger over the picture. "It contains a code. I can tell by the pattern of background pixels." After scanning it into her soahl, she continued, "It's called 'a pretty good pirate code' and it was generated by Ket's soahl." It took Lacy less than a minute to decode it. She read the message to the others. "Corvus is planning something. Somehow Margie convinced him to let her use Ket's soahl to create this coded photo, and she got the app from the daughter of a BSP member. We're watched constantly, but Corvus weds wife two in Tahoe, May fourteenth. Send a robo-limo for us and get us out of California, please!"

"Wife two?" Rube said.

"I'm searching for that," Lacy said. She flicked her dark glasses down over her eyes.

"What's Corvus up to?" Quasi asked.

"I don't have any idea," Harlow said, "but maybe you guys are going to California after all? Though, if you'd told me what you were planning yesterday—"

"Tahoe is a lot less dangerous than Big Sur," Rube said. "Maybe *we* can pick them up at the wedding." He studied Quasi's face. "It would be another chance for you to practice driving."

Quasi noticed that Rube was looking at him. "I reckon—"

"Though maybe we should send a car without a driver," Rube continued, "as suggested."

"You can't just send a robo-car to California," Lacy said. "Besides, I think it's a trap."

"Of course, you're right," Rube said. "Ket's mom wouldn't have let Margie use Ket's soahl and neither would Corvus."

"Look," Lacy said. A pink wedding announcement appeared on the lenses of her glasses. "I found it on a soahl rumor page, but no name is given for the bride. And Corvus hasn't announced anything in public. I'll bet there's no wedding. It's a ruse to get you to go to Tahoe."

"It's a rhino-hair's width too obvious," Quasi said, "using a code that's so easy to break."

"I don't think this is Whitesmith's work," Rube said. "It sounds like another plan Corvus would come up with. We should stay here."

"Mobius would never let us go to California, regardless," Quasi said.

"Unless?" Rube smiled. "I have to appear in court in two months. After that I am going to visit my brother. Mobius doesn't like it, but Africa is far away. I've convinced Mobius if I travel with guards I'll be fine. Maybe I can also convince Mobius an *old* friend should go on a visit to California, and see what's really going on."

"You're going back to the disguise plan?" Quasi rubbed his forehead.

"I'm getting dizzy," Lacy said. "Rearranging plans is like rearranging the deck chairs on the Titanic after it hit the iceberg."

"Well, if it's a wedding, there'll be cake," Harlow said. "Maybe I should go too."

"Let's wait and see what more we learn," Rube said. Like he was relieved to find a rope that would pull him to safety, he said the one thing he was sure of—the one thing that gave him hope. "We also should discuss this with Ket."

This time she'd have to make time to talk with him.

Chapter 28
Just When You Thought You Had It All Figured Out

Slog::Bad Wave:: More notes about Kay Cees.

I have been walking around the Kay Cees compound for two months, but unfortunately, only for a few hours per day.

Kay Cee Biotechnology: I've learned that most of the habitats, in fact all the buildings, and also my v-bod body there, are grown from seeds. Their AI can bioengineer the DNA needed to grow any product. I've seen furniture, tools, and homes growing inside domed biospheres. Their portals to their AI grow like plants too. Imagine talking to a daffodil. I haven't seen how the actual AI is produced, and the Kay Cees said that it simply exists. However, I'm told artificial life forms with a nervous system are banned. For that, they need to start with the animal DNA of an existing species. And I was asked again if I would donate mine, with a partner.

Other Species on the Kay Cee Colony World: Up to today, I've cataloged twenty-one intelligent species living in different areas. All the inhabitants, so far, seem content. I'm starting to wonder though, since their AI seems to do a much better job translating English into the various languages than vice-versa, which is strange. For one thing, all the aliens refer to me as 'least naked' even though I have asked them to call me Ket. I've gathered I'm called 'least naked' because I have a lot of hair on my head. However, I would think the translator software could call me human easily enough. But names do not translate very well. I can't pronounce the names of any of the Kay Cees I've met. I'll have to talk to the Kay Cees about this. But, as I've pointed out before, they don't seem to understand much about technology themselves. For now, I will continue to catalog the characteristics of the various species.

Ket stopped writing. She thought about how lucky she was to have access to the control room each evening to conduct her v-bod visits to the Kay Cees' colony. None of the other students knew what she was doing, and she missed out on many of the social events. It scared her to think that bonding with them might have to wait until the actual eight and a half month journey to Mars. She didn't know which of the thirty-two novices, twenty males and twelve females, would be selected for the mission. But they already knew that she and Prasham were going, which made her a definite outsider. No one showed open resentment toward her, and Prasham assured the novices that extra slots could be added if someone showed exceptional talent, or if anyone chose to bring a significant other with them, as per Mobius's new rules.

She did surmise, from their whispers and their stares, that the other students assumed she and Prasham were spending their free time with each other. Since she couldn't tell them about her research, she didn't correct this perception. However, when Prasham was not consumed with training her and the other students, he worked on his own research.

She knew that Prasham had always obsessed over work, but he now seemed more reclusive than ever. The gravitino burst paper had been submitted, but she was surprised to see that only Mobius, Prasham, and Harlow were listed as authors, while she was only thanked in the acknowledgment for helping record the bursts. Prasham told her she would be the lead author on the ET discovery paper after she arrived on Mars, and he would catch up on her work when there was time. But there never was time.

Mobius said he too wanted to catch up on her ET work. But he was busy giving virtual outreach talks on Earth and arranging for dignitaries to do virtual travel to Mars, routing their soahls through the antenna in Antarctica. He was schmoozing with politicians and building support for his case to keep the gravitino antenna operating, in preparation for the court case with the ICA. It wasn't that Ket hadn't seen Mobius at all. He'd visited the novices twice. He'd even shaken her hand with one of the new heated v-bods. And she'd appeared virtually with him on a few of the outreach events. But in each of these meetings, he'd been all business.

Ket began to think about what she should tell Mobius and Prasham in the summary of her notes. Could she really explain how hard it was too understand one alien culture, let alone the twenty-one she had encountered? She imagined explaining to them it was like visiting a wildlife sanctuary, though all the inhabitants seemed to be co-equals and not like animals in captivity. They'd been raised there, along with their native foods. They could travel virtually to other planets, including their home worlds. Most spent their lives studying other species. There were millions on the gravitino network, but the aliens she'd met so far tended to specialize, as humans did. No one in the universe, it seemed, could learn everything about everything.

That's why Ket concentrated on the Kay Cees in her summary. It was already information overload. So she wrote what she had learned about their obsession with obtaining DNA and their religion of descendent worship, realizing she was likely getting it all wrong.

Then she decided she should at least try to discuss a little comparative anatomy.

Common Characteristics of the Colony Species: Of the intelligent species I've seen so far, all are land-based and all have some sort of hands, with a Fibonacci number of appendages, and binocular vision on at least one side of one of their heads. Otherwise, the number of eyes, ears, noses, and limbs varies, as does the source of nutrition. Speaking of which, most of the habitats seem insect free—a bonus of living on a controlled environment—except for that of a large panda-like, red-fly eating species. All would be classified by appearance as animals, though a few are different enough to be classified as belonging to kingdoms unknown on Earth. My Kay Cee provided v-bod doesn't have a camera, but I'll ask for pictures and videos.

Some kind of covering, like hair or fur, is common. None are as hairless as humans. Almost all wear some kind of jewelry or clothing, though less of the latter than most humans. I'm told all have undergone genetic modifications to adapt to the colony world. None seem aggressive. Though a group that looked like tiny hummingbirds with iridescent, bioluminescent arms, turned into flying, feathered sharks with claws when I reached to touch one. They continued to act friendly, but aloof. Perhaps docile behavior is selected for or added to the exchanged DNA? Overall, species interaction seems intellectual not social.

Ket stopped writing and thought about how she'd not seen any interspecies hand-holding or cuddling, even with the Kay Cees, the most social of them all. Even after hundreds of millennia of interspecies colonization, it was hard to overcome differences. She also learned that despite very efficient seed-grown solar power, resources limited a single planet to no more than a few dozen species exchanges. Though maybe politics did too.

For one thing, the colony planet was not unified under a single government. It was this fact that brought up the indigenous inhabitants for the first time. Ket had hoped the Kay Cees would bring them up first. She'd feared that maybe the Kay Cees had disposed of them. If true, she didn't want to know about that yet.

However, the Kay Cees were happy to show her a video of the locals. Tree Jesters, she thought. Their python-shaped bodies, covered with harlequin patches of black and white fur surrounding peacock-like eyespots, curved around branches and ended in multicolored striped heads with prehensile stalks. And the stalks ended in seashell-like bells that actually jingled and could wrap around and manipulate objects. But Ket did not write about them in her summary. She decided that would wait until she'd met one, and until she understood why the Kay Cees had avoided introducing her to them.

Instead, Ket started to write about alien family relationships. But tiredness sifted through her and a wave of loneliness emanated from her heart.

It had been good to hear from Lacy about her mother, sister, and nieces. She'd watched the video of them on the Soahl-7 clip herself. She agreed—her mother wouldn't send a coded message in a picture. However, only her family knew her mother used to call her Mrs. McGillicuddy. Whitesmith could have been told that, but the message seemed more like another stupid idea from Corvus. She also didn't want Rube, or Quasi, or Harlow risking their lives by going to California. Her gut told her that her mother would find her own way to escape Corvus.

For a moment, she missed her friends so much the urge to leave Antarctica for Seattle overwhelmed her. But she was the focal point of a discovery of singular importance. Once she was on Mars, other scientists would take over some of the work, including those more adept at anthropology than her. But this was her time to do the extraordinary.

She mustered her strength. Mars was her future. She had waited years to escape Corvus. She had waited years to find the good people of the universe. Some of those good people were depending on her right now. Some would join her on Mars a few years after her arrival. Others would travel with her. She vowed to get to know them better.

She was about to go find the other students, when a chime sounded from her display. Mobius needed to see her.

* * *

Ket had quickly gathered her hand-written notes from the control room and brought them back to her room, putting them on her desk for transcribing into her soahl. Before she could sit, there was a knock and her door opened, revealing Mobius.

He glided into the room and around her. Ket thought he moved quite well in his v-bod body. The extra training from Rube had really paid off. She staggered back, turned, and saw him ease onto her bed. She attempted to change the frustrated look she felt on her face into a smile. Then she tried to do her own glide to the opposite side of the room and tripped, landing on the side of her bed next to Mobius. She couldn't help but look into his eyes.

"Sorry, I should have warned you I was about to arrive when I sent that message."

She realized she should say something in response. "No problem. But is everything all right? I—"

"Of course, I should have explained. I wanted to make a social visit. I've been so busy, and I know we've not had much of a chance to talk since Fiji."

"I want to thank you again. It was so strange. You rescued me … you and Rube … and then you swam out to sea. I should have done more to tell you what that meant to me. I mean we've talked a little during training here and at outreach events, but I should have come to see you on Mars. I've … I've been learning so much about the Kay Cees. I'm writing a summary for you and Prasham." Ket realized she was rambling, and that Mobius was smiling at her. "Uh … you said you *needed* to see me?"

"Again, sorry. I was in a hurry. I didn't mean to make it sound urgent, it's not."

"That's good to hear." Ket felt the tension in her back relax. She noticed a very slight difference in his voice, a small deviation from its usual confidence. Even so, it was always intimidating to be around Mobius.

"Ket, to be honest with you, I want to hear about the Kay Cees …"

Ket stood up to get her papers from her desk. "Good, I can read you my summary—"

"But I'm worried the Kay Cees might cause people to lose interest in Mars. When people find out there are ways to travel through the universe, virtually, through the elsewhere, Mars will become boring. And if they learn we can transmit DNA to other worlds to start human colonies, will the Mars Mission still make sense to them?"

"It might raise some questions, but it will also reignite interest in space and the universe. I expect it will increase funding for space travel."

"But to Mars?"

"Mars is still the logical first step. Besides, would you want me to keep the Kay Cees a secret? I'm not sure I could—"

"No, no … I just needed someone to talk with … about worries I have."

Ket had never really thought about Mobius and worries before. He looked a little nervous now. "Sure. I guess if you have concerns about the Kay Cees, I'm the one to talk to."

"I do want to hear all about them."

"Good, so back to my summary—"

"Yes, I'll read that later. But … to be honest, I am here to discuss previous business."

"Oh?" Ket sat at her desk.

"Remember how I told you about going on dates?"

Ket wondered if she should admit remembering this, but said, "Platonic ones, as I recall."

"Right, even with a heated v-bod, every date I've had has been entirely platonic. I also said that I planned to date lots of women before finding the right mate." Mobius motioned for her to sit by him again. His utter confidence had returned.

"You said that you were kidding." She wondered where this was going.

Mobius registered a deep laugh. He seemed extremely please with himself. "I said I was looking for the right person, and you were allowed to look too."

"What about Nickie?" Ket thought about stopping the conversation right now. Just when she thought she had it all figured out, just when she thought she had pushed her loneliness far away, she felt very unsure of herself.

"She's not the right person. But don't get the wrong idea."

"What?"

"I'm not saying you are either."

Ket tried to process this. One of the most compelling persons in the entire universe seemed about to put the moves on her, and then maybe he wasn't. He was too old, but should age matter? It flattered and annoyed her. How could she be on the verge of getting a Ph.D. and winning the Nobel Prize and feel so confused? How could she go to Mars, knowing the 'boss' did not recognize professional boundaries? But then again, this wasn't about a job—this was about her life. She had to show she was in control. "Look, my plan is to go to Mars, on my own terms. Maybe even stay there. I think I've made it clear to you, and to Rube, that I'm not interested in a relationship right now."

"I'm not either. But with Rube out of the picture, all I am asking for is a platonic date. You can say no. No strings attached, as always."

Ket's mind reeled: the arrogant bastard. Can there really be no strings attached? But something in her said to not react out of fear. A part of her was interested. Why not get to know him better? She thought about living on Mars with him for the rest of her life. Even if this were a rationalization, wouldn't it be irrational to not see where this was going? "All right, Mobius," she said. "I'll admit I'm scared of you. But maybe we should find out if we're right for each other before I blast myself two hundred fifty million miles around the sun just to meet up with a crazy old man."

"Good. I'll meet you on the track tomorrow after training. We can walk a few laps."

"And I'll tell you about the Kay Cees. They're all I think about." Ket lied. She really needed someone to talk to, about everything. She could have v-bod travelled to Rube, but her feelings for him were too complicated. How could she admit loneliness and still tell Rube she was going to Mars without him? She could have confided in Lacy, or even Quasi, but anything she said to them would get to Rube. She could have gone to Prasham, but he was her mentor, not her counselor. No, Mobius was her only option right now. Ket woke up from her daydream and realized Mobius was still there. "And you can tell me more about yourself too," she added.

"It's a date then." Mobius stood up and walked across the room. He took her hand, bowed, and kissed it.

This time his lips felt warm.

Chapter 29
Meaningless From Another Point Of View

Rube raised his display to block the cold icy stare of Evelyn Hatter. Next to him stood his bodyguard, and they all stood before a judge in a small courtroom in Cairo. Rube hoped she thought the bodyguard was there because of her.

When they'd met on a virtual quest, Evelyn had seemed eager to follow him through flights of fancy about science and philosophy. Though after they finally met face-to-face, she flirted in an indifferent sort of way. She said she'd been scarred by her father's abandonment and asked for tangible symbols of attachment, like expensive jewelry. Then she seemed to open up to him. But within a month, the warning signs were apparent. She lured him into promising to marry her in a virtual world and asked for a dowry in the real one. Rube told her she didn't know what she was talking about. And she told him that she was glad that he had switched from astronomy to computer science. Computer scientists made much more money. He never did tell her about the dream that had led to that switch.

Still, Rube thought they were having fun watching old comedies that he liked. But she revealed to him her fascination with torture movies, saying it was a catharsis for her fantasies about her father—about anyone that would abandon her. She ordered Rube to promise that he'd never leave her. He pulled back, saying they had to get to know each other better. It was too soon for that kind of commitment.

That's when she blew up, saying she always knew he was not the one, that he'd always be a minion working for the real men that created the world. She demanded a divorce. That only confused Rube. Ironically, he retreated into a virtual world, feeling lucky to have escaped physically unscathed. It seemed she wanted to extract pounds of money, not flesh.

So here he was, in court, listening to the judge explain virtual world contracts and the value of his assets accumulated there in the real one. Rube was told his contract with Ms. Hatter was binding, but Rube could counter sue if he thought he could prove fraud on her part.

After two seconds of thought, Rube told his lawyer he would pay if Evelyn agreed to stay completely out of his life. The settlement was worked out over lunch, and he signed a check to her for his entire savings. He heard what he could only identify as a fake cackle outside the room. Through the window, he saw Evelyn run in her stiletto heels toward a robo-limo. Speckled dots from her laser-pointer eyes bounced upon its rear door and it opened. She hopped in and disappeared. He hoped forever.

The good news was that he could still catch the evening flight to Nairobi.

* * *

"So, Evelyn took your dough and Ket stomped on your heart? Here, have a beer, bro."

"Ket didn't stomp on my heart," Rube said. "She realized it was happening too fast."

"And she wanted to ... just ... be ... friends. Bummer."

"Vic, she also realized that if she chose to take me to Mars, it would never feel right. I have to make it there on my own."

"Sounds like stupid pride to me."

Vic's daughter Tepi came in. "Uncle Rube, you're not a doll this time. Did you bring me a new one?"

"Sorry Tepi, I didn't bring a doll, but I did bring you a treat." Rube pulled some red licorice out his pocket. Then he pulled out his n-cloth and flicked it into a display. "I can also show you some cartoons, if your Dad doesn't object."

"No problem. We're connected to the network this week because the generator's running. But Tepi needs to go to the village and find her mother. She's visiting a friend, and I think she's forgotten we have company. We need her home to cook."

"What?" Rube protested. "We can fix ourselves dinner."

"No, we need her. After a few more beers, we won't be fit to touch knives and hot stoves. Go Tepi. Go fetch your mom."

Tepi laughed and ran out the door.

Vic turned to Rube. "Will your bodyguard outside be joining us?"

"Yes, unfortunately he's stuck with me." Rube looked down at his display and saw a message from Quasi, pointing him to a link. He tapped on it and opened a video. His brother came over to watch.

Mobius appeared on the display. His v-bod avatar stood next to Ket in Antarctica, and he spoke to the camera. "Kids, I want to introduce you to a special friend of mine. Here she is, way back when she was twelve-years-old."

The video switched to an old homemade movie. Rube saw a classroom. "Can anyone guess how long will it take to travel to Mars?" a much younger Dr. Mateni asked. A hand shot up in the front row. "Ooh, ooh, I know," a young girl said.

"Who's that?" Vic asked.

"That's Ket and her teacher," Rube replied. "Shh."

On the video, Ket walked to the chalkboard and continued, "You draw an ellipse from Earth on one side of the sun to Mars on the other." She drew as she talked. "That's called a Hohmann orbit. Mars is one point five times the distance of the Earth from the Sun, so the average distance is two point five over two, or one point two five. To get the time, cube that, to get about one point seven five, and then take the square root, to get one point three seven five, and divide by two to get point six eight seven five. That's from Kepler's Third Law. Multiplying by twelve gives about eight months."

"Pretty smart for a twelve year old." Vic rubbed his head. "Maybe too smart."

"Not too smart, just very smart. And pretty much perfect in every way imaginable."

The video switched back to Ket and Mobius. "Now Ms. Betti Keturah is all grown up. She's studied hard and is about to become a renowned scientist. She is preparing to lead the next mission and join me on Mars. She's also an adjunct instructor for the Math Monks of Mars, and she's going to tell you little more about Mars and our mission there. Take it way, Ms. Keturah." The view switched to a classroom watching Mobius and Ket on a holo-screen. As the camera zoomed in, Ket began to tell them, in her most compelling way, about the adventure she was about to undertake. She was wonderful with children, even on a holo-screen. Then the camera panned back for a moment to reveal her taking Mobius's hand. He looked at her with affection. Rube hit the pause button and collapsed his n-cloth.

"That's harsh dude. After telling you she wasn't interested in a relationship."

"It may not be how it looked."

"It looked to me like she's thinking about sharing a cup of *coffee* on Mars."

"What?"

"You know, with Mr. n-cloth-head. Though I've never understood why you call it that. Seems to me it should be called e-cloth."

"As in 'e' for electrical-cloth? It's the nano-tech that—"

"No, no, I mean, e-cloth for erectile-cloth, since it has its flaccid and erect states. I'm only saying—that would make Mobius a dick head."

Rube didn't respond.

"Bro, you should stay for a while. Working here again would do you good. Going to Mars—it's like you said, it could be meaningless from another point of view. And given the view we've seen, I'd say more than meaningless ... a real waste of time. Right?"

"I need to find out what's going on."

"Don't do that. Have more beer." Vic pulled another bottle from the case on the floor and popped off the top.

"Yeah, I really need to find out what's going on." Rube took the beer from Vic. "Right after I have this beer."

Chapter 30
Sending Mrs. McGillicuddy Everywhere

Slog::Bad Wave:: More notes about Kay Cees.

A local and the bad Kay Cees: My Kay Cee friends were chirping with each other and lost track of me. There, just outside a yellow fence of vines, was a Tree Jester. She asked me if I wanted to meet the other Kay Cees—the good ones. (I'll call her a she, based on how she waved her stalks and the voice the translator gave her, though I'm ashamed to admit my biased interpretation.) She also said her pets could acquire exotic DNA for me if I so desired. It could be used to grant any wish, cure any disease, even my body-baldness. Before I could ask what she meant by pets, with a shriek, my Kay Cee friends grabbed me. The translator kept repeating, "expletive deleted," until things calmed down. It turns out there was another faction of Kay Cees here—unethical ones who deal in illicit DNA and who do not subscribe to the DNA non-proliferation treaties. They are bad Kay Cees—and they would steal my DNA in a heartbeat.

* * *

Private Slog::Bad Wave:: What is still needed.

I've been telling Mobius all about the Kay Cees. He's still not sure how the news will affect the Mars mission. Will it cause a loss of interest in Mars once people know we can talk to ET and establish colonies on other planets, or will it create more enthusiasm for Mars? He says humans on Earth could kill themselves off before establishing a colony anywhere else. Mars is still needed. Of course, he's preaching to the choir with me.

He's so confident. It's very alluring. Except, he let a video out without careful editing. The private video of me at age twelve can no longer get Dr. Mateni in trouble, but he should have asked first. More disturbingly, it shows us sharing a bit of affection. That was my fault too. I lost myself for a moment. But it should have been edited out. However, I now know that Mobius, as charming as he can be, is not my perfect bra. I know because whenever I see him there's a moment of disappointment—a moment of longing, wishing it were Rube.

Ket closed her display and left her room. She knew Mobius was waiting for her on the track again. She walked down the hall to the elevator. Everyone else had gone to bed. It was the perfect time to talk, the perfect time to put his 'no strings attached' promise to the test. He was a big boy. She would find a way to say they could 'just be friends' without sounding like she'd led him on. She was sure he could take it.

* * *

"That's great news, Lacy." Rube looked at her on his display. "How did they get away?"

"They didn't have to escape. It seems that Ket's mother agreed to sign all of Abraham's money over to Corvus. He let them go and had the pirates drop them off near the border. They were arrested when trying to cross from California into Oregon. Luckily, she convinced immigration to allow her to send one message, and she had them contact Dr. Mateni. He talked to us, and Quasi arranged to have them bailed out and picked up."

"So a robo-car is on its way to pick them up? Could it be trap?"

"A search of my soahl says we can trust Oregon immigration."

"Corvus is now the richest person on Earth. Never underestimate what money can buy."

"Well, if it is a trap, if they are expecting one of us to show up, they'll be disappointed."

"I'll feel better when they're here."

"Don't worry, Rube. And don't worry about Ket either. She doesn't have time to keep in touch very often. But she did tell me that Mobius was pursuing her." Lacy hesitated. "At first she decided to see where it might lead. I replied, of course, that if fate had anything to do with it she'd end up with you. But I'm biased. Her latest message, though, said she didn't believe, to put it in my terms, that he was her destiny. So there's hope, Rube."

Rube pictured hope as a hammer that might sock him in the gut again. But he still needed to talk to her. "Have you told her that her family is free?"

"I sent the message, but for some reason it bounced. There's a problem between the soahliverse and Antarctica today. I'll resend it later."

* * *

Ket approached Mobius on the track. His broad-shouldered back looked a little slimmer than usual. But why was he wearing an athletic robe and hood? He looked ready for a workout, but how would that make sense? Maybe it was for some new test of the v-bod. He'd really seemed to enjoy their walks together and was always excited to tell her about his latest ideas. She hoped he wouldn't feel too deflated when she let him down. After coming up behind him, she took a deep breath and tapped him on the shoulder. "Hello, Mobius."

The v-bod whirled with predatory swiftness and grabbed Ket's arm. Searing pain shot through her body. She fought. Before she could cry out, the v-bod's other hand clamped over her mouth. Now she could see under the hood, into the v-bod's charming blue eyes. *No, it can't be!*

Corvus dragged her like a rag doll down the track and into the elevator. She made as much noise as she could muster, but only a moan came out, drowned out by the ventilation system. His v-bod hands jerked her out of the elevator and snapped her wrists back. She was unable to resist and tried to collapse to the floor, but he pulled her into the control room and forced her onto one of the beds. "Lie down or everyone here will die."

"But how?"

Corvus didn't answer. He pulled from his robe a spool of high strength packing tape, maybe taken from the shipping area. Ket decided to play along, but it was a mistake. He strapped her to the table then locked the door. Returning to her, he took the soahl from the hem of her dress. "You keep underestimating my intelligence. Whitesmith is working with me, and we've deciphered the message you're planning to send the aliens ... and your plan to spread sin throughout the universe by mating with that boy." He took out a needle attached to some sort of analyzer and pulled an n-cloth mask over her face. After scraping the inside of her nose with it, he must have sensed her confusion. "It's a DNA analyzer, from the med-lab here. I've already scraped my cheek and uploaded my DNA sequence into this v-bod from my location. Now I'll add yours. In moments, it will be our combined DNA that spreads throughout the universe."

"How do you know about this?" Ket finally got some words out. She realized she'd confirmed things she shouldn't have. "I mean, what makes you think there are aliens?"

"When Whitesmith hijacked this v-bod earlier today, we downloaded videos. I've seen the Kay Cees. I know they want DNA. Now they'll get ours. Think of it—a million little Corvus and Mrs. McGillicuddies out there. It came to me in a dream. The Spirit wants me to use your own technology against your evil plan, to spread, instead of evil, the word of the Spirit."

"Corvus, stop. I'll go back with you ... just stop."

He ignored her. "You've turned off authentication in the control room, haven't you? You didn't think anyone could get in here."

Ket heard him lay on the other bed and the faint sound of an n-cloth mask fitting itself over his v-bod face. Then she felt the room dissolve around her, and she found herself with Corvus in front of two Kay Cees. They were not the ones she called friends.

* * *

Rube looked around the home. It was on fire and an alarm was sounding. For some reason, he couldn't move. His insides lurched in panic. Why wouldn't his legs work? The flames engulfed him, but he felt no pain.

Then he woke up. The alarm was still going. It was coming from his soahl.

Vic stumbled in. "What's going on? It's the middle of the night."

"I don't know." Rube grabbed his shirt from chair next to his sleeping mat. He squeezed the soahl in its hem to silence the alarm. Then, from his pants pocket, he took his n-cloth display and flicked it open. There was Lacy. "What's wrong? Is there a problem getting Ket's family?"

"Much worse. Someone is California is sending signals to one of the v-bods in Antarctica. Do you have a travel kit?"

"Yes, let me find it." Rube searched his suitcase.

Lacy continued to speak. "Put on the mask and gloves and fall back. I'll patch you in to the other v-bod in Antarctica."

"How do you know how to do that? Never mind, just do it."

"I was investigating why I couldn't get a message to Ket and traced signals going into Antarctica from California. I sent Mobius a message via ordinary radio, and he replied that he couldn't make contact either or connect to either v-bod there. That took a while, given the ordinary time delay to Mars. I can't tell what's going on. However, I can connect you to the other v-bod in Antarctica—doing that now ..."

* * *

Rube found himself sitting on the floor in the control room in Antarctica. He stood up and saw Ket lying on one bed and a v-bod lying on the other. It sat up.

"Done, my impure one." Corvus tore the n-cloth mask off his v-bod and dropped it on the floor. "So, there was one more thing the Spirit told me. I have to cut out your heart and offer it as a sacrifice. It was in the dream. I hope you don't mind." He pulled out a knife.

Rube recognized it from the kitchen. Though nothing else made sense. Using an n-cloth mask on a v-bod for double virtual travel was unbelievable. Except, there was Corvus, so he had to believe. Rube crept toward him. At least he had the element of surprise. Clamping his hands together, he swung to give Corvus a body blow from behind. But a forearm blocked his fists.

"Soulless soahl boy? You're here? Well, you can be sacrificed too."

Rube dodged the stabbing blade. But it came back rapidly and stuck in his ribs.

For a moment Rube thought he was lying on the floor of the control room in Antarctica, dead. But he felt no pain. Another dream? He sat up. It was dark. He wished he had died.

Of course, there was no way Corvus could have killed him. The same could not be said for Ket. He'd failed to save her.

Then the lights came on and he was back in Antarctica. He heard Lacy's voice.

"Sorry, Rube. I hacked into the remote management console at the base in Antarctica and shut off the power to everything, disconnecting you and Corvus. I should have thought of that earlier. I've brought the power back online. You'll need to disable the other v-bod before Corvus catches on and returns."

Rube sprang up and took the knife from the v-bod that had been Corvus. He used it to pry open an access panel on its abdomen. The v-bod's eyes flashed to life for a moment, and he saw Corvus blink. But Rube yanked out a pair of wires. Corvus vanished and the v-bod fell back. Then Rube rushed over to Ket and used the knife to slice away the tape holding her to the table.

She shook so hard, Rube wondered if she'd been cut. He checked for wounds, but found none. "It's all right now," he said.

"No, no, it's not. He gave them our DNA sequences." Ket swallowed. "We have to get them back. Put on the mask and lie on that table."

"What?"

Ket, with her mask still on, found her soahl on the floor, and lay back. "Do it."

Rube found the other mask on the floor and followed Ket's order.

The room dissolved and Rube found himself sitting with her and two Kay Cees.

"Please," Ket begged, "erase the DNA sequences you were just given."

"We were about to transmit them," the smaller Kay Cee said. "What will you give us?"

"What do you want?"

"DNA."

"No, it's wrong. It's not ethical," Ket explained.

Shrieking chirps, which the translating device failed to block, threatened to split Rube's eardrums. These were followed by "expletive deleted" five times and "ready to transmit."

"Wait!" Ket's yell stopped the Kay Cees' outburst. "If we give you ours," she continued, "will you erase the DNA sequences the other human gave you, from the one called Corvus?"

"We can do that, but only if you send us your combined DNA sequences."

Rube muted his mike for everyone but Ket. "I don't have my mine."

"Is there a DNA sequencer where you are? Please, Rube." Ket sounded desperate.

* * *

Rube sat up in the control room and pulled off the mask. Then he pulled off his mask in Africa. "Vic, I need help!"

A sleepy Vic appeared. "I was going back to bed. What's wrong?"

"Do you have a DNA analyzer?"

"Yes, at the clinic. Why?"

"Get it—fast. I'll explain later."

* * *

The transitions made Rube nauseous—Africa, Antarctica, and back again to the Kay Cee planet, this time with his DNA sequence. He hoped he wasn't too late. "Is this really the only way?"

"Yes," Ket replied. "They want our DNA before they'll erase what Corvus gave them."

"You always said you didn't want children."

Ket stared at Rube. Did he see turmoil … or something else?

"If I have to have them," she said, "I want them with you." She turned to the Kay Cees. "I have our sequences."

The larger Kay Cee held up a cube. "This is designed to hold the sequences from only one mating pair. It will not allow us to hold or transmit more than one pair because of our obscene rules. Your new combined sequences will supplant the existing pair only if you initiate the replacement. Otherwise, we'd have to purchase another device and start over. These cubes are very expensive, designed for a single use in a thousand-orbit protocol. But we are ready to send this one now, with the DNA replaced, if you so desire."

Ket nodded. "Then let's do it."

"Wait, the male almost-naked mole rat must initiate the replacement."

"What?" Ket was surprised they knew which of them was male. She still had no idea about the sexes of the Kay Cees, though the translator made them sound like young males.

"The uglier one. What you call a he. He must touch the device for authorization, like your earlier mate did."

Rube hadn't been there, but he knew Corvus had done everything against Ket's will. Apparently her approval hadn't mattered. He focused on Ket, pouring every ounce of his being through the elsewhere to her. "I'll do it … if you want me to."

"Do it, Rube," Ket looked at him with exigent need and love. "I want you to do it."

And he did.

Chapter 31
For Captain Ket

"Where are you going?"

Rube felt a sense of déjà vu as he called out to his friends up the street, outside the Mars Explorer Building. They had returned to the spaceport on Sriharikota Island to meet up with Ket for the first time since she had returned to India from Antarctica. She and the rest of the crew for Mission Fourteen were about to go into quarantine. The launch was in three weeks. That alone was amazing to think about. Though so much had happened in the last twenty-six months, Rube thought some stability would be good. But what would that mean without Ket?

Quasi stopped massaging his brow under a maroon headband and replied to Rube. "To the launch pad."

"Do you think that's a good idea?"

"Relax, I have the codes for the robo-car and the gate," Lacy replied.

"With permission from Mobius," Quasi added.

"And Corvus isn't a threat anymore," Lacy said.

"I know," Rube said. He walked to his friends. At least they weren't going to the beach. "It's a miracle he and Whitesmith were arrested in Tahoe last month. Did Mobius tell you the whole story? He says he wants to meet with me later this afternoon, without Ket."

"I guess he wants to meet, v-bod to man," Quasi said. "Maybe explain his feelings for—"

"No way." Lacy shook her head. "Mobius never feels the need to explain himself. But that's also not her fate. I feel it in my—"

"Bones?" Quasi asked.

"In my finger," Lacy replied. She pointed her tattooed finger at Rube and tapped him on his breastbone. "But the arrest changes everything."

Rube could guess what changes Lacy meant, but he carried on with what he had been about to say. "Tahoe was a trap for us, and they knew we knew this. But they moved the supposed second wedding date to January and sent out a formal announcement. I think they thought one of us might still show up, that we wouldn't be able to resist. For once the international police were able to step in, in California. If Corvus and Whitesmith had remained in Big Sur they would've been untouchable. But after Ket's mom gave her deposition, the evidence was too great. Corvus never saw that coming, or that Mobius would show up."

"He was able to grab them as a v-bod, without tripping?" Quasi asked.

"Rube's a good teacher," Lacy said.

Rube gave a little bow. "The other good news is that the BSP didn't help transfer a nuke from India to Fiji, whatever that crazy plan was about. After the arrest, both countries backed out. And the BSP have gone back to routine piracy."

With a hum, a robo-car pulled up next to them. Quasi opened the door and let Lacy in the back seat. He motioned for Rube to join her and took the driver's seat.

"Robo-car, emergency over-ride." Quasi turned to the backseat. "Lacy, do you have the passphrase?"

"If I am a massless neutrino, then you are not a Higgs boson."

Quasi repeated what Lacy said and started driving.

"So," Rube said, "we'll go take a look and come back to meet Ket and Mobius?"

"Better," Quasi said.

Rube's neck snapped back as the car lurched off. "Better?"

"You'll see." Quasi turned and grinned. The car veered a bit, but he corrected its path.

Rube decided to keep quiet. He absorbed the smear of beach that sped by, and then, looking farther out, let his vision melt into memory. He imagined the launch pads, sixteen kilometers from the Mars Explorer Building, and what he'd say to Ket when he saw her. His head swung forward and his shoulder belt caught him before his head hit the front seat. He looked up. They had stopped at a guardhouse with a wooden gate across the road. No guard was on duty. "Lacy?"

"Fourteen," Lacy replied. "Though, for this mission, I would have picked lucky number forty-two." She glanced at Rube.

Quasi typed in a one and four on the keypad. "Not very secure, but the gate then waits fifteen seconds, while cameras scan the car." He turned back at Rube. "The same code works for the launch tower lifts. I know because I had to use it to inspect the fuel systems last week."

Rube saw the gate open.

"See," Quasi said, "I told you Mobius is on board with this."

Rube's neck muscles responded to the rapid acceleration.

"Relax and enjoy the ride," Lacy said. "I always do."

Rube did feel a bit more relaxed. If they were in trouble, surely the gate wouldn't have opened. Everything was fine, he thought. Corvus and Whitesmith were locked up, he was on track for Mars, and he would see Ket later today. He drifted back into his bittersweet thoughts. A few minutes later he heard Quasi's excited voice.

"Here we are, and there they are!"

The car stopped abruptly. Out the front window, two rockets appeared, less than a mile away. To his left, Rube saw cables coming down from the direction of the launch pad. These ended in a sand pit next to a concrete bunker.

And beside the bunker, eight robo-cars were parked in row. "Why are we stopping here?"

"This is where we leave the car. You'll see," Quasi said. He opened his door and hopped out. Lacy joined him.

Rube thought about staying put, foiling their plan to get him into trouble. But he got out. "So there are the rockets." He pointed. "Now can we go back?"

"No, friend. Now we walk to pad two with the crewed rocket and take the lift to the top."

* * *

On the gantry between the MLV rocket and the launch tower Rube took in the view.

"If I am a massless neutrino, then you are not a Higgs boson ..." He shook his head and looked at Quasi and Lacy. "I once thought I might spend the rest of my life trying to understand stuff like that. If I had, I wouldn't have friends like you, and I wouldn't be here right now."

"You'd have ended up a bit of a sterile neutrino, don't you think?" Lacy smiled.

"Probably," Rube replied. "What I'm saying is, this is a good thing. This view. This time. Having friends like you. This is better."

After an awkward silence, Quasi took his flask out of his satchel. "Well, I reckon there's no better place to have a sip of rocket fuel than here." While he worked to unscrew the top, Rube and Lacy turned inland. Lacy took off her dark glasses and twirled them in her hand.

"I wonder how far we can see from up here?" Rube asked.

"I'm sure Ket could figure that out in her head in a second."

The high booming voice almost made Rube fall off the gantry. Lacy almost dropped her glasses. And Quasi did a spit take. They all turned to see Prasham at the tower end of the gantry. He motioned to the steel door behind him. "I was in there, checking on supplies." He walked over to the group of friends.

"Uh, Prasham, it's good to see you." Rube meant it, and he extended his hand for a shake. Prasham took it, so everything must be fine. But he decided to make sure. "Did you know we'd be up here?"

"Ket told me to meet you here." Prasham's face lit up. "She said I should make sure you didn't get into trouble. She's captain now, you know."

"She is?" Rube laughed. "Of course, she is."

"Well, it's her nickname," Prasham said. "I'm really in charge."

"Whatever she wants you to believe." Lacy winked.

Prasham ignored this. "But she did convince Mobius and the Indian authorities to let you come up here." He turned to Quasi. "And she convinced me to authorize your safety test too."

"Safety test?" Rube started to feel queasy. Quasi and queasy, they seemed to go together.

"I may be a sterile neutrino to you, and you may be know-nothings from the back row to me, but even I know when its time to let my hair down a bit." Prasham took the flask from Quasi and raised it in a toast. "To great friends of the Mars Mission. When this candle lights in three weeks, sing happy burn-day to us." He took a sip. "That's rocket humor."

He laughed and then everyone else did too.

"Here, here," Quasi said. He took back the flask.

"Thank you, Prasham," Rube said. He shook Prasham's hand again.

"I knew that Math Monk stuff was just an act," Lacy said. "You should get a tattoo before the launch. I know the perfect—"

"Don't let your wave functions get too carried away," Prasham interrupted. "I'll take my leave before your 'test' and if anyone asks, I wasn't here." He bowed and walked way.

Rube and his friends stood silently until Rube asked again, "Safety test?"

"When I said better, I meant it," Quasi said. He pointed to the right, where the gantry joined the tower. There, a gate was labeled 'Emergency Exit.'

Rube had noticed it, but now wondered what that meant. He followed Quasi and Lacy back down the gantry and, with them, pushed through the gate. There he saw eight escape baskets attached to cables.

"The ultimate zipline," Quasi announced.

"Whoopee!" Lacy spiraled her hands from above her head like falling maple seeds.

"As you heard," Quasi continued, "Captain Ket says we can test them. We can pretend we are escaping from a burning rocket."

Lacy reached over and tweaked Quasi's headband. "If the rocket was on fire, we'd use the launch escape system to fire emergency rockets in the nose-cone to eject the command capsule for a landing in the sea."

"What?" Rube asked.

"Haven't you seen the video of the Soyuz T-10-1 launch? In 1983, spilled fuel caught on fire. And two seconds before things exploded the crew used that type of system to get away." Lacy started to pull out her n-cloth display.

"That's fine, I believe you," Rube said.

"I've seen it," Quasi said. "But these baskets are for emergency evacuation before the engines have started."

"Right," Lacy said. "In that case, the crew blows the hatch, and they run to the baskets and fly down the cables to the bunker, where they take shelter, or the vehicles back to mainland."

"Still, it would be cool to think we are escaping from a burning rocket." Quasi motioned for Rube and Lacy to hop in a basket. "Let's go."

"Uh, the elevator seemed fine to me," Rube said.

"This will get you back to the car," Lacy said, getting into the basket next to Quasi. "And the faster we get back, the sooner you'll see Ket. I hear she has a surprise for you."

Rube saw Quasi and Lacy take hold of a lever. Reluctantly, he got into a basket and did the same. With a quick pull, each of them was on their way. At first, Rube felt more like he was falling than flying. His stomach set sail within his chest. But the wind settled into a steady stream, and it was fun. It was really fun.

* * *

The Indian police at the bottom of the zipline did not seem amused.

"Captain Ket gave us permission," Lacy said. "I mean Betti Keturah."

"And Prasham too," Quasi said. "Really, how should I say it? It is all *coupersetique*."

Rube didn't think Quasi's use of his French accent was helping. But he added, "Mobius knew we'd be up there too."

The stone-faced police in their drab uniforms and white helmets didn't respond. Instead, they studied their displays and muttered. Finally, the oldest looking one, with stripes on his shoulder, looked at Rube and said, "Are you Reuben Duel?"

"Yes," Rube said.

"You're the only one we want."

"What, did I scream louder than the others?"

"We don't care about the zipline. Prasham told us about that. It's you we want. You're under arrest." One of the younger officers forced Rube to turn around. He handcuffed Rube and patted him down.

"Why?" Rube wanted his friends to hear the charges before he was taken away.

"For international spying using a v-bod," the oldest officer said.

Rube felt like saying, wait—they went skinning dipping—how can you arrest me for something trivial like spying? He felt like saying, he'd done it for Captain Ket. But he said nothing. He knew anything he said would get his friends in trouble.

The party was over. And this time there hadn't even been talk of cake.

CHAPTER 32
NEVER AND ALWAYS

Sitting in a small cell, Rube saw the soft orange glow of a dress. Its wearer approached down the darkened hall. She carried something rolled up in her hand.

"What's that?" Rube asked when she got closer.

"It's the poster from Lacy," Ket replied. "She wanted you to have it."

"Ah, the universe, unfolding as it should." Rube tried to sound lighthearted.

"Apparently not."

"But tell Lacy thanks." Rube searched for a way to make sense of everything. "Corvus and Whitesmith are in jail. Maybe my being here was meant to happen, to make that happen."

"That's a good thing—a very good thing. But I'm sure you are not supposed to be in there." Ket touched the bars. "Besides … I owe you so much."

"You don't owe me a thing. I'd do it all again. Not just for you, but for me. You deserve Mars. When I get out of here, we can still talk, still meet in the elsewhere."

"I hope so. But there's the ICA. Did you hear the news?"

"I'm not allowed to send or receive messages. What's happened?"

"Rube … we lost the court case."

"What?"

"The ICA convinced the international court that communication with Mars violated encryption laws. The fact that

Corvus was able to break into Antarctica really clinched it. Proved, the ICA said, that the Mars Program could not be trusted with cybersecurity. All communication with Mars is going to be shut down. They'll decide the exact date soon."

"All communication?"

"Until we quantum-encrypt the transmissions. For radio communications, it can be done in a few weeks. But for sending gravitinos through the elsewhere, the quantum encryption process will destroy the entanglement. Prasham is working on it, but it may be impossible. We'd have to develop a new satellite, if he figures something out. After my launch, the gravitino antennas in Antarctica will be impounded."

"We can appeal."

"Even in jail, Corvus has friends with money and power to keep that going for years. I can continue my research on Mars. But with you on Earth ... I'll never be able to talk with you again." Ket's face became torn. "I wish you could come with me."

Rube studied her eyes. What was in her heart? Maybe his had been hurt enough.

"Listen," Ket said, "we'll get you out. Then you'll come to Mars."

"I will. I will, when it's my turn. That is, if I'm not in here."

"Mobius is working on it. He can hire the best lawyers." Ket looked very worried.

"Mobius wants to help? Do you know how they found out?" Rube felt he had blurted out more than he wanted to admit. "I hear he turned me in." Rube calmed himself. He was mad at Mobius but knew Ket was going to be with him on Mars. "Sorry. Whatever has happened, I'm here because of my own decisions."

"Mobius had to tell them what he knew." There was hurt in Ket's voice. She looked down. "You know, to support the case against Corvus and Whitesmith. They had the doll, Rube."

"Who did?"

Ket looked up. "Corvus had it with him when he was arrested. Whitesmith had figured some things out. Do you know it's sitting out front in the evidence box with the officer?"

Rube shook his head. "I was brought in from the back. Wherever this is."

"It's a small station, a few blocks from my old Bangalore apartment. Lacy says the records show v-bod network traffic to Fiji from there, and you'll be prosecuted in this district. With Mobius's help, you'll get a slap on the wrist and be out right after the trial."

Rube started to believe all hope was not lost. "Where are Quasi and Lacy?"

"Lacy is chatting up the one guard on duty here. It's not a very high security place. As I was saying, it's not going to be a big deal."

"So why aren't they back here?"

"You're allowed only one visitor."

"And there's just one guard?" Rube tried to see past Ket. "I guess I'm not such a big international criminal after all."

"We are being watched."

"Of course, I know that. But I'll see you again in a few years?"

"Maybe ..." Ket was hesitant.

Rube saw the uncertainty in her eyes. He felt like needles were stuck into his own. "Unless you and Mobius ..." His sadness leaked out. He'd wanted to not fail again, at life's choices ... at love. But in this universe, entanglement was unavoidable.

Then Ket looked straight at him. "Do you love me?"

Inside, he said yes with infinite force. He'd thought about this more times than he could count. But he hadn't expected to hear this question. Not today. Not given recent events. Was it fair she was asking it now?

After they'd given the Kay Cees their DNA, he'd started to meet with her for virtual dates. She said she wanted him to join her. He thought maybe the trauma they'd been through caused her to say this. It was really too late for him to join her mission. He mentioned the possibility of her staying with him and trying for the next one. But she was unsure and said they probably needed to slow things down and see how their relationship developed.

They talked all night about relationships and everything. They agreed their friendship would last, no matter what. They also agreed they should be just friends, again. Rube didn't push her. Though the more they talked, the more he fell in love with her, but the more he knew it wouldn't be fair to ask her to give up Mars. And there was still Mobius to contend with. Even though Ket insisted she was never more than his friend, and friendship with him was all she wanted, Rube wasn't sure she'd dare admit more than this.

Now, here he was, wanting to answer her question, trying not to tremble. He had to say something. "Corvus isn't a threat anymore. That changes things."

"I know. I could stay here. I don't have to escape from him anymore. That's why I need to know. Do you love me?"

"What about Mobius?"

"Like I told you—for a while he was in the picture as potentially more than a friend. But that's all he was—all he'll ever be." Ket's lips quivered, but she didn't look away. It was clear she needed to say that. "Forget the past. What I want to know is—do you love me?"

Rube realized she too was caught in a storm of reason and emotion. He decided to rely on the only thing that made sense to him in a situation like this, his mind, not his heart. "Because of Corvus, circumstances kept bringing us together. But that's over now. We need to learn to be together without all the drama and see what happens. Like we've discussed."

"Rube, I'm not asking for a re-analysis of the nonsense we've said before. I *need* to know … do you love me?"

"Of course, I do." Rube wanted his answer to shatter the bars in front of him. But was it nonsense to face reality? "It's clear Mobius does too. Even if you won't admit it, you still have some feelings for him. So the question is, do you love him?" He hoped Ket would step closer to him, but she did the opposite.

"I thought maybe I did. Or that maybe in time I would. I've never wanted to admit that before … that I've not known what I want. Rube, when I came here, I came to tell you goodbye. But when I saw you, I knew I wanted something more. I want to go to Mars. I want to …" Ket paused for moment and seemed to choose her words carefully. "I want to continue my research. No, not my research, but continue my search, for something deeper. I'm confused … but I want to be confused … if you get it. There's a whole universe out there waiting for me. But I would wait for you." She stepped toward Rube. "Just ask me to stay."

"Stay for the next launch? There'd be no guarantees. You have to follow your dreams."

"But I could wait."

"I'm not asking you to do that. You can't do that. When I get out, I'll come to Mars on the next mission. That's always been the plan."

"I'm afraid it might be a bit longer than that."

"You said I'd be out right after the trial."

"Yes, that's how is should work out. But …"

"But?"

"The trial might not happen for two to three years. And …"

"And? Don't sugarcoat it."

"Worst case, you could get life in prison." Ket looked down. "It's to do with those laws my father and Mobius worked to pass. But Mobius won't let that happen."

Rube felt his hope sink to the center of the Earth. If Ket stayed, her chance for Mars would be lost. If she went, he would be in prison, with no way to see her for years or maybe forever. At best, it would be at least a half-decade before he could get to Mars. She and Mobius would be Adam and Eve by then, regardless of what she said she wanted. "We need more time to talk. God, there is so much we need to talk about. Our children ..."

"The Kay Cees tell me even though our DNA went out, it will not be used for a thousand years, whatever that means through the elsewhere. We can take a breather for now."

"But in a thousand years, we'll be the parents of millions of kids living in alien sanctuaries throughout the universe."

"If our species survives. It's part of the protocol. No spreading of technological species until they prove they can survive. We've less than two hundred years under our belts. Besides, the Kay Cees need to study us further, to understand what kind of habitat our kids will need."

"Well, then Mars is even more important, not only to us but also to humanity. Who knows, humans might blow up the Earth. With you on Mars, you can help ensure humans will survive far into the future, far enough to see our children born."

"Yes, Rube. No matter what happens, we'll always have our kids. But when I think of them, I think I should stay ... if I only knew—"

"But you can't. None of us can know anything for sure. You have to go. You want another reason to go to Mars, here's one ... I can tell when you talk about Mobius there's something there, even if it's not love. I can see it. He needs you. And it's not just the future of humanity that needs you, maybe the entire universe needs you."

Ket teared up. "Either way, if I stay or go, I need to really know. Do you love me?"

Rube thought about repeating his answer. Of course, he did. But it didn't matter. He knew what he had to do. "The thing is, you know that song your Mother likes, *As Time*

Goes By, I think it's called. It was used in a movie called *Casablanca*."

"Yes, I know. It's still famous in the soahliverse."

"Well, to paraphrase ..." Rube gave Ket his bravest look. "If you don't get on that rocket, you'll regret it. Maybe not today, maybe not tomorrow, but soon, and for the rest of your life."

"But I just need to know," she squeaked out. "Do you—"

Rube raised an index finger to his lips. "Here's looking at you, Ket."

Both were silent until it became unbearable.

Then they both fell down and laughed. They laughed so hard from either side of the bars that Rube felt the tension pour out of them like they'd spent a night making love. After reaching through the bars and touching hands for a moment, Rube stood up with Ket. "We'll always have the other side of the universe," he said.

Ket nodded. She turned and walked away ... away to quarantine.

Rube knew that Ket had tried to give him hope. He also knew he'd never get out of prison. He wanted to cry. He wanted to call out to her. If the universe was unfolding as it should, then the universe sucked. But he knew he had to let her go.

A tear escaped down his cheek. He would never see her again, never talk to her again—his life, from now on, always empty, always meaningless.

Chapter 33
The Good, The Bad, And The Fluffy

Ket tasted bitterness in her mouth. Seated with her back to the ground next to Prasham at the top of the MLV rocket, she couldn't relax. Her last conversation with Rube interrupted her thoughts.

In quarantine for the past three weeks, she'd kept busy during the day, going through checklists and safety drills. But at night, her mind wandered. Did he love her? Of course, he had said it, qualified in a way that it didn't count. She knew he'd wanted to make it easier for her to leave. But would someone in love really do that? Yes. After all, she'd decided the same thing, to be brave and carry on. It was what they had to do. And she had given him a chance, hadn't she? After he'd saved her in Antarctica, she'd discussed his joining her on this mission. But he'd hesitated. He'd said he wanted to earn his own way. They'd both agreed that was best.

So it was decided even before Rube was in jail. It made sense. He would join her later.

Except now there was no hope of that. He was scheduled for transfer to a maximum-security prison to await trial in a court with a two-year backlog. The charges were over blown, but he had done it. He would spend at least another two years in jail, probably more. It wasn't like she'd planned to stay if he wasn't in prison, and staying now wouldn't solve anything.

So why did she feel guilt? He had done a lot for her, for the mission, and even when Mobius pursued her that hadn't stopped him. But did that make him stupid or persistent?

He'd been right about a lot of things. It was too late for him to go and too late for her to stay. And the future of humanity and their unborn children were at stake. The one thing he'd got wrong, though, was his assertion that she still had feelings for Mobius. That was definitely stupid, right? But if he was stupid, so was she. In reality, she and Rube had not spent much time together face-to-face, and she'd only spent time with Mobius using v-bods. It always came back to this. Her going to Mars was the right thing to do.

It helped that everyone else thought so too. Prasham reminded her that given the political climate, she could safely announce her discovery of the Kay Cees only from Mars, even if she had to do it by old-fashioned radio. Otherwise, she would be imprisoned, too, for contacting them against international treaty. And Dr. Mateni said he would work with the Fijian authorities and get them to not ask for the maximum sentence of life, while Lacy and Quasi would fly to India to visit Rube every year until he was out of prison. After that, Rube and his friends would join her on Mars. But she needed to lead the way.

Mobius agreed—her role was essential to the success of the Mars Program. But he was less optimistic about Rube. He pointed out that Corvus had friends in high places in Fiji and in India, and they were causing problems with Rube's case. Mobius said he would do what he could to help Rube, but only as long as it didn't jeopardize the mission. He also said he had seen greatness in her from the start, the courage to step toward the future and the curiosity to face the universe head on. Rube, he said, hadn't wanted her to squander this opportunity, and she'd been right not to give him false hopes. She imagined again being with Mobius on Mars, but all it made her think of was Rube. It was fitting then. If he lived in prison, alone, for the rest of his life, she would live on a cold world, alone, for the rest of hers.

Ket shuddered. *Snap out of it.* On her display she saw the unmanned partner rocket, a kilometer closer to the sea, being filled with the hydrogen that would be used to synthesize fuel for the return trip of the next launch. The cryogenic tanks sent vapors into the air.

All systems were a go. She would lift off in less than six hours. This was it, her mission, Mission 14, what she'd always wanted. It was time to push all the old worries out her mind.

Unfortunately, this only let new worries rush in. Had she paid attention enough during training? Would she really adapt to zero-g and the point-three-eight g's on Mars? Still, she should be thankful there were some things she didn't have to worry about. New protocols and drugs, developed since the first mission, dealt with bone loss and radiation, and proven engineering and safety systems now made sending regular persons to Mars possible.

Though there wasn't anything regular about the crew of six, four women and two men, seated behind her. She had finally bonded with them. They had even made her nickname somewhat more official, voting her captain of the team. She'd also earned the copilot seat next to Prasham, receiving top scores in the simulators. Of course, computers would do most of the flying. Only if these and their backups failed, and something happened to Prasham, would she have to do anything besides enjoy the ride. And after the eight and a half month journey to Mars, and the fifteen months there, she would have more than bonded with the crew. By then, some of them would be her best friends. But they would only add to, not replace the ones she already had.

On another display she saw the empty bleachers atop the Mars Explorer Building where a crowd would gather later. Quasi and Lacy would be there, as would Harlow. So would Dr. Mateni and his family, and her mother, sister, and nieces. There would also be the students for the next mission. Even Rube's brother would be there. Everyone would be there, except Rube.

Prasham read down his checklist. "LOX status green. Fuel intake green."

Ket and the crew had been ordered to rest in their couches for the next three hours. Behind her, some of them snored. But Prasham was always eager. So she brought up her own list on her display. A message appeared without a header.

Good Sine says, break a leg Bad Wave.

"How?"

* * *

Rube paced in his cell.

Three weeks of lying on a hard cot with only a weekly sponge bath made him wonder how someone could survive a trip to Mars. At least today he had been given a display to watch the launch. All controls for sending or receiving messages were locked out, but he would get to see Ket fulfill her dream, and maybe see his friends and his brother in the crowd shots. After his arrest, he'd asked Vic to attend in his place. Then, in five hours, it would all be over. He was scheduled for transfer to somewhere else in India. The guard wouldn't tell him where.

It almost made him feel nostalgic for his current cell. It was true that the one jailer on night watch here, Biswanath, liked to make cruel remarks. But he seemed do this more out of the need to talk to someone rather than sadism. He had never harmed him, though he liked to explain all the methods of torture he'd learned in the army. Biswanath had even given him the display to use—an act of kindness Rube was sure would never occur at the next facility.

Speaking of the devil, Rube saw Biswanath walking to his cell carrying a bakery box.

"It's from someone named Harlow, for your birthday." Biswanath opened the box.

Inside, Rube could see a cake. There was a cut in its middle.

"You want some?" Biswanath asked.

Rube's birthday was two months ago, but he played along. He didn't want to sound too excited, because he wasn't. He'd be over thirty before his trial even started. How strange was it that he'd once feared turning thirty on Mars. But he replied, "Sure."

"I'm sure you would. Problem is, no gifts allowed." Biswanath looked happy. "Also, when I sliced into the cake, I found this." He held up a broken soahl. "I'm afraid I'll have to eat the cake myself, after I scan it for knives, or explosives … or poison." He considered this for a moment. "Hmm, better not risk it. Pity." He threw the cake into the trash and walked away.

* * *

Ket attached her display to the control panel and touched a button to connect to her soahl. She forwarded the message to Lacy.

"Are you getting through your checklist?" Prasham asked.

"Just a short diversion. We've got hours."

"I don't know how the young get anything done, searching their soahl every moment, gazing at their displays all the time. I was up at one a.m. today to prepare."

"Hmm, hmm." She angled her display away from Prasham.

A message popped up.

soahl-touched::private::to Bad Wave::from Tattoo Girl:: "Urgent! Corvus extradited to Fiji last night. Whitesmith found dead in his cell this morning. Good you touched my soahl. Almost no mention of this in the soahliverse, I would have missed it. Quasi and I are on our way to watch the launch. Yours, Lacy."

Ket knew Fiji wanted to put Corvus on trial for fraud. Charges for kidnapping her had never happened, though she had hoped he would be charged in Seattle, along with Whitesmith, for the break-in to her apartment. Somehow the fact that Whitesmith was dead didn't shock her. He was wanted for so many other crimes his death would have been his only way out. Corvus, on the other hand, might be able to maneuver his way back to freedom one day. But if he'd been taken to Fiji last night, he would be in prison there now. So it didn't matter. Fiji was a long way from India, and she'd be on Mars long before he was ever released.

She continued with the checklist, when another urgent message appeared.

soahl-touched::to Ket::from Mobius:: "ICA shutdown."

* * *

Rube was starting to feel a little lightheaded. He stopped pacing. Maybe he had spent too much time lying down the past three weeks. Then he looked down the hall. He was hallucinating too.

* * *

"We do not need communication with Mars for the launch," Prasham said. "And we can re-establish radio and gravitino contact once in space."

"But why is the ICA shutting things down this morning?" Ket asked.

"Many of your father's supporters believe the propaganda—that Corvus's arrest was a setup by the Mars Program. And your father had friends at the ICA."

"I should've known. Just locking up Corvus wouldn't make the problems he's caused go away. I suppose that's why there's still ten times the usual security for this launch."

"You're father's supporters are angry but peaceful. We're not worried about them. But even with the bad guys locked up ... or dead ... one can never be too safe."

Ket thought Prasham was right, even if it was presumptuous of him to think he knew how her father's supporters would act. She'd thought about telling Prasham, after Corvus and Whitesmith had been arrested, that the extra guards weren't needed. Even Sunjay, who'd gone to California to join the Big Sur Pirates, was out of the picture. It was expected the pirates would go back to drinking, looting, and seeking comfort women. She imagined Sunjay being used as one of the latter. It was a bad thought, she knew, below her standards. But it amused her, distracting her from her real concern—the earlier message. How could Rube have contacted her?

* * *

Rube rubbed his eyes. The doll—the v-bod doll—was walking down the hall. It did a little hop and almost fell over. So did Rube. He felt so unsteady.

"Stay awake," the doll called out.

Rube grabbed the bars. When the doll reached him he looked down. It was Mobius ... holding keys. Rube slid down to his knees. His mind wasn't working right and he wasn't sure he could get up again. "You're cute. But how?"

"When Ket visited you, the guard pulled out the evidence box for your case and asked her if she wanted to claim any of the non-tagged items. It seems the guard thought Ket was your wife. Quasi and Lacy were with her and saw the doll. Quasi noted it was pulled apart. When Ket went to visit you, Quasi snapped it back together while Lacy showed the guard her tattoos. They thought we might need it. Intuition, I guess. But …"

"But?"

"Listen, there was no way I was going to leave you in here. We had to wait for the box to be taken out again today, for your transfer. So I had Harlow send over a special cake. It's harmless, but once cut its aroma makes a person suggestible. When I sat up in that box I convinced the guard to go to the airport to meet his mother. It's having an effect on you too."

"You're rescuing me as a teeny-weeny little doll?" Rube felt drunk. "Did I say cute?"

"Shut up and listen. The ICA is shutting down all transmissions to Mars any minute now. Take these keys and get out of here."

Rube swiped his hands at the keys and missed. "Hold still."

"I'm holding still. Take the keys and get out of here. It may be four a.m., but you're being monitored. Someone will notice if you're gone. You'll have to have your wits about you."

"Can I take my poster with me?" Rube pointed to the one on his cell's wall.

The doll looked toward the poster. "That show? *Star Trek* I think it was called."

"Never heard of it." Or had he? Rube tried to remember. "The show was about a poem?"

"I don't mean the poem. But the man on the poster—he was on the show."

"He's a witch doctor, I think. Lacy said she liked the ear body-art."

"Yes—he was on the show. It still has a following at sci-fi conventions. I talked to some fans at one, once. I wanted to talk about Mars, so I told them I hadn't come to go on about *Star Trek*. Space, I said, was the enemy! Aargh. Listen to me!"

"That wasn't nice, Mobius. I like that pointy-eared guy." Besides, the poster was his only possession. Well, almost his only possession. He felt for his harmonica in his shirt pocket. After careful scanning, they'd decided he could keep it. He took it out. "Wanna hear a tune?"

"No. Take the key!"

"Key? Hee-hee. I have to pee."

"Stop goofing around. There's one more thing. The most important thing, though I wasn't sure I should tell you this. I received a message from Lacy. Corvus was extradited to Fiji last night. But his plane never showed up."

Rube mustered something inside himself. "Ket's in danger?"

"No one can get to her now. She launches in four hours. But be on watch. He could be after you. Now take the key, dammit! Time is running out."

Rube's head started to clear. Ket needed him. With extreme effort, he grabbed the key.

The doll fell over and Mobius was gone.

* * *

Ket checked. No new message for the last two hours.

She'd learned from Lacy that Corvus had never arrived in Fiji. He'd probably bribed someone to escape. But what could he do alone? She looked back at the display of the stands. They were starting to fill up. Quasi and Lacy were there. And in came her mother, sister, and nieces. Then she caught a glimpse of Dr. Mateni and his family. And there was Rube's brother, and Harlow looking fitter than ever. Then another message came in.

soahl-touched::to Ket:: "On my way. –Good Sine"

It was on her public account, for fans. The message had no return handle. She sent it to Lacy, this time specifically asking her how could Rube be doing this.

"We are completely fueled," Prasham said. "If Corvus does try to come to India he'll be stopped at the border. I'm sure he'll hide in Fiji to stay out of prison."

Ket thought he was right. She should just relax. Except now she needed the restroom. Crawling down the rungs in the floor in their vertical configuration to get to the facilities was awkward, but at least the toilet swiveled for use. It was either that or she'd have to use her suit-vac. After having to do that during training, she wanted to avoid the latter.

* * *

When Rube got off the mag-train at Sullurupeta he had no idea how he would get to Sriharikota Island or to the Mars Explorer Building. Security was everywhere, and all the signs said to have your pass and ID displayed. He had no idea why he hadn't been caught yet. On the train he had borrowed a passenger's soahl and sent Ket a message using the public protocol of her fan site. He hoped she'd got it. After the launch, he'd turn himself in. Mobius must have lost his mind. He wouldn't tell anyone how he got out, but if they figured it out, Mobius was safe on Mars. Soon Ket would be safe too, on her way there.

Right now he wanted to get to Lacy. She was the one to most likely to know what was up with Corvus. Rube could also borrow her soahl and send Ket a private message. Just a good luck wish, he thought. No sense going into more than that. He could also say a proper good bye to his friends and Vic. He hadn't had a chance to do that before.

But how could he get to them? He exited the station and saw his answer. A bus by the curb was loading instruments and band members. It was a multicultural group wearing mufti outfits with flag lapels from many nations. There were dancers too, all Indian, like those at the last launch.

Luckily the prison had given him a plain black shirt and pants. He walked over to the bus. He didn't have shoes, though almost everyone else did. He'd decide to try Quasi's type of charm as best as he could. He knocked and the bus driver swung open the door.

"Hello, mate." Rube climbed the steps to the driver's level. "May I get on?"

The driver looked at Rube like he didn't care. "Wait for the group leader. He has the list for the roll call. Then you can load up."

"I reckon he won't mind if I get on first. I need the restroom at the back." Rube crossed his legs and squirmed like he might go right where he was.

"Go," said the driver. "But then come back and get off."

* * *

Ket returned to her seat. It was still an hour and fifty minutes before the launch. The control tower and Prasham were checking all the engine circuits. Her job was to double-check his list.

A message flashed on her display.

Good Sine says goodbye Bad Wave.

It was like the first message, without headers. She tried to reply, but got, "No reply allowed." Maybe Rube was sending her secret messages. She forwarded it to Lacy and hoped she would sort this out.

* * *

Rube sat in the restroom, hearing the thuds of instruments loading under the bus. Maybe the driver would forget he was in there. But someone knocked on the door.

"Open."

It was not the driver's voice. Rube slid the door across. There stood a tall, blond, middle-aged man in a green suede jacket with a nametag identifying him as the band coordinator. He also wore a security badge and a stern expression.

"Vat you doing?"

"Just needed to go." Rube said. He didn't try his faux Scottish on this guy. "Can I take my seat?"

"Is your instrument stowed? Vat do you play?"

Rube thought for a moment. He patted his shirt. "Harmonica."

"Very funny." The coordinator snarled.

Rube smiled. "You caught me." But he hung his head in despair. He'd have to get off the bus and try something else.

"You must be a dancer. Sit here. I must go roll call the band."

Rube was stunned but sat down. He realized he perhaps looked like a local.

A male dancer sat next to Rube. "Everything is so disorganized this year. Where's your robe? You look like you just got out of prison."

Rube pointed to his throat, indicating he couldn't talk.

"You're sick?" The dancer got up and moved to another seat.

Soon after that the musicians got on. A band member sat next to him but said nothing. And they were on their way.

* * *

At the Mars Explorer Building Rube followed the dancers to the roof. They waited in the wings. Behind him, snaking down the stairs was the band. Rube decided he would head for the bleachers as soon as they went on stage.

Then he saw Nickie and Twiddle out by the podium. Twiddle was flapping his arms in his corduroy suit. He went to the mic and announced the dance group. Rube tried to split off, but the guy who'd sat next to him pushed him toward the stage. Half way out, without thinking, he committed to staying with the dancers.

Bollywood music blared over the sound system. The dancers brought their hands together in prayer position and then pushed them up like rockets lifting off. Rube followed along. The men flexed their broad shoulders, slapped their knees, and stamped their feet. Rube couldn't see what the women were doing. He was too busy trying to copy the other males. At least he was in the back row. He remembered from last time that the group was about to break formation, exposing him to the crowd. He wasn't sure what he would do. Then he heard Lacy.

"Get him out of there!"

Rube didn't look up, but seconds later someone grabbed his shirt from behind.

"No worries," Quasi said as he dragged Rube away from the dancers. "He's an old mate of mine who's had a few too many, trying to join in on the fun." He turned to Rube. "No more Bollywood movies for you, mister." He took off his flat newsboy cap and pushed it down over Rube's face. "Hide behind this," he whispered. "Security's everywhere."

Rube pushed the hat down to his nose. He followed Quasi to the bleachers, where he was greeted with hugs from Vic, Dr. Mateni, and Lacy, who had her dark glasses on.

"How did you get here?" Lacy asked.

Rube was about to answer, but Harlow spoke.

"Piece of cake. Right?"

"Right." Rube turned to Lacy. "I can explain later. But about Corvus?"

"I only know he's escaped. Why are you messaging Ket from a no-reply account?"

"What do you mean? I sent one message from the train, as an anonymous user on another passenger's soahl."

"Damn," Quasi said. "That means someone else has her private soahl handle."

"Corvus?" Lacy said.

"Of course," Rube said. "It has to be him. Her handle was on the soahl Whitesmith stole."

"I thought she erased that before giving it to Whitesmith," Quasi said. "Otherwise, why hasn't Corvus sent her a message before?"

"I'm afraid he probably got it from a video I reposted," Dr. Mateni said. "After they were arrested, I've been a bit lax when sending out things about Ket." He looked very disturbed. "In this case, I'm not Dr. OK."

"It's no problem," Rube said. "She can change her soahl handle or block him from sending more messages. He's probably in Fiji somewhere, trying to scare her one more time."

* * *

Ket was astonished to get an encrypted message from Lacy saying that Rube had escaped with help from Harlow and Mobius, and he had made it to the bleachers. Ket immediately sent Lacy an encrypted reply: "There's a time to do the right thing and a time to do the smart thing. This time be smart and get Rube away as soon as possible. And don't let him give you an ends-don't-justify-the-means argument. We're not talking about covering up mass murder, just a v-bod spy mission. Corvus stacked the deck. What choice do we have? Yours always, Ket"

"Everything all right?" Prasham asked.

"Almost," Ket replied. She wasn't sure which was racing faster, her heart or her thoughts.

Then she heard the announcer on the bleacher display talk about the visiting dignitaries. "Fiji," he said, "is very proud to have their largest naval ship here to farewell their very own Betti Keturah Boni. They send her a big *Ni sa bula vinaka.*" A picture of the ship appeared.

"That looks close," Ket said to Prasham.

"The Indian navy is keeping all ships a hundred miles off shore."

Ket exhaled. "Well, just over an hour to go." Then another message came in.

Good Sine to Bad Wave: BS BS BS BS BS BS BS BS BS BS BS BS BS BS BS BS BS BS BS BS BS BS BS BS BS BS BS BS BS BETTER RUN

* * *

Rube studied the message on Lacy's display. "That has to be Corvus. But why all the swearing?"

"What swearing?" It was Ket's mother leaning over now. "What's it say?"

"Just swearing," Rube said.

"What kind? Don't worry, I grew up in the Bronx."

"It says BS over and over. Or it's to do with the Big Sur Pirates. I heard him say it when he was taking to Abraham about Whitesmith."

"Let me see." Ket's mother sounded incredulous. Lacy handed her the display.

"Oh my, I think I know what this means. Corvus would never swear. But I once heard him say BS to someone on the phone. I was shocked. That's why I remember it. But then he said, Big Scare. BS, it means Big Scare."

Rube watched as Lacy took back her display and started to search. He saw another message come in from Ket.

soahl-touched::private::to Tattoo Girl::from Bad Wave:: "Something's not right about the Fijian ship."

Lacy searched for ten minutes. Then she looked at Rube. "This is bad, really bad."

"What?" Quasi and Rube asked at the same time.

"Here's a live satellite image of the Fijian vessel. Ket suggested I measure its angular size. It's wrong. That ship is twenty feet too long. I've matched it against all known ships. Its disguised, but it's a BSP frigate, the one that went to Fiji. I don't know how I missed this before. There's also a coded message—something about the salvage of B-41's. What's it mean?"

"Nukes." Rube felt the color leave his face.

"Nukes?" Quasi asked. "What's that malignant sidewinding maggot up to this time?"

"Corvus must have planned this all along," Rube continued. "Lacy, tell Ket to launch now." The fear in his voice burned his throat. "Hurry—before it's too late!"

The building shook then swayed. The roof listed and everyone in the bleachers fell over. From beneath a pile of bodies, Rube heard screams.

"Earthquake," someone yelled.

Rube struggled to his feet. There were groans, but no one seemed hurt.

"A quake off the coast, magnitude eight-point-three." That was Lacy.

"Maybe Corvus blew himself up," Dr. Mateni said. "That'd be OK with Doctor OK."

"No, it was deep down." Lacy's glasses were missing, but she was studying her display.

"In the seabed?" Quasi asked. He brushed the dust off his clothing.

"Of course," Rube said. "Tsu—" Before he could finish the alarms went off, along with klaxons and rotating blue lights. A message scrolled across the large holo-screens:

... TSUNAMI ALERT ... EVACUATE TO MAINLAND ...

The crowd, now spread out across the roof, had become a disarrayed mass of confusion. Now, a horrified calm swept through them and everyone moved toward the exits.

"Lacy, get me voice to Ket."

Lacy touched a few buttons and handed her display to Rube.

"Ket, Corvus has triggered a tsunami. Launch now."

"Rube, we know. My panels are lit up like a Christmas tree and the control tower is in my ear. We need at least thirty minutes to secure all moorings from the tower for a safe launch."

"That'll be about one minute too late." Quasi had a Tsunami tracker up on his display.

"Can the rockets ride it out?" Rube asked.

"A sixty-foot surge hitting a three-hundred-foot rocket. I don't think so," Quasi replied.

"We are ordered to abort." It was Ket on Lacy's display. Then it went black.

Rube gave his friends a quick hug, telling them what he was about to do.

"Go get her, bro," Vic said. He handed Rube his shoes.

"I will. Now evacuate. We'll see you on the mainland." Rube left them, but heard Lacy call out that a mini-sub had been spotted on the beach near the launch pad. He ran.

When Rube reached the stairs he found them clogged with musicians and dropped instruments. He put the shoes over his hands and pushed his way down, leaping four stairs at time whenever there was a gap. He landed on a trombone on the third floor landing and almost went head over heels. But he made it to the lobby. There, he slipped the shoes onto his feet and zigzagged through the tuba players. It seemed they had never gone up the stairs and now were unsure what to do with the metal life preservers worn around their waists.

Once out on the street, Rube ran to one of the building's robo-cars. He hopped into the driver's seat and said, "If I'm a massless neutrino, then you're not a Higgs boson."

Nothing happened. Panic engulfed him. But then he said, "If I am a massless neutrino, then you are not a Higgs boson."

The car started and he drove off, tires squealing. Time seemed to stop and fear clawed inside him like a monster trying to rip its way out. "Go, go, go!" Faster than he could believe, he saw the checkpoint and wooden gate approaching. He knew the code, but there was still a fifteen second wait for the gate to open. He took over control of the car and floored it.

The wooden gate exploded into splinters. He sped on, the pedal pressed to the floor, until the bunker zoomed into view. There, crew members from the rocket were hopping out of the escape baskets and heading to the robo-cars.

He slammed the brakes, skidded sideways to a stop, and ran to Prasham. "Where's Ket?"

"She was right behind me."

Rube looked up at the rocket and saw a struggle between two figures on the gantry.

* * *

"My betrothed. I finally have you."

Ket fought against the hand across her mouth as she was dragged backward. Another hand had her arm bent behind her back. After blowing the hatches, she was the last to exit the rocket. She was the captain, after all. Prasham had protested, but she told him she would be right behind him. But before she could get through the gate to the escape baskets, she heard a steel door open behind her. She stopped for a moment then turned to follow Prasham. He was gone. And that's when someone grabbed her, the sickening sound of his breath in her ear.

"Isn't the sea lovely from up here?" Corvus let her go and walked back to the tower, picking up his cane.

Ket noticed the shore looked very odd. The sea had rushed out much farther than it did during low tide. "We need to get out of here. There's a tsunami coming."

"Funny that—a tsunami—your biggest fear. Well, here's how I see it, bitch. Either you come with me or we both die here."

Ket weighed her options. Dying seemed the better one. Then she saw Rube come up behind Corvus. She was so shocked she couldn't control her reaction. "Rube, run!"

Corvus whirled around. "Soulless soahl boy. Aren't you supposed to be in prison?"

"Aren't you?" Rube replied.

Corvus moved along the gantry to Ket. "Leave or she dies." At first Ket seemed to let him seized her. But then she kicked Corvus hard in the shin and fell back toward the rocket.

Rube saw his chance. He moved forward, conscious that the cane could drop him like stuck pig. He took hold of the gantry railings and swung his feet at Corvus.

Corvus lurched to one side but managed to strike his cane hard across Rube's ankles.

Rube's feet clanked onto the steel walkway, and he ran back to the tower. He saw Ket by the rocket's blown hatch. He hoped she would go in and initiate the launch escape system rockets. Then he could go down the tower, back to the robo-car. But she stayed put and there was no time to explain. Corvus was coming for him.

With mindless fury, Rube charged like a ram to meet Corvus halfway. In a desperate move, he grappled for the wooden part of the cane before it could zap him. His arm muscles bulged to the limit as he and Corvus fell down. After rolling along the narrow pathway, Rube found his head sticking out beneath the guardrail. The ground was a hundred meters below. Corvus had pulled away. But before Rube could stand, Corvus was back, positioned over him with his cane inches from Rube's nose. Rube grabbed the cane again, but Corvus was in control.

"Give up. I'll pray for the Spirit to have mercy on you." Corvus leaned in close and his cobalt eyes seemed to burn with hate.

Rube spit at them. This was no time to fight fair.

"So now you are possessed?"

Rube suppressed his rage. He had to try something. "This isn't about me. You can't make someone love you, Corvus."

"Listen to me, Corvus. Abraham wouldn't want this." Ket had come down the gantry.

Corvus straightened himself and put his foot against Rube's chest.

Rube quickly grasped a strut and tried to get up. But he couldn't get leverage, with Corvus trying to push him over the edge. Rube battled to hold on, the steel cutting into his hands. One jolt from the cane and he'd fall to his death, unconscious. Then Rube saw Ket had a wrench. She swung it chest high. Corvus dodged out of the way, and the wrench broke away a piece of the railing. Corvus steadied himself and managed to graze Ket's calf with his cane. She screamed and retreated, her leg convulsing.

Rube knew it was his turn. He came at Corvus, but stopped short of another cane strike.

From behind, Ket shouted. "Look at the sea! The tsunami. It's coming!"

Rube used the distraction to wrap his arms around Corvus. He tried to shake the cane loose, but Corvus was too strong. Limping forward, Ket wielded the wrench like a machete, slashing Corvus at knee level. He didn't go down, but kicked at her, forcing her to back off.

In the confusion, Rube pulled the cane away. Holding it, he stepped back, his body aching. He tried not to show he was out of breath, out of strength. "It's over. Let's get in the rocket and use the launch escape system to get out of here."

"Never. We will all die. Only my soul will live forever, while you and the bitch will be consumed by flames." Corvus leapt at Rube.

Rube stiff-armed Corvus with the cane, like putting a stake to his sternum, and pushed the button. Corvus's cheeks sucked in, his hair stuck out, and he staggered backward. Incredibly, he didn't fall down. Rube finally released his anger. "Corvus, that last name of yours—is it McCluff as in fluff, or McClow as in cow? Right now, you're a bit of a fluffy cow."

"It doesn't matter," Corvus replied. "Look."

Rube glanced down for a split-second. Water rushed across the ground below. Then he was surprised to see Corvus move toward him once more. Rube stepped back and stopped, brandishing the cane. But Corvus held a derringer.

"I didn't think I'd need this. It's been modified to put down a deer at twenty yards. Let's see how it does at stopping sin from spreading through the universe." Corvus took aim.

Rube was too far from the tower to turn and run, too far from Corvus to get him with the cane. He prepared to charge again, to go down with a fight … to die.

An orange dress appeared like a parachute over Corvus. It covered him like a shroud and lit up for a moment before it sloughed off into the breeze. Corvus dropped his gun and fell to his knees. His face was now completely contorted. He reached for where the railing had broken away, but grabbed only air and wobbled like a top about to fall over.

Rube dropped the cane and reached out. "Give me your hand."

It was too late. Corvus fell through the gap. It was a long fall, and Rube had time to get to Ket before seeing Corvus hit the rising water below. "He's gone. Your dress, it really was electrified?"

Ket held her display. "Before Corvus was arrested, Prasham had Harlow make some modifications to it." She pointed to an orange button. "He added a protect mode. He always said the dress was a bit of a menace, but I decided to take it along as a good luck charm." Then her leg gave out, and she collapsed into Rube's arms.

After Rube helped her into the rocket, he took Prasham's seat. "Fire up the launch escape rocket," he said. "Let's get this capsule out of here."

"We can't. With the hatch blown, we'll take on water, sink, and drown."

"Can't we launch toward land?"

"It's fixed to land in the sea. No steering mechanism. And the parachute is too small for landing on a hard surface."

"Well, we can't launch into space either. Not with the door open. At least with a water landing we have a chance."

"Right." Ket flipped open the emergency launch escape system panel, and put her hand on the abort lever. "Oh, oh," she said, indicating one of the displays.

Rube saw it showed a mighty big wave. "Ket, just so you know. I really do love you."

"And I love you too, Rube."

Rube embraced Ket as best he could. Then he waited for her to pull the abort lever.

"Wait!" A voice ricocheted around the cabin.

"What?" Rube looked around, then down. Two military-grade v-bods with the faces of Quasi and Lacy were working on the hatch.

"Quasi activated the v-bods at the Mars Explorer Building before we left," Lacy explained. "We're on the mainland now, high and dry."

"And then," Quasi said, "Lacy hacked into the v-bods, and voila, here we are."

"Actually, it took a while for us to drive them here and find the tools," Lacy said.

"And new O-rings and bolts for the door," Quasi said. "But we're sealing you in now."

The hatch closed. There was the sound of riveting.

"We'll never make it," Rube said.

"Look," Ket said. She pointed to the display. The rocket closer to the sea tilted under the dynamic force of the tsunami. It leaned over and broke in two, ripping open the hydrogen filled upper stage. There was a flash, and a second later the reverberations from the explosion hit.

"That wasn't good," Rube said. His seat rumbled beneath him.

"No, not good," Ket said. Her hair had fallen around her face.

Quasi appeared on another display. "You're at full mast, maties." Lacy pushed in beside him. "He means you're air tight. Initiate the abort."

"Or not," Ket said.

"Huh?" Rube turned to her.

"I said we couldn't launch in less than thirty minutes safely. I didn't say we couldn't launch." She smiled.

Rube wanted to point to the display showing the large amount of debris flying toward them from the other rocket. But he said, "You're the captain."

Ket took her hand off the abort lever. She entered a code into the main control panel.

"Main engine start," the computer said.

A deafening roar filled Rube's ears. He became heavier. The shaking was so hard it didn't just seem that all hell was breaking loose, but every layer below it as well, from here to the other side of the universe. Then he heard a voice from heaven.

"Nnnice rrrescue," Ket said.

"Cccool eeescape ppplan," Rube said. "Ccccrazy too."

"Aaand thanksss for the card with the flowerrrr." Ket pulled it from her seat pocket and opened it.

Rube saw where he'd written the story of seeing her for the first time. He remembered everything, from the beginning.

Ket truly was the smartest and most unattainable woman in the entire universe.

Unless?

What if they were together on Mission Fourteen to Mars?

Rube reached for her, and she placed her warm hand in his.

Chapter 34
Baby, It's Mars

Lacy walked out onto the balcony of her Seattle apartment.

Quasi joined her. "You're up early."

"It's a special day." She stared up at the sky. It was an oddly warm and clear night. She could see Mars in the west and patted her bulging tummy. "Look baby, it's Mars."

* * *

More than fifty million miles from Earth, Rube floated beside Ket.

After eight and a half months of travel, space was no longer the enemy. They'd found their own special elsewhere—a region of space and time all to themselves. They'd also reached into each other's souls, pondering every aspect of life, discussing their core philosophies, some of which had changed, while daring the other to reveal what drove them to search for their place in the universe.

Rube decided to not worry so much about what gave life meaning … or made it meaningless. Instead, he said, "It matters not what you do, as long at it harms no one and has meaning to you. Finding you is what matters to me."

Ket called that cute. "And I'm no longer trying to find the good people of the universe … or my perfect bra," she added.

"You mean I'm not perfect?"

"I mean, I've found the best bra for me, the only one I'll need for the rest of my life."

Then the baby cried. Rube thought Ket looked terrific for someone who had given birth a few hours ago. Just a couple of weeks early, but precisely on time for today's landing.

Ket floated over to the crib made from duck-taped seat cushions. When constructing the crib, they'd worried about suffocation. But weightlessness had it advantages and disadvantages. Keeping the baby from floating away was more of a problem than keeping her face from getting pushed into a cushion. She pulled the newborn, wrapped tightly in a clean white towel, into her arms. Then Ket floated with her to one of the port windows.

"Our first born," Rube said. "I saw how great you were with kids on Earth, even though you said you didn't want any of your own."

"You said the same thing. But that was before we had this precious little girl." Ket snuggled her face into the baby's.

"I'm sure we'll have lots of boys in about a thousand years." Rube had never smiled so hard. It brought tears of joy.

Ket burst out laughing.

Rube laughed too. He loved how they made each other laugh. He floated over to join Ket and his daughter. So much was uncertain, so many challenges lay ahead. But now was not the time to worry about the future. With his harmonica, he began to play a soft lullaby.

Ket swayed with the music and pointed out the window.

"Look baby, it's Mars."

The End

Acknowledgements

Thanks to my family, critique group, beta readers, editors, artists, designers, and everyone who helped make this book possible.

About the Author

Gregory Allen Mendell works on relativistic astrophysics and has contributed to some well-known discoveries. He's lived in several counties. When writing, he likes to interweave stories about space, human relationships, and cross-cultural experiences while exploring key mysteries about the future and the meaning of it all. He loves spending time with his wife and son somewhere in the multiverse.

Made in the USA
Middletown, DE
22 December 2019